A man for mum!

Three of our leading Mills & Boon® authors bring you three brand new full-length stories full of passion, family and fun with the added bonus of giving you a taste of the stories from three of our most popular lines:

Presents™   Penny Jordan

Enchanted™   Leigh Michaels

Temptation®   Vicki Lewis Thompson

For our three unsuspecting heroines, Verity, Molly and Rose, kids are a great focus in their lives and the fathers of those children end up being part of the package. In A MAN FOR MUM! three doesn't make a crowd, it makes a family. And what better gift for any single mum or mum-to-be than to fall in love with a single sexy guy to complete the picture.

So relax, sit back and enjoy the fun and romance as our three deserving heroines find the man (and the family) of their dreams.

A man for mum!

WANTING HIS CHILD
by
Penny Jordan

THE BOSS AND THE BABY
by
Leigh Michaels

ONE MUM TOO MANY
by
Vicki Lewis Thompson

MILLS & BOON®

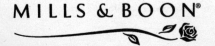

*MILLS & BOON and MILLS & BOON with the Rose Device
are registered trademarks of the publisher.*

*First published in Great Britain 1999 by
Harlequin Mills & Boon Limited,
Eton House, 18-24 Paradise Road,
Richmond, Surrey, TW9 1SR*

A MAN FOR MUM! © by Harlequin Enterprises II B.V. 1999

The publisher ackowledges the copyright holders of the
individual work as follows:

Wanting His Child © Penny Jordan 1999
The Boss and the Baby © Leigh Michaels 1999
One Mum Too Many © Vicki Lewis Thompson 1997

ISBN 0 263 81706 7
103-9901

*Printed and bound in Great Britain
by Caledonian Book Manufacturing Ltd, Glasgow*

WANTING HIS CHILD
by
Penny Jordan

CHAPTER ONE

VERITY MAITLAND grimaced as she directed the long nose of the top-of-the-range BMW sports car she was driving through the outskirts of what had once been her home town.

It may have been over a decade since she had originally left but, from what she could see, nothing much seemed to have changed—but then why should it have done? Just because so much had changed in *her* life, that didn't mean…

The car was attracting a good deal of covert attention, and no wonder: from its immaculate shiny paintwork to its sporty wheels and its sleek soft-top hood it screamed look at me…admire me…*want* me.

She would never in a thousand years have deliberately chosen a car so blatantly attention seeking and expensive and had, in fact, only bought it as a favour to a friend. Her friend, a modern wunderkind spawned by the eighties, had recently taken the decision to 'downsize' and move herself, her man, and her two children to a remote area of the Scottish Highlands where, as she had explained ruefully to Verity, the BMW would be a luxury she simply couldn't afford. What she had also not been able to afford had been the time to look around for a private buyer prepared to pay a good price for the almost new vehicle and so, heroically, Verity had stepped in and offered to buy the car from her. After all, it was hardly as though she couldn't afford to—she could have afforded a round dozen or so new cars had she wished.

Along with the nearly new car she had also acquired from the same friend a nearly-new wardrobe of clothes, all purchased from Bond Street's finest.

'I'm hardly going to be wearing Gucci, Lauren, Prada or Donna Karan where we're going,' Charlotte had sighed, 'and we are the same size.'

Well aware, although her friend hadn't said so and despite her cheerful optimistic attitude, that her 'downsizing' had not been totally voluntary and that money was going to be tight for her, Verity had equably picked up on Charlotte's hints about selling off her wardrobe and had stepped in as purchaser.

She could, of course, have simply offered to give her friend the money; as a multimillionairess, even if only on a temporary basis, she could after all afford it, but she knew how Charlotte's pride would be hurt by such an offer and their friendship meant too much to her for her to risk damaging it.

'After all, it isn't just *me* who's being done a favour,' Charlotte had commented enthusiastically as they had stood together in the large bedroom of her soon to be ex-Knightsbridge house, viewing Verity's appearance in the white Gucci trouser suit she had just pulled on.

'Now that you've sold the business and you aren't going to be working non-stop virtually twenty-four hours a day, you're going to need a decent wardrobe. You're going to have to watch out for fortune hunters, though,' she warned Verity sternly. 'I know you're in your thirties now, but you're still a very attractive woman…'

'And the fact that I'm currently worth over forty million pounds makes me even more attractive,' Verity suggested dryly.

'Not to me, it doesn't,' Charlotte assured her with a warm hug. 'But there are men…'

'*Please*… You sound just like my uncle,' Verity told her.

Her uncle. Verity was thinking about him now as she drove through the town and headed out towards her destination. It had been an ironic touch of fate that the very house where she had grown up under the guardianship of her late uncle should have been one of the ones the estate agent had sent her details of as a possible house for her to rent.

When people had asked her what she intended to do, having finally taken the decision to sell off the business she had inherited from her uncle—a business which she had been groomed by him to manage and run virtually from the moment she had gone to live with him following her parents' death; a business which she had been brought up by him to look upon as a sacred trust, as the whole focus of her life and as something far, far more important than any personal desires or needs she might have—she had told them, with the calmness for which she was fabled, that so far she had made no plans. That she simply intended to take some time out in order to give proper consideration to what she wanted to do with the rest of her life. After all, at thirty-three she might not be old, but then neither was she young, and she was certainly wise enough to be able to keep her own counsel—it was not completely true that she hadn't made any plans. She had. It was just that she knew exactly how her advisers, both financial and emotional, would look upon them.

To divest herself of virtually all of the money she had received from the sale of the company was not a step they would consider well thought out or logical, but for once in her life she wanted to do what felt right for *her*, to be motivated by her *own* judgement rather than simply complying with the needs and demands of others.

She had fought a long battle to retain ownership of the business—not because she had particularly wanted to, but because she had known it was what her late uncle would have expected—but that battle was now over. As she herself had known and her financial advisers had warned her, there had been a very great danger that, if she had not accepted one of the excellent offers she had received for the sale of the business, she could have found herself in a position where a sale had been forced upon her. She had at least managed to ensure that her uncle's name remained linked to that of the business for perpetuity.

Verity frowned, automatically checking her speed as she realised she was approaching the local school and that it was that time in the afternoon when the children were coming out.

It was the same school she had attended herself, although her memories of being there were not entirely happy due, in the main, to the fact that her uncle's strictness and obsession with her school grades had meant that she had not been allowed to mingle freely with her classmates. During the long summer evenings when they had gone out to play, she had had to sit working at home under her uncle's eagle eye.

It had been his intention that her father, who had worked alongside him in the business and who had been his much younger brother, would ultimately take over from him, but her father's untimely death had put an end to that and to the possibility that he might have further children—sons.

Her uncle's own inability to father children had been something that Verity had only discovered after his death and had, she suspected, been the reason why he had never married himself.

She was clear of the school now and the houses had become more widely spaced apart, set in large private gardens.

Knowing that she would shortly be turning off the main road, Verity automatically started to brake and ten seconds later was all too thankful that she had done so as, totally unexpectedly, out of a small newsagent's a young girl suddenly appeared on a pair of roller blades, skidded and shot out into the road right in front of Verity's car.

Instinctively and immediately Verity reacted, braking sharply, turning the car to one side, but sickeningly she still heard the appalling sound of a thud against the front wing of the car as the girl collided with it.

Frantically Verity tugged at her seat belt with trembling fingers, her heart thudding with adrenalin-induced horror and fear as she ran to the front of the car.

The girl was struggling to her feet, her face as ashen as Verity knew her own to be.

'What happened? Are you hurt? Can you walk…?'

As she gabbled the frantic questions, Verity forced herself to take a deep breath.

The girl was on her feet now but leaning over the side of the car. She looked all right, but perhaps she had been hurt internally, Verity worried anxiously as she went to put her arm around her to support her.

She felt heartbreakingly thin beneath the bulkiness of her clothes and Verity guessed that she wouldn't be much above ten. Her grey eyes were huge in her small, pointed white face, and as she raised her hand to push the weight of her long dark hair off her face Verity saw with a thrill of fear that there was blood on her hand.

'It's okay,' the girl told her hesitantly, 'it's just a scratch. I'm fine really… It was all my fault… I didn't look. Dad's always telling me…'

She stopped talking, her eyes suddenly brimming with tears, her whole body starting to shake with sobs.

'It's all right,' Verity assured her, instinctively taking her in her arms and holding her tight. 'You're in shock. Come and sit in the car…'

Glancing up towards the shop the girl had just come from, she asked her gently, 'Is your mother with you? Shall I…?'

'I don't have a mother,' the girl told her, allowing Verity to help her into the passenger seat of the car where she slumped back, her eyes closed, before adding, 'She's dead. She died when I was born. You don't have to feel sorry for me,' she added without opening her eyes. 'I don't mind because I never knew her and I've got Dad and he's…'

'*I* don't feel sorry for you,' Verity assured her, adding with an openness that she could only put down to the fact that she too was suffering the disorientating and disturbing effects of shock, 'I lost *both* my parents in a car accident when I was six.'

The girl opened her eyes and looked thoughtfully at her. Now that she was beginning to get over her ordeal she looked very alert and intelligent and, in some odd way that Verity couldn't quite put her finger on, slightly familiar.

'It's horrid having people feeling sorry for you, isn't it?' the girl said with evident emotion.

'People don't mean to be patronising,' Verity responded. 'But I do know what you mean…'

'Dad told me I wasn't to go outside the garden on my rollers.' She gave Verity an assessing look. 'He'll ground me for ages—probably for ever.' Verity waited, guessing what was coming next.

'I don't suppose… Well, he doesn't *have* to know, does he…? I could pay for the damage to your car from my pocket money and…'

What kind of man was he, this father, who so patently made his daughter feel unloved and afraid? A man like her uncle, perhaps? A man who, whilst providing a child with all the material benefits he or she could possibly want, did not provide the far more important emotional ones?

'No, he doesn't *have* to know,' Verity agreed, 'as long as the hospital gives you the all clear.'

'The *hospital*?' The girl's eyes widened apprehensively.

'Yes, the hospital,' Verity said firmly, closing her own door and re-starting the car.

She would be being extremely negligent in her duty as a responsible adult if she didn't do everything

within her power to make sure the girl was as physically undamaged as she looked.

'You have to turn left here,' the girl began and then
looked closely at Verity as she realised she had started
to turn without her directions. 'Do you know
the way?'

'Yes. I know it,' Verity agreed.

She ought to. She had gone there often enough with
her uncle. Before he had moved the company's head-
quarters to London, the highly specialised medical
equipment he had invented and designed had been
tried out in their local hospital and Verity had often
accompanied him on his visits there.

One of the things she intended to do with the
money from the sale of the company was to finance
a special ward at the hospital named after her uncle.
The rest of it... The rest of it would be used in equally
philanthropic ways. That was why she had come back
here to her old home town, to take time out to think
about what she wanted to do with the rest of her life
and to decide how other people could benefit the most
from her late uncle's money.

When they arrived at the casualty department of the
hospital they were lucky in that there was no one else
waiting to be seen.

The nurse, who frowned whilst Verity explained
what had happened, then turned to Verity's companion and asked her, 'Right... Let's start with your
name.'

'It's... It's Honor—Honor Stevens.'

Honor Stevens. Verity felt her heart start to plum-
met with the sickening speed of an out-of-control lift.

She was being stupid, of course. Stevens wasn't that unusual a name, and she was taking her own apprehension and coincidence too far to assume that just because of a shared surname that meant...

'Address?' the nurse asked crisply.

Dutifully Honor gave it.

'Parents?' she demanded.

'Parent. I only have one—my father,' Honor began weakly. 'His name's Silas. Well, really Silas Stevens.' She pulled a face and looked at Verity, and unexpectedly told her, 'You look...' She stopped, looked at her again speculatively, but Verity didn't notice.

Silas Stevens. Honor was Silas' daughter. Why on earth hadn't she known? Guessed? She could see so clearly now that the reason she had found Honor's features so oddly familiar was because she was Silas' daughter. She even had his thick, dark, unruly hair, for heaven's sake, and those long-lashed grey eyes— *they* were his, no doubts about it. That disconcertingly level look was his as well and...

'Are you feeling all right?'

Verity flushed as she realised that both Honor and the nurse were watching her.

'I'm fine,' she fibbed, adding dryly, 'but it isn't every day that I get an out-of-control roller blader courting death under my car wheels.'

And it certainly wasn't every day that she learned that that child was the daughter of a man...of *the* man... What would Honor think if she knew that once Verity had believed that Silas' children would be hers, that *she* would be the one to bear his babies, wear his ring, share his life...? But that had been before... Before her uncle had reminded her of where her real

duty lay, and before Silas had told her so unequivo-
cally that he had his own plans for his life and that
they did not include playing second fiddle to another's
wishes, another man's rules, another man's business.

'But I can't just walk away and leave him, leave
it,' Verity had protested shakily when Silas had delivered an ultimatum to her. 'He needs me, Silas, he
expects me to take over the business...'

'And what of my needs, my expectations?' Silas
had asked her angrily.

In the end they had made up their quarrel, but six
weeks later her uncle had announced that he had made
arrangements for her to go to America where she
would work for a firm manufacturing a similar range
of medical equipment to their own, since he believed
the experience would stand her in good stead when
she took over his own business. She had been tempted
to refuse, to rebel, but the strictness with which he
had brought her up had stopped her—that and her
sense of responsibility and duty towards not just him
but the business as well. The twenty-year gap which
had existed between him and her father, despite the
fact that they had been brothers, had meant that her
father himself had been a little in awe of him, and
Verity, entering his household as a shy six-year-old
suddenly bereft of her parents, had been too nervous,
too despairingly unhappy over the loss of her mother
and father, too intimidated to even think of rebelling
against his stern dictatorship so that the seeds had
been sown then for her to be taught by him to obey.

Later, away from his oppressive presence, she had
started to mature into her own person, to feel able to
make her own judgements and have her own values

and she had known then, tried then...but it had been too late...

Quickly she veiled her eyes with her lashes just in case either Honor or the nurse might read what she was feeling.

'We'll need to take some X-rays and of course she'll have to see the doctor, although it doesn't look as though anything's wrong,' the nurse assured Verity.

'You'll wait here for me. You won't leave without me, will you?' Honor begged Verity as the nurse indicated that she was to follow her.

'I...' Verity hesitated. She too knew what it was like to feel alone, to feel abandoned, to feel that you had no one.

'Your father—' the nurse was beginning firmly, but Honor shook her head.

'No,' she said quickly. 'I don't want... He's away...on business and he won't be back until...until next week,' she responded.

The nurse was pursing her lips.

'Look, if it helps, I'll wait...and take full responsibility,' Verity offered.

'Well, I don't really know. It is most unorthodox,' the nurse began. 'Are you a relative, or—?'

'She's...she's going to be my new mother,' Honor cut in before Verity could say anything, and then looked pleadingly at her as the nurse looked questioningly at Verity, seeking confirmation of what she had just been told.

'I...I'll, er...I'll just wait here for you,' Verity responded, knowing that she ought by rights to have corrected Honor's outrageous untruth, but suspecting

that there was more to the girl's fib than a mere desire
to short-circuit officialdom and avoid waiting whilst
the hospital contacted whoever it was that her father
had left in official charge of her.

It baffled Verity that a parent—any parent, male or
female—could be so grossly neglectful of their child's
welfare, but she knew, of course, that it did happen,
and one of the things she intended to do with her new-
found wealth was to make sure that children in
Honor's situation were not exposed to the kind of danger Honor had just suffered. What Verity wanted to
do was to establish a network of secure, outside-
school, protective care for children whose parents for
one reason or another simply could not be there for
them. She knew that what she was taking on was a
mammoth task, but she was determined and it was
also one that was extremely dear to her heart.

It was almost an hour before the nurse returned
with Honor, pronouncing briskly that she was fine.

'I'll run you home,' Verity offered as they walked
back out into the early summer sunshine.

Honor had paused and was drawing a picture in the
dust with the toe of her shoe.

'What is it? What's wrong?' Verity asked her.

'Er... Dad doesn't have to know about any of this,
does he?' Honor asked her uncomfortably. 'It's just...
Well...'

Verity watched her gravely for a few seconds, her
heart going out to her, although she kept her feelings
to herself as she told her quietly, 'Well, *I'm* certainly
not going to say anything to him.'

Wasn't that the truth? The thought of having anything...*anything* whatsoever to do with Silas Stevens

was enough to bring her out in a cold panic-induced sweat, despite the fact that she would dearly have loved to have given him a piece of her mind about his appalling neglect of his daughter's welfare.

'You're not. That's great…' A huge smile split Honor's face as she started to hurry towards Verity's car.

When they did get there, though, her face fell a little as she saw the dent and scraped paintwork where she had collided with the car.

'It's a BMW, isn't it? That means it's going to be expensive to repair…'

'I'm afraid it does,' Verity agreed cordially.

She sternly refused to allow her mouth to twitch into anything remotely suspicious of a smile as Honor told her gravely, 'I *will* pay you back for however much it costs, but it could take an awfully long time. Dad's always docking my pocket money,' she added with an aggrieved expression. 'It isn't fair. He can be really mean…'

You too, Verity wanted to sympathise. She knew all about that kind of meanness. Her uncle had kept her very short of money when she'd been growing up, and even now she often found it difficult to spend money on herself without imagining his reaction— which was why her cupboards had been so bare of designer clothes and the car she had driven before kind-heartedness had driven her to purchase Charlotte's BMW had been a second-hand run-of-the-mill compact model.

'I get my spending money every week. I wanted to have a proper allowance but Dad says I'm still too young… Where do you live?' she asked Verity.

Calmly Verity told her, watching as she carefully memorised the address.

'Can you stop here?' Honor suddenly demanded urgently, adding, when Verity looked quizzically at her, 'I...I'd rather you didn't take me all the way home...just in case...well...'

'I won't take you all the way home,' Verity agreed, 'but I'm not going to stop until I can see that you get home safely from where I'm parked.'

To her relief Honor seemed to accept this ruling, allowing Verity to pull into the side of the road within eyesight of her drive.

'Will there be someone there?' Verity felt bound to ask her.

'Oh, yes,' Honor assured her sunnily. 'Anna will be there. Anna looks after me...us... She works for Dad at the garden centre when I'm at school... I won't forget about the money,' she promised Verity solemnly as she got out of the car.

'I'm sure you won't,' Verity agreed, equally seriously.

So Silas still had the garden centre.

She remembered how full of plans he had been for it when he had first managed to raise the money to buy it. Her uncle had been scornful of what Silas had planned to do.

'A gardener?' he had demanded when Verity had first told him about Silas' plans. 'You're dating a gardener? Where did you meet him?'

Verity could remember how her heart had sunk when she had been forced to admit that she had met Silas when he had come to do the gardens at the house. She had hung her head in shame and distress when her uncle had demanded to know what on earth she, with her background and her education, could possibly see in someone who mowed lawns for a living.

'It isn't like that,' Verity had protested, flying to the protection of her new-found love and her new-found lover. 'He's been to university but...'

'But what?' her uncle had demanded tersely.

'He...he found out when he was there that it wasn't what he wanted to do...'

'What university has taught me more than anything else,' Silas had told her, 'is to know myself, and what I know is that I would hate to be stuck in some stuffy office somewhere. I want to be in the fresh air, growing things... It's in my blood, after all. My great-grandfather was a gardener. He worked for the Duke of Hartbourne as his head gardener. I don't *want* to work for someone else, though—I want to work for myself. I want to buy a plot of land, develop it, build a garden centre...'

Enthusiastically he had started to tell Verity all about his plans. Six years older than her, he had possessed a maturity, a masculinity, which had alternately enthralled and enticed her. He had represented everything that she had not had in her own life and she had fallen completely and utterly in love with him.

Automatically, she turned the car into the narrow road that led to the house originally owned by her uncle—the house where she had grown up; the house where she had first met Silas; the house where she had tearfully told him that her responsibility, her duty towards her uncle had to take precedence over their love. And so he had married someone else.

The someone else who must have been Honor's mother. He must have loved her a great deal not to have married for a second time. And he had quite obviously cherished her memory and his love for her far longer than he had cherished his much-proclaimed love for *her,* Verity acknowledged tiredly as she reached her destination and drove in through the ornate wrought-iron gates which were a new feature since she had lived in the house. Outwardly, though, in other ways, it remained very much the same. A large, turn-of-the-century house, of no particular aesthetic appeal or design.

Both her uncle and her father had spent their childhood in it but it had never, to Verity, seemed to be a family house, despite its size. Her uncle had changed very little in it since his own parents' death, and to Verity it had always possessed a dark, semi-brooding, solitary air, totally unlike the pretty warmth she remembered from the much smaller but far happier home she had shared with her parents.

After her return from America her uncle had sold the house. His own health had started to deteriorate, during Verity's absence, so he had set in motion arrangements to move the manufacturing side of the business to London. It had seemed to make good sense for both he and Verity to move there as well, Verity to her small mews house close to the river and her uncle to a comfortable apartment and the care of a devoted housekeeper.

Stopping her car, she reached into her handbag for the keys the letting agent had given her and then, taking a deep breath, she got out and headed for the house.

She wasn't really sure herself just why she had chosen to come back, not just to this house but to this town. There was, after all, nothing here for her, no one here for her.

Perhaps one of the reasons was to reassure herself that she *was* now her own person—that she had her own life; that she was finally free; that she had the right to make her own decision. She had done her duty to her uncle and to the business and now, at thirty-three, she stood on the threshold of a whole new way of life, even if she had not decided, as yet, quite what form or shape that life would take.

'What you need is a man...to fall in love,' Charlotte had teasingly advised her the previous summer when Verity had protested that it was impossible for her to take time off to go on holiday with her friend and her family. 'If you fell in love then you would have to find time...'

'Fall in love? Me? Don't be ridiculous,' Verity had chided her.

'Why not?' Charlotte had countered. 'Other people do—even other workaholics like you. You're an attractive, loving, lovable woman, Verity,' she had told her determinedly.

'Tell that to my shareholders,' Verity had joked, adding more seriously, 'I don't *need* any more complications in my life Charlie. I've already got enough and, besides, the men I get to meet aren't interested in the real me. They're only interested in the Verity Maitland who's the head of Maitland Medical...'

'Has there *ever* been anyone, Verity?' Charlotte had asked her gently. 'Any special someone...an old flame...?'

'No. No one,' Verity had lied, hardening her heart against the memories she'd been able to feel threatening to push past the barriers she had put in place against them.

She'd had her share of opportunities, of course—dates…men who had wanted to get to know her better—but…but she had never really been sure whether it had been her they had wanted or the business, and she had simply never cared enough to take the risk of finding out. She had already been hurt once by believing a man who had told her that he loved her. She wasn't going to allow it to happen a second time.

Squaring her shoulders, she inserted the key into the lock and turned the handle.

CHAPTER TWO

As SHE stepped into the house's long narrow hallway, Verity blinked in astonished surprise. Gone was the dark paint and equally dark carpet she remembered, the air of cold unwelcome and austere disapproval, and in their place the hallway glowed with soft warm colours, natural creams warmed by the sunlight pouring in through the window halfway up the stairs. The house felt different, she acknowledged.

Half an hour later, having subjected it to a thorough inspection, she had to admit that its present owners had done a wonderful job of transforming it. Her uncle would, of course, have been horrified both by the luxury and the total impracticality of the warm cream carpet that covered virtually every floor surface. Verity, on the other hand, found it both heart-warming and deliciously sensual, if one could use such a word about something so mundane as mere carpet. The bedroom carpet, for instance, with its particularly thick and soft pile, was so warm-looking that she had had to fight an urge to slip off her shoes and curl her bare toes into it. And as for the wonderful pseudo-Victorian bathroom with its huge, deep tub and luxurious fitments, not to mention the separate shower room that went with it—it was a feast for the eyes.

'It's the best we've got on our books,' the agent had told her. 'The couple who own it had it renovated to the highest standard and if his company hadn't transferred him to California they would still be living there themselves.'

Well, at least she had plenty of wardrobe space, Verity acknowledged a couple of hours later, having lugged the last of her suitcases up the stairs and started to remove their contents.

It had been Charlotte who had decided that they should have a ceremonial clear-out of all the plain, businesslike suits Verity had worn during her years as Chief Executive and Chairperson of the company.

'Throw them out!'

Verity gasped in shock as she listened to what Charlotte was proposing.

'They're far too good for that. That cloth…'

'…will last forever. I know. I remember you telling me so when you originally ordered them—and that was five years ago.'

'Just after Uncle Toby died, yes, I know,' Verity agreed sombrely.

'I hated them on you then and they don't have any place in your life now,' Charlotte reminded her, adding, 'and, whilst we're on the subject, I just never, ever, want to see you wearing your hair up again—especially when it looks so wonderful down. Nature is very, very unfair,' she continued. 'Not only has she given you the most wonderful skin, a profile to die for and naturally navy blue eyes, she's also given you the most glorious honey-blonde hair. It's every bit as thick and gorgeous-looking as Cindy Crawford's and it curls naturally…'

'Cindy who?' Verity teased, laughing when Charlotte began to look appalled and holding her hands up in defeat as she admitted, 'It's okay. I do know who she is…'

'What *you* need to do is to cultivate a more natural, approachable look,' Charlotte counselled her. 'Think jeans and white tees, a navy blazer and loafers, with your hair left down and just a smidgen of make-up.'

'Charlie,' Verity warned, telling her friend, 'I've been in business far too long not to recognise someone trying to package an item for sale.'

'The only person *you* need selling to is yourself,' Charlotte countered. 'I've lost count of the number of men I've introduced you to who you've simply frozen out… One day you're going to wake up on your own heading for forty and—'

'Is that such a very bad deal?' Verity objected.

'Well, there *are* other things in life,' Charlotte reminded her, 'and I've watched you often enough with my two to know how good you are with children.'

It wasn't a subject which Verity wanted to pursue. Not even Charlie, who was arguably her closest friend, knew about Silas and the pain he had caused her, the hopes she had once had…the love she had once given him, only to have it thrown back in her face when he had married someone else, despite telling her… But what was the point in going back over old ground?

She had been nineteen when she and Silas had first met; twenty-two when he had married—someone else—and what time they had had together had been snatched between her years at university, followed by a brief halcyon period of less than six months between her finishing university and being sent to America by her uncle. Halcyon to her, that was. For Silas?

Face it, she told herself sternly now as she hung the last of her spectacular new clothes into the wardrobe. He was never really serious about you, despite everything he said. If he had been he'd have done as he promised.

'I'll love you forever,' he had told her the first time they had made love. 'You're everything I've ever wanted, everything I *will* ever want…'

But he had been lying to her, Verity acknowledged dry-eyed. He had never really loved her at all. And why on earth he had encouraged her to believe that he did, she really could not understand. He had never struck her as the kind of man who needed the ego-boost of making sexual conquests. He was tall, brown-haired and grey-eyed, with the kind of physique that came from working hard out of doors, and Verity had fallen in love with him without needing any encouragement or coaxing. She had just finished her first year at university and come home for the holidays to find him working in her uncle's garden. He had introduced himself to her and had watched her quizzically as she had been too inexperienced, too besotted, to hide her immediate reaction to him, her face and her body blushing a deep vivid pink.

Verity tensed, remembering just how betrayingly her over-sensitive young body *had* revealed her reaction to him, her nipples underneath the thin tee shirt she had been wearing hardening so that she had instinctively crossed her arms over her breasts to hide their flaunting wantonness. He, Silas, had affected not to notice what had happened to her or how embarrassed she had been by it, tactfully turning his head and gently directing her attention to the flower bed he had been weeding, making some easy, relaxed comment about the design of the garden, giving her time to recover her equilibrium and yet, somehow, at the same time, closing the distance between them so that when he'd started to draw her attention to another part of the garden he'd been close enough to her to be able to touch her bare arm with his hand.

Verity could remember even now how violently she had quivered in immediate reaction to his touch.

Fatefully she had turned her head to look at him, her wide-eyed gaze going first to his eyes and then helplessly to his mouth.

He had told her later that the only thing that had stopped him from snatching her up and kissing her there and then had been his fear of frightening her away.

'You looked so young and innocent that I was afraid you might... I was afraid that if I let you see just how much I wanted you, I'd frighten you, terrify the life out of you,' he had told her rawly, weeks later, as he'd held her in his arms and kissed her over and over again, the way she had secretly wanted him to and equally secretly been afraid that he might that first day in the garden.

Looking back with the maturity she had since gained, she could still see no signs, no warnings of what was to be or the full enormity of how badly she was going to be hurt.

She had believed Silas implicitly when he had told her that he loved her. Why should she not have done? *He*, after all, had been the one who had pursued her, courted her, laid seige to her heart and her emotions, her life.

That first summer had been a brilliant kaleidoscope of warmth, love and laughter, or so it seemed looking back on it. She had still been talking to Silas hours later when her uncle had returned home, her bags still standing on the drive where the taxi driver had dropped them and her off. She had been blissfully unaware of just how late it had been until she'd seen her uncle draw up.

'Still here?' he asked Silas curtly, nodding dismissively to him as he turned to Verity and demanded frowningly, 'I should have thought you'd have too much studying to do to waste your time out here, Verity...'

Chastened, Verity bade Silas a mumbled 'goodbye' and turned to follow her uncle into the house. But when she went to pick up her bags, Silas had got there first, gathering up the two heaviest cases as though they weighed a mere nothing.

To Verity, used as she was to the far more frail frame of her elderly uncle, the sight of so much raw, sexual, male strength was dizzyingly exciting.

Her uncle lectured her over supper about the need for her to allocate time during her summer vacation for working hard at her studies.

'Of course, you'll come to the factory with me during the day,' he informed her, and Verity did not attempt to argue. Every holiday since she had turned sixteen had been spent thus, with her learning every aspect of the business from the factory floor upwards, under her uncle's critical eye.

But fate, it seemed, had had other plans for her. The following morning when she went downstairs— her uncle always insisted on leaving for the factory

well before seven so that he could be there before the
first workers arrived at eight—she learned that her
uncle had received a telephone call late the previous
evening informing him that the firm's Sales Director
had been taken to hospital with acute appendicitis,
which meant that her uncle was going to have to step
into his shoes and fly to the Middle East to head a
sales delegation.

He would, he informed Verity, be gone for almost
a month.

'I shall have to leave you here to your own de-
vices,' he told her. 'I can't have you going into the
factory without my supervision. Had this happened a
little earlier I could have made arrangements for you
to come with me. It would have been excellent experience for you but, unfortunately, it's far too late
now for you to have the necessary inoculations and
for me to get a visa for you. Still, you must have
brought work home with you from university.'

'Yes,' she agreed meekly, eyes downcast, her heart
suddenly bounding so frantically fast against her chest
wall that she felt positively light-headed.

Even with her uncle gone she was still unable to
acknowledge the real reason for her excitement and
sense of freedom, nor for her sudden decision to work
in the sitting room which overlooked the part of the
garden which Silas had been working on the previous
day and to wear a pair of cotton shorts which showed
off her long slim legs.

Silas arrived within an hour of her uncle's depar-
ture, and from her strategic position in the sitting
room Verity was able to discreetly watch him as he
worked. As the day grew hotter he stopped working

and stood up, stretching his back before removing his
soft cotton tee shirt.

Dry-mouthed, Verity watched him, her body shaking with the most disturbing sensation she had ever
experienced.

'Lust,' she told herself angrily now as she folded
the last few pairs of briefs and put them neatly into
one of the wardrobe drawers.

Lust: she had been too naive to know just what that
was or how powerful it could be *then*. All she *had*
known was that, no matter how hard she tried to concentrate on her work and the words on the paper in
front of her, all that she could really see was Silas'
image imprinted on her eyeball.

At lunch time she had gone outside to offer him a
cold drink and something to eat. Gravely he had accepted, following her into the kitchen, and it had only
been later that he had admitted to her that he had
brought his own refreshments with him but that the
opportunity to spend some time with her had been too
much of a temptation for him to resist.

Over the light salad lunch she had quickly and nervously prepared for him—Verity had possessed very
few domestic skills in those days; her uncle had considered that learning them was a waste of time when
she was going to take over his business and they had
a housekeeper who lived in, but who fortuitously was
away at that time taking her annual period of leave—
Verity had listened wide-eyed whilst Silas had de-
scribed to her his work and his plans.

'That's enough about me,' he announced gruffly
when they had both finished eating. 'What about you?
What do you intend to do with your life?'

'Me? I'm going to take over my uncle's business,' Verity told him gravely. 'That's what he's training me for. I'm the only person he's got to inherit it, you see. It's his life's work and—'

'*His* life's work, but *you* have your own life and the right to make your own choices, surely?' Silas interrupted her sharply, before telling her pointedly, '*My* parents originally wanted me to train as a doctor like my father, but they would never impose that kind of decision on me, nor would I allow them to…'

'I…my uncle… My uncle took me in when my parents were killed,' Verity explained low-voiced to him. 'I've always known that he expects me…that he wants me… I'm very lucky, really, it's a wonderful opportunity…'

'It's a wonderful opportunity if it's what you really want,' Silas agreed, 'otherwise it's… *Is* it what you want, Verity?'

'I… I… It's what's expected of me,' Verity told him a little unsteadily. It was proving virtually impossible to concentrate on what he was saying with him sitting so close to her—close enough for her to be intensely, embarrassingly aware of his body and its evident physical masculinity, its tantalising male scent. He had asked her permission to 'clean up' before sitting down to lunch with her and his discarded shirt was now back on.

Every time she dared to look at him she was swept with such an intense and heightened awareness of him that she could feel her face starting to flush with hot self-consciousness.

'What's *expected* of you? Listen,' Silas commanded her, reaching out and taking hold of her hand, keeping it between his own with an open easiness which robbed her of the ability to object or protest. 'No one has the right to *expect* anything of you. *You* have the right to choose for yourself what you do with your life. It is *your* life you're living you know, and not your uncle's...'

Verity bit her lip.

'I... I know,' she responded uncertainly, 'but...'

'I'm having a day off tomorrow,' Silas told her, changing the subject. 'There's a garden that's open to the public twenty miles away—I was planning to go and see it. Would you like to come with me?'

Shiny-eyed and flushed with delighted happiness, Verity nodded.

'Good,' he told her. 'I'll pick you up at nine, if that's okay.'

Once again Verity nodded, not trusting herself to speak.

Silas was still holding her hand and she had to tug it before he released it, giving her a rueful smile as he did so.

Of course, she didn't do any work for the rest of the day, nor did she sleep that night.

Three outfits were tried on and discarded before Silas arrived to pick her up, and she blushed betrayingly at the appraising look he gave her as he studied her jeans-clad figure and the neat way the denim hugged her small firm bottom.

Jeans. How long had it been since she had worn a pair of those? Verity wondered grimly now, as the rest of her underwear joined the items she had already put away.

She had acquired a couple of pairs from Charlotte, designer labelled and immaculately tailored.

'You could have taken these with you,' Verity had protested when Charlotte had handed them over to her.

'What? Wear Lauren where *we're* going? Do you mind? The jeans *I'll* be wearing now are a pair of sturdy 501s,' she had told Verity, her face breaking into a wide grin as she had caught sight of the raised-eyebrowed look her friend had been giving her.

'Oh, 501s. Poor you,' Verity had commented dryly.

'Well, they might be "in" fashion-wise but they are also ideally designed for working in and, besides, the Lauren ones are too tight. I can barely move in them. They'll fit you much better—you're slimmer than I am right now.'

Jeans. Verity went to the wardrobe and pulled them out, touching the fabric exploratively, smoothing it beneath her fingertips.

The jeans she had worn on that first date with Silas had been a pair she had bought from her allowance. Thus far, she had not worn them in front of her uncle, knowing that he would not have approved. He had been a rather old-fashioned man who had not liked to see women wearing 'trousers'—of any kind.

Courteously Silas had held the door open for her on the passenger side of his small pick-up. The inside of the vehicle had been spotlessly clean, Verity had noticed, just as she had noticed that Silas was a good and considerate driver.

The gardens they had gone to see had been spectacularly beautiful, she acknowledged, but she had to admit that she had not paid as much attention as she ought to have done to them, nor to Silas' explanation of how the borders had been planted and the colour combinations in them constructed. She had been far too busy studying how he was constructed, far too busy noticing just how wonderfully dedicated to her task nature had been when she had put *him* together with such spectacular sensuality. Even the way he'd walked had made her heart lurch against her ribs, and just to look at his mouth, never mind imagining how it might feel to be kissed by it...by him...

'What's wrong? Are you feeling okay?' Silas asked her at one point.

'I'm fine,' Verity managed to croak, petrified of him guessing what she was really feeling.

He had brought them both a packed lunch—far more tasty and enjoyable than the meal *she* had prepared for him the previous day, Verity acknowledged, assuming, until he told her otherwise, that his mother had prepared it for them.

'Ma? No way,' he told her. 'She believes in us all being self-sufficient and, besides, she works—she's a nurse. My two brothers are both married now and I'm the only one left at home, but Ma still insists on me making my own packed lunches. One thing she did teach us all as a nurse, though, was the importance of good nutrition. Take these sandwiches. They're on wholemeal bread with a low-fat spread, the tuna provides very important nutrients and the salad I've put with it is good and healthy.'

'Like these,' Verity teased him, waving in front of him the two chocolate bars he had packed.

Silas laughed.

'Chocolate *is* good for you,' he told her solemnly,

adding with a wicked smile, 'It's the food of love, did you know that...?'

'Want me to prove it?' he tempted when Verity shook her head.

He enjoyed teasing her, he admitted later, but what he enjoyed even more, he added, was the discovery that beneath her shyness she possessed not just intelligence but, even more importantly, a good sense of humour.

They certainly laughed a lot together that first summer; laughed a lot and loved a lot too.

She could still remember the first time he kissed her. It wasn't sunny that day. There was thunder in the air, the sky brassy and overcast, and then late in the afternoon it suddenly came on to rain, huge, pelting drops, causing them to take refuge in the small summer house several yards away at the bottom of the garden.

They ran there, Silas holding her hand, both of them bursting into the small, stuffy room, out of breath and laughing.

As the door swung closed behind them, enclosing them in the half-light of the small, airless room, Silas turned towards her, brushing her hair off her face. His hands were cool and wet and, without thinking what she was doing, she turned her head to lick a raindrop off him, an instinctive, almost childish gesture, but one which marked the end of her childhood, turning her within the space of an afternoon from a child to a woman.

Even without closing her eyes she could still visualise the expression in Silas' eyes, feel the tension that suddenly gripped his body. Outwardly, nothing had

changed. He was still cupping her face, they were still
standing with their bodies apart, but inwardly *everything* had changed, Verity acknowledged.

Looking into Silas' eyes, she felt herself starting to
tremble—not with cold and certainly not with fear.

'Verity.'

Her name, which Silas started saying inches from
her face, he finished mouthing with his lips against
her own, his *body* against her own. And there was
nothing remotely childish about the way she reached
out to him—for him—Verity remembered; nothing remotely childish at all in the way she opened her
mouth beneath his and deliberately invited him to explore its intimacy. They kissed frantically, feverishly,
whispering incomprehensible words of love and
praise to one another, she making small keening
sounds of pleasure against Silas' skin, he muttering
rawly to her that he loved her, adored her, wanted
her. Over and over again they kissed and touched and
Verity felt incandescent with the joy of what she was
experiencing; of being loved; of knowing that Silas
loved her as much as she knew she loved him.

They weren't lovers that day. She wanted to but
Silas shook his head, telling her huskily, 'We can't…
I can't… I don't have… I could make you pregnant,'
he explained to her, adding gruffly, 'The truth is I
would *want* to make you pregnant, Verity. That's how
much I love you and I know that once I had you in
my arms, once my body was inside yours, there's no
way I could… I want to come inside you,' he told her
openly when she looked uncertainly at him, explaining in a low, emotional voice, 'I want to have that
kind of intimacy with you. It's man's most basic in-

stinct to regenerate himself, to seed the fertility of his woman, especially when he loves her as much as I love you.'

'I… I could go on the pill…' Verity offered, but Silas shook his head.

'No,' he told her gently, 'taking care of that side of things is *my* responsibility. And besides,' he continued softly, looking around the cramped, stuffy summer house, 'this isn't really the right place. When you and I make love I want it to be…I want it to be special for you…perfect.'

Verity moistened her lips.

'My uncle is still away,' she offered awkwardly. 'We could…'

'No. Not here in another man's house. Yes, I know that it's your home, but no, not here,' Silas said quietly.

'Where, then?' Verity breathed eagerly.

'Leave it to me,' Silas told her. 'Leave everything to me…'

And like the dutiful person she had been raised to be she dipped her head and agreed.

CHAPTER THREE

THE doorbell rang just as Verity had finished her unpacking. Frowning, she went downstairs to answer it. Who on earth could that be? She certainly wasn't expecting anyone.

She was still frowning when she opened the door, a small gasp of shock escaping her lips as she saw who was standing there and recognised him immediately.

'Silas!'

Instinctively her hand went to her throat as she tried, too late, to suppress that betraying whisper of sound.

'Verity,' her visitor responded grimly. 'May I come in?'

Without waiting for her assent he was shouldering his way into the hallway.

'How...how did you know I was back?' Verity managed to ask him huskily. Was it possible that he had actually grown taller *and* broader in the years they had been apart? Surely not, and yet she couldn't remember him ever filling the space of the hallway quite so imposingly before. He might be over ten years older but he was *still* as magnetically male as she remembered, she recognised unwillingly, and perhaps even more so—as a young man he had worn his sexuality very carelessly, softening it with the tenderness and consideration he had shown her.

Now… She took a deep breath and tried to steady her jittery nerves. Now there was *nothing* remotely soft nor tender about the way he was looking at her. Far from it.

'I didn't until I did a check at the hospital and found out that *you* had accompanied Honor there. What the hell kind of person *are* you, Verity? First you damn near run my daughter over and then you don't even bother to let *me* know that she's had an accident. What am I saying? I know *exactly* what kind of woman you are, don't I? Why should I be surprised at *anything* you might choose to do, after all I know?'

Verity couldn't utter a word. What was he saying? What was he trying to accuse her of doing? She… He made it sound as though she had deliberately tried to hit Honor, when the truth was…

'I did what I thought was best,' she told him coolly. There was no way she was going to let him see just how much he had caught her off guard, or how agitated and ill-equipped to deal with him she actually felt.

Thinking about him earlier had done nothing to prepare her for the reality of him. She had been thinking about, remembering, a young man in his twenties. *This* was a mature adult male in his late thirties and a man who…

'What *you* thought was best?' He gave her an incredulously angry look as he repeated her words. 'Didn't it strike you that as Honor's father *I* had the right to know what had happened? Didn't it cross that cold little mind of yours that *you* had a responsibility to let me know what had happened? After all, you used to be very big on responsibility, didn't you? Oh, but I was forgetting, the kind of responsibility you favoured was the kind that meant—'

'I didn't get in touch with you because I had no idea that you were Honor's father until we got to the hospital,' Verity interrupted him quickly, 'and by then…'

By then Honor had begged her not to let her father know what had happened and, additionally, untruthfully told both her and the nurse that Silas was unavailable and out of the country. But she certainly wasn't going to tell Silas *that*. Against all the odds, and ridiculously, she felt a certain sense of kinship, of female bonding with Honor.

Female *bonding* with a *ten*-year-old? And she was supposed to be intelligent? Charlotte was right—she *did* need to get a grip on her life.

'Presumably, though, you knew by the time Honor had informed the nurse that *you* were going to be her stepmother,' he informed her with deadly acidness.

She was surely far too old and had far too much self-control to be betrayed now by the kind of hot-faced blush which had betrayed her so readily all those years ago, but nonetheless Verity found herself hurriedly looking away from the anger she could see in Silas' eyes and curling her toes into her shoes as she fibbed, 'Uh…did she…? I really don't remember…the casualty department was busy,' she embroidered. 'I just wanted to make sure that Honor got some medical attention—'

'Liar.' Silas cut across her stumbled explanation in a brutally incisive voice that made her wince. 'And don't think I don't know *exactly* why you laid claim to a non-existent relationship between us.'

This was worse than her worst possible nightmare, worse by far than the most embarrassing and humiliating thing she could ever have imagined happening to her, Verity decided. She could *never* remember feeling so exposed and vulnerable, so horribly conscious of having her deepest and most private emotions laid bare to be derided and scorned. No, not even the first time she had had to stand up in front of her late uncle's board of directors, knowing how much each and every one of them must secretly have been resenting her appointment as their leader, as the person to whom they would have to defer.

In that one sentence Silas had torn down, trampled, flattened, all the delicate defences she had worked so hard to weave together to protect herself with—defences she had created with patience and teeth-gritting determination; defences she had bonded together with good humour and cheerful smiles, determined never to allow *anyone* to guess what she was really feeling, or to guess how empty her life sometimes felt, how far short of her once idealistic expectations it had fallen. Other people's compassion and pity were something she had always shrunk from and gently rejected. Her lack of a man to share her life, a child to share her love—these had been things she had determinedly told herself she was not going to allow herself to yearn for. She had her *life*, her *friends*, her *health*.

But now, pitilessly and brutally, Silas had destroyed that precious, fragile peace of mind she had worked with gentle determination to achieve.

Silas had guessed, unearthed, exhumed the pitiful little secret she had so safely hidden from other eyes.

Bravely Verity lifted her head. She wasn't going to let him have a *total* victory. Something could be salvaged from the wreckage, the destruction he had caused, even if it was only her pride.

'Contrary to what you seem to think—' she began, but once again Silas wouldn't let her finish.

He cut her off with a furious, 'I don't *think*. I *know*. You let the nurse believe that you had the right to sign Honor's consent form because you thought it would get you off the hook, that that way you wouldn't have to face up to what you had done, nor suffer any potential legal consequences.

'My God, what kind of woman are you to be driving so carelessly in a built-up area in the first place, and at school-leaving time? But, then, we both already know the answer to that, don't we? Such mundane matters as children's safety, children's lives, simply don't matter to you, do they? You've got far more important things to concern yourself with. How many millions are you worth these days, Verity? No doubt that car outside is just *one* of the perks that comes with being a very rich woman.

'Funny—I knew, of course, that the business came first, second and third with you, but I never had you down as a woman who needed to surround herself with all the trappings of a materialistic lifestyle.'

Verity gave him a dazed, almost semi-blind look. What was he saying—something about her car? About her wealth? It didn't matter. All that mattered was the intense feeling of relief she felt on realising that he hadn't, after all, meant what she had thought he had meant by that comment about knowing why she had not refuted Honor's outrageous claim that she was soon to become her stepmother. That he had thought she had allowed his daughter's fib to stand so that no questions could be asked about the accident, not because secretly she still yearned for...still wanted...

'My God, but you've changed,' she heard him breathing angrily. 'That car...this house...those clothes...'

Her clothes... Verity pushed aside her euphoric sense of relief—there would be time for her to luxuriate in that later when she was on her own.

'I'm wearing jeans,' she managed to point out in quiet self-defence.

'Designer jeans,' Silas told her curtly, nodding in the direction of the logo sewn on them.

Designer jeans? How had Silas known that? The Silas she remembered simply wouldn't have known or cared where her clothes had come from. The Silas *she* knew and remembered would, in fact, have been far more interested in what lay beneath her clothes rather than the name of the design house they had originated from.

Quickly, Verity redirected her thoughts, telling him dryly what her own quick eye had already noticed.

'Your own clothes are hardly basic chain store stuff.'

Was that just a hint of betraying caught-out colour seeping up under his skin? Verity wondered triumphantly.

'I didn't choose them,' he told her stiffly.

Then who had? A woman? For some reason his admission took all her original pleasure at catching him out away from her, Verity acknowledged dismally.

'I suppose you thought you were being pretty clever and that you'd got away with damn near killing my daughter,' Silas was demanding to know, back on the attack again. 'Well, unfortunately for you a…a friend of mine just happened to see you at the scene of the accident and she took a note of your car's registration number.'

'Really? How very neighbourly of her,' Verity gritted. 'I don't suppose it occurred to her that she might have been more usefully employed trying to help Honor rather than playing at amateur detective?'

'Myra was on her way to a very important meeting. She's on the board of several local charities and, as she said, she could hardly expect busy business people who are already giving their time to feel inclined to make a generous cash donation to a charity when its chairperson can't even be on time for a meeting…'

Whoever this Myra was, Silas obviously thought an awful lot of her, Verity reflected. He made her sound like a positive angel.

'You aren't going to deny that you *were* responsible for Honor's accident, I hope?' Silas continued, returning to the attack.

Verity was beginning to get angry herself now. How dared he speak to her like this? Would he have done so had he not already known her, judged her…had she been a stranger? Somehow she doubted it. He was being unfairly critical of her, unfairly caustic towards her because of who she was, because once she had been foolish enough to love him, and he had been— Quickly she gathered up her dangerously out-of-control thoughts.

Deny that she was responsible? But she *hadn't* been

responsible. It was… On the point of opening her mouth to vigorously inform him just how wrong he was, Verity abruptly remembered her conversation with Honor and the little girl's anxiety. Quickly she closed it again.

'It *was* an *accident*,' was all she could permit herself to say.

'An accident caused by the fact that *you* were driving too selfishly and too fast along a suburban road, in a car more properly designed for fast driving on an *autobahn*, or in your case, probably more truthfully, for showing off amongst your friends.'

Verity gasped.

'For your information,' she began, 'I bought that car…' On the point of telling him just why she had bought the BMW, she suddenly changed her mind. After all, what explanations did she possibly owe *him*? None. None at all.

'I bought that car because I wanted to buy it—because I liked it. No doubt your *friend* prefers to drive something ecologically sound, modest and economical. She has a Beetle, perhaps, or maybe a carefully looked after Morris Minor which she inherited from some aged aunt…' she suggested acidly.

'As a matter of fact—not that it's any business of yours, Myra drives a Jaguar. It was part of the settlement she received when she divorced her husband… But I'm not here to talk about my friends or my private life. You do realise, don't you, that I could report you to the police for dangerous driving?'

Immediately Verity froze, unable to control her expression.

'Yes, you may well look shocked,' Silas told her grimly.

'You can't do that,' Verity protested, thinking of Honor.

'Can't I? I've certainly got a damned good mind to, although, given your cavalier attitude towards the truth and the fact that there were no witnesses to the *whole* event, no doubt you'd manage to find a way of extricating yourself.'

'*Me* cavalier with the truth? That's rich coming from you,' Verity retorted bitterly.

'What the hell do you mean by that?' Silas challenged her.

Verity glared at him, her own temper as hot as his now. After all, she could hardly remind him that he had once told her he loved her; that he would always love her; that there would never be anyone else.

'Why have you come back here?' he demanded abruptly.

Verity turned her face away from him so that he couldn't fully see her expression.

'I grew up here. It's my home town,' she reminded him quietly.

'Sentiment. You've come back out of sentiment. My God, now I really have heard everything!'

'My roots are here,' Verity continued, praying that nothing in her voice or her expression would reveal to him how very, very much his cruelty was hurting her.

'Roots, maybe,' Silas allowed in a biting voice. 'But if you're hoping to revisit the past or resurrect old—'

'I'm not hoping to do any such thing,' Verity interrupted him passionately. 'So far as I'm concerned, the past is the past and that's exactly how I intend it to stay. There's *nothing* in it that I miss.'

'Nothing in it that you miss and certainly nothing in it that you ever valued,' Silas agreed.

And then to Verity's shock he suddenly took a step towards her.

'Silas.' Dizzily Verity moved too, but not back away from him putting more distance between them as she had planned. No. Instead what she actually did was take a step towards him. A step that brought her within intimate reach of his body, within his private body space, and close enough to him not just to see the dark shadowing along his jaw where his beard would grow but also to reach out and touch it, to feel it prickling against her palm as she had done all those years ago, the first time they had shared a bed together, and she had woken up in the opalescent light of a summer morning in the euphoric knowledge that he was there beside her, that she had the blissful, awesome right to simply turn her head and watch him as he slept, knowing that he was *hers*; that *she* was his, that nothing and no one could cause them to part—ever.

Silas!

Verity closed her eyes. She could feel the deep, uneven, heavy thud thud of her own heartbeat, pounding through her body in urgent summons. Was it *that* that was making her feel so weak, so…?

'I'm warning you, Verity, stay away from me. Stay out of my life…'

The ugly words hit her like blows aimed viciously into her unprotected vulnerable emotions. Instinctively she tried to protect herself from them by wrapping her arms around her body, but Silas was already turning away from her and heading for the door.

'I mean it,' he warned her as he paused to open it. 'Stay out of my life.'

She must be suffering some kind of shock, Verity decided dazedly ten minutes later as she slowly made her way back upstairs.

Stay out of *his* life? Did he *really* think he needed to warn her off, that she didn't *know* that there was no place there for her, no love there for her?

Numbly she stared out of her bedroom window and into the garden below. From this window she could just about see the roof of the little summer house where they had sheltered from the rain, and it had been here in this room, if not on this bed, that she had lain dreaming her foolish, idealistic, heated, adoring, loving, girlish dreams of him.

And it had been here too that she had lain in the days after he had fully made love to her, feeling and believing that the reality of his lovemaking had far, far outstripped even her most feverish and sensually exciting daydreams.

It had been here too in this room, this sanctuary, that she had come after that dreadful quarrel when he had challenged her to choose between her love for him and her duty to her uncle, and here too that she had cried her tears of relief and happiness when he had told her, with remorse and regret, that the last thing he had wanted to do was to hurt her; that hurting her had hurt him even more and that, of course, he had understood that she had to at least attempt, as a matter of duty and honour, to accede to her uncle's wishes.

'It won't be for long,' she had promised him as he had held her face and her tears had flowed down onto his hands. 'America isn't really so very far away and when I come back…'

'When you come back I'm never ever going to let you out of my sight again,' he had told her savagely. 'If you weren't so damned stubborn I wouldn't be letting you go now.'

'I have to go,' she had wept. 'I owe it to my uncle…' And yet she had known even as she had said the words that a part of her had longed for him to snatch her away, to refuse to allow her to leave him, to, however implausible it would have been, insist.

'You could come with me,' she had even suggested. 'You could work over there…'

'Come with you? As what?' He had balked immediately, telling her, 'I'm a independent man, Verity. I *can't* live on your coat tails and, besides, what about our plans to buy the small holding we visited last week—to develop the garden centre…?

Verity closed her eyes now and leant her hot face against the cool glass.

'I'll wait for you,' he had promised her when she had left. 'I'll wait for you, no matter how long it takes…'

Only he hadn't…he hadn't waited. Hadn't loved her. Hadn't given her the wedding ring nor the child he had promised her so passionately and, she had believed, so meaningfully.

Oh, God! Had he guessed just now in the hallway,

when she had stepped towards him instead of stepping away, just what was going through her mind, her body? How *easy* it would have been for her to…? Had he known that a foolish, idiotic part of her had actually thought that he *was* going to kiss her, that he had *wanted* to kiss her? That that same foolish, idiotic part of her remembered with such aching intensity that that was exactly how he used to move towards her when…?

'No,' Verity protested despairingly beneath her breath. 'No…please, no…' But it was already too late, already the memories were flooding back, swamping her. The first time he had made love to her… She could remember it as clearly and intensely as though it had only happened yesterday.

They had been out together for the day. Another visit to a famous garden—Silas, as she had discovered by this time, was a passionate advocate of the importance of good garden structure.

'Not having a proper structure to me is like…like…well, imagine trying to clothe a human body if all the limbs had simply been stuck on haphazardly here and there and everywhere, or if a house had been designed simply by adding one room next to another…'

And he produced books and then drawings to show Verity to reinforce his point. Completely head over heels in love with him by this stage, Verity acknowledged that she was probably spending longer gazing adoringly at the way his hair curled into his collar and flopped over his forehead than studying the designs he was showing her, but she took on board all that he was saying and she was as impressed and excited as he was by the elegant simplicity of the gardens they went to see.

'Every garden has a right to be properly designed,' he told her passionately, 'and you only have to read one of Sir Roy Strong's books to see just how the concept of good architectural design can be transferred to even the smallest urban garden.'

They were sitting eating their sandwiches at the time.

'Mmm...' Verity agreed, smiling lovingly at him.

And then he put down his sandwich and removed hers from her, and took her in his arms and kissed her lingeringly and very, very thoroughly, but very gently, before lifting his head and looking from her love-dazed eyes to her kiss softened mouth before telling her rawly, 'You don't know what I'd give right now to be somewhere alone with you and private...'

Very slowly he reached out and traced the shape of her lips with his fingertip.

'Perfect,' he whispered tenderly.

'Good architectural design,' Verity whispered teasingly back.

'Better than that. The best,' Silas told her solemnly, but then the laughter died out of his eyes as the tip of his finger touched the centre of her bottom lip and Verity could feel it and him starting to shake with need—a need which she fully reciprocated.

'Couldn't we do that—be together?' Verity asked him huskily.

They talked about becoming lovers but Silas told her that he had applied the brakes to his plans to find them the perfect hideaway because he wanted to wait until he was sure it was what she wanted—he was what she wanted—and that he didn't want to rush her.

'We could…there's my bedroom,' Verity boldly offered her home again. Her uncle was away on another trip. The Sales Director's appendicitis had proved more problematic than his doctors had first expected, causing a delay in his recovery, and her uncle had had to take over his duties and was consequently away on business far more than usual.

'No, not there,' Silas answered firmly, 'but if you're sure…'

His hand was holding the back of her head, caressing her scalp through her hair. Shivering with excitement and emotion, Verity smiled tremulously at him. The look in his eyes made her face burn—and not with the embarrassment of coy self-consciousness of a young woman who was still a virgin.

'I'm sure,' she told him positively. 'Oh, Silas, I'm so sure…'

'I want everything to be right—special,' he told her gruffly. 'I've looked into some of the hotels in the area and I could book us a room—for tonight…'

'Oh, yes, yes,' Verity breathed.

Tenderly she reached out and touched his face, feeling the warmth of his skin beneath her fingertips, the hard firmness of the bones and muscles that lay below it. She might not have been physically experienced, might never have had a previous lover, but she had no sense of fear nor trepidation, simply a deep inner knowledge of how right this was, of how right Silas was!

Silas found them a hotel several miles away from the garden they had visited. Small and privately owned, it was set in its own gardens but, for once, after they had booked in, Silas showed no inclination to explore.

'I…I thought you might like to…to see the gardens,' Verity had protested a little uncertainly once they were alone in the room.

Silas shook his head quietly, locking the door before turning back to her.

'No. Right now there's only one thing I want to do, one garden I want to explore,' he said softly, and Verity knew from the way he looked at her, his glance slowly caressing every inch of her, just exactly what he meant.

'I…what…? I don't know what to do,' she told him finally and honestly, blushing and then laughing. 'Well, I do, at least I think I do, but…'

'Come here,' Silas commanded her and, her colour still high, Verity walked unsteadily into his arms.

They had kissed before of course, and touched intimately so, but never like this, Verity acknowledged as Silas kissed his way slowly along the soft line of her lips and then, repeating the gesture he had made earlier, pressed the pad of his thumb to the centre of her bottom lip, hungrily nibbling the tender flesh he had exposed, his arms tightening possessively around her as Verity trembled in response to his touch. His tongue slowly caressed the inner sweetness of her mouth as hers did his and then he slowly and rhythmically sucked on her tongue and taught her to do the same to his.

As she repeated his sensual, intimate caress, Verity could feel the jolt that ran through his body and the sexual hardening and arousal that went with it.

Wrapping her arms around him, she pressed herself just as close to him as she could get, instinctively rubbing her body lovingly against his and making little purring sounds of pleasure as she did so, her eyes closing.

'Verity, Verity,' she heard Silas groaning as his hands gripped her waist half as though he was going to put her slightly away from him, but then he changed his mind, his hands sliding down her body to cup her buttocks and grind his own hips into her receptive body.

A delicious shiver of pleasure convulsed her and Silas removed one of his hands from her bottom to gently rub and knead the length of her spine in a caress that was so tenderly soothing that it made Verity open her eyes and look dazedly up at him.

'I don't want to take things too fast,' Silas told her rawly in response to her unspoken question. 'This will be your first time and I want...I want to make it perfect for you—in every way, Verity.'

'It will be,' she promised him, knowing as she spoke the words that they were true, with some deep rooted primal feminine wisdom that didn't need to be analysed or questioned.

Gently and lovingly, Silas undressed her, pausing to caress and kiss each bit of flesh he exposed, but once he got to her breasts, Verity felt his self-control beginning to slip away. As he slowly circled one taut, hard, flushed nipple with the pad of his thumb she knew it wasn't just her who was trembling so violently in sensual reaction.

'These are the most beautiful...you are the most perfect thing I have ever seen,' he whispered throatily as he picked her up and carried her over to the huge king-sized bed.

'More perfect than one of Sir Roy Strong's gardens,' Verity teased him remembering their earlier shared humour.

An answering smile crinkled the corners of his mouth and momentarily lightened the passion that had darkened his eyes as he teased back, 'Who's Sir Roy Strong?'

Their laughter immediately banished whatever small feeling of self-consciousness Verity felt she might otherwise have had and very soon her fingers were equally busy as Silas', if not perhaps quite as patient, as she tugged at the buttons of his shirt and then closed her eyes in mute pleasure when she had finally revealed the tanned male expanse of his chest.

Lovingly she buried her face against him, closing her eyes and breathing in his scent before delicately licking at the small indentation in the middle of his chest, discovering the faintly salty male taste that was exclusively his.

'Verity,' Silas groaned.

'I want to,' Verity protested. 'I want to know every bit of you, Silas. I want to hold you, touch you, taste you. I want…'

'You don't know what you're saying,' Silas warned her.

But gravely and seriously and suddenly completely adult and mature, suddenly totally sensually a woman, Verity told him quietly, 'Oh, yes, I do. I want you, Silas,' she told him, lifting one of his hands and placing it first against her heart and then against her sex, saying, 'Here,' and 'here,' and then finally lifting his hand to her temple and repeating softly, 'and here.'

'With all my heart I thee love,' Silas whispered back, taking hold of her hand and pressing a kiss into the palm before placing it against his chest. 'With my body I thee worship.'

Watching her eyes, he placed her hand intimately on his own body. Verity drew in a quick sharp breath of feminine appreciation and urgency, the pulse in her wrist thudding every bit as fiercely as the pulse she could feel throbbing through the urgent shaft of male flesh she was touching. Instinctively her fingers closed over him, delicately learning and knowing him, whilst Silas continued in a thickly changed voice, lifting not the hand that was holding his sex with such feminine tenderness and love, but her other to his own forehead. 'With my mind I thee honour, with everything that is me I commit myself to you now, Verity. Nothing ever can and ever will break the bond we are forming between us tonight. Nothing…'

'Nothing…' Verity repeated softly, and beneath her fingertips she could feel the hot, hard shaft of his sex harden even further and begin to pulse in ever fiercer demand.

The first time he entered her Verity cried out, not in pain but in exultation, clinging passionately to him, welcoming him within her with a heart full of love and joy, her emotions so charged and heightened that the feel of him within her, the knowledge of the intimacy, the love they were sharing, the bond they were creating, brought quick, emotional tears to her eyes.

Seeing them, Silas immediately cursed himself under his breath and started to withdraw from her, believing that he had hurt her. Quickly Verity reassured him, explaining in a choked voice that it was the pleasure of having him within her that had caused them, and not the pain.

Later he told her that what they had shared was just the beginning of the pleasure he intended to give her, the special sensual intimacy they would share.

'*You* are my *special* garden, Verity,' he told her as he lovingly caressed her warmly naked body. 'My most private, secret garden where what flowers between us is special and magical and for us alone.'

'And which, one day, hopefully will bear fruit,' Verity continued, picking up on his theme as she blissfully ran her fingertips down his spine, revelling in her right to touch him and to be with him. 'But not for a long time yet,' she added drowsily. 'And I don't suppose that Uncle Toby will want me to have more than the most basic maternity leave…'

'Maternity leave?' Silas checked her, his body suddenly tensing as he started to frown. 'I know you've said that your uncle expects you to work in the business once you've finished university, but surely what's happened between us changes that? I'm not so sexist that I'd want to prevent you from working if that's what you want, but…'

'It isn't a matter of what *I* want, Silas,' Verity told him slowly. 'My uncle *expects* me to work alongside him in the business and then to take over from him. It means *everything* to him…'

'More than *you* or *your* happiness,' Silas challenged her. 'Or are you trying to tell me that it and he mean more to you than me and our children…?'

'No, of course not…but I owe him so much and he…'

'More than you owe our love?' Silas demanded.

They were on the verge of quarrelling and Verity's eyes filled with hot, hurt tears. Couldn't Silas understand how *difficult* things were for her? Of course she wanted to be with him. How could she not do?

'Please, don't let's spoil things by fighting,' she begged him. Although she sensed that he wanted to continue their discussion, instead he gave a small sigh and said, 'No, you're right. This isn't the time…nor the place…'

'Make love to me again, Silas,' she urged him, and it wasn't until many, many months later that she was mature enough to recognise how dangerously she had begun the habit then—a way of avoiding the issue and sidelining it, and Silas, by distracting his attention away from the future through lovemaking. In fact, it wasn't until Silas himself accused her of it that she was forced to recognise just what she was doing and by then…

'I'll love you for ever. You're everything I've ever wanted, everything I *will* ever want,' Silas promised her the following morning as they lay entwined with one another in bed, her body still sleek and damp from the passion of their recent lovemaking.

Only it hadn't been a promise which he had kept. It had been a promise he had broken, just as he had broken her heart and almost broken her.

CHAPTER FOUR

HER first impression that the town hadn't changed had been an erroneous one, Verity acknowledged as she dumped the supermarket carrier bags on the kitchen table.

She had spent the afternoon exploring her old environment before calling in at an out-of-town supermarket to fill her car with petrol and buy some food.

The layout of the town centre might essentially be the same but many of the small shops she remembered from her girlhood had gone, to be replaced with what she privately considered to be an over-representation of building society and estate agents offices. The pedestrianisation of the town centre itself, though, she had to admit, was an improvement, and she had particularly liked the way shady trees had been planted and huge tubs of brightly coloured tumbling summer bedding plants grouped artistically around them. Along with the strategically placed benches, they had created a relaxed, informal, almost continental air to the town centre, which today had been heightened by the fact that the warm summer weather had meant that people had been able to eat outside the square's several restaurants and cafés under the umbrellas decorating the tables and chairs on the pavement. It had been disconcerting, though, to read from a small plaque that the square had been re-designed by Silas as a gift to the town.

If the town centre itself had looked disconcertingly unfamiliar, then so had the faces of the people she had seen around her. She had never made any really close friends during her school-days. The regime imposed by her uncle had prevented that, but there had been girls whose company she could have enjoyed.

Tonight she would ring Charlotte, she promised herself as she started to unpack her provisions. It would be good to hear a friendly voice. She didn't want to think about the consequences of the fact that one of the few adult voices she had heard since her return had been that of her ex-lover and that it had been far from friendly.

A 'friend' had told him about the accident, he had told her tersely. What exactly did *that* mean? The term 'friend' applied to a member of the opposite sex could cover so many possibilities. Anyway, why should *she* care who or what this woman was to Silas?

Removing the jacket of the Gucci trouser suit she was wearing, she opened the fridge door.

Wearing Gucci to do the supermarket shopping was perhaps a trifle over the top, especially outside Knightsbridge, and even more especially when the suit in question was white and had featured extremely prominently in all the glossies early on in the season, but having given into Charlotte's pleas and bought the dratted thing she could hardly leave it hanging in her wardrobe... Even so... She had fully registered the several double takes she had received from other shoppers, women clad in the main in the busy suburban women's uniform of immaculate neat jeans, white shirt and navy blazer.

She supposed her hair didn't help either, she acknowledged, flipping it back over her shoulder, then taking a clip from her pocket and pinning it up. She had worn it long ever since she could remember. As a teenager she had wanted to have it cut but for once her uncle and Silas had been unanimous in their veto—albeit for very different reasons. Her uncle had always insisted that her hair was neatly tucked into an old-fashioned bun—the kind he remembered his mother wearing—whilst Silas... Silas had whispered to her that first night they had shared together that he had fantasised about taking her hair and wrapping it around his body, feeling its supple silkiness caressing his skin.

She had made that fantasy come true for him, even if she had blushed a little to do so that very first time.

In the years that had passed since then, she had still not had her hair cut—trimmed occasionally, yes, but cut, never—and, until she had sold the company, in obedience to her uncle's wishes she had always worn it rolled into an elegant knot.

She had lost count of the times Charlotte had tried to persuade her to wear it down.

'I'm too old for long, loose hair,' she had protested determinedly.

'Are you crazy?' Charlotte had argued back, adding, 'Have you seen the latest round of jeans ads—the one featuring the back view of a woman with hair down to her waist? She's seventy and she's making one hell of a positive statement about the way women have the right to view ourselves, besides which she looks absolutely stunning. If I had hair like yours—thick, wavy—there's no way you'd ever get me to hide it away.'

'In business, big business, men view long hair on a woman as a sign of weakness. It's probably some kind of Narcissus complex,' Verity had remarked wryly. 'They see long hair and immediately they think, Ah ha...gotcha...she's going to be spending more time in front of the mirror than in front of any sales figures, and then they start rubbing their hands together in glee because they think they're going to put one over on you.'

'Oh, yeah. Let me tell you something, lady,' Charlotte had corrected her after she had finished laughing. 'The reason they're rubbing their hands together in glee is because they're thinking, Wow, that's some woman, *I* want to take her to bed...'

'In other words to them long hair equals bimbo, victim...weakness.'

'Why do I get the distinct impression that somewhere, some time, some man has hurt you very badly?' Charlotte had asked intuitively. But Verity had simply shaken her head. The past, her past, was simply something she was not prepared to talk about—not even to her closest friend.

One thing Verity had noticed, though, when she had been out, and it was something that had caught painfully at her unguarded, vulnerable emotions, had been the number of couples shopping together—and not all of them young. Seeing the loving, tenderly amused looks one couple had exchanged, as the man had reached up to a higher shelf for something the woman had wanted and she had surreptitiously stroked his thigh whilst he did so, had made Verity look away in hot-cheeked sharp awareness of the emotional emptiness of her own life. It didn't have to be that way. Once she had had time to think, to assess and to plan; once she became fully involved in the charities she intended to set up with her uncle's money, then there would be no time for painful regrets about what might have been.

It was seeing Silas that had unsettled her so distressingly, she told herself angrily. Seeing him and listening to him making those outrageous accusations against her.

She stiffened as she heard the doorbell ring. There was no reason for her to think that it might be Silas, of course, but just in case... Forcing her face to assume the expression she normally reserved for the boardroom—the one that said 'Don't even *think* about trying to mess with me'—she headed determinedly for the front door and yanked it open.

'Honor,' she squeaked in startled surprise. 'What on earth are you doing here?'

'I got my pocket money today and I've come to pay the first instalment of the money I owe you for the damage to your car,' Honor told her sturdily, adding before Verity could say anything, 'May I come in? It's so hot...'

'Yes. Of course. Let me get you a cold drink,' Verity offered, leading the way to the kitchen. 'Did you walk here?'

'Mmm...' Honor mumbled as she took a deep gulp of the iced orange juice Verity had poured for her.

'Mmm...real juice!' Honor exclaimed blissfully. 'Wonderful, but it's very expensive,' she told Verity sternly. 'Dad won't buy it—he says I waste it because I never finish it and it's too expensive. He buys it when Myra comes round, though.' She pulled a face.

'Apparently she likes it for breakfast—not that she's ever stayed overnight. She'd like to, though. She thinks I don't know what her game is but I do—a woman always knows,' she concluded wisely. 'She wants to get married again and she wants to marry Dad. He'd be mad if he did—she's poison.' Honor pulled an expressive face. 'She didn't even like the new clothes I made him buy, and I know why—she doesn't want any other woman looking at him.'

Honor had chosen Silas' designer clothes! But Verity didn't have time to digest this information properly before Honor was continuing, 'I've tried to warn him but Dad just can't see it... I suppose he can't see the truth beneath all that make-up she wears. She hates kids as well. That's why she left her first husband. I know... But Dad thinks it's because he wouldn't let her get pregnant...'

Verity gave her a wary look.

'Oh, it's okay, Dad didn't tell me that. He's a great father, the best, but we don't have that kind of relationship. He's pretty much for keeping what he thinks of grown-up things to himself, but I'm not a kid...and I've got my ear to the ground. She's just not good enough for him.'

'How old are you exactly, Honor?' Verity asked her faintly, automatically refilling the now empty glass Honor had extended.

'Ten...' Honor told her promptly.

Ten going on ninety, Verity decided. Did Silas have any inkling of how his daughter felt about her prospective stepmother? she wondered. At least she now knew exactly what the word 'friend' meant when applied to Silas' relationship with his tell-tale girlfriend.

'I'm starving,' Honor told her winningly, 'and Dad's gone out for dinner tonight. I don't suppose…?'

Her aplomb really was extraordinary for someone so young, and perhaps Verity ought to very firmly remind her of the age gap that lay between them and the inadvisability of inviting herself into other people's lives—but she *liked* her, Verity acknowledged, and even if it *was* a weakness within herself she simply couldn't bring herself to dent that luminous youthful pride by pointing out such facts to her.

'I'm afraid I *can't* offer you anything to eat,' she replied gravely instead, intending to tell Honor that she rather thought that her father would disapprove of them having any kind of contact with one another— and not just because *he* obviously considered that she had more or less callously practically run Honor down, thanks to the evidence of his 'girlfriend'. She amended her private thoughts to say gently instead, 'I was planning to eat out.'

'Oh, good.' Honor grinned, telling her frankly, 'I hate cooking too.'

Verity blinked.

'Honor, I *don't* hate cooking,' she protested. 'It's just…'

'There's a terrific Italian place just opened up in town. Italian's my favourite, I love their ice cream puddings,' Honor volunteered.

Totally against her better judgement, Verity knew that she was weakening.

'Mmm…' she agreed. 'I like Italian too…'

Woman to woman they looked at one another.

'You're right,' Verity heard herself saying, a little

to her own bemusement. 'Why cook at home when you can eat Italian somewhere else?'

What was she thinking? What was she *doing*? Verity asked herself grimly ten minutes later when she had parked the car in the town centre car park. There would be hell to pay if Silas ever found out, she acknowledged fatalistically, frowning a little as she waited for Honor to get out of the car before activating the central-locking system.

That wasn't by any chance *why* she was doing this, was it? To get at Silas? She was way, way above those kind of childish tit-for-tat manoeuvres, wasn't she? Wasn't she…?

'It's this way,' Honor told her, happily linking her arm through Verity's.

'You should wear your hair down,' she advised Verity seriously as she checked their reflections in a shop window. 'Men like it.'

'Uh-huh…er…do they?'

Heavens, what was wrong with her? *She* shouldn't be the one acting flustered and self-conscious, Verity derided herself.

'The purpose, the point, of being a woman is not to please men or to seek their approval,' she told Honor sternly.

'No, but it sure helps when you want your own way,' Honor told her practically.

Verity gave her an old-fashioned look. 'Your father came to see me,' she told Honor quietly. 'His…friend…Myra…saw the accident and told him about it.'

Honor grimaced. 'Yes, I know. He hasn't grounded me, though, but he was pretty angry about it. He just got angry, though, because he feels guilty that he can't be there all the time for me,' Honor told her with a maturity that caught at Verity's sensitive heart. 'He worries about me—I worry too,' Honor admitted un-expectedly, showing heart-rending vulnerability as she confided reluctantly, 'It isn't much fun—not having a mother. It hurts a lot sometimes.'

'I know,' Verity agreed quietly.

For a moment they looked at one another and then Honor told her quickly, 'Look, the restaurant's here,' directing Verity's attention to the building in front of them. 'Don't let them give us a bad table just because we're two women eating alone without a man,' Honor hissed to Verity as they walked inside.

'Two *what…*?' Verity started to question, but the *maître d'* was already approaching them and, mindful not only of Honor's stern admonition but also of the fact that as a potential mentor—not to mention role model—to the young girl, it behoved her to set a good example, she looked him firmly in the eye and said, 'We'd like a table for two, please. That one over there,' she added, pointing to what was obviously their 'best' table.

Without batting an eyelid the *maître d'* swept them both a small bow and agreed, 'Very well, Madam, if you would just follow me.'

'That was good,' Honor acknowledged gleefully when they had been seated.

'No,' Verity corrected her wryly with a grin, '*that* was Gucci,' she told her flicking her fingertips over her suit. 'It isn't *just* long hair that men are susceptible to, you know,' she pointed out drolly, before picking up her menu.

'Ready to order?' she asked Honor several minutes later.

'Mmm…' the young girl agreed.

Raising her hand discreetly, Verity summoned the *maître d'*, waiting until Honor had given him her order before giving her own.

'Oh, and I'd like a glass of the house red as well,' Honor included decidedly.

The *maître d'* was visibly and seriously impressed, as well he might be, Verity acknowledged as, considerably less so, *she* gave Honor a thoughtful look.

'Er…with water,' Honor amended hastily, obviously sensing the veto that was about to leave Verity's lips.

'It's okay,' she told Verity defensively when the waiter had gone. 'Dad lets me—he says it's important for me to grow up learning how to handle alcohol. He says it makes for less mistakes later.'

'Dad said that you used to live here, in town,' Honor commented to Verity once they were eating their starter.

'Er, yes. Yes, I did,' Verity agreed.

'Did you know him then?' Honor asked her.

Verity paused, the forkful of food she had been lifting towards her mouth suddenly unappetising for all its rich, delicious smell.

'Er…no, I don't think so,' she prevaricated. How much had Silas told his daughter? Not the truth. How could he?

'Did you know my mother?' Honor asked her, startling Verity with the unexpectedness of the question.

'No. No, I didn't,' she told her truthfully. Poor child, and she *was* a child still, for all her quaintly grown-up ways and determined independence, Verity recognised. It couldn't be easy for her, growing up without any real personal knowledge of the woman who had given birth to her.

'She and Dad met when he was staying in London,' Honor told her pragmatically, 'so I didn't think you would. I don't look very much like her.'

'No, you look like your father,' Verity agreed, her heart suddenly jolting against her ribs as the restaurant door opened and the subject of their conversation walked in, accompanied by a woman whom Verity didn't recognise but who she guessed must be his 'friend' Myra.

'What is it?' Honor asked her innocently.

'Your father's just walked in,' Verity told her warningly, but to her surprise, instead of reacting as she had expected, the little girl simply dimpled a wide smile that caused sharp alarm bells to ring in Verity's brain.

'You *knew* he was coming here,' she breathed.

'It's the "in" place to be seen, but Myra won't be very pleased that *we've* got the best table,' Honor told her sunnily.

No, she certainly wasn't, Verity acknowledged, quickly assessing the other woman's angry-mouthed expression, and, what was more, Verity suspected that it wasn't simply the fact that the best table wasn't free that was angering her. *Their* presence—full stop— Verity rather guessed had a very definite something to do with the other woman's ire.

In any other circumstances the sternly condemnatory look Silas was sending her would probably have had her scuttling for the exit, Verity reflected ruefully, but she could hardly leave Honor to face her father's wrath alone, even if perhaps she did semi-deserve it.

Silas was heading for their table, having bent his head to say something first to his girlfriend, who was now standing glaring viciously, not so much at her as at Honor, Verity recognised with a strong surge of protection towards the young girl.

'Mmm, this is yummy… Hi, Dad,' Honor acknowledged her father, turning her head to give him a wide beam.

'Would you like to explain to me what the *hell* you think you're doing?' Silas asked Verity in a dangerously quiet voice, totally ignoring his daughter's sunny greeting.

'Riccardo gave us the best table, Dad,' Honor chattered on, apparently oblivious to both Verity's tension and her father's fury. 'Verity said it was because of her suit. It's Gucci, you know, but I think it was probably because Riccardo fancied her. He likes strawberry blondes,' she added warmly to Verity. 'That's probably why he never gives Myra a good table,' she told her father, whilst Verity closed her eyes and sent up a mental prayer, not just for her own safe deliverance from Silas' very evident ire, but Honor's as well. 'He doesn't like brunettes… Dad…' She paused judiciously before refilling her fork '…do you suppose Myra dyes her hair? *I* think she must because it's such a very hard shade of dark brown. What do you think, Verity?'

Verity gulped and shook her head, totally incapable of making any kind of logical response. She was torn between giving way to the fit of extremely inappropriate giggles of feminine appreciation of Honor's

masterly undermining of a woman whom Verity could
see quite plainly she considered to be a rival for her
father's attention, and a rather more adult awareness
of the danger of her own situation and just how little
Silas would relish the fact that *she* was the one to
witness his daughter's artful stratagems.

'What are you doing here, Honor?' Silas turned to
his daughter to ask with awful calmness.

'I...I...er...invited her to have dinner with me,'
Verity began, immediately rushing to the little girl's
defence, but Honor, it transpired, didn't need any defending—rather she seemed positively to enjoy courting her father's fury, looking him straight in the eye.

'I invited Verity to have dinner with me,' she told
her father challengingly. 'It was the least I could do
after—'

'The least *you* could do?' Shaking his head, he
turned from Honor to Verity and told her acidly, 'First
you damn near kill my daughter with your dangerous
driving and then you, God alone knows by what
means, persuade her to have dinner with you. What
were you intending to do? Trick her into changing her
story just in case I *did* decide to report you to the
police? You run her down and then—'

'No, Dad... It wasn't like that...' Honor pushed
away her plate and looked quickly from Verity's
white face to her father's. 'I... It wasn't Verity's
fault... I...' She swallowed and then continued
bravely, 'It was mine...'

'Yours? But Myra said—'

'It happened exactly how you'd warned me it
would,' Honor ploughed on doggedly. 'I did just what

you told me not to do. I was on my blades and I didn't think to stop or look and then I lost control and—'

'Is this true?' Silas asked Verity coldly.

For a moment Verity was tempted to lie and take the blame, but before she could do so Honor was speaking again, reaching out to touch her father's arm.

'Yes. It is true, Dad,' she told him quietly. 'I…I'm sorry… Please don't be mad. I…I went to see Verity because I want to pay for the damage to her car out of my spending money. It was my idea for us to come out for dinner…'

'Honor. You *know* the rules. What on earth…? You were *supposed* to be going straight to Catherine's from school and staying there tonight.'

'I know that, Dad, but today Catherine said that her aunt and uncle were coming to stay and I knew it was going to be a family sort of thing… I didn't want…' She hung her head before saying gruffly, 'I just wouldn't have felt right being there.'

As she listened to her, Verity's heart went out to her. Underneath her amazingly streetwise exterior she was still, after all, a very vulnerable little girl at heart. A little girl who had never known the love of her mother; a little girl who quite plainly and understandably was jealously protective of her own place in her father's life, to the extent that she quite obviously did not like the woman who she had told Verity was angling to become her father's second wife.

'I think perhaps we should go, Honor,' Verity intervened, gently touching the little girl's arm, summoning the quiet strength of will she had often been forced to use in her boardroom battles. It had never been Verity's style to assume the manner of a 'man'—there *were* other ways of making one's point and any man, anyone, who thought that she could be bullied or pushed around just because she didn't hector or argue very quickly discovered just how wrong they had been.

'I haven't had my pudding,' Honor reminded her stoutly, but Verity could see that she was glad of her protective intervention.

'I've got some fruit and ice cream,' she told her, before turning to Silas and looking him straight in the eye as she said, 'You're quite right, I *should* have checked with you before bringing Honor out—that was *my* mistake. Yours…' She paused and reminded herself that with Honor as an interested audience, never mind the *maître d'* and the now very obviously fuming Myra, this was not the time nor the place to point out where *he* had gone wrong or what his misjudgement had been.

'I'm quite prepared to drive Honor round to her friend's, but I wonder if she might be permitted to finish her supper with me?'

'Oh, yes, Dad. And then you could pick me up from Verity's on the way home,' Honor interrupted her eagerly. 'I'd much rather do that than go to Catherine's.'

'If your pudding is ordered, then I'll ask the *maître d'* to bring another chair and you can stay with Myra and me. I take it *you've* finished your meal,' Silas demanded of Verity coldly.

'No. She hasn't… She hasn't had *her* pudding,' Honor told him indignantly, adding, 'Besides, I don't *want* to be with you and Myra, you know she doesn't like me…'

'Honor,' Silas began warningly, twin bands of anger beginning to burn high on his cheek-bones, although, as Verity could see, she herself was more alarmed by his fury than Honor.

'Look, *what's* going on? When are we going to eat?'

All three of them looked up as Myra finally grew tired of waiting on the sidelines and came to join battle.

'I'm sorry,' Silas apologised, giving her a warm smile. But Myra wasn't looking at him. Instead, her eyes were flashing warning signs in Verity's direction, narrowing angrily as she studied Verity's suit.

'I was just explaining to Honor that she could finish her meal with us,' Silas told Myra.

'What? But you're coming back with me so that I can show you that video I've got of my cousin's wedding…' Myra protested, darting a fulminating look at Honor.

'If I stay with you, can I have cappuccino to finish with?' Honor asked Silas.

'Er…' Silas was looking uncertainly from his daughter's face to his girlfriend's. In any other circumstances and with any other man, Verity knew she would have felt quite sympathetic towards him. As it was, tucking down the corners of her mouth so that no one could see the smile curling there, she caught Honor's attention.

'Remember the Bible story of Solomon?' she asked the little girl *sotto voce*.

'Solomon?' Honor whispered back whilst Silas and Myra removed themselves slightly from the table to engage in what looked like a very heated conversation. 'Oh, you mean the one where the two women both claimed the baby and Solomon threatened to cut it in two and let them have half each?' Honor asked her.

'That's the one,' Verity agreed dulcetly. Honor frowned and then suddenly burst out laughing as she saw Verity glance over towards Silas.

'Oh, but Dad isn't a baby,' she protested.

'No, but he *is* your father and sometimes loving someone means letting them make their own decisions,' Verity told her gently.

'But she's not right for him,' Honor protested, and then shrugged her shoulders. 'Okay.'

'Dad…'

'Honor…'

Verity waited as they both started to speak and then both stopped.

'If you're sure you don't mind giving Honor supper and keeping her with you until I can collect her,' Silas told Verity distantly.

'*I* don't mind at all,' Verity responded truthfully, adding as she smiled at Honor, 'In fact, it will be a pleasure.'

'Goodie… There goes Myra's plan for showing my father the tempting prospect of getting married via her cousin's wedding video,' Honor exulted several minutes later as she and Verity exited the restaurant, Honor clutching a huge double portion of rich ice cream that the now-besotted *maître d'* had insisted on giving her complete with a bowl of ice to keep it chilled until they got home.

'I shouldn't be too sure about that,' Verity warned her. 'Myra looks one very determined lady to me…'

'Determined she might be, but Dad is catastrophically old-fashioned about me going to bed early on school nights. There's no way he's going to be able to go home with Myra tonight.'

Verity stopped walking and swung round to glance incredulously at Honor.

'Did you deliberately plan all of this?' she asked her bluntly.

Honor's face assumed a hurt expression.

'Me... I'm ten years old,' she reminded Verity.

'Yeah...but somehow you seem so much older,' Verity responded feelingly.

As they walked in amicable female companionship towards Verity's parked car, Honor allowed herself to relax.

Part one of her plan was working. What would Verity say, she wondered, if she told her that she had recognised her straight away on the day of the accident from a photograph of her she had found in her father's desk? Her father needed rescuing from Myra and it was high time, Honor had already decided, that she had a mother—one of her own choosing!

She looked sideways at Verity—why had she fibbed about not knowing her father? She was tempted to ask but she decided it might be best not to rush things so much...not yet. Honestly, grown-ups, they were so slow... But it was just as she and her friend Catherine had said earlier this afternoon when she had jubilantly told her all about Verity. Sometimes grown-ups didn't know where their own best interests lay, so it was just as well that she, Honor, was here to show them.

What she needed to do now was to keep her father and Myra apart, but if her plans worked out as she

knew they would that shouldn't prove too difficult—
Catherine had her instructions!

Verity gave her a surprised look as Honor suddenly
slipped a small, slightly grubby hand into her own and
beamed a huge smile up at her.

'It's no good trying to get round me like that,'
Verity warned her severely, adding untruthfully, 'and,
besides, I can't make cappuccino…'

'No, but I bet Myra can,' Honor told her. 'She was
really frothing at the mouth, wasn't she?' she ob-
served dispassionately.

'Honor…' Verity warned, and then spoiled it by
suddenly giving way to an uncontrollable fit of the
giggles.

'Verity…just a moment, please…'

Verity's body tensed in shock as she heard Silas
calling out curtly from behind her. She had already
unlocked the car for Honor to get inside it and now,
as she too saw her father, Honor opened the door.

Silas shook his head and told her crisply, 'You stay
where you are, please, Honor. I want to have a few
words with Verity…in private!'

Verity wasn't sure which of them looked the more
wary—herself or Honor. What she *was* sure of,
though, was that she could feel her skin turning a very
definite shade of mollified pink as Honor, after one
look at her father's stern 'I mean business' expression,
quietly closed the passenger door of Verity's car.

Equally reprehensibly feebly, Verity discovered
that she herself was moving several yards away from
her car, mirroring the way that Silas was moving out
of Honor's potential earshot. Just to make sure that
Silas knew and understood that, unlike his daughter,

she was not someone he could talk down to or tell what to do, before he could tell her whatever it was that had brought him hotfoot out of the restaurant and away from Myra's side, Verity demanded coldly, 'Please be quick, Silas, I still haven't eaten my pudding.'

'Ice cream?' His mouth took on a mocking twist. 'As *I* remember it you were always more of a cheese and biscuits woman and—'

Immediately Verity's eyes flashed. How dared he remind her of the intimacy they had once shared; of everything they had once been to one another, now when he…?

'Is *that* why you came running after us—to remind me because *I* opted for ice cream over cheese and biscuits? *My* tastes have changed, Silas…just like yours…'

But sharp though her words were, for some unaccountable reason, as she said them, Verity discovered that she was looking at his mouth and remembering…

A shudder of self-contempt shook her as she acknowledged just *what* she was remembering, her eyes darkening as she did so.

Did Silas remember that ice cream they had shared so long ago, and, if he did, did he remember too the way he had teased her by offering her the last mouthful of it and then, when she had taken it, kissing her through the icy-cold taste, his lips, his mouth, his tongue, so velvet-hot and sensuous against her lips, and then when the ice cream had melted his kiss becoming so passionate that *it* had practically melted *her*?

Her face on fire, Verity made to take a step back

from him, but to her consternation Silas immediately reached out to stop her, his hand grasping her upper arm in a grip she knew it would be impossible for her to break.

'Verity,' he began, his voice unexpectedly thick and husky as though…

Quickly Verity cast a lash-veiled look at him. Surely his own colour was slightly higher than it should have been?

Because he was angry? It certainly couldn't be because he was aroused, could it?

Unexpectedly he gave his head a small shake, as though trying to dispel some unwanted thought, and when he spoke again his voice was much crisper.

'Honor is ten years old…a child… I don't want her getting hurt…' he began warningly.

Immediately Verity took umbrage. How dared he suggest that *she* might hurt Honor?

'If you're implying that I might hurt her,' she told him furiously, 'then you're wrong. In fact, if you believe that Honor *is* being hurt I should look far closer to home for the source if I were you.'

There was a moment's shocked pause before he demanded in disbelief, 'Are you trying to say that *I* might hurt her…?'

Taking advantage of his momentary lapse in concentration, Verity pulled herself free of his grip and started to turn towards the car.

'Verity, I haven't finished—' she heard him saying furiously to her, but Verity had had enough—more than enough if the way her body, her senses, were still responding to the memory of that shared ice cream so long ago was anything to go by.

'Oh, but I think you have,' she corrected him through gritted teeth and then stopped abruptly, shocked to discover that for some reason all his attention seemed to be focused on her mouth. Instinctively she raised protective fingers to her lips, her whole body starting to tremble.

'Verity…' she heard him saying roughly, but she shook her head, unable to listen to whatever it was he wanted to say, whatever further contemptuous criticism he wanted to hurl at her unprotected heart.

'Go away, Silas,' she demanded shakily. 'Go back to Myra…'

And without waiting to see his reaction she hurried quickly towards her car and opened the door.

'What did Dad want?' Honor asked uncertainly several minutes later, once Verity had negotiated their way out of the car park.

'Er…he wanted to tell me that you weren't to have too much ice cream,' Verity fibbed, making up the first excuse she could think of.

'Not much chance of that. By the time we get back it will all be melted…gone…' Honor told her in disgust.

Gone…like their love… Verity bit down hard on her bottom lip. Ice cream and Silas' kisses. Funny how sharply painful the sweetest things could sometimes become!

CHAPTER FIVE

'IT'S gone ten o'clock,' Verity told Honor worriedly. 'I thought your father would have been here by now— you said he wouldn't want you to be out late.'

'Mmm… I know.'

Honor seemed far less perturbed about her father's absence than she was, Verity noticed, which surprised her. She would have thought that, given Honor's obvious dislike of Myra, she would have become at least a little anxious about the fact that Silas was quite obviously lingering with the woman rather longer than Honor had originally intimated.

Perhaps Myra had prevailed on him to take her home after all, and, once there, no doubt she had insisted that he remain for a nightcap and of course, whilst he was drinking it, she had no doubt put on the video. 'Just so that he could see a few minutes of it.' And then, of course, it would be a small step—a *very* small step for her kind of woman—from that to turning down the lights and refilling Silas' glass, insisting that there was no need for him to rush and that surely Honor could miss a morning of school for once…

Verity could virtually hear the enticing personal arguments she would purr into his ear as she slipped onto the sofa beside him and placed her hand on his jacket, supposedly to remove a bit of non-existent fluff, before sliding it up onto his shoulder and then caressing the back of his neck where his hair curled

81

thick and dark. Verity closed her eyes. She could remember so clearly just how that felt—how *she* had
felt, how just the intimacy simply of touching him like
that had made her go weak at the knees, all melting,
yielding, wanting womanhood.

'Verity, are you all right?'

'What…? Er…' guiltily Verity opened her eyes
'…er, yes…' she fibbed, hot-cheeked, hurriedly getting up so that she could avoid meeting the innocence
of Honor's eyes.

'Perhaps we should ring the restaurant,' she began
hurriedly. 'I—'

'No… No… I don't think that would be a good
idea,' Honor instantly denied. 'I mean, Dad was so
angry, wasn't he? And…' But despite what she had
said Verity couldn't help noticing that Honor herself
did keep looking at the silent telephone.

'Perhaps he's been delayed…a flat tyre or something like that,' she offered comfortingly.

'How long is your hair?' Honor asked, moving their
conversation away from her father's late arrival.

'Er…'

'Take it down now,' Honor urged her, reaching out
to tweak some of the constraining pins from Verity's
hair before she could stop her.

Suspecting that the little girl was more disturbed by
her father's non-appearance than she wanted to admit,
Verity gave in.

'Oh, it's lovely,' Honor told her in open and honest
admiration when all the pins were finally removed and
Verity had quickly pulled the small brush she kept in
her handbag through her soft curls.

'It's getting too long. I should really have it cut,' Verity said ruefully.

'Oh, no, you mustn't,' Honor told her, gently stroking her fingers through it.

Verity felt her heart jerk and then almost stop. Once, a long time ago, a *lifetime* ago it seemed now, Silas had touched her hair just like that and spoken similar words to her.

'No, don't ever have it cut,' he had whispered to her. 'I love it so much—I love *you* so much.'

Instinctively she closed her eyes.

'What's the matter? You look awfully sad,' Honor told her.

There was a huge lump in Verity's throat.

'I—' she began, and then stopped as the phone suddenly rang. Honor reached it first but, a little to Verity's surprise, she waited for her to pick up the receiver.

'Verity?'

There was no mistaking the crisp tones of Silas' voice.

'Yes. Yes, Silas…'

'Look, I can't talk now. There's been an emergency. I'm at the garden centre. The police called me out. Someone reported seeing intruders trying to break in. So far we haven't found any signs of anyone but it looks as though I could be tied up here for some time. Honor…'

'Honor's fine with me, unless you want me to take her to her friend's,' Verity assured him as calmly as she could. Why was her heart beating so frantically fast, her pulse racing, her mouth dry, her whole body reacting to the sound of his voice as if…as though…?

'No. It's probably best if she stays with you. I don't know what time I'm going to be through here…'

'Don't worry,' Verity assured him. 'She'll be fine here with me. Would you like to speak with her?'

Without waiting for his response, she handed the receiver over to Honor, before walking over to the window and putting her hands to her suddenly hot face.

What on *earth* was the matter with her? She was reacting like…like a woman in love… A deep shudder ran through her. Impossible. No. No way. Not again. Not a second time.

'Not a second time what?' Honor asked her curiously.

Wide-eyed, Verity turned round and looked at her. She hadn't heard Honor replace the telephone receiver, never mind realised that she had spoken out loud.

'Er…nothing… Look, it could be some time before your father gets here. If you want to go to bed…'

'No. Well, yes, perhaps that might be a good idea,' Honor allowed. 'I haven't got anything to wear, though,' she reminded Verity.

'That's okay, you can sleep in your undies for tonight,' Verity told her practically.

'I don't very much like the dark,' Honor said as they walked upstairs. 'Will you…will you stay with me until I go to sleep?'

Once again Verity was reminded of the fact that Honor was only a very young girl—a motherless young girl—and Verity herself knew what that meant and all about the private desperate tears cried into one's pillow at night. Tears for the love and want of a mother's arms—a mother's care. Honor had her pride, Verity could see, but she could see as well that she also had her vulnerability, her need to be reassured, her need to be mothered.

'Yes, of course I will,' Verity agreed warmly, giving her hand a small squeeze.

'I'm not very keen on the dark myself,' she added.

In the end it was another hour before Honor was finally in bed—Verity's bed, since it was the only one that was made up and since Honor had announced that she liked Verity's room best of all. 'Because it smells of you,' she had so engagingly told Verity.

Who could resist that kind of persuasion? And, for the second time, Verity had been all too intimately reminded of hearing Honor's father make just such a similar comment, although in a vastly different context—a context far too intimate and personal to *even* allow herself to think about in the presence of anyone else, never mind Silas' young daughter.

'Why not? Why don't you want me to?' he had asked her thickly when she had tried to push him away the first time he had bent his head towards the most intimate part of her body.

'Because…because…' Awkwardly she had struggled to explain how both shocked and excited she had felt at the thought of being caressed so, so personally by him, of having his lips, his mouth, kiss the most delicate and sensitive part of her body.

'It just doesn't seem right,' she had told him shakily in the end. 'I mean, it's…' Pleadingly she had lifted her gaze to his. 'Silas, I don't…it's…'

'It's just another way of showing you how much I

love you,' Silas had told her gently. 'If you don't want me to then I won't, but I want to enjoy the scent and taste of you—the real you—so much, Verity. I know what you're thinking...how you're feeling...but I promise you that it will be all right.'

'It seems so... It makes me feel so...so nervous and afraid and so...excited at the same time,' she had confessed. 'All sort of squirmy and...and...'

'It makes me feel the same,' Silas had told her in a deep voice. 'Only even more so. Will you let me, Verity? I promise I'll stop if you want me to. It's just...' He had paused and looked deep into her eyes, making her heart thump against her chest wall in great shuddering thuds.

'I want to make you mine in every way there is. To know you so completely; to love you so completely.'

And when eventually he had lain her tenderly on the bed and bent his head over her body, when she had felt his tongue tip gently rimming the very centre of her sexual being, Verity hadn't wanted him to stop at all, not at all, not ever, as she had cried out frantically to him when the racking paroxysms of pleasure had seized hold of her, caught her up and dislodged from her mind any thought she might ever have had about not wanting the pleasure that Silas had been giving her, the intimacy...

'Verity...'

With a start Verity dragged her mind and her thoughts back to the present.

'It's a very big bed, isn't it?' Honor told her in a small voice. 'Do you always sleep in a big bed like this?'

'M...mostly,' Verity confirmed.

'It must feel very lonely. Haven't you ever wanted to get married, have children?' Honor asked her.

'It's after eleven o'clock,' Verity warned her, side-stepping the question, knowing that the only honest answer she could give her was no answer to give the ten-year-old daughter of the man whose wife she had hoped to be.

'Stay with me,' Honor whispered again, a small hand creeping out from beneath the bedclothes to hold onto Verity's.

Watching her ten minutes later as she lay next to her, Verity felt a tug of love on her heartstrings so strong that Honor's small hand might actually have been physically wrapped around them.

'Stop it,' she warned herself sternly. 'Don't you dare start daydreaming along those lines... Don't you dare!'

Very gingerly Verity eased her arm from beneath Honor's sleeping body. It ached slightly and had started to go a little numb. Disconcertingly, though, she discovered as she slid carefully off the bed, she actually missed the warm young weight of Honor's body.

The knowledge that she would probably never marry and have children of her own had been something she had pushed to the back of her mind in recent years. A child or children that she would have to bring up on her own had never been an option for her—her own childhood had given her extremely strong views about a child's need to feel secure and, to Verity, the kind of security *she* had craved so desperately as a child had come all neatly wrapped up with two parents.

In the early years after her breakup with Silas she'd had virtually only to see a young couple out with a small child to feel pierced with misery and envy.

Another woman, a different woman, might, on learning that the man she had loved, the man who had promised always to love her, had married someone else, have hardened her heart against her own emotions and made herself find someone else, built a new life for herself with a new man in it, but Verity had never been able to do that. For one thing the business had meant that she simply hadn't had the time to form new relationships and for another… For another, for a long time she had felt so hurt and betrayed, so convinced that Silas was the only man she could ever love, that she simply hadn't tried.

But there had still been that sense of loss, that small, sharp ache of envy for other young women who'd had what she hadn't: a man to love and their child.

But now she felt she was far too mature to give in to such feelings.

'What rubbish,' Charlotte had told her forthrightly recently when she had brought up the matter and Verity had said as much to her.

'For one thing you are not even in your late thirties, and for another, women in their early forties are giving birth to their first child nowadays. Neither can you start telling me that you can't spare the time and that the business is too demanding—you don't *have* the business any more.'

'I don't have a partner either,' Verity had felt bound to point out.

'That could easily be remedied,' Charlotte had told her firmly, 'and you know it!'

'Perhaps I'm simply not the maternal type.' Verity had shrugged, anxious to change the subject.

'Come off it,' Charlotte had scoffed. 'You know my two adore you.'

And she loved them, Verity acknowledged now as she tiptoed towards the bedroom door, but something about Honor had touched her heart and her emotions had really shaken her.

Because she was Silas' child?

If anything, surely that should make her resent and dislike her and not…? It was certainly plain that Myra did not feel in the least bit maternal towards her intended future stepdaughter. Was it Honor herself she didn't like, or did she perhaps simply resent the fact that she was the physical evidence that Silas had loved another woman? Myra certainly hadn't struck her as the emotionally insecure type.

As Verity opened the bedroom door, Honor moved in her sleep and muttered something. Holding her breath, Verity waited until she was sure she had settled down again and, leaving the bedroom door open and the landing light on, she went quickly downstairs.

It was gone twelve. How much longer would Silas be?

Her discarded suit jacket was lying on the chair where she had left it. Automatically she picked it up and folded it neatly, smoothing the soft fabric. Her uncle would have thoroughly disapproved of her buying something so impractical in white and in a delicately luxurious fabric. Clothes to him had simply been a necessary practicality. Verity could still remember how surprised and thrilled she had been when she and Silas had been walking through town one day and he had stopped her outside a boutique window and, indicating the dress inside, told her tenderly, 'That would suit you…'

The dress in question had been a silky halter-necked affair, backless, the fabric scattered with pretty feminine flowers, and it had also been a world away from the type of clothes she had normally worn: sturdy jeans, neatly pleated skirts, dully sensible clothes bought under the stern eye of her uncle's sixty-year-old Scottish housekeeper.

'Oh, Silas, it's lovely,' she had breathed, 'but it's far too…too pretty for me…'

'*Nothing* could ever be *too* pretty for you,' Silas had returned softly, adding huskily, 'Not pretty enough, maybe…'

'Oh, Silas…' she had whispered, blushing.

'Oh, Verity,' he had teased her back but, later in the week, when he had arrived with a present for her that had turned out to be the dress, the look in his eyes when he had persuaded her to model it for him had made her blush for a very, very different reason.

She had protested, of course, that he shouldn't have bought her something so personal nor so expensive.

'Why not?' he had countered. 'You're the woman I love, the woman I'm going to marry.'

She had been so young and naive then, assuming that he'd accepted that even as Silas' wife she'd owe it to her uncle to do as he wished and take her place in his business. She had known too, of course, that

Silas hadn't been happy about the silent but ostrich-like way she had convinced herself that it would all work out and had pushed it to the back of her mind. Silas would surely come to respect her point of view. They were young and in love—how could anything so mundane as duty come between them? She had been too dazed with love and happiness to guess that Silas might still see her role as his future wife in a far different light from that in which she did herself.

Through the sitting-room window Verity saw the headlights of a car coming up the drive. Silas! It had to be.

She opened the front door to him, putting her finger to her lips as she warned him, 'Honor's asleep.'

He looked tired, she recognised, deep lines etched either side of his mouth and tension very evident in the way he moved as he followed her into the house. For some inexplicable reason these indications of the fact that he was no longer a carefree young man in his twenties increased rather than detracted from his masculinity, Verity realised, her heartbeat quickening as the adrenalin kicked into her system and sent a surge of dangerous emotion racing through her veins.

'Was everything all right at the garden centre?' she asked him shakily as he followed her into the kitchen.

Best not to look at him. Not yet. Not until she had herself fully and properly under control. Not that that shuddery, all-too-familiar sensation within her body *meant* anything, of course, it was just…just… Well, she certainly didn't want him looking at her face and recognising anything that might possibly be familiar to him.

'Well, there were no signs of anyone having broken

in,' Silas told her tiredly. 'I checked and then double-checked the place and the alarm and everything seemed okay, but the police say that they had a definite tip-off that the place was being broken into and it always leaves you worrying. You know the sort of thing—create a false alarm and then when all the fuss has died down... We've got a hell of a lot of valuable young plants there at the moment, plus a delivery of antique garden statues which I've acquired for one of my clients. It's insured but...' He changed the subject. 'Thanks for looking after Honor for me.' He stopped and grimaced as his obviously empty stomach gave a protesting growl.

'You're hungry.' Verity looked at him. 'Would you like something to eat...?'

He started to shake his head and then stopped as his stomach gave another, louder, protest.

'It isn't anything much,' Verity warned him without waiting for him to make any refusal. 'Just some pâté and French bread...'

Behind her as she busied herself at the fridge, Verity could hear him groan.

'That sounds marvellous,' he told her, admitting, 'I'm famished and I missed out on lunch altogether today.'

'But you *had* dinner,' Verity began as she removed the pâté and some salad, 'and you always used to enjoy Italian.'

'So did you... Remember when I flew out to New York to see you and you took me all around the Italian restaurants you'd discovered...?'

Verity looked at him.

'Yes,' she agreed huskily. 'Yes, I do.'

It had been a brief, a far too brief, visit—a cheap flight he had managed to get, involving only a two-night stay, his visit a surprise to her on her birthday.

She had cried with joy when he'd arrived and she had cried again—*wept* with misery when he had left, but those tears had been nothing to the ones she had cried the day she had read of his marriage to someone else.

'Unfortunately Myra isn't as keen on Italian food as I am and after… Well, we left the restaurant shortly after you—the call came through from the police on my mobile before we could order.'

'It isn't much,' Verity told him again as she put the plate of pâté and salad she had just prepared onto the table in front of him and then went to cut the bread.

'Not much! It's *wonderful*, manna from heaven,' Silas told her fervently.

'Cappuccino?' Verity asked him quizzically as she handed him the bread basket.

It had always been a bit of a joke between them that he had loved the rich chocolate-sprinkled coffee so much. She didn't need to guess where Honor had got *her* sweet tooth from.

'Mmm…this pâté's good. Did you buy it locally?' Silas asked her.

Shaking her head, Verity turned away from him. Despite what Honor had assumed, she was, in fact, a very good self-taught cook.

'Actually, I made it myself,' she told him truthfully, and she could see what he was thinking from the way he looked from his plate to her expensive and im-practical white trousers.

'Not wearing this,' she told him slightly tartly.

He had almost finished eating and had started to frown again. 'I'd better go up and get Honor,' he told her. 'I'm sorry you got landed with her this evening… It's one of the trials of being a single parent that…'

'Yes. It must have been hard for you, losing your wife,' Verity forced herself to acknowledge.

'Nowhere near as hard as it was for her to lose her life, nor Honor to lose her mother,' he countered harshly, before adding equally grimly, as he glanced at her unbanded wedding finger. 'Obviously, you've never married.'

'No,' Verity agreed coolly. 'The business—' she began, but Silas wouldn't allow her to finish.

He interrupted her with a harsh, 'Don't tell me. *I* know…remember?'

He started to get up as Verity reached to remove his plate, her hair accidentally falling forward and brushing his face as they both moved at the same time.

Immediately Verity tensed, lifting her hand to push her hair off her face, but Silas, on his feet by this time, got there first. The sensation of his fingers in her hair was so familiar, so intimate, that she instinctively closed her eyes.

'Verity…' she heard Silas groan, and then the next minute she was in his arms and he was kissing her with a fierce, hungry, angry, passion that brought her defences crashing down so that immediately and helplessly she was responding to him, the years rolling back so that she was a girl again, so that they were a couple, a *pair* again, so that there was nowhere that it was more natural for her to be than here in his arms, *nothing* that was more natural for her to *feel* than what she was feeling right now, nothing it was more natural for her to *want* than what she was wanting right now.

Beneath his mouth and hands her body threw off the shackles she had so sternly imposed on it—he was hers again and she was his. Hers to reach out and touch, as she was doing right now, slipping her fingertips into the gap she had miraculously found between the buttons on his shirt, feeling the solid, familiar heat of his skin. Without realising what she was doing, she unfastened one of the shirt buttons that was preventing her from touching him as she wanted to do.

Beneath his mouth she made a small, contented sound of triumph and pleasure at being able to spread her hands fully over his chest with nothing in the way to bar her sensual exploration of his naked skin.

He felt so good, so Silas, so wonderfully familiar. He even tasted just as she had remembered. Automatically Verity pressed closer to him, shuddering deliciously as she felt his hands slide down her back to cup her bottom, lifting her even deeper into his body.

She could feel the urgency, the hunger, the need, in the way he touched her, running his hands over all her body as he continued to kiss her with increasing passion.

The kitchen was full of the sound of their heightened breathing, the electric crackle of hands against cloth, the silky whisper of skin against skin.

'It's been so long,' Verity whispered emotionally between their kisses. 'I've wanted…'

I've wanted you so much, she was just about to say, but suddenly she stiffened. From upstairs Verity heard the bathroom door open. Silas must have heard it too because he immediately released her, saying tautly, 'This shouldn't be happening. Blame it on the frustration of the evening…'

The frustration? Verity's hands were shaking so much she had to hold them out of sight behind her back as she came back down to earth with a sickening jolt.

What was Silas *saying* to her? That it was *his* sexual frustration at having to leave Myra which had caused him to kiss her?

For a moment she thought she was actually going to be sick. A pain, like red-hot twisting knives, was shredding her emotions. Silas hadn't been thinking about *her* at all. All that passion, all that need, all that *wanting* she had felt in him, had *not* been for her at all and she, like a complete idiot, had virtually been on the point of telling him, revealing to him…

Turning away from him so that he couldn't see her face, she told him quietly, 'Honor's obviously awake.'

'I'll go up and get her,' Silas announced curtly. 'Thanks for looking after her for me.'

'I didn't do it for *you*,' Verity told him fiercely. 'I did it for *her*.'

She still couldn't risk turning round. She daredn't, just in case… Just in case what? Just in case Silas guessed what she had been thinking…feeling… wanting…? His pity was something she couldn't bear. His scorn and his rejection would be hard enough to stomach—almost as hard as the knowledge that for the second time he was rejecting her in favour of another woman, letting her *know* that he simply didn't

want her—but if she should look at him now and see
pity in his eyes…

Quickly she headed for the kitchen door.

'I'll show you which room Honor's in,' she told
him without looking at him.

Honor was back in bed when Verity pushed open
the bedroom door. When she saw her father she
smiled winningly at him.

'Can I stay here with Verity tonight?' she asked.

'No, you can't,' Silas denied sharply, softening his
denial by explaining, 'I'm sure Verity's far too
busy…'

'You're not, are you, Verity?' Honor appealed.

Verity hesitated. What could she say?

'Perhaps another time,' she offered as Silas gathered up Honor's clothes and stood waiting determinedly with them.

The house felt empty once they had gone.

Oh, but how could she have been so stupid as to
overreact like that just because…? No wonder Silas
had felt it necessary to make it clear to her that there
had been nothing personal in that kiss he had given
her. She could feel her face starting to burn with humiliation and pain. As she began to tidy up the
kitchen, a small item on the floor caught her eye.
Frowning, she bent to pick it up. It was a button—a
man's shirt button. Her face burned even more hotly.
She must have *ripped* it off when she had… Quickly
she swallowed. She had never been driven by her sexuality and even when she and Silas had been lovers
she had always been the more passive partner. She
could certainly never remember having virtually

ripped the shirt off his back before. Angrily she put her hands to her hot face. The last thing she needed was for Silas to start thinking that she was holding some kind of torch for him…that she still *wanted* him, that she was stupid enough to still be hurting over the way he had treated her.

From now on, when they met—*if* they met—she was going to have to make it very clear to him that tonight's kiss was something as little wanted or relished by her as it had been by him!

CHAPTER SIX

'DAD.'

'Mmm…' Silas glanced down at his daughter's head as she sat next to him in the car.

'When Verity lived here before, were you friends?'

'What makes you ask that?' Silas questioned her sharply.

'Nothing.' Honor smiled, looking up at him. 'Well, were you?'

'No.' Silas told her curtly.

'Yes. That's what she said.'

Silas frowned.

'She's very pretty, though, isn't she?' Honor continued sunnily. 'Riccardo certainly thought so.'

'Very,' Silas agreed through gritted teeth. As a young girl Verity has possessed a natural, wholesome, sweet prettiness, but as a woman she had matured into someone whose subtle sensuality…

His favourite plants were always those that took a little bit of knowing; whose attractions were not necessarily flashingly visible at first glance. He had never liked anything overblown nor obvious and Verity… Just now, kissing her, he had been overwhelmed by the urge, by the memory of a certain night they had spent together in the heat of her small New York flat when, during their lovemaking, she had wrapped her legs around him and…

Tonight, watching the way she had moved in that

silky white suit she had been wearing, remembering just how lovely and equally silky and feminine her legs were...

'I really like her and she's going to be *my* friend,' Honor informed him. 'Can I invite her round for tea tomorrow?'

'What? No, you can't. You've got school in the morning and homework.'

'No, I haven't. We're having a leave day—I told you last week.'

'What?' Silas looked at her and groaned.

'Honor, why on earth didn't you remind me of that earlier?' he demanded. 'I've got a site meeting in the morning that I can't put off.'

'You should have left me at Verity's,' Honor told him practically. 'You'll have to ring her and ask her if she can look after me tomorrow.'

'What? No way. What about Catherine?'

'No.' Honor shook her head firmly. 'She's got her aunt and uncle staying, remember?'

Silas groaned again.

When Honor had been a baby he had employed a succession of full-time live-in nannies to take care of her when he wasn't there, also taking her into work with him when he could, but the situation was more complicated now that Honor was growing up. For one thing she was extremely independent and diabolically good at getting her own way so that finding the right kind of person—someone firm enough for her to respect and yet young enough not to be too restrictive with her—was proving increasingly difficult. Anna helped out when he could spare her from the garden centre, but they were too busy just now for her to be away from the centre all day.

His last housekeeper had left after Silas had made it plain that she was employed to take care of Honor's needs and not his own, and since then he had been relying increasingly on a patchwork of haphazard arrangements, getting by on a wing and a prayer and the good offices of kind friends.

If he hadn't hit such a busy patch with the business, he would have had time to advertise and sort something more permanent out, but as it was…

'I expect Myra was really cross when you had to leave to go to the garden centre,' Honor commented.

Silas gave her a wry look.

'Just a little,' he agreed.

The truth was that Myra had been furious. She was not a particularly maternal woman. In fact, her own two sons from her marriage lived with their father and his new partner. Silas knew perfectly well that becoming his wife was Myra's goal but being Honor's doting stepmother was the last thing the woman wanted.

She was a woman who, as she had told him quite openly, had a very high sex drive—so far, despite all the encouragement she had given him, Silas had kept their relationship on a purely platonic footing. Perhaps he was out of step with modern times, but sex for sex's sake was something that didn't appeal to him. It never had, which was why…

Silas looked down again at his daughter's dark head. As always when he thought of Honor's mother he was filled with a mixture of guilt and regret.

Neither of them had ever imagined when Sarah had

conceived Honor that giving birth to her would result in Sarah losing her own life. If they had…

It had been Sarah herself who had suggested that they should have the pregnancy terminated—neither of them, after all, had been thinking of a baby when Honor had been conceived—but Silas had persuaded her not to go ahead with it.

'I can't afford to bring up a baby,' she had told him frantically.

'I can,' Silas had replied.

A week later they had been married and just over seven months after that Honor had been born.

Forty-eight hours after giving birth Sarah had been dead despite everything that the doctors had done to try and save her. Nothing had been able to stop the massive haemorrhaging which had ended her life and, in the end, the doctors had told Silas that there was simply nothing they could do, that no amount of blood transfusions were going to help, that her body was too far in shock for them to be able to risk any kind of emergency surgery.

She had died without ever seeing Honor.

It hadn't been easy in those early years being totally responsible for a motherless girl child. His own parents had been retired and living abroad, and he had been determined that since he was Honor's only parent he was going to be as involved in her life and as much 'there' for her as he possibly could be, and so he had learned to change nappies without flinching, to bring up wind and to correctly interpret what all those different baby cries meant. But then, almost as soon as he had mastered those complexities, Honor had found new ways to tax his parenting skills—was still finding new ways to tax them, he admitted ten minutes later as he ushered her upstairs to her own bedroom, newly decorated last year for her birthday since she had announced that the 'Barbie' colour scheme and decor she had insisted on having for her sixth birthday was now totally passé and far too babyish for a girl of her new maturity.

In its place her room was now resplendent with everything necessary for a devout and ardent fan of the latest popular 'girl band'.

'I really like Verity,' Honor told him drowsily as he was tucking her up. 'I wish…'

'Go to sleep,' Silas said.

He had reached the doorway and was just about to switch off the light when she called out, 'Da-ad.'

'Yes.' Silas waited.

Honor sat bolt upright in her bed and eyed him seriously. 'You do know, don't you, that I'm getting to an age where I need to have a woman to talk to?'

Silas wasn't deceived. Honor, as he well knew, could run rings around a woman four times her age— could and, exasperatingly, very often did.

'You know what I mean,' Honor stressed. 'There are things I need to know…girl-type things…'

Silas gave her a sceptical look. He and Honor had always had a very open and honest relationship, no subject was taboo between them, and he had assumed that when the time came the subject of Honor's burgeoning womanhood and sexuality would be one they would cope with together. Honor, or so she was implying, had other ideas.

'Go to sleep,' he advised his daughter thoughtfully before switching off the light and going downstairs.

He only wished he could go to bed himself, but he had some paperwork to do. The landscaping business, which he had built up from nothing, had thrived—two years running he had won critical acclaim from the judges at the Chelsea Flower Show and he was now fully booked up with design commissions for the next eighteen months.

Add to that the garden centre side of his business and it was no wonder that, increasingly, he was finding it difficult to juggle all the various demands on his time.

It had hurt him more than he liked to think about even now when Verity had made it plain that taking over from her uncle in his business meant more to her than being with him—had *hurt* him and had damn near *destroyed* him. It wasn't that he was arrogant enough to think that a woman, his woman, should not want to have a career or run her own life, it was just… It was just that he had assumed that their relationship, their love, had meant as much to her as it had to him and that…

Plainly, though, he had been wrong.

'Give me time,' she had begged him, and because he had loved her so much he had.

'I have to go to New York,' she had told him. 'But I'll be back… It won't be for ever and there'll be holidays.' But too many months had come and gone without her coming back and in the end he had been the one to go to her. A meagre forty-eight hours was all they had had together—all he'd been able to afford to pay for and he had only managed that because he had picked up the short break as a special tour operator's bargain.

'Don't make me wait too long,' he had begged her.
'Please understand,' she had asked him.

Finally, pushed to the limits of his pride and his love, he had given her an ultimatum.

'Come home, we need to talk,' he had written to her, but she had ignored his letter—and when he had rung her apartment a strange male voice had answered the phone, claiming not to know where she was.

He hadn't rung again and then, four weeks later, he had met Sarah, and the rest, as they said, was history.

The local paper had carried several articles about Verity's uncle five years ago when he had died—he had been, after all, probably the town's most successful and wealthy inhabitant—but Silas had never expected that Verity would come back.

If it hadn't been for that incident with Honor and her roller blades, he doubted that they would even have seen one another. And he wished to God that they hadn't. Tonight had resurrected too many painful memories. Grimly he switched his thoughts back to the present.

He was going to have to find someone to take care of Honor tomorrow. But who? He had used up all his credit with his normal 'babysitters'. If worse came to worst, he would have to take her to the garden centre with him and ask Anna to keep an eye on her.

He groaned. Sometimes she made him feel as old as Methuselah, and at others her maturity filled him with both awe and apprehension.

Earlier this evening, walking into the restaurant and seeing her there with Verity, he had felt such a confusing and powerful mixture of emotions and when they had both looked at him, identical womanly expressions of hauteur and dismissal in their eyes, he had felt, he had felt... Grimly he pushed his hand into his hair. They certainly made a formidable team.

A team... Oh, no. No! No! No way. No way...

Silas looked enquiringly at Honor as she replaced the telephone receiver as he walked into the kitchen.

She looked enviably fresh and alert in view of how late it had been when she had finally gone to bed last night.

'I've just checked with Verity,' she told Silas with a very grown-up air as she poured herself some cereal, 'and she says it's okay for me to stay with her today. I've arranged for her to come and collect me at ten o'clock.'

Silas opened his mouth and then closed it again and, going to make himself a cup of coffee, waited until he had poured the boiling water on the coffee grains before trusting himself to speak.

'Correct me if I'm wrong, Honor,' he began pleasantly, 'but I rather thought that *I* was the adult in this household and that as such *I* am the one who makes the decisions.'

'I knew you probably wouldn't have time to drive me over to Verity's,' Honor told him virtuously, 'that's why I asked *her* if she could come *here* to pick me up.'

'Honor!' Silas warned and then cursed under his breath as the phone rang.

By the time he had dealt with the call, Honor had made a strategic retreat to her bedroom.

The phone rang again as he snatched a quick gulp of his now cold coffee. Sooner rather than later he and Honor were going to have a serious talk—a *very* serious talk.

Honor waited until her father had gone out, leaving her in the temporary care of their cleaning lady, before making her second call of the morning.

'It's me,' she announced when she heard her friend Catherine pick up the receiver. 'Guess what?'

'Is it working?' Catherine asked her excitedly. 'Did your father…did they…?'

'Both of them are pretending that they've never met before,' Honor told her friend. 'I haven't told them about finding that photograph. I got Verity to take me out for supper last night like we planned—to the same place where Dad was taking Myra. You should have seen her face…'

'What, Verity's? Did she look as though she still loved him? Did he—'

'No, not *Verity*,' Honor interrupted her. 'I meant you should have seen *Myra's* face—she was furious.'

'I bet she wasn't too pleased later when your dad got that phone call about the garden centre being broken into either.' Catherine giggled.

'Mmm…that worked really well. Tell your cousin I'll pay him what I owe him when I get more pocket money. I can't stay on the phone too long. Verity's coming round for me at ten. I'm spending the day with her. When she gets here we're going to do some womanly bonding.'

'What's that?' Catherine asked her uncertainly.

'I'm not sure, I read about it in a magazine. I think it's when you sit round and talk about babies and things,' Honor told her grandly.

'Oh. I'd rather talk about the boys,' Catherine informed her. 'Are you sure that your dad's still in love with her?'

'Positive. Last night they were kissing,' Honor informed her smugly.

'What? Did you see them?'

'No, but Dad had got lipstick on his mouth.'

'It could have been Myra's…'

'No. Myra wears red. This was pink…'

'But if they really love one another like you told me, how come he married your mother?'

'I don't know. I suppose they must have fallen out. Just think, if I hadn't found that photograph I'd never have discovered Dad and Verity knew each other before. I can't wait for them to get married.'

'Will you be a bridesmaid?' Catherine asked her wistfully.

'I'll be *the* bridesmaid,' Honor responded firmly, unaware of a touch of wistfulness in her voice too.

'They'll go away on one of those honeymoon things and leave you at home,' Catherine warned her, retaliating for Honor's comment about being 'the' bridesmaid and squashing her own hopes of wafting down the aisle alongside her friend in a cloud of pink tulle. Despite all Honor's chivvying, Catherine still retained regrettable fondness for their shared Barbie days.

'My uncle left Charlie at home when *he* remarried.'

'No, they won't,' Honor said adding, 'Verity would never let Dad leave me behind. She's so exactly right.' She smiled happily. 'I could tell the moment I met her.'

Catherine knew from experience when her friend's mind was on other things.

'I've got a new video,' she told her. 'We could watch it together on Saturday...'

'Maybe,' Honor hedged. 'I might not be very well...'

'Not very well? What do you mean?' Catherine demanded.

'Wait and see,' Honor responded mysteriously, before adding quickly, 'Verity's just driven up, I've got to go...'

'Daddy said to say thank you very much for looking after me,' Honor told Verity in a serious tone when she had opened the front door to her. 'He said he was very, very grateful to you and he couldn't think of anyone he could trust more to look after me.'

Verity blinked. To say she had been surprised to receive a telephone call from Honor asking if she could possibly spend the day with her because she was off school and Silas had to go out was something of an understatement. After what had happened between them last night she would have thought that *she* was the last person Silas would want around his daughter—and around himself.

What kind of a father *was* he exactly, if he could so easily entrust his only child to a woman he himself did not even pretend to like? she wondered critically as Honor skipped off to collect her coat.

Thoughtfully she waited for Honor to return.

'Your father *does* know that you're spending the day with me, doesn't he?' she questioned her dryly.

Honor gave her an injured look.

'Of course he does. You can ring him on his mobile if you like...'

'No. It's all right,' Verity assured her, adding palliatively, 'I'm not used to looking after little...*young* women... What would you like to do?'

'Could you take me shopping?' Honor asked her. 'I don't have any nice clothes,' she confided. 'Dad isn't very good at buying me the right kind of things. She looked down at her jeans and tee shirt and told Honor, 'I think sometimes he forgets that I'm a girl.'

Honor couldn't have said anything more guaranteed to touch her own heart, Verity acknowledged. She too had suffered from hopelessly inaccurate male assessment of what kind of clothes were suitable for a young girl.

Even so...

'Your father...' she began uncertainly, but Honor shook her head.

'Dad won't mind,' she answered Verity excitedly. 'He'll be pleased. He *hates* taking me shopping. In fact...' She paused and gave Verity an assessing look, wondering how far she should try her luck. Not too far if that unexpectedly shrewd question Verity had asked her earlier was anything to go by. 'Well, he *has* been saying that he would have to try and find someone—a woman—to take me out shopping.' Honor gazed up pleadingly at Verity.

'Wouldn't Myra...?' Verity began cautiously.

But Honor immediately shook her head and pulled a face before informing Verity tremulously, 'Myra doesn't like me... I think she...if she ever married my father, she would try to send me away...'

The horrified look Verity gave her reassured Honor. Everything was going to work out. Verity was going to make the *perfect* mother for her.

Prior to receiving Honor's telephone call Verity had planned to spend the day working, and a couple of hours after she had picked Honor up she was beginning to wonder if working might not have proved to be the easier option.

They were in the pre-teen department of a well-known chain of clothes shops, Verity waiting outside the cubicle area whilst Honor tried on the clothes she had chosen.

'And I thought having *teenagers* was bad,' another woman standing next to Verity groaned. 'My youngest...' she nodded in the direction of one of the changing rooms '...isn't speaking to her father because he refused to allow her to have her navel pierced. She's eleven next week. So far, the only clothes she's said she'll wear are the ones that her father will have forty fits if he sees her in, and I've got to admit he does have a point. Of course, we all know that fathers don't like to see their little girls growing up, but—'

'Verity, what do you think?' Honor demanded, suddenly emerging from the changing cubicle dressed in a tiny cut-off top that clung lovingly to her mercifully still flat chest and a pair of stretch Lycra leggings in a mixture of colours that made Verity's eyeballs ache.

'It's... I don't think your father will like it very much,' Verity began.

But she was out-manoeuvred as Honor informed her sunnily, 'No, I don't suppose he will, but you'll soon be able to talk him round.'

She could talk him round? Verity opened her mouth and then closed it again.

'Honor…' she began, but Honor was already disappearing in the direction of the changing cubicle.

It was another three hours before Honor pronounced herself reasonably satisfied with her purchases, declaring that she was hungry and suggesting that they made their way to the nearest McDonald's.

They were settled at a table when Honor asked Verity her most searching question yet. 'Have you ever been in love?'

Verity put down her cup of coffee.

'Once,' she admitted quietly, after a few long seconds had passed. 'A good many years ago.'

'What happened?' Honor asked her curiously.

Verity focused on her. What on earth was she *doing*? This wasn't a suitable topic of conversation to have with a ten-year-old girl even when the girl was the daughter of the man she had loved—especially when that ten-year-old was the daughter of the man she had loved, she corrected herself quickly—and yet, to her consternation, she still heard herself saying huskily, 'He…He married someone else!'

'Perhaps he married someone else because *he* thought *you'd* stopped loving him,' Honor told her quickly. 'Perhaps he really still loves you,' she said eagerly.

Verity started to frown. It was quite definitely time to change the subject.

'It's half past four,' she told Honor. 'What time did you say your father would be back?'

Silas' meeting had ended a little earlier than he had anticipated, and since he needed petrol he headed for the large out-of-town supermarket where he normally did his grocery shopping.

Catherine's mother was heading for the checkout with a full trolley-load when he walked in. Smiling at him, she asked, 'Did your aunt enjoy seeing Honor? Catherine was disappointed that she couldn't stay with us after all.'

Silas frowned.

'I'm sorry?' he began and then checked. What exactly was going on? Honor had told *him* that she couldn't stay at Catherine's because her friend had family visiting, but from what Catherine's mother had just said she seemed to be under the impression that it was *Honor* who had had the family commitment.

'Oh, and thanks for the invitation to dinner next week, we'd love to come.'

The invitation to dinner...? Next week? Silas opened his mouth and then closed it again. His daughter, he decided grimly, was going to have some serious explaining to do.

It was five o'clock when Verity finally pulled into Silas' drive, empty thankfully of his car, but she knew she couldn't escape until he returned home to care for his daughter. Besides, Honor was not feeling very well.

'My stomach hurts,' she told Verity.

'I'm not surprised. You *did* have two milk shakes,' Verity reminded her.

'It's not that kind of pain,' Honor came back quickly. 'It's the kind you get when you feel sad and...and lonely.'

Once they were inside the house, though, Honor

suddenly remembered something she had to do out-side.

'You stay here,' she told Verity, pushing open the kitchen door. 'I won't be long.'

The kitchen was generously proportioned and com-fortable. In the adjoining laundry room Verity could see a basket perched on top of the tumble-dryer, a pile of clean laundry next to it as though someone had pulled it from the machine and not had time to fold it.

Automatically she walked through and started to smooth out the crumpled garments. Honor's under-wear and school clothes and...

Her fingers tensed as she picked up a pair of soft male briefs, white and well styled. Her hands were trembling so much she almost dropped them. Quickly she put them down as though they had scalded her. She could hear Honor coming back.

'*I* bought Dad those for Christmas,' she told Verity, picking up the briefs.

'I'm learning to cook at school. You should have dinner parties and invite people round.'

Verity looked at her.

'Dinner parties?' she questioned warily.

'Mmm... Catherine's mother has them all the time. Dad was saying last week how embarrassed *he* felt because he wants to invite them round here but he doesn't have anyone to help him. I mean, he's okay really with the food, but it's the other things, isn't it?' Honor asked her earnestly. 'The flowers and the...the placements. Myra says that those are very important.'

The placements. Verity bit her inner lip to keep her mouth straight. It would never do to laugh and hurt

Honor's feelings. The last time she had heard someone referring to the importance of their placements had been at a stuffy Washington diplomatic dinner.

'Er…yes,' she agreed. 'Well, I'm sure that Myra would be only too pleased to act as hostess for your father.'

'She can't,' Honor told her quickly, 'It's… Catherine's mother doesn't like her… Perhaps you could do it?' Honor suggested.

Verity's eyes widened.

'Me? But…'

'I don't know how well you can cook, but I could help.'

Verity automatically continued to fold the laundry. Now she stopped and turned to Honor.

'Honor,' she began gently, 'I don't think—'

'Dad's back, I just heard the car,' Honor interrupted her, adding quickly, 'Don't say anything to him about the dinner party… He doesn't like people thinking that he can't do things.'

Outside the kitchen door Silas hesitated. Just the sight of Verity's BMW had raised his heartbeat. What the hell was the matter with him? Hadn't he learned his lesson the *first* time around? Eleven years ago Verity had rejected him in favour of her uncle's business and he was a fool if he allowed himself to forget that fact.

Even so, the sight that met his eyes when he finally pushed open the kitchen door was one that made him check and curl his hand into a hard warning fist. Verity and Honor were standing in the laundry room deep in conversation, Honor holding the end of the sheet that Verity was busily folding.

'Dad always says that it's a waste of time to iron them because no one but us ever sees them.'

No one! Verity's heart gave a quick thud. Did that mean that Myra and he...? Or was it simply that he discreetly chose not to share a bed with his lover in the same house where his daughter slept?

'Dad!' Honor cried, releasing the sheet as she saw her father and bounding across the kitchen to hug him with such very evident love that Verity's heart gave another and even more painful lurch.

It was so obvious, watching the two of them together, not just that Honor was Silas' daughter but also how much they loved one another. There was nothing false or artificial about the way Silas held his daughter.

'Thank you for helping out,' he told Verity formally. 'I—'

'Dad, Verity took me shopping. Just wait until you see what we bought. I told her you'd pay her,' Honor hurried on, 'but she still wouldn't let me have some of the things I wanted. There was this top and these leggings...' She began enthusiastically explaining the eye-popping ensemble to Silas before adding, 'But Verity didn't think they were my colours.'

Over her head Silas' eyes met Verity's.

Thank you, he mouthed silently before turning his attention back to Honor and telling her gravely, 'I'm sure she was right.'

'Well, that's what I thought because her own clothes are so beautiful,' Honor agreed. 'Don't you think she looks luscious in that suit, Dad?'

Luscious...

Verity could feel her face starting to grow warm as

two identical pairs of eyes studied her Donna-Karan-clad body.

'She certainly looks very…elegant…and success-ful,' Silas agreed quietly. But somehow, instead of sounding like a compliment, the words sounded much more like condemnation, Verity recognised grimly.

'I was just telling Verity how much you want to have a dinner party,' Honor chattered on, apparently oblivious to the tension growing between the two si-lent adults. 'She said she'd love to come and help you and it will help her to get to know people as well, won't it?'

'Honor…'

As they both spoke at once, Verity and Silas looked at one another.

'Now you're both cross with me…'

Bright tears shimmered in Honor's hurt eyes as her bottom lip wobbled and she turned her head away.

Verity was immediately filled with guilt and con-trition. Out of her own embarrassment and reluctance to have Silas think that she was deliberately inveigling her way back into his life, she had inadvertently hurt Honor.

Silas looked less concerned but he was still frown-ing.

'This dinner party,' he began, ignoring his daugh-ter's tear-filled eyes. 'It wouldn't be the same one that Catherine's mother informed me she would be de-lighted to attend, when I bumped into her in the su-permarket earlier, would it, Honor?'

Honor gave him a sunny smile.

'Oh, can they come? Good… Catherine's mother is a brilliant cook,' she informed Verity, 'and—'

'Honor!' Silas began warningly.

Quickly Verity picked up her handbag.

'I think I'd better go,' she announced quietly.

'Go? Oh, no, not yet. I wanted you to stay for supper,' Honor pleaded.

'I'm afraid I can't… I… I have another appointment,' Verity fibbed.

Honor's eyes widened.

'But this afternoon you said that you were staying in tonight by yourself,' she reminded Verity in a confused little voice.

'I'll see you out,' Silas told her, shooting Honor a quelling look.

'Thank you once again for looking after Honor,' he told Verity formally as he accompanied her politely to her car.

Verity daredn't allow herself to look at him but suddenly he was striding past her, examining the front wheel of her car.

'You've got a flat tyre,' he told her sharply.

Disbelievingly Verity looked at her car.

'I…I've got a spare,' she told him, but he was shaking his head,

'*That* won't do much good,' he said curtly. 'The back one's flat as well. They've both got nails in them,' he informed her. 'You must have driven over them.'

'Yes, I must,' Verity agreed, shaking her head. 'But I don't know where. If I could use your phone to ring a garage…'

'You can, but I doubt you'll be able to get it fixed until the morning,' he told her dryly. 'It's more likely the garages round here will all be shut now.'

Helplessly Verity studied her now immobile car.

How on earth had she managed to run over two nails—and where? She certainly hadn't been aware of doing so, nor of driving anywhere where she might have expected loose nails to be lying on the ground.

'Let's go back inside. I know the local dealer, I'll give him a ring,' Silas suggested.

Silently Verity followed Silas back into the house.

Watching them from the sitting-room window, Honor surreptitiously crossed her fingers. So far, so good—the plan to get them together was working beautifully. It had been hard work driving those nails into the tyres, though—much harder than she had expected.

'You *can't* do that,' Catherine had protested, her eyes widening in a mixture of shock and excitement when Honor had told her what she had planned to do.

'Watch me,' Honor had challenged her, bravado covering her brief twinge of guilt at what she had to do.

Verity waited in the kitchen with Honor whilst Silas went into his study to ring the garage. When he came back his expression was grave.

'The garage can't come out until tomorrow, I'm afraid, which means that you're going to have to spend the night here.'

Verity opened her mouth to protest and say that if he couldn't run her home she could get a taxi, and then, for some inadmissible and dangerous reason, she found that she was closing it again.

'Oh, good, now we can play Scrabble and you can share my bedroom,' Honor was saying excitedly.

'Verity can sleep in the guest bedroom,' Silas reproved crisply, 'and as for Scrabble—'

Verity smiled. Honor had told her earlier in the day how much she enjoyed the game.

'I'd love to play with her,' she interrupted Silas pacifically, adding truthfully, 'It's always been one of my favourite games.'

'Yes. I… I enjoy it as well,' Silas agreed.

Her heart hammering too fast for comfort, Verity wondered if that slight hesitation in his voice had been her imagination. Had he, as she had momentarily felt, been about to say that he remembered how much she had enjoyed Scrabble?

Ridiculous to feel such a warm, fuzzy, sentimental, inappropriate surge of happiness at the thought.

'I still can't understand where I managed to pick up those nails,' Verity commented, shaking her head.

They had just cleared away after supper and Honor had gone upstairs to get the Scrabble.

'Where they came from is immaterial now,' Silas pointed out. 'The damage is done…'

'Mmm…'

'More wine?' Silas offered her, picking up the still half-full bottle from the kitchen table.

On the point of refusing, Verity changed her mind. What harm could it do, after all, and since she wasn't driving…? The meal they had eaten had been a simple one of chicken and vegetables, prepared by Silas with Honor's rather erratic assistance.

It had touched Verity, though, when Honor had insisted on dragging her out to the garden with her so that they could find some flowers to put on the table.

'Dad, when you have the dinner party, you'll have to use the dining room,' she told her father whilst they were eating. 'I'll show you the dining room afterwards, Verity,' she informed Verity with a woman-to-woman look. 'You'll need to know where everything is.'

'Honor,' Silas began, 'I don't think—'

But Honor refused to listen to him, turning instead to Verity and demanding passionately, 'You will do it, won't you, Verity? Please,' before telling her father, 'You don't understand... I *hate* it at school when the others talk about the parties their mothers give. I can tell that they're all feeling sorry for me. I know that Verity may not be able to cook, but *we* can have just as good a dinner party here as they have.'

After such a passionate outburst, what else could Verity do other than swallow her own feelings and give in? Silas, she suspected, must be swallowing equally hard—harder, perhaps, if the frowning look on his face was anything to go by.

'You had no business inviting Catherine's mother and father round, though, no matter the circumstances...' Pausing, Silas shook his head before adding sternly, 'No business at all. But since you *have*, I agree that we can hardly tell Catherine's mother the truth. Please don't feel that *you* have to get involved, though—' he told Verity.

'I'd be happy to help,' Verity cut him off, looking him straight in the eye as she told him quietly, 'I know how Honor feels, but, of course, if there's someone else you would prefer to act as your hostess...?'

She waited. Would he tell her that, by rights, Myra ought to be the one hostessing his dinner party? And what if he did? Why should that concern *her*?

'No. There's no one,' he denied before adding, 'Besides, this will be *Honor's* dinner party, I suspect, not mine…'

'You can choose the wine, Dad,' Honor informed him in a kind voice. 'That's the man's job. What will we do about food?' she asked Verity excitedly.

'We'll sort something out,' Verity promised her whilst she mentally reviewed which of her favourite dishes she should serve.

In London she had had little time for giving dinner parties, but when she had they had been occasions she had thoroughly enjoyed.

Good food, good wine and good friends—most of all good friends; they were a recipe for the very best kind of entertaining. But she didn't know Silas' friends and the situation was bound to be both uncomfortable and awkward. He was being polite about it now, just as he had been good-mannered about the accident to her tyres and the fact that he had been forced to offer her a bed for the night. But they both knew how he really felt about her.

Quickly now, Verity reached for her wine and took a deep gulp, grimacing a little as the wine's sharpness hit her palate.

'You never did have much of a head for alcohol,' Silas commented, watching her.

Silently their glances met and held.

'That was over ten years ago,' Verity finally managed to tell him huskily. 'My…tastes have changed since then.'

'Here it is…'

Both of them looked round as Honor came bounding into the room carrying the Scrabble.

CHAPTER SEVEN

'RIGHT, time for bed...'

'Oh, Dad, just *one* more game,' Honor protested, but Silas was already shaking his head.

'You said that last time,' he reminded her sternly.

Diplomatically Verity busied herself tidying up the letters and putting everything away. Honor had needed no allowances made for her and she had thoroughly trounced them, not once, but twice—perhaps because in Verity's own case, at least, her concentration had been more on the words that Honor had formed than matching them, she admitted, quickly glancing away from Honor to the board.

Love... Tiff... Quarrel... Mama... Surely she was being over-sensitive in her reaction to seeing those words? After all, Honor knew nothing about the past, their shared past.

Quickly Verity broke up the words and folded the board.

'You will come up and say goodnight to me, won't you?' Honor begged Verity, adding determinedly, 'I want you both to come up...together...'

Verity couldn't bring herself to look at Silas. Instead she went to wash the empty coffee mugs whilst Silas took Honor upstairs.

She was just about to remove their wineglasses when he came back down.

'No, leave those,' he told her. 'We might as well finish off the bottle.'

'I'll just go up and say goodnight to Honor,' Verity told him huskily.

Standing in the kitchen on her own whilst he'd been upstairs with Honor had given her too much time to think, to remember…to regret…

If things had been different Honor could have been *her* child… If things had been different… If Silas had not rejected her… If… If… But what use were 'ifs'? No use whatsoever to an aching, lonely, yearning heart. A heart that still beat ridiculously fast for a man who had hurt it so badly.

Honor was lying flat beneath the bedclothes, her hair a dark mass on the pillow. Automatically as she bent to kiss her Verity smoothed it back off her face.

'I do like you, Verity,' Honor told her softly. 'I wish you could be here with us for always…'

Sharp tears pricked Verity's eyes. She wasn't totally gullible, and she was perfectly well aware that Honor wasn't averse to using soft soap and flattery to get her own way, but for once there was no mistaking the very real emotion in the little girl's voice. The real emotion and the real need, Verity recognised.

Honor was looking, if not for a mother, then certainly for a mentor, a role model, a woman with whom she could bond. None knew better than she herself just how it felt to be on the verge of young womanhood without any guiding female influence in one's life, Verity acknowledged. It was one of the loneliest and most isolated places on earth—almost as lonely and heartache inducing as being without the man you had given your heart to.

Her uncle, although providing for her material welfare, had been oblivious to the emotional needs of a young girl, and Verity remembered with painful clarity how she as a young adolescent had tried desperately to attach herself to the mother of a school friend, and then, when that had been gently discouraged by the woman in question, she had turned instead to one of her schoolteachers. But both women, although kind and caring, had had their own families and their own lives, and their distancing of themselves from her had left Verity feeling even more bereft than before—and not just bereft, but sensitively aware of being gently held at a distance.

Honor, she suspected, although on the surface a very different girl from the one she had been, was going through a similar stage. There was no doubting Silas' love for his daughter, nor his caring paternal concern for her. He was, Verity could see, a father who was very actively involved in his daughter's life, but Honor was making it plain that she wanted a *woman's* influence in her life as well as her father's.

'You will stay the night, won't you?' she whispered now, clutching Verity's hand. 'I want you to be here when I wake up in the morning...'

'I'll be here,' Verity promised her.

'I like your hair best when it's down,' Honor told her sleepily. 'It makes you look...more huggy. Catherine, my friend, has got two brothers and loads and loads of cousins...' Her eyes closed. Very gently, Verity bent and kissed her.

For all her outer layer of sturdy independence, inside she was still very much a little girl. Silas' little girl.

Quietly Verity got up and headed for the bedroom door.

Alone in the kitchen, Silas allowed himself to relax for the first time since he had come home. He didn't know what kind of game Honor thought she was playing by inveigling Verity into agreeing to hosting that damned dinner party, and the only reason he hadn't given her a thorough dressing down over it was because he was well aware that she had reached that sensitive and delicate stage in her development where her burgeoning pride and sense of self could be very easily bruised. He would have to talk to her about it, of course, and explain that she had put Verity in a very embarrassing and difficult position.

It had been hard to guess exactly what Verity's real feelings about the situation were. She had developed a disconcerting, calm, distancing and very womanly maturity which, very effectively, drew a line over which no one was allowed to cross, but he certainly knew how he was going to feel, sitting at the opposite end of the dining table from her whilst she acted as his hostess. It was going to be sheer hell, total purgatory, an evening filled with excruciating pain of 'could have beens' and all because his darling daughter wanted to be on a par with her school friends.

Well, he couldn't blame her for that. It was all part and parcel of growing up. Honor was getting ready to grow into womanhood and she was making it clear to him that she wanted a woman in her life to pattern herself on.

He had, at one stage, wondered if Myra—but the pair of them would never accept one another.

Had Verity been anyone other than who she was he suspected that by now he would have been thanking fate for bringing her into their lives. It was glaringly obvious how Honor felt about her—and not just from the determined way she was attaching herself to Verity. If he was honest with himself, which he always tried to be, without the past to cast its unhappy shadow he knew perfectly well that, had he been meeting Verity for the first time now, he would have been instantly and immediately attracted to her.

She had still, despite the life she had lived, an air of soft and gentle femininity, an aura of natural womanly strength melded with compassion and love.

He found it hard to picture her as the head of a multi-million-pound business making corporate decisions based purely on profits and completely without emotion. It wasn't that he doubted her skills or abilities, it was just that, to him, even now, she still possessed that certain something that made him want to look after her and protect her.

Protect her? Was he crazy? She *had* all the protection she needed in the shape of the material assets she had chosen above their love.

'It's my duty, I owe it to him,' she had told him sadly when she had allowed her uncle to part them and send her away to New York, but those had been words he hadn't wanted to hear.

Last night, holding her in his arms, kissing her... She'd been back less than a week and already... He wasn't going to make the same mistake he had made last time. This time he was going to be on his guard and stay on it...

He had known, of course, of her uncle's plans for

Verity's future and the way her uncle had deliberately fostered and used her strong sense of duty for his own ends.

One of the first things he had decided when he had found himself widowed and the father of a baby girl was that he would never ever manipulate her feelings and cause her to feel that she was in debt to him for anything in the way he had witnessed Verity's uncle manipulating hers.

But, naively perhaps, he had assumed that Verity had shared his feelings, his belief that their future lay together.

'Do you love me?' he had demanded, and shyly she had nodded.

Had she ever loved him or...?

'I'll be back soon from New York and then...then we can be together,' she told him.

And he had taken that to mean that she had wanted to marry him, and share his dream of establishing a business together.

He could still remember the sense of excitement and pride he had felt the day he had first taken her to see the small run-down market garden he had hoped to buy. She had seemed as thrilled and excited as him.

'There's a real market locally for a garden centre and a landscaping service, but it won't be easy,' he warned her. 'I've been through all the figures with the bank and for the first few years we're going to have to plough back every penny we make into the business. I won't be able to buy us a big house or give you a nice car.'

'I don't care about things like that,' Verity assured him softly, making one of those lightning changes she could make from a girl's *naïveté* to a woman's maturity and shaking his heart to its roots in the process. It fascinated and delighted him, held him in thrall with awe to be privileged to see these glimpses of the woman she was going to be. She was so gentle, so loving, so everything that most appealed to him in a woman.

'I don't care where we live just so long as we're together…'

'Well, I should certainly make enough to support a wife and our child, our children…' he had whispered. It was all he wanted then. His parents were away on holiday with friends and he took her home with him, making love to her in the warm shadows of the summer evening. He was twenty-seven and considered himself already a man; she was twenty-one.

'I'm going to see the bank manager tomorrow,' he whispered to her as he slowly licked and then kissed her pretty pink fingertips, 'and then I'm going to put a formal offer in on the business. Once it's ours, we can start to make plans for our wedding.'

He thought that the quick tears that filled her eyes were tears of love and pleasure—she often wept huge silent tears of bliss after their lovemaking—and it was only later that he realised that she had wept because she had known that, by the time he was the owner of the small plot of land, she would be on the other side of the Atlantic.

Silas warned her repeatedly that her uncle was trying to separate them, that he had his own selfish reasons for not wanting them to marry, but Verity refused to listen.

Her uncle wasn't like that, she protested, white-faced. He didn't push the matter, thinking he knew how vulnerable she was, how much she needed to believe that the man who had brought her up did care more about her than his business, not wanting to do anything that might potentially hurt her.

Hurt her! Did *she* care about hurting *him* when she ignored his letter, his pleas to her to come home? She didn't even care enough to write to him and tell him that it was over. She simply ignored his letter.

And then her uncle called round, supposedly to buy some plants but in reality to tell him that Verity had decided to stay on in New York for a further year.

The business wasn't building up as fast as Silas had expected. He was struggling to service the bank borrowing he had taken out to buy and develop the garden centre, and when his bank manager telephoned him a week later to inform him that they had had an anonymous offer from someone wanting to buy the newly established garden centre from him he was so tempted to take it, to move away and make a fresh start somewhere else. What, after all, was there to keep him in the area any longer? His parents had decided to retire to Portugal, and he knew there was no way he could bear to live in the same town as Verity once she *did* return to take over her uncle's business—but then fate stepped in, throwing him a wild card.

He had obtained tickets for the annual prestigious Chelsea Flower Show—two of them—because he had assumed by then that Verity would be back from New York and he had wanted to take her with him.

Almost, he decided not to go. He had lost his love, and it looked very much as if he could soon be losing his business as well, but the tickets were bought and paid for and so he set out for London.

He saw Sarah when he was booking in at his hotel. She was staying there too, a thin, too pale girl who looked nothing like Verity and whom, if he was honest, he felt more sympathy for than desire. Her attempts to pick him up were so obvious and awkward that he had took pity on her and offered to buy her a drink. She was, she told him, originally from Australia where she had lived with foster parents, and she had come to England trying to trace her birth mother.

Whilst living in London she had met and fallen in love with a fellow Australian who had now left the country to continue his round-the-world tour, refusing to take Sarah with him.

'I thought he loved me,' she told Silas sadly, 'but he didn't, he was just using me.'

Her words and her sadness struck a sombre chord within Silas. In an attempt to cheer her up he offered her his spare ticket for the flower show, which she accepted.

They spent all that day together and the next, although there was nothing remotely sexual between them. Silas simply didn't feel that way about her. Verity was the only woman he wanted. Emotionally he might hate her for what she had done to him, but physically, at night alone in his bed, he still ached and yearned for her.

Even now he still didn't know what prompted him to knock on Sarah's door the second night after they had met. She didn't answer his knock but when, driven by some sixth sense, he turned the handle and pushed open the door, he found her seated on the bed, a glass of water in one hand and a bottle of pills on the bed beside her.

He shook her so savagely as he demanded to know how many she had taken that it was a wonder her neck didn't snap, he acknowledged later.

'None,' she told him dull-eyed, 'not yet...'

'Not yet. Not ever!' Silas told her sharply, picking up the bottle and going through to the bathroom to flush the contents down the lavatory.

When he came back she was crying soullessly into her hands.

'Don't go,' she begged him. 'I don't want to be on my own.'

And so he stayed and, inevitably perhaps, they had sex, out of compassion and pity on his part and loneliness and need on hers.

In the morning they went their separate ways, but not before Silas had insisted on giving Sarah his telephone number and getting her own address from her.

He was concerned enough about her to telephone her as soon as he got home and to ring her regularly twice a week after that.

Always, at the back of his mind, was the concern that she might succumb and try a second time to take her own life. She had told him sadly that when her boyfriend had moved on she had felt she had nothing left to live for. His own pain at losing Verity had enabled him to understand what she had been feeling. He had counselled her to think about returning to Australia and her foster parents and friends, and she had promised him she would think about doing so, and then he received the tearful telephone call that was to completely change his life—to change both their lives.

She was pregnant, she told him, an accident. She was on the pill but had forgotten to take it. He was not to worry, she said, she intended to have the pregnancy terminated.

Silas reacted immediately and instinctively, taking the first train to York where she was living.

'I can't afford a baby,' she protested when he told her that he didn't want her to have a termination.

'This is *my* baby as well as yours,' Silas reminded her sombrely. 'We could get married and share the responsibility.'

'Get married? *Us*…? You and me? But you don't… It was just sex,' she protested shakily.

Just sex maybe, but they had still created a new life between them, and in the end she gave way and they were married very quickly and very quietly.

From the start Honor had been an independent, cheerful child. Until she had started school Silas had often taken her to work with him and the bond between them was very close and strong. She had asked about her mother, of course, and Silas had told her what little he knew, but until recently she had always seemed perfectly happy for there just to be the two of them.

He had named her Honor as a form of promise to Sarah that he would always honour the bargain they had made between them to put the welfare of the child they had created first, and he believed that he had always honoured that bargain.

He could hear Verity coming back downstairs now.

'I… I'm sorry about…about the car…' she told him awkwardly as she walked into the kitchen.

'It's hardly your fault,' Silas pointed out.

'Do you plan to stay in town long?' he asked her politely as he handed her the glass of wine he had poured her.

'I… I'm not really sure yet.'

Silas frowned. 'Surely the business—?' he began, but Verity cut him off, shaking her head.

'I sold it… It was either that or risk being forcibly taken over. I plan to use the money to establish a charitable trust in my uncle's name,' she told him.

Silas fought hard not to let his shock show. What had happened to the woman who had put the business before their love? Verity must have changed dramatically—or perhaps weakened. Quickly he caught himself up. There was no point in allowing his thoughts to travel down *that* road, or in hoping, *wishing*— what? That she had had such a change of heart earlier, that their love…that he had been more important to her, that they could have… Stop it, he warned himself.

'It must have been hard for you, making the decision to sell,' he commented as unemotionally as he could. 'After all, it's been your life…'

Her *life*. Had he any idea how cruel he was being? Verity wondered. Did he know what it did to her to be told by him, of all people, that her life was so cold and empty and lacking in real emotion? She stiffened her spine and put down her glass.

'No more than *your* business has been yours,' she pointed out quietly.

It wasn't true, of course—his work had been something that he loved, that he had chosen *freely* for himself, whilst hers… Not even with him could she be able to discuss how it had felt to finally step out from beneath the heavy burden that the business had always been to her, to feel free, to be her own person for the first time in her life.

Verity drew in her breath with a small hiss of pain.

'I think I'd like to go to bed,' she told him shakily. 'It's been a long day.'

Meaning, of course, that she didn't want to spend any time with him, Silas recognised.

'I'll take you up,' he told her curtly.

The guest room, Verity discovered, was more of a small, private suite on the top floor of the house in what must have originally been the attics—a pretty, good-sized bedroom with sloping ceiling and its own bathroom plus a small sitting room.

'I had this conversion done for Honor,' Silas informed her. 'She's getting to an age where she needs her own space and her own privacy.'

As he turned and walked towards the door Verity had a strong compulsion to run after him and stop him.

'Silas…'

He stopped and turned round, waiting in silence.

'Goodnight,' she told him shakily.

'Goodnight,' he returned.

After showering and brushing her hair, Verity crept into bed. It felt so strange being here in Silas' house. During the years they had been apart she had resisted the temptation to think about Silas and what might have been. She thought she had learnt to live with the pain, but seeing him again had reawakened not just

the pain she had felt but all her other emotions as
well. She couldn't possibly still love him. Hadn't she
learned her lesson? Verity could feel the back of her
throat beginning to ache with the weight of her sup-
pressed tears as she closed her eyes and willed herself
to go to sleep.

CHAPTER EIGHT

SILAS woke up abruptly. There was a sour taste in his mouth from the wine he had drunk and his head ached. Swinging his legs out of bed, he stood up and reached for his robe. His weight was much the same now as it had always been but his body was far more heavily muscled than it had been when he was in his twenties—the work he did was responsible for that, of course. Shaking his head, he padded barefoot out onto the landing and into the bathroom. He needed a glass of water.

He was just reaching into the bathroom cabinet for an aspirin when he heard a familiar sound. Putting down the glass of water he had been holding, he walked quickly towards Honor's door. When she was younger she had often woken in the night in tears, frightened by some bad monster disturbing her dreams, but when he gently opened her bedroom door she was sleeping deeply and peacefully.

Still frowning, he glanced towards the stairs that led to the guest suite.

The noise was clearer now, a soft, heart-tearing sobbing. Verity was crying?

Immediately, taking the stairs two at a time, Silas hurried to her room, pushing open the door.

Like Honor she was asleep, but unlike Honor her sleep wasn't peaceful. The bedclothes were tangled and the duvet half off the bed, exposing the creamy softness of her skin. As he realised that, like him, she slept in the nude, Silas hastily willed himself to ignore the temptation to let his gaze stray to her body, concentrating instead on her pale, tear-stained face.

Without her make-up and with her hair down she looked no different now than she had done at nineteen and, for a moment, the temptation to gather her up in his arms and hold her close was so strong that he had to take a step back from the bed to prevent himself from doing so.

In her sleep Verity gave a small, heartbreaking little cry, fresh tears rolling down her face from her closed eyes.

Silas could remember how rarely she had cried, how brave and independent she had always tried to be. Once, when they had quarrelled about something—he had forgotten what, some minor disagreement—she had turned her face away from him in the car and he had thought she had been sulking until he had looked in the wing mirror and seen the tears streaming from her eyes.

'I didn't want you to see me cry,' she had told him when he had stopped the car and taken her in his arms. 'It hurts so much.'

'The last thing I want to do is hurt you,' Silas had told her and meant it.

In her sleep Verity was reliving the events of the final summer of her relationship with Silas. After the two days they had spent together, New York had seemed even more lonely than ever. The work she had been doing with her uncle's old friend had been mentally and physically demanding and yet, at the same time somehow, very unsatisfying. She hadn't got the heart for it, Verity had acknowledged. Her heart had been given to Silas. Just how empty her life had been without him had been brought home to her during the two days they had spent together. Then, she had felt alive, whole, complete... When he had gone... It had been less than a week since he had flown home, having begged her to tell her uncle that she had changed her mind and that her future now lay with Silas.

'I can't do it,' she protested.

'It's business, Verity,' Silas argued, 'that's all. *We're* human beings with feelings, needs... I miss you and I want us to be together.'

'I miss you too,' Verity told him.

Initially she had been supposed to be spending four months in New York, but the original four had stretched to eight and then twelve, and every time she mentioned coming home her uncle procrastinated and said that, according to his friend, there was a great deal she still had to learn.

Sometimes the temptation to tell him that she simply couldn't do what he wanted her to do was so strong that she almost gave in to it, and then she would remember how he had taken her in.

Although it had never been discussed between them, Verity had the feeling that her uncle blamed her for her father's death. He and her mother had been on their way to collect her from a birthday party she had insisted on going to when they had been involved in the fatal accident which had killed them both, and she felt as though, in taking his place, she was doing some kind of penance, making some kind of restitution.

She had tried to say as much to Silas but he always
got so angry when they discussed her uncle that she
had simply not been able to do so. And her uncle
seemed to dislike and resent Silas as much as Silas
did him.

'Have you any idea just how wealthy you are going
to be?' he demanded of Verity when she begged him
to allow her to return home. 'You must be very careful, Verity,' he warned her. 'There are always going
to be hungry and ambitious men out there who will
try to convince you that they love you. Don't listen
to them.'

'Silas isn't like that,' she protested defensively.

'Isn't he?' her uncle countered grimly. 'Well, he is
certainly a young man with an awful lot of debts—
far too many to be able to support a wife.'

'Come home,' Silas begged her.

But she said, 'No...not until I have fulfilled my
debt to my uncle.'

Shortly after Silas returned to England, the murder
of one of her fellow tenants in the block where she
rented an apartment resulted in her uncle insisting that
she moved to a safer address.

Verity tried to telephone Silas to tell him that she
was moving but, when she wasn't able to get any
reply either from Silas' home telephone or the garden
centre, she had to ask her uncle to pass on to him her
new address and telephone number.

She knew from what Silas had told her during his
visit that he had several new commissions and was
working virtually eighteen hours a day, which explained why she was unable to get hold of him.

A month later when she had still not heard from

him she finally made herself acknowledge the truth. She loved him and missed him—dreadfully. He was the most important thing, the most important person in her life, and even though it meant disappointing her uncle she knew that it was impossible for her to go on denying her feelings, her love, any longer. She wanted to go home.

She rang her uncle, who assured her that he had passed on to Silas her new address and telephone number.

Silas was angry and upset with her, Verity acknowledged. It had taken a lot for him to beg her to come home as he had done and, no doubt, she had hurt his pride when she had been unable to say yes.

She knew how little he had been able to afford either the time or the money for his spur-of-the-moment flying visit to her, and she wished she had been able to tell him then how much she was missing him and how much she wished she could be with him.

When another two months passed without him getting in touch with her, she finally acknowledged the truth. She had lost weight; she couldn't sleep; she thought about him night and day; she ached so badly for him that the pain of missing him was with her all the time. She loved him so much that, even if it meant letting her uncle down, she knew that it was impossible for her to go on denying her feelings. There must surely be a way that she could be with Silas and do as her uncle wished, a way she did not have to choose between them, but if there wasn't…

If there wasn't, then she had made up her mind, selfish though it might be: being with Silas was more important to her than pleasing her uncle. She wanted

to go home; she wanted to be with Silas; she wanted
to be held in his arms close to his heart; she wanted
to hear him telling her in that gruff, sexy voice he
used after they had made love that he loved her and
needed her and that he would never ever let her go.
She wanted to hear him telling her how much he
wanted her to be his wife, how much he wanted them
to spend their lives together.

Reliving the times they had had together over and
over again in the empty loneliness of her apartment
was no substitute for the reality of being with him.

Without giving herself time to change her mind, she
booked herself on the first available flight home, without telling anyone what she was doing. She wanted
to surprise Silas, to see the look in his eyes when she
walked into his arms, to show him that he meant more
to her than anything else, than anyone else, in the
world.

Confronting her uncle wasn't going to be easy, she
knew that. She was twenty-two, old enough to know
her own mind and to make her own decisions.

She bought a copy of the local newspaper whilst
she waited for a taxi to take her from the station to
the garden centre. Without that, without seeing that
small, bare announcement of Silas' marriage to another woman, she wouldn't have known, would have
walked into a situation for which she was totally un-
prepared.

The taxi driver, seeing her white face, was concerned enough to ask her if she was ill.

Verity looked at him blankly, her gaze returning to
the newsprint in front of her. Silas was *married*. How
could that be possible? He had been going to marry

her. Was she suffering from some kind of madness, some kind of delusion? Was it all just a bad dream? How *could* Silas be married to someone else? There must have been a mistake, and yet she knew that there was no mistake, just as she now knew the reason for his silence during these last long weeks.

The pain was like nothing she had ever imagined experiencing: a tearing, wrenching, soul-destroying agony that made her want to scream and howl and tear at herself and her clothes, to ease a grief she could neither control nor contain.

She made the taxi driver take her back to the station. *En route* to Heathrow and a transatlantic flight back to New York she couldn't understand why, despite the heat of the day, her fingers and toes felt as cold as ice, so cold that they hurt, her movements those of a very, very old woman.

Back in New York she applied herself to her work with a grim concentration, throwing up a barrier around herself that she would allow no one to pass through.

Silas hadn't loved her at all. Silas had lied to her. Her uncle was right. From now on she was going to devote herself to the business. What else, after all, was there for her?

Fresh tears rolled down Verity's face—the tears she had never allowed herself to cry during the reality of her heartbreak at losing Silas but which now, reliving those days in her sleep, she had no power to suppress.

Silas. Not even in the privacy of her apartment had she allowed herself the weakness of whispering his

name, of reliving all the times they had shared together.

'Silas…'

As he heard her say his name Silas closed his eyes.
It hurt him to hear the emotion in her voice and to
see the evidence of the distress on her damp face.

Very gently he reached out and touched her wet
cheek. Her skin felt cool beneath his fingertips, her
eyelashes ridiculously long as they fanned darkly on
her cheek. She was lying half on and half off the
pillow and automatically he slid his hand beneath the
nape of her neck intending to make her more comfortable, just as he often did for Honor. But Verity
wasn't Honor, a child…his child… She was a
woman…his woman…

The shudder that galvanised his body was its own
warning but it was a warning that came far too late.
He stiffened as Verity suddenly opened her eyes.

'Silas…'

The husky wonderment in her voice held him spellbound.

'Silas.'

She said his name again, breathing it as unsteadily
as an uncertain swimmer gulping air. As she struggled
to sit up, the duvet slid further from her body, leaving
it clothed only in the soft silver moonlight coming in
through the window.

Silas caught his breath. In her early twenties she
had had the body of a girl, slender and gently curved,
only hinting at what it would be in maturity, but now
she was fully a woman, her curves were so richly
sensuous that he had to close his eyes to stop himself
from reaching out to touch her just to make sure that

she was real. He could feel the beads of sweat beginning to pearl his skin as he was flooded with hungry desire for her.

Even though he had looked away immediately, every detail of her was already imprinted on his eyeballs and his emotions. His hands ached to cup the ripe softness of her breasts, to stroke the taut warmth of her belly, to cover the feminine crispness of her pubic curls, to…

The power of his reaction to her, not just sexually but emotionally as well, shocked him into immobility.

'Silas…'

Reluctantly he opened his eyes as she whispered his name. Her mouth looked soft and warm, her eyes confused and unhappy. He lifted his hand to touch her hair and let it slide silkily through his fingers, his body shuddering as he started to release her.

Verity watched wide-eyed, still caught up in the intensity of her dream, her glance following Silas' every movement. Pleadingly she raised her hand to touch the side of his face, her palm flat against his jaw where she could feel his beard prickling her skin.

Silas closed his eyes as he moaned her name, a tortured, haunted sound of denial, but Verity was too lost in what she was doing to respond to it. Her fingertips trembled as she pressed them against his mouth, exploring its familiar shape, feeling them move as he mouthed her name. Instinctively she slipped them between his lips.

Immediately her nipples hardened, the muscles in her belly and thighs tautening as she shook with the force of what she was feeling.

Helplessly Silas opened his mouth, his tongue tip

caressing the smooth warmth of her fingertips. He could see as well as feel her whole body trembling in reaction to his caress. Holding her arm, he sucked slowly on her fingers.

Beneath her breath Verity made a small, familiar keening noise as she lifted her other hand to his face, stroking him with frantic little movements, far more sensual and exciting for all their lack of open sexuality than a more calculatedly sexual caress could ever have been.

His self-control breaking, Silas caught hold of her hands, bearing her back against the softness of the pillow, his hands now cupping her face as he started to kiss her, opening her mouth with his lips, his tongue, feeding rather than satisfying his hunger for her with passionate, deeply intimate kisses.

As she opened her mouth to him, Verity caught back a small sob of relief. It had been so awful, dreaming that she had lost Silas, but here he was, with her, holding her, loving her, showing her that she was safe.

The smell of him, the sight of him, the *feel* of him, totally overwhelmed her starved senses, her body, so sensitive to him that her breasts were aching for his touch even before she felt his hands reaching out to cup them. Eagerly she moved to accommodate and help him, shivering in mute pleasure as she felt the hard familiarity of his palms against the taut peaks of her nipples.

Beneath his robe he was naked and it was heaven to have the luxury of sliding her hands up over his shoulders and down his back, to feel the solid male warmth of his skin, his *body* beneath her hands, to have the longed-for male reality of his flesh against her own, to feel that she was totally and completely surrounded and protected by him.

'Silas.' As she said his name she moved beneath him, silently inviting him to increase the intimacy between them.

As he felt her lifting her body towards his Silas groaned. He could feel her trembling as he touched her and he knew that he was shaking just as much. There hadn't been this much sexual tension between them even the first time they had made love. It felt as though their bodies were waiting to explode, to meld, to come together so completely that they could never be parted again.

She felt so good, so right...so...so Verity. He wanted to touch her, kiss her, possess her so completely that she would never be able to leave him again.

His hand touched her stomach and she rose up eagerly against him. He bent his mouth towards her breast, holding his breath as he started to lick delicately at her nipple, half afraid he might accidentally hurt her as he forced himself to go slowly, but Verity seemed to have no such inhibitions, her hand going to the back of his head as she pulled him closer to her body so that his mouth opened fully over her damp nipple.

Shuddering, he drew it deeply into his mouth and started to suck rhythmically on her. Beneath his hand he could feel the flesh of her belly grow hot and damp. Her face was flushed with desire, her body trembling as she made small, pleading cries deep in her throat.

Wordlessly he parted her thighs. The room was light enough for him to be able to see her naked body, and her sex. He could remember how shy she had been the first time he had whispered to her how much he wanted to see her, to look at her. But she had still let him and he could still remember the sense of awe and love he had felt, knowing just how much she trusted him.

He could see that same trust in her eyes now and, even though he knew he was deluding himself, it was almost as though there had never been anyone else for her but him, as though her body had never known any other lover, as though it had memories of only him, his touch, his need, his love.

Sombrely he parted her soft outer lips, exposing the secret kernel of her sex. His heart was thudding frantically fast, his own body stiff with arousal and need. He could see her looking at him, silent and wide-eyed as she reached out to caress him with her fingertips.

Very gently he touched her, coaxing, caressing.

Verity gave a low, aching groan, her hand tightening around him. She could feel her body responding to him, aching for him. It had been without him for so long that it needed no preliminaries, hungry and eager now for the longed-for feel of him within it.

'I want you, Silas,' she told him jerkily. 'I need you…now… Oh, yes, now…' she whispered frantically. 'Now. Now…now…'

The rhythm of their lovemaking was fast and intense, their shared climax a juddering, explosive catalyst of release that left them both trembling as Silas held Verity in his arms.

'Stay with me,' Verity whispered to him as her exhausted body slid into sleep. 'Don't leave me, Silas. Please don't leave me... Not this time...'

As she slept Silas looked down into her face. She was a woman now, a woman with a woman's needs, a woman's sexuality. If she hadn't loved him enough to put their love first before, she was hardly likely to do so now. She might want him sexually, she might even stay for a while, but it wasn't just his own emotions she was likely to hurt this time, his own heart she could easily break. There was Honor to consider as well.

'Stay with me,' she had begged him. But she was the one who had left *him*. *She* was the one who had refused to stay.

Very slowly he eased himself away from her, picking up his discarded robe as he looked down at her.

'Stay with me,' she had said. As he bent and kissed her cheek a single tear rolled down her face, but it wasn't one of her own.

Clenching his jaw, Silas walked towards the door, closing it quietly behind him without daring to look back.

CHAPTER NINE

VERITY surfaced slowly from the deepest and most relaxing sleep she could remember having in a long time. She stretched luxuriously, a womanly knowing smile curling her mouth. Her body felt deliciously, blissfully satisfied. Even her skin where the sunlight shone warmly on her exposed arm on top of the duvet seemed to have a silken, sensuous shimmer to it. She closed her eyes and made a purring sound of female happiness deep in her throat as she savoured the novelty of feeling so good. It was as if she had opened a present, spilling out from it a glowing, sparkling, magical gift of happiness and love. Mmm… Her eyes still closed, she rolled over and reached out for Silas.

Abruptly, Verity opened her eyes properly, her body tensing as her hand rested on the cold empty space on the other half of the bed. Of course. She had known Silas wouldn't be there in bed beside her—he had Honor to think of, after all—but the pristine smoothness of the unused pillow next to her own suggested that he had left her on her own as speedily as he could, not even pausing for a few moments to savour their closeness, and that hurt!

Her happiness and joy evaporated immediately.

Once before, he had left her like this and she had woken up alone. Then, he had returned carrying arms full of flowers and fresh bagels he had bought from a bakery in her New York neighbourhood.

Then they had shared a breakfast of kisses and bagels in her bed.

Then…

But this was now and instinct told her that the reason for his absence from her bed had nothing to do
with any plans he had to surprise her with early morning flowers or other gifts of love.

She could hear footsteps on the stairs leading to her
bedroom but she knew, even before the door was
pushed open and Honor's dark head appeared around
it, that they did not belong to Silas.

'Are you awake?' Honor asked her.

Forcing a smile, Verity nodded.

'I wanted you to sleep with *me* last night,' Honor
told her reproachfully as she ran across the room and
scrambled up onto the bed next to Verity, snuggling
up to her.

Automatically Verity reached out her arm to draw
her close and hold her. Her body, which such a short
space of time ago had felt so good, so female, so
loved, now felt cold and empty, her muscles aching
and tense. But it wasn't *Honor's* fault that she wasn't
her father.

Verity could hear fresh footsteps on the stairs but,
unlike Honor's, these stopped halfway and she heard
Silas call out, 'Honor… Breakfast…'

'Coming, Dad,' Honor called back, scrambling off
the bed and starting to head for the door, and then
unexpectedly turning round and rushing back to fling
her arms around Verity's neck and give her a brief
little girl kiss.

Blinking fiercely, Verity watched her leave. The
fact that Silas had not chosen to come into her room

had told her everything she needed to know about how he felt about last night, as though she *needed* any extra underlining of the fact that it had meant so little to him.

Fresh tears welled and once again she forced them back, but these had nothing to do with the tenderness she had felt at Honor's kiss.

She might only have the haziest memory of how she and Silas had come to be making love last night—she could remember waking up to the touch of his fingers on her face, the warmth of his body next to hers. Presumably he must have had some reason to come up to her room.

She might not know what that was, but she certainly knew why he had made love to her—made love! Had *sex*, she told herself brutally. She might not be able to remember what had brought him to her bed, but she could certainly remember what had kept him there. She couldn't have made her feelings, her need of him, more plain if she'd written them on a ten-foot banner, she told herself bitterly. He'd have to be made of granite not to have taken what she had so stupidly put on offer for him.

Sexual desire, sexual frustration, could do all manner of things to a man—even make him feel the need for a woman he did not like, never mind love, and that was quite plainly what had happened last night. Silas had used her to vent his sexual frustration. No *wonder* he hadn't stayed with her. No *wonder* he was keeping his distance from her this morning.

The plain, ugly truth was that he had used her and she had let him—and not merely let him but positively encouraged him. And to think that when she'd woken up she had thought…felt…believed…

Would she *never* learn? She had believed once before that he had loved her, cared for her, *about* her, and she had been wrong. Now, here she was, eleven years down the line, still hoping, still feeling…still *loving*.

Verity closed her eyes. No. She did *not* still love him. She could not still love him. She *would* not still love him. She opened them again and stared dully at the wall. Just who did she think she was kidding? She loved him all right!

Drearily she got out of bed and headed for the bathroom. Coming back to town had been a total mistake. And she was not even convinced any more about her real motives in having done so.

Or perhaps she was. *Had* it been at the back of her mind all the time that she would see Silas? Even though she knew he was married to someone else?

She gave a small, hollow groan. She had come back because this was her home, the place where she had grown up.

Once she had dressed, reluctantly she made her way downstairs.

When she pushed open the kitchen door, Honor was seated at the table eating her cereal whilst Silas stood at the counter making coffee.

As she walked in he turned and looked at her and then looked quickly away again.

'I've just checked with the garage. They're going to make picking up your car a priority,' he told her, his attention on the kettle he was refilling, asking her briefly, 'Tea or coffee?'

'Coffee, please,' Verity responded. Did he really need to ask? Had he really forgotten how he had teased her in the past about her urgent need for her morning caffeine, or was he underlining the fact that, although her preferences mattered, they were of as little importance to him as she was herself.

'I'll drop you off at your place when I take Honor to school,' he told her as he made her coffee.

'Toast…cereal?'

'No, nothing, thanks,' Verity told him coolly.

As he brought the coffee to her she deliberately turned away from him. He smelled of soap and coffee and her stomach muscles churned frantically as he stood next to her. Inside she was trembling and she had to wrap both her hands around the mug of coffee he had brought her, just in case he might see how much he was affecting her.

'When are we going to do the shopping for the dinner party?' Honor was keen to know.

They were in Silas' car on the way to Honor's school, Verity seated in the front passenger seat next to Silas, at Honor's insistence and very much against her own inclinations. The dinner party! Verity had forgotten all about that.

'That's enough, Honor,' Silas told her crisply as he pulled up at the school gate.

As she hopped out of the car Honor said, 'Look, there's my friend Catherine. I want her to meet you,' and then she was tugging open Verity's door and leaving Verity with no alternative other than to unfasten her seat belt and go with her to where the young girl was standing watching.

'Catherine, this is Verity,' Honor announced importantly. Catherine was smaller and fairer than Honor and it was plain to see which of them was the leader of their twosome, Verity acknowledged as Catherine gave her a shy look and started to giggle.

'Goodbye.' Honor reached up and gave Verity a fierce hug before telling her, 'And don't forget, will you, about the dinner party?'

Verity watched her race out of sight with her friend before turning to walk back to the car. Bending down, she told Silas through the open window, 'I can walk home from here, thank you…'

And before he could say anything she turned smartly on her heel and proceeded to do just that.

She wasn't going to give him another opportunity to humiliate her by keeping his distance from her, she decided proudly, as she lifted her chin and willed herself not to look back at him.

As he watched Verity walking away through his rear-view mirror, Silas hit the steering wheel with the flat of his hand.

He was the one who was in danger of being hurt, rejected, used, so how come it was *Verity* who was behaving as though he were the one treating her badly?

He had known all along that last night had been a mistake and there, this morning, was the proof of it. Verity was treating him as distantly as though they were two strangers. It was perfectly obvious that she regretted what had happened between them, and that she intended to make it very plain to him that neither it nor he meant anything to her. Last night she might have wanted him, but this morning…

* * *

'But you promised…' Honor insisted, tears clustering on her lashes as she stared across the table at her father.

'Honor. I've just explained. I don't have the time to get involved in giving dinner parties and—'

'*Verity's* going to do it…'

'*Verity* is far too busy with her own life to want to get involved in ours,' Silas told her curtly. 'And, whilst we're on the subject, I want you to promise me that you won't go round there any more. Verity has her own life to live.'

Watching the tears run pathetically down his daughter's face, Silas cursed silently to himself.

He hated having to disappoint and hurt her like this but what other option did he have? The more he allowed her to get involved with Verity, the more she was going to be hurt in the end.

'Now hurry up and finish your homework,' Silas admonished her sternly. 'I've got to go out at eight and Mrs Simmonds is coming round to babysit you…'

'Mrs Simmonds.' Honor glared at him. She liked the elderly widow who normally came to sit with her on the rare occasions when Silas went out in the evening, but she wasn't Verity.

'Why can't I have Verity? Where are you going anyway?' she demanded suspiciously. 'Not to see Myra?'

Silas gritted his teeth.

'No. I am not.'

He knew perfectly well what was in Honor's mind. She had made it more than plain that she didn't want Myra as a stepmother—not that there had been any real danger of that happening. Myra was not good stepmother material, Silas acknowledged, especially not for Honor who needed a much more compassionate hand on the reins; a much more gentle touch— like Verity's! Now where had that thought come from?

Watching him under her lashes, Honor held her breath. For her, Verity would make the perfect stepmother. She remembered the message she had seen on the back of the photo in her father's desk.

'To my beloved Silas, with all my love for ever and always.'

'Why did they say they didn't know each other, do you suppose?' Catherine had asked, wide-eyed, when Honor had related this interesting fact to her.

Honor had rolled her eyes and told her severely, 'Because they're still in love with one another stupid…'

'How can they be?' Catherine had objected naively. 'Your father married your mother…'

'It happens!' Honor had assured her wisely.

'Maybe they just stopped being in love,' Catherine had suggested, adding, 'Anyway, why do you want to have Verity as your stepmother?'

'Because…' Honor had told her with quelling dismissal.

If she had to have a stepmother, and it seemed that she did, then Verity was quite definitely the one she wanted, and so she had mounted her own special campaign towards that end.

Now, though, things weren't going at all according to plan and the tears filling her eyes weren't entirely manufactured. Cuddled up in Verity's arms this morning, she had experienced an emotion which had broken through the tough, protective outer shell she had created around herself. From being very young she had resented the pity she had seen in the eyes of the women who had cooed at her father and said how hard it must be for him to bring up a little girl like her on his own, scowling horribly at them when she had digested what they'd been saying. Gradually, she had come to see the adult members of her own sex not as potential allies, but as adversaries who wanted to come between her and her father.

With Verity it was different. Honor didn't know why. She just knew that it was, that there was something soft and comforting and lovely about Verity and about being with her. She now wanted Verity as her stepmother, not just to protect her from the likes of Myra, but for herself as herself, and now, just as things were beginning to work out, here was her father being awkward and upsetting all her plans.

His suggestion that Verity might be too busy with her own life to have time for her was one she dismissed out of hand. She knew, of course, that it wasn't true. Verity *liked* her. She could see it in her eyes when she looked at her; there was no mistaking that special loving look. She had seen it in Catherine's mother's eyes when *she* looked at Catherine and felt envious of her because of it.

Silas was driving past Verity's house on his way home. Her BMW was parked in the drive. On impulse he stopped his own car and got out.

The gardens looked very much the same now as they had done when he had worked in them. There

was the border he had been working on the first time
he had seen Verity. Grimly he looked away and then,
almost against his will, he found himself turning back,
walking across the lawn.

The house might have changed since she had lived
here, but the gardens hadn't, Verity acknowledged as
she paused by the fish pond, peering into it in the dusk
of the summer's evening.

Her uncle had used to threaten to have it filled in,
complaining that the carp attracted the attentions of a
local tom-cat, but Verity had pleaded with him not to
do so. She used to love sitting here watching the fish.
It was one of her favourite places.

From here she could see the small summer house
where she and Silas had exchanged their first earth-
shattering kiss.

An unexpected miaow made her jump and then put
her hand on her heart as, out of the shadows of the
shrubbery, a small, black cat stalked, weaving his way
towards her to rub purringly against her legs.

Laughing, Verity bent to stroke him.

'Well, *you* certainly aren't old Tom,' she told him
as she rubbed behind his ear, 'but you could be one
of his offspring.'

Miaowing as if in assent, the cat jumped up onto
the stone edge of the pond where she was sitting and
peered into the darkness of the water.

'Ah ha. Yes, you definitely *must* be related to him,'
Verity teased.

As a child she would have loved a pet but her uncle
had always refused, and once she had become adult
the business had kept her too busy and away from

home too often for her to feel it would be fair for her to have one.

Now, though, things were different. When she finally decided where she was going to spend the rest of her life, there was nothing to stop her having a cat or a dog if she so chose… A cat, I suppose it would have to be, she mused. After all, cats and lonely single women were supposed to go together weren't they? A dog somehow or other suggested someone with friends, a family…a full, vigorous life.

Bending her head over the cat, she tickled behind his ear.

'Verity…'

'Silas…' Quickly Verity stood up, her stance unknowingly defensive as though she was trying to hold him off, Silas noted, as she held her hands up in front of her body.

Immediately he took a step back from her.

He couldn't even bear to be within feet of her, never mind inches, Verity recognised achingly as she saw the way Silas distanced himself from her.

'I was just thinking that this cat could be one of old Tom's descendants,' she told Silas huskily, trying to fill the tensioned silence.

'Mmm…from the looks of him he very probably is,' Silas agreed.

'Look, Verity, I wonder if I could have a few words with you.'

Verity's heart sank.

'Yes… Yes, of course,' she managed to agree. Whatever it was Silas wanted to say to her, she could see from his expression that it wasn't anything particularly pleasant.

'It's about Honor,' Silas told her, still keeping his distance from her. 'I've had a talk with her this evening about…about the way she's…she's been trying to involve you in our lives… I've explained to her that *you* have your own life to live and—'

'You've come here to tell me that you don't want her to see me any more,' Verity interrupted flatly, guessing what he was about to say and praying that he wouldn't be able to tell just how much what he was saying was hurting her.

'I… I think it would be best if she didn't,' Silas agreed heavily. 'She's at a very vulnerable age and…'

'Do you think that *I* don't know that?' Verity told him swiftly, her face paling with the intensity of her emotions. 'I've been there, Silas,' she advised him jerkily, 'remember…?'

It was the wrong thing to say, the very worst thing she could have said, she realised as she saw his mouth twist and heard the inflection in his voice as he told her curtly, 'Yes, *I* remember… Honor's got it into her head that she needs a woman's influence in her life,' Silas admitted slowly, 'but…'

'But there's no way you want that woman to be *me*,' Verity guessed angrily.

'I don't want Honor to be *hurt*,' Silas interrupted her bluntly.

Verity stared at him. She could feel the too-fast beat of her own heart and wondered dizzily if Silas too could hear the sound it made as it thudded against her chest wall.

Was he really trying to imply that *she* would stoop so low as to try to hurt *Honor*? A *child*…? Did he really think…?

For a moment Verity felt too outraged to speak. Quickly she swallowed, drawing herself up to her full height as she challenged him, 'Are you suggesting that *I* would hurt Honor? Is that *really* what you think of me, Silas?' she questioned him carefully. 'Do you really think of me as being so…so *vengeful*?'

Half blinded by the tears that suddenly filled her eyes, she turned away from him and started to walk quickly towards the house, breaking into a run when she heard him calling her name.

'Verity,' Silas protested, cursing himself under his breath. She had every right to be angry with him, he knew that. But surely she could see that he had every right to protect his child?

'Verity,' he protested again, but he knew it was too late. She was already running up the steps and into the house.

Quickly Verity dabbed at her hot face with the cold water she had run to stop her tears.

How *could* Silas imply that she would hurt Honor? How *dared* he imply it after what *he* had done to her, the way *he* had hurt *her*? It must be his own guilty conscience that was motivating him.

She would *never* do anything like that. Not to a child, not to *anyone*… She had wanted to help Honor for Honor's sake alone. Her sense of kinship with her had nothing to do with the fact that she was his daughter.

Hadn't it? Slowly she straightened up and looked at herself in the bathroom mirror. Hadn't a part of her recognised how easily *she* might have been Honor's mother? Hadn't she felt somehow honour-bound herself to reach out and help the girl because of that inner knowledge?

To *help* her, yes, but to *hurt* her, never. Never…never…

She couldn't stay here in this town. Not after this. She would ring the agent tomorrow, tell him that she was terminating her lease on the house; the charitable trust she had wanted to establish in her uncle's name in the town could still go ahead—the details of that could be dealt with as easily from London as from here. She had been a fool ever to have come back. She *was* a fool. A stupid, idiotic, heartbroken fool!

CHAPTER TEN

'VERITY... Verity... It is you, isn't it?'

Verity put down the shopping she had just been about to put in the back of the car and looked uncertainly at the woman hailing her, her face breaking into a warm smile as she recognised a girl who had been at school with her.

'Gwen!' she exclaimed warmly. 'Good heavens. How *are* you...?'

'Fine. If you don't count the fact that I'm thirty-three, ten pounds overweight and just about to do a supermarket shop for a husband and three kids,' the other woman groaned. 'When did you get back to town? You look wonderful, by the way...'

'Only very recently. I—'

'Look, I'm in a bit of a rush now. We've got the in-laws coming round for supper.' She pulled a wry face. 'I'd love to have a proper chat with you, catch up on what you've been doing... Can I give you a ring?'

'Yes. Yes, that would be nice,' Verity acknowledged, quickly writing down her telephone number for her before climbing into her car.

It was ironic that she should bump into one of the few girls she had made friends with at school just as she had decided she was going to leave town, she thought as she started her car.

* * *

Honor looked sideways at the telephone in the garden centre office. It was Saturday morning and, instead of going swimming with Catherine and her mother, she had opted to come to work with her father. He was outside dealing with a customer. Glancing over her shoulder, Honor reached for the telephone receiver and quickly punched in Verity's telephone number.

Verity heard the telephone ringing as she unlocked the front door, putting down her bag as she went to answer it.

'Verity, is that you?'

Her heart lurched as she recognised Honor's voice and heard its forlorn note.

'Honor… Where are you? Are you all right?' she asked anxiously.

'Mmm…sort of… I'm at the garden centre. Verity, can I come and see you?'

Verity leaned back against the hall wall and closed her eyes.

'Oh, Honor,' she whispered sadly beneath her breath. Opening her eyes, she said as steadily as she could, 'Honor, I don't think that would be a good idea, do you? I—'

'You've spoken to Dad, haven't you?' Honor demanded in a flat, accusing voice. 'I thought you *liked* me… I thought we were *friends*…'

Verity could hear the tears in her voice.

'Honor,' she pleaded. 'Please…'

'I thought you *liked* me…' Honor was repeating, crying in earnest now.

Verity pushed her hand into her hair. She had left it down this morning, oblivious to the admiring male glances she had attracted as she'd walked across the supermarket car park, the bright sunlight burnishing it to honey-gold.

'Honor. Honor, I do... I do... but I shan't be staying in town very much longer. I only intended to make a very short visit here,' Verity began, but Honor was no longer listening to her.

'You're leaving? No, you can't. You mustn't. I need you, Verity.' Then the phone went down.

Leaning against the wall, Verity took a deep breath.

Honor looked at her father. He was still talking to his customer. Sometimes grown-ups just didn't know what was good for them!

She went up to him.

'Dad, I've changed my mind and I want to go swimming with Catherine after all.'

'All right,' Silas agreed. 'Give me five minutes and then I'll drive you round to Catherine's.'

'I'll need to go home first to get my swimming things,' Honor reminded him.

'Fine...' Silas replied.

He was well aware that he was in his daughter's bad books—and why. His only comfort was that one day she would understand and thank him for protecting her. One day... but quite definitely not *today*.

'So what are you going to do?' Catherine asked Honor interestedly. They were sitting in Catherine's bedroom eating Marmite sandwiches and drying one another's hair after their trip to the leisure centre.

'I don't know yet,' Honor replied in despair.

'You could always try to find someone else to be your stepmother,' Catherine suggested cautiously.

'I don't *want* anyone else,' Honor retorted passionately. 'Would you want to change your mother?'

Catherine looked at her.

'Sometimes I would,' she reflected. 'Specially when she won't let me stay up late to watch television.'

'Goodbye, Honor.'

Honor turned dutifully to smile and wave as she got out of Catherine's mother's car.

The latter had just brought her home and Honor could see her father opening the front door for her. Dragging her bag behind her, she headed towards him.

'No kiss for me...?' Silas asked her with forced joviality as she stalked past him and into the house.

Honor turned to give him a withering, womanly look.

'Honor, I was thinking, you know that puppy you wanted...'

'I don't want a puppy,' Honor told him coldly. 'I want *Verity*.'

Silas gritted his teeth. He knew when he was being punished and given the cold-shoulder treatment. How best to handle it? In situations like this he'd benefit from a woman's advice. Verity's? He checked abruptly. Damn Honor. Now she'd got him doing it.

'I've got your favourite for supper,' he told her heartily as he followed her into the kitchen.

'I'm not hungry,' Honor replied. 'We're having an end-of-term play at school... I'm going to be a pop singer but I'm going to have to have a costume.'

'Well, I'm sure we'll be able to find you one,' Silas

offered, ignoring for the moment the dubious merits of a ten-year-old aping the manners of a much older pop-singer star, sensing that he was being led onto very treacherous ground indeed, but not as yet quite sure just where the danger was coming from. He soon found out.

'All the other girls are having outfits made by their mothers,' Honor informed him.

'Well, perhaps Mrs Simmonds might...' Silas began, but it was obvious that Honor was not going to be so easily put off.

'*Verity* would know how to make mine,' she informed him coldly. Silas held his breath.

'Now, look, Honor—' he began, but as he watched his daughter's eyes fill with tears which then ran slowly down her face he closed his eyes. This was the very situation which he had hoped to avoid.

'Honor,' he began more gently, but his daughter was refusing to listen to him, whirling round and running out of the room and upstairs.

Silas heard the slam of her bedroom door and sighed.

Verity...

God, but even thinking her name hurt, and not just on Honor's account.

Ever since the night she had spent here he had been fighting not to think about her, not to give in to his compelling, compulsive urge to relive every single second of the time he had held her in his arms, every single heartbeat...

Closing his eyes, he acknowledged what he had been fighting to deny ever since he had walked away, leaving her alone in bed.

It was too late to tell himself not to fall into the trap of loving her again. It had always been too late, for the simple reason that he had never stopped.

'Honor, I've got to go out for half an hour. Will you be all right or shall I phone Mrs Simmonds?'

Honor looked up from the book she was reading. It was Monday teatime and Silas had just received a phone call from one of his customers who wanted to see him urgently.

'No, I'll be fine,' Honor assured him instantly.

Honor waited until she was sure her father had gone before going into the study and rifling through his desk until she found what she was looking for. Yes, there it was, the photograph of Verity.

Picking it up, she turned it over, quickly reading the message on the back.

Desperate situations called for desperate measures. Squaring her shoulders, she went upstairs to her bedroom and packed a haversack with a change of clothes. In the kitchen she added a bar of chocolate to it and then, after thoughtful consideration, added another—for Verity.

Having packed her bag, she then sat down and wrote her father a brief note.

Slowly she read it.

'I am going to live with Verity.'

It didn't take her very long to walk round to Verity's, but even her stout heart gave a small bound of relief when she finally got there and saw that Verity's car was outside. She wasn't sure what she would have done if Verity hadn't been in.

The unexpected ring on the doorbell brought Verity to the door with a small frown.

'Honor!' she exclaimed as she saw the small lone figure. 'What…?'

'I've come to live with you,' Honor told her stoically, walking quickly into the hall and then bursting into tears and flinging herself into Verity's arms as she told her between sobs, 'It's horrid not being able to see you.'

By the time Verity had managed to calm her down she was comfortably ensconced in the kitchen eating home-made biscuits and drinking juice whilst the cat, who had decided to adopt Verity, sat purring on her knee.

'Honor, you *know* you can't stay here, don't you?' Verity asked her gently. 'Your father—'

'He doesn't care,' Honor interrupted her.

'You know that isn't true,' Verity chided her. 'He loves you very much…'

'Like you love him?' Honor asked her, looking her straight in the eye.

Verity opened her mouth and then closed it again. Her legs, she discovered, had gone strangely weak. She sat down and was soon extremely glad that she had done so.

Honor was rifling through the haversack she had brought in with her. Triumphantly she produced the photograph she had taken from her father's desk.

'I found this,' she told Verity, watching her.

'Oh, Honor,' was all Verity could say as she stared at the familiar picture. She could remember the day Silas had taken it—it was the day after they had made love for the first time and Silas had told her he would always keep the photograph in memory of all that they had shared.

'Not that I shall ever need any reminding,' he had whispered passionately to her as he had abandoned the camera and taken her in his arms.

'It says "To my beloved Silas, with all my love for ever and always",' Honor told her solemnly.

Verity looked away from her.

'Yes. Yes, I know,' she agreed weakly.

'You said you didn't *know* my father…' Honor reminded her.

'Yes. Yes, I know,' Verity agreed again.

'And *he* said that *he* didn't know you, but you wrote here that you love him. Why did you stop loving him, Verity?'

'I… It wasn't…' Verity shook her head. 'It was all a long time ago, Honor.'

'But I want to know,' Honor persisted stubbornly.

Verity shook her head, but she sensed that Honor wasn't going to be satisfied until she had dragged the whole sorry story out of her.

'There isn't a lot *to* know,' she told her. 'Your father and I were young. I thought… He said… I had to go away to New York to work and whilst I was there your father met someone else—your mother…'

Silas cursed as he found the note Honor had left for him. Angrily he picked up his discarded car keys and headed for the door. She was coming home with him right now and no nonsense, and once he got her home he was going to have a serious talk with her—a *very* serious talk.

Parking his car behind Verity's, Silas got out and

headed for the front door and then, changing his mind, turned to go around the back of the house instead.

The kitchen door was half open—Verity had been outside hanging out some washing when Honor had arrived. Neither of the two occupants of the room could see him and Silas paused in the act of pushing open the door as he heard Verity saying huskily, 'I thought your father loved me. I didn't know about your mother… I suppose I should have guessed that something was wrong when he didn't get in touch with me, but I just thought that he…that he was cross with me because…' She stopped and shook her head. 'I came home to tell him how much I loved him, to tell him that he was right and that our love was more important than any duty I owed my uncle, but I discovered that your father had married your mother.'

Helplessly Verity spread her hands.

'I thought he loved me but he didn't really love me at all.' Her voice shook with emotion and the cat stopped purring.

Honor looked up, her eyes widening as she saw her father standing in the doorway.

Verity turned round to see what had attracted Honor's attention, her face paling as she too saw Silas.

For a moment none of them spoke and then Silas marched across the room and took hold of Honor's arm, saying firmly to her, 'Honor, you're coming with me—right now and no arguments.'

He hadn't said a word to Verity. He hadn't even looked at her, Verity acknowledged as he walked Honor out of the back door, firmly closing it behind him.

She could hear the engine of his car firing. Her hand shook as she reached across the table for the photograph that Honor had left.

Tears blurred her eyes. Tipping back her head, she blinked them away. She was not going to cry...not now, not again...not ever...

Catherine's mother looked surprised when she opened the door to find Silas and Honor outside.

'Jane, I'm sorry to do this to you but something very urgent's cropped up. Can Honor stay with you for...until I can get back for her...?'

'Of course she can,' she agreed warmly, ushering Honor inside. What, she wondered, was going on? There had been a lot of whispering being done between the two girls recently and Catherine was rather obviously 'big with news', as the saying went, announcing importantly to anyone who would listen that she and Honor had a special secret.

Having coldly inclined her cheek for her father to kiss, Honor marched inside with all the regal bearing of a grand dowager—a highly offended grand dowager, Jane Alders reflected ruefully.

Silas, however, was looking far too grim-faced for her to think of questioning him.

Verity was just finishing pegging out the last of the washing she had abandoned when Honor had arrived when Silas came back, walking soft-footed across the grass so that she had no inkling of his presence until she suddenly saw his shadow.

'Si...Silas...' To her chagrin the unexpected shock

of seeing him made her stammer. 'Wha…what do you want? What are you doing here?'

'Do you want the abridged version?' Silas asked her tersely and then, shaking his head without waiting for her to respond, he demanded abruptly, '*Why* did you tell Honor that you came from New York to tell me how much you loved me?'

'Because it was the truth,' Verity admitted huskily. Why on earth was he asking her that? What could it possibly matter now?

'No, it isn't,' Silas argued flatly. 'Your *uncle* told me the *truth*. He told me that you had asked him to tell me that you didn't want to see me again; that it was all over between us.'

Verity stared at him. Suddenly she felt extremely cold.

'No,' she whispered, her hand going to her throat. 'No, that's not true, he *couldn't* have told you that. I don't believe it…'

'Believe it,' Silas told her harshly, 'because I can assure you that he did. Not that I was in any mood to listen to him. Not then. I even wrote to you begging you to change your mind, pleading with you to write back to me, giving what I suppose was an ultimatum in that I wrote that if *I* didn't hear from you then I would have to accept that it was over between us.'

Verity badly needed to sit down.

'Is this some kind of joke?' she asked Silas weakly. His mouth hardened.

'Can you see me laughing?' he demanded.

Verity shook her head. She could see that he was telling her the truth, but the full enormity of just what her uncle had done, of what he had set in motion, was still too much for her to fully comprehend.

'I never got your letter,' she whispered. 'There was a murder in the apartment block and my uncle insisted that I had to move out. He promised me that he would give you my new address and telephone number. I... I waited and waited for you to get in touch and then, when you didn't...for a while I... You were right. Our love was more important than doing what my uncle wanted. I... I came home to tell you that. To tell you how much I loved you and...' To her horror Verity felt hot tears spill down her cheeks as she relived the full trauma of that time.

'I read about your marriage in the taxi on the way from the station. After that I knew there was no point in trying to see you,' she told him bleakly.

Verity looked down at the ground. *Why* was he doing this to her, dragging her through this...this humiliation? What could it matter now?

'Look, let's put aside the issue of my marriage for the moment,' she heard Silas telling her huskily. 'I want to concentrate on something else, on something far more important... Did you really love me so much, Verity?'

For a moment she was tempted to lie, but why should she? Proudly she lifted her head and looked at him.

'Yes. I did,' she acknowledged. 'I...' Quickly she swallowed, knowing that she could not admit to him that she had never stopped loving him; that she still loved him and that, if anything, that love was even deeper and more painful to her now than it had been then.

'I didn't marry Sarah because I loved her,' she heard Silas telling her rawly. 'I married her because she was pregnant.'

Disbelievingly, Verity focused on him.

'But...' she whispered, shaking her head. 'You would never do something like that. You would never make love to someone you didn't...you didn't care about...'

'I didn't make love to her,' he told her bluntly. 'We just had sex.'

Briefly, without allowing her to stop him, Silas told her exactly what had happened.

After he had finished speaking Verity looked searchingly into his eyes. There was no doubting the veracity of what he had just told her. Her stomach felt as though it had just done a fast cycle in a washing machine, her heart was banging so hard against her ribs she thought it was going to break them, and as for her legs...

'I...I need to sit down,' she told Silas weakly.

'And I need to lie down,' he countered gruffly, 'preferably in bed with you in my arms with nothing between us, with nothing to separate us. Oh, Verity,' he groaned as he suddenly reached for her, wrapping her in his arms as he kissed her eyes, her face, her mouth. 'Oh, Verity, Verity,' he whispered rawly to her. 'You are the only woman I've ever loved, the only woman I ever *will* love...'

'No, that can't be true,' Verity whispered back through kiss-swollen lips. 'It can't be... Not after the way you left me the other night...not after I'd begged you to stay...'

Tears filled her eyes and rolled down her cheeks.

'Oh, no, my darling, don't cry. Please don't cry.' Silas groaned, holding her tight and rocking her in his arms, his cheek pressed against her head. 'It wasn't like that, it really wasn't. I left you because…because I was afraid, not just for myself or for the pain I knew I would feel if I let you back into my life, but for the pain I thought you might cause Honor.'

'I would *never* hurt Honor,' Verity protested fiercely.

'No,' Silas agreed softly. 'Forgive me for that.'

'She reminds me so much of the way I was…' Verity told him shakily. 'Oh, I know how much you love her, Silas…and you *couldn't* be more different from my uncle—'

'But I'm not enough,' Silas interrupted her ruefully, adding before she could protest, 'I know, so my darling daughter has already informed me.'

'Did you really think that of me…that I might hurt you both…?'

'You'd already hurt me very badly once,' Silas reminded her softly. 'Or, at least, so I thought.'

'I felt the same way about you,' Verity admitted. 'It hurt so much knowing that when you'd told me you loved me, when you said that you'd love me for ever, you didn't mean it…'

'I *did* mean it,' Silas corrected her. 'I still mean it, Verity. Is it too late for us to start again?' he asked her seriously.

Verity looked at him, her heart in her eyes.

'I… Oh, Silas…' she whispered.

'Let's go inside,' he whispered back. 'There's a phone call I want to make…'

Even to make his telephone call to Jane Alders, Silas refused to let Verity move out of his arms.

'You stay right where you are,' he mock growled at her when she did try to move away.

'Jane, it's Silas,' he announced when Catherine's mother answered his call, tucking the receiver in the crook of his neck whilst he bent his head to feather a soft kiss against Verity's mouth. 'Would it be asking too much for you to keep Honor there with you tonight? I wouldn't ask but... You don't mind...? No, it's okay, I don't need to speak with her,' he continued, 'but if you could just give her a message from me, if you wouldn't mind. Could you tell her that I think she might be going to get what she wanted? What she wanted more than a puppy,' he stressed, smiling.

'What was all that about?' Verity asked him when he had replaced the receiver.

Smiling at her, Silas said, 'Honor has been begging and pleading with me to let her have a puppy. The other day when I ill-advisedly offered her one as a peace-offering, she informed me that she didn't want a puppy, she wanted you.'

Verity looked at him.

'Oh, Silas,' she protested, torn between laughter and tears.

'I want to take you to bed,' Silas told her huskily, cupping her face in both his hands. 'I want to make love to you, Verity... I want to make love with you. I want to re-affirm all those vows and promises we made to each other years ago, but if you think it is too soon, if you want to wait...if you feel...'

Putting her fingertips against his lips to silence him,

Verity told him softly, 'What I feel right now is that I want you. I want you in all the ways that a woman wants a man she loves, Silas. You can't imagine how empty my life has been without you, how—'

'Can't I?' he checked her gruffly. 'There hasn't been a day in the years we've been apart when *I* haven't thought about you. Even on the day of Sarah's funeral… As I stood at her graveside all I could think was how much I needed and wanted you.'

'Poor girl,' Verity whispered compassionately.

'Yes, poor girl,' Silas agreed.

'Take me to bed,' Verity begged him urgently. 'Take me to bed, Silas, and…'

She didn't have to say any more, *couldn't* have said any more because suddenly he was picking her up and carrying her towards the stairs.

'You are the most beautiful woman on earth,' Silas whispered extravagantly as he threaded his fingers through Verity's hair.

Smiling lazily up at him in the aftermath of their lovemaking, Verity reached out and touched his face, wriggling appreciatively against the muscled warmth of his naked body.

'Hey, don't do that,' Silas warned her as he slowly kissed the palm of her hand. 'At least, not unless you want…'

'Not unless I want what?' Verity teased, deliberately moving even closer.

'Not unless you want this,' Silas told her huskily, taking her hand and placing it against his hardening body.

'Silas, we can't,' Verity protested unconvincingly

as her fingers stroked instinctively down the hard strength of the silky, hot-skinned shaft of male pleasure she was caressing.

It felt so good to be able to touch him like this, to know how much he wanted and needed her, to know how much he loved her.

'Oh, no?' Silas challenged softly, cupping her breast in his hand and bending his head to trail tiny provocative kisses all the way down from her collarbone to her navel.

'Don't…' Verity whispered.

'Don't what?' Silas asked her as he circled her navel with the tip of his tongue, gently biting at her flesh.

'Don't…don't stop,' Verity breathed.

'I'm not going to,' Silas assured her as his head dipped lower and his hand slid between her thighs.

This was bliss, heaven, every delight she had ever known or imagined knowing, Verity decided shakily as she gave in to the gentle caress of Silas' hand against her body and the slow, sensual search of his mouth as it homed in on the sensitive female heart of her.

The orgasmic contractions gripping her body were, if anything, even stronger this second time. Just for a second she tried to resist them, wanting to share what she was experiencing with Silas, but he wouldn't let her.

'Let it happen, Verity,' he begged her, his voice shaking with male arousal. 'I want to see it happen for you, feel it happen…'

'Silas,' she protested, but it was already too late.

With a small cry she gave in to the urgency of Silas' plea and her body's own demands.

'Have you thought...?' Silas questioned her later, when they were sitting up in bed eating the smoked salmon sandwiches he had gone down to make for them and drinking the bottle of white wine they had decided would have to stand in lieu of celebratory champagne.

They probably looked more like a couple of naughty children, sitting side by side in the nest they had made of the duvet and pillows, Verity acknowledged, than adults, but she felt almost childlike, full of all the youthful hope and shining joy that she had lost when she had thought she had lost Silas. She felt, she recognised, like a girl again, only this time she was able to appreciate what she had, what they had, with all the maturity of a woman.

'Have I thought what?' she prompted, taking a bite of the sandwich he was proffering her and giggling when he withdrew it so that her teeth grazed his skin, and then teasingly licking at his fingers as though she hadn't known all along that that was just what he'd wanted her to do.

'Mmm...' he retaliated, bending to nibble on her own fingertips. 'Tastes good, but not as good as—'

'Silas,' Verity reproved. 'Have I thought what?'

'Well, I don't know about you,' he told her seriously, 'but I certainly wasn't using any precautions.' He shook his head. 'To be truthful, that was the last thing on my mind, irresponsible though it sounds.'

Verity gave him a concerned look.

'I'm not protected from conceiving,' she admitted,

adding semi-shyly, 'I don't… Well, there's never been any need, not since… Not since, well, not since you and I…'

The sandwiches were pushed to one side as he took her in his arms and groaned.

'Oh, Verity, I never expected… I couldn't, and I love you just the same no matter what… Have you any idea just how much that means to me? It's the same for me, you know,' he told her quietly. 'I haven't…'

'Not even with Myra?' Verity asked him.

'Most especially not with Myra.' Silas grinned.

'She wanted you,' Verity told him.

'Mmm…but she didn't get me. There wasn't anything here for her,' he told her seriously, touching his own heart lightly and then adding, 'and so there couldn't be anything here either…' Verity watched as he touched his sex.

'I thought it didn't work like that for men,' was all she could manage to say.

'For some men, but not for me. Perhaps that's why I'm so hungry for you now,' he told her with a soft groan. 'I've got a lot of lonely nights to make up for…'

'I don't want to get pregnant,' Verity told him, explaining when she saw the look in his eyes, 'I mean, not just yet. Not until Honor has had a chance to…to adjust…to know that she'll always be very special to both of us… We need time together as a unit, a family… We need to bond properly together as a threesome, Silas, before we introduce a new baby into our family. We owe it to Honor to wait until *she's* ready.'

When she looked at him she saw that his eyes were bright with emotion.

'What is it?' she asked him warily. 'Have I...?'

'You're perfect, just perfect, do you know that?' he told her passionately. 'No wonder Honor is so determined to have you as her stepmother. Come here and let me kiss you...'

Smiling at him, Verity complied...

EPILOGUE

'WHAT are you doing?' Catherine asked Honor curiously.

They were both standing in Verity's bedroom, still wearing their bridesmaid's dresses from the afternoon wedding ceremony which had taken place in the garden. Honor was writing something down on a piece of paper, shielding it with her hand as she kept a weather eye on the half-open bedroom door.

Down below them, in the garden, Verity and Silas were mingling with their guests, Silas' arm wrapped protectively around his new wife's waist.

'I'm writing a list of babies' names,' Honor informed her friend loftily.

'Babies names... What for? *You* won't be having a baby for ages yet,' Catherine told her.

'It's not for me, stupid,' Honor told her. 'It's for Verity.'

'Is Verity having a baby?' Catherine asked her, looking confused.

'Maybe not quite yet. But she soon will be now that she and Dad are married,' Honor told her confidently. 'I think, if it's a girl we should call her Mel and if it's a boy...I think Adam...'

'Why Adam?' Catherine asked her.

'It's a nice name for a baby brother.'

Down below them in the garden, happily oblivious to the plans that were being made for their future, Verity leaned a little closer into Silas' body.

'Looking forward to tonight?' he teased her wickedly as he felt the soft warmth of her body.

Laughing ruefully, Verity wrinkled her nose at him.

'You're the one who's supposed not to be able to wait to get *me* into bed, not the other way around,' she reminded him.

'What makes you think I'm not?' Silas challenged her. 'We're going to have to make the most of tonight,' he warned her. 'It's the last night we're going to have to ourselves for quite some time.'

'Mmm... I know,' Verity agreed, closing her eyes as she dwelt blissfully on the thought of the luxurious suite at the hotel where he had once made love to her that Silas had booked in their names for their wedding night. She smiled as she remembered that on their first stay there they had a much smaller room.

'If I ever thought about where I'd spend a honeymoon, it certainly wasn't Disneyland,' he told Verity dryly.

She opened her eyes and laughed.

'No, me neither,' she admitted.

'So how come *you* were the one who insisted that we make the booking?' Silas asked her gently. 'Or can I guess?'

'We couldn't have gone away without her,' she told him quickly.

'Maybe *you* couldn't,' Silas agreed roundly, 'but I certainly could!'

'You don't mean that.'

'Don't I?' He gave her a wide, almost boyish grin that made him look heartachingly young. 'We must be mad. Three *weeks* in Disneyland with Honor in tow…'

'Either that or we must be grateful,' Verity acknowledged, whispering the words into a soft kiss. 'After all, without her…'

'Yes,' he admitted. 'Without her…'

Both of them glanced up towards Verity's open bedroom window where they could hear the sound of raised voices.

'Well, I think Adam is a stupid name for a baby,' Catherine was shouting.

'I don't care what *you* think,' Honor was retaliating in an equally loud voice. 'I like it and he's going to be *my* brother.'

Her what? Verity and Silas looked at one another whilst all around them their guests started to grin.

'Honor,' Silas began sternly.

Verity touched his arm and shook her head.

'Don't say anything to her,' she begged him. 'I think this is probably my fault.'

'Your fault? How can it be?'

'She came into the bathroom this morning whilst I was being sick,' Verity told him quietly.

'You were being *sick*…?' Silas stared at her, his face changing colour and then becoming suffused with tender emotion as he took hold of her gently and asked, 'Are you?'

'I don't know…not yet… But Honor seems to have made up her mind what *she* thinks if it proves to be true,' she told him ruefully. 'She was thrilled—so much for us waiting.'

Silas gave a small sigh.

'You do realise that this baby is going to make her

completely impossible, don't you?' He groaned. 'She'll never let either of us near her or him...'

Glancing towards the upper window and her small stepdaughter, Verity smiled.

'She's going to be the best sister that any baby could have,' she told him softly—and meant it.

THE BOSS AND THE BABY
by
Leigh Michaels

Leigh Michaels has always loved happy endings.
Even when she was a child, if a book's conclusion
didn't please her, she'd make up her own. And,
though she always wanted to write fiction, she very
sensibly planned to earn her living as a newspaper
reporter. That career didn't work out, however,
and she found herself writing for Mills & Boon®
instead—in the kind of happy ending only a
romance novelist could dream up!

Now the acclaimed author of over fifty titles, and
most recently her renowned trilogy *Finding Mr
Right*, she has become one of the most loved
authors in the Enchanted™ line.

Leigh likes to hear from readers; you can write to
her at PO Box 935, Ottumwa, Iowa, 52501–0935
USA.

CHAPTER ONE

MOLLY MATTHEWS straightened the lapels of her jacket and took a deep breath as she looked herself over in the guest room mirror. Her suit was stylishly cut, but the neutral beige wool didn't scream for attention. The pale yellow blouse was softly feminine, but it was neither lacy nor revealing. Her jewelry was limited to tiny gold earrings and the slightly splashier pin nestled in the geometric pattern of the scarf tucked casually around her throat. Her hair was swept back and up into a neat twist, revealing a slim, straight neck…

And a bruise on the left side of her jawline, halfway between chin and ear.

Molly sighed. She'd done the best she could to camouflage the yellowing stain with makeup, and she'd just have to hope that the casual observer would think the shadow on her jaw was no more than a reflection of the darkest color in the brilliant scarf.

She gave a final pat to the folds of the scarf and turned away from the mirror. As job applicants went, she was as well turned out as it was possible to be—tasteful instead of high-fashion, with nothing about her clothes or manner that could create a bad first impression with an interviewer. "Unless he's put off by someone who looks so seriously vanilla," she told herself, and tried to laugh. But this appointment was too important to make into a joke. The job she was seeking…

Though, to be technical, she wasn't interviewing for a job at all, she was vying for a contract. And she wasn't an applicant, exactly. She was a business proprietor contacting a prospective client who had indicated an interest in her skills.

If Warren Hudson liked her ideas and was impressed enough with her abilities to give her this assignment, she'd have a few months of work ahead of her. Enough, perhaps—if she was careful—to build a foundation under her new small business.

Matthews and Associates was, at the moment, very new and very small. Molly could see the whole of it, in fact, from where she stood. The bed in her parents' guest room had been pushed aside to leave room for a folding table, which held a telephone so newly installed that Molly hadn't yet memorized the number and a computer with the sales stickers still attached. Under the table was a box of office supplies in untouched wrappings and a bag containing business cards on which the ink was barely dry.

She had bought carefully and frugally, but that corner of the room represented a good chunk of her worldly resources. Which was why it was so important for Molly Matthews and her fictional associates to impress Warren Hudson this afternoon.

That was the truly frightening part, Molly thought—being so very clearly on her own. Always before, even during a few weeks when she'd been between jobs, she'd had a safety net of sorts. But this time, instead of using her last paycheck as a cushion while she sought another corporate position, she'd invested it in her future. And—of course—Bailey's future, too.

Remember Bailey, she told herself. *You'd take a bigger risk than this for her sake.*

Molly picked up the dark brown calfskin portfolio that contained the best examples of her work, tucked it under her arm and closed the guest room door behind her.

From the kitchen, Bailey called, ''Mommy! Come and see!''

Molly paused in the arched doorway between kitchen

and hall. For a moment her eyes rested on her daughter, kneeling on a kitchen chair so she was tall enough to work on the tabletop, industriously wielding a blue crayon. Bailey's dark brown hair, a couple of shades deeper than her mother's, was combed into twin ponytails today, each adorned with a big pink bow that matched her corduroy overalls.

Bailey looked at her mother and grinned, and Molly's heart turned over. *Yes,* she thought. *I'd take a much bigger risk than this—for Bailey.*

"What a pretty picture, darling," she said.

From across the table came a light, almost brittle laugh. "Since no one could possibly guess what it's supposed to be, I'd say that's a safe comment."

Molly moved the crayon into a position where Bailey had better control and looked levelly at her sister. "Hello, Megan. It's good to see you."

Her sister, she noted, had pushed her chair well back from the table. Molly wasn't surprised that Megan Matthews Bannister would maintain a safe distance between her creamy white cashmere sweater and Bailey's crayon. If Bailey had chosen paints this afternoon, Megan would probably have retreated all the way to the deck, despite the crisp breeze coming off Lake Superior.

Megan tossed her head. The golden highlights in her light brown hair almost shimmered with the movement. Though it was only April, the streaks in her hair and the tone of her skin made it seem as if she'd spent weeks in the sun.

But of course she had, Molly remembered. Their mother had written, in her dutiful once-a-month letter, about Megan's winter vacation in the Caribbean.

"I dropped by to ask Mom some last-minute questions about the anniversary party," Megan said. "I've been gone so much that everything's been on hold, but the details have to be wrapped up this week."

Of course you wouldn't be coming to visit me, Molly

thought. *Even if we haven't seen each other in years. Even if you've never met your niece before. Even if we've been home only a few days...*

She was startled at the bitterness she felt—though the reaction was really nothing new. Even in their teenage years, Megan—popular, beautiful and graceful—had never had much time to spare for a younger sister who had still been gangly and awkward, an unwelcome tagalong. And now that they were adults...

Megan's still the socialite, Molly reflected, almost wryly. Megan had married a wealthy man from a good family. She belonged to all the best clubs, went to all the best parties, worked for all the best charities, vacationed in all the best spots, knew all the best people.

While I... Molly's gaze rested thoughtfully on the top of Bailey's head. The part that separated the child's ponytails was crooked, and one of her bows had slipped, but when Molly tried to straighten it, Bailey squirmed away, more interested in her drawing than her appearance.

Molly gave up and looked around the kitchen. "Where is Mother, by the way? She said she'd watch Bailey this afternoon while I go to my appointment."

Bailey's lower lip crept out, and her chin trembled. "Don't want Gramma," she said. "I want you to stay, Mommy."

Molly's heart twisted. *Of course she doesn't want Gramma. The child hardly knows her. It's only been four days—*

She leaned over Bailey and dropped a kiss on her hair. "I know, darling, and I'd stay here with you if I could. But remember we talked about my new job? I have to go see a man—"

Megan drew a breath that sounded like a sharp hiss. "What happened to your face? You look as if you've been in a brawl."

Molly's hand went automatically to the dark spot on her jaw. "Oh, this. It's nothing, really."

Her mother spoke from the doorway. "*Nothing?* She says Bailey kicked her." Alix Matthews's dark tone implied that she had her doubts about the explanation.

"Kicked—" Megan's tone was speculative.

Alix nodded and walked briskly across the kitchen. "In my day a child who did that—if, of course, she really did…"

"I told you it was a somersault that went wrong, Mother. Bailey didn't mean to hurt me, it was an accident."

Bailey frowned. She held up her drawing to look at it and then put her blue crayon down and selected a green one.

Megan didn't look convinced.

Alix's gaze skimmed over Molly. "That suit's all right, I suppose. At least it fits. You're not going to wear a ring?"

Molly wanted to groan. Instead, she said dryly, "Remember, Mother? I'm divorced."

"I still think that a discreet little gold band…"

Molly didn't want to listen to any more. "I don't expect to be gone for more than a couple of hours, Mom. Thanks for taking care of Bailey."

Alix didn't answer, but she looked at her watch.

Molly leaned over the little girl, and the scent of baby shampoo tickled her nose. Bailey was almost four, but she was small for her age, and her wiry little body still fit perfectly in her mother's arms. "I'll come back just as soon as I can, Bailey," she said. "You be good for Grandma, all right? And maybe tonight we'll go get ice cream."

Bailey's eyes lit. "Pink ice cream?"

"Bribing a child," Alix said, "is never a good idea."

Molly bit her tongue. The tip of it was beginning to feel sore after four days of Alix's advice, but she absolutely would not argue with her mother about how to raise her child as long as she was living under the woman's roof. And if Molly pointed out the fact that she'd been doing quite well on her own, Alix would probably just sniff and say that opinions differed—so why bother to say it?

One more reason, Molly told herself, *that I have to do well in this presentation.* If Warren Hudson liked her work enough to give her a contract to produce his company's publications, then before long she and Bailey could move to a place of their own.

And that day couldn't come fast enough for Molly.

Her father had warned her that Warren Hudson's business had changed a great deal in the years since she'd left Duluth. Still, Molly wasn't fully prepared for Meditronics' complex of sleek new buildings, nestled close together and tucked almost into the side of the steep and rugged hill that pressed the city close to Lake Superior. And she certainly wasn't prepared for the security post at the main entrance.

There had always been a gate house, of course. In the days when her father had been a line worker in Meditronics' factory, building medical machinery, there had been around-the-clock guards who checked each employee and visitor in and out. Now, in a well-sheltered niche at the side of the main drive was what looked like a parking-lot ticket machine with a keyboard attached. Molly lowered her car window and eyed the machine, which beeped, clicked and said, in a pleasant—though mechanical—masculine voice, "Please enter your name, last name first."

Molly obediently tapped the keys. The machine digested the information and said, "Please enter the name of the person you wish to visit, last name first."

"I liked the old days better," she murmured as she started to type. "All the guards knew me, and there was

never any fuss about getting inside where it was warm
to wait for the end of Dad's shift.''

The machine ignored her protest and with an asth-
matic whir thrust a card down a chute in its front, announcing, ''While you are inside the plant, please wear
this identification badge at all times. You will find Mr.
Warren Hudson in the administration building, to your
left at the first intersection.''

Molly picked up the card. Its laminated surface was
still warm. Under the plastic coating was her name,
along with Warren Hudson's, an elaborate bar code and
a small photograph of her with her mouth open and her
eyes half shut, obviously taken just moments before.

''That's what you get for talking back to the machine,'' she muttered. ''It exacted revenge.'' She fastened the card to her jacket lapel with a clip, which the
machine had thoughtfully dispensed, and let her car
creep up the main drive to the parking lot outside the
administration building.

It isn't too late to back out, said a little voice in the
far corner of her brain.

She shook her head almost in surprise. Of course it
was too late to cancel this appointment, and she
wouldn't back out even if she could. She needed this
job, this client.

There are other clients, the voice murmured. *You
don't have to go in there and face Warren Hudson.*

That was crazy. There was no reason not to go, she
told herself. The only thing Warren Hudson knew about
her was that Bernie Matthews was her father.

Are you sure about that?

''Of course that's all he knows,'' she said to herself.
''He'd hardly be interested in the fact that you used to
have a terrific crush on his son.'' Molly rubbed her temples and dragged her portfolio from the back seat. She
was only suffering from last-minute butterflies. There
was always this breathless sensation right before a pre-

sentation, when it was too late to do another thing to make the package better.

She was five minutes early when she walked into the executive office suite, and Warren Hudson, his secretary said, was waiting for her. Molly wondered uneasily if that was a good sign or a bad one. Was he simply eager to talk to her because he was excited about this project? Or…

There wasn't time to speculate. The secretary tapped on the half-open walnut door and said, "Ms. Matthews, sir." She stood aside to let Molly pass and added, "Shall I bring the coffee tray in now?"

Molly's gaze went straight to the massive desk set at right angles to the window, which framed a view of the aerial lift bridge and the lake beyond. The water looked gray today, under a halfhearted April sun, and mist hid the far side of the lake.

But Warren Hudson wasn't at his desk. He was seated in a wing chair in a little conversation area nearby, with the *Wall Street Journal* open on his knee. He stood up, folded the newspaper and laid it aside and held out a hand to Molly. "Your father tells me you're just what I'm looking for. Come in, my dear, and let's talk."

He was as big and gruff as Molly remembered, though his hair was entirely silver now, his shoulders stooped a bit, and there was a tremor in his outstretched hand. He waved her to the chair that matched his, and Molly set her portfolio on the deep gray carpet at her feet.

Warren Hudson settled into his chair once more. "So you're back in Duluth. You know, all the time I hear people saying they can't wait to leave this town. The funny thing is how many of them end up coming back here. You've been in Chicago the last few years, right?"

She'd started to wonder when—or if—he was going to let her get a word in. "Most of the time. I worked for a couple of corporations in their publications divisions, doing product brochures and catalogs and annual reports.''

"But with downsizing—'' he prompted.

Molly nodded. She wasn't surprised he knew how she'd lost her job. Her father would have told him, just to make it clear that she hadn't been fired for incompetence. "The company decided to eliminate the division and farm out the work to independents.''

"So you elected to start your own business.''

"I'd been thinking about it for a while, and this seemed the right time to give it a try.''

The secretary came in with a delicate china coffee service, and Warren waved a hand toward Molly. The secretary set the tray on the low table in front of her and disappeared once more into her office. Molly noticed that she left the door half-open, and told herself not to fret about it. This conversation was hardly top secret.

Warren said, "Would you pour? I'd appreciate it. I'm a clumsy old soul since I had a stroke a few months back.''

"I'm sorry to hear that. Not a severe one, I hope?'' The scent of the rich, dark brew rose from the china cups as she poured, tugging at Molly's senses.

"Oh, I'm doing all right.'' He put out his left hand for his cup and saucer and sat back, frowning. "I'm still not sure I understand, though. You had contacts in Chicago. People in the business who knew your skills. A possibility of actually doing the same work for the same people, though under a different set of circumstances. Here, you'll have to start from scratch.'' There was a challenge in his voice. "So what really brings you back to Duluth, Molly Matthews?''

It was a question she should have anticipated, and Molly could have kicked herself for not having an answer prepared. To buy a little time, she leaned forward to pour cream into her coffee. "I can still do some of

that work from here, you know. With faxes and overnight delivery services—''

He shrugged. ''Easier yet to do it there. Besides, if
people don't see your face regularly, they tend to forget
you exist.''

''But it's less expensive to start a business here than
in a larger city and to live till it gets off the ground. And
my family offered help in the meantime.'' The image of
Alix looking at her watch as if she was starting a mental
timer flashed into Molly's mind, and she tried to shrug
it off.

He didn't look satisfied, but he didn't press.

''And I have a little girl now,'' she went on. ''I didn't
want to raise her in the city, and this was the best time
to make the move.''

Warren's brow cleared. ''That's right. Your father told
me your marriage didn't work out. I'm sorry.''

Apparently, she thought grimly, *there isn't much my
father didn't tell you.* ''Thank you, sir.'' She kept her
eyes focused on the coffee tray. Would she ever be able
to hear that damned divorce mentioned without feeling
as if she was choking?

It's part of the price of coming home, she reminded
herself.

''When I lost my wife,'' Warren mused. ''Of course,
it was a different sort of ache, but I expect the feeling
of being abandoned is a fairly universal one, don't
you?''

The feeling of being abandoned… Molly could certainly identify with that, but the last thing she wanted
was to be drawn into a discussion about it. ''I'm sure
you understand how painful it is for me to talk about.''

''Of course. There for a minute I forgot you're not
just Bernie Matthews's daughter stopping by for a social
chat.''

Molly forced herself to smile, to play along. ''No, that
would have been Megan.'' She leaned forward to pick

up the coffeepot. "Tell me about the changes at Meditronics since I left."

"How long do you have?" Warren Hudson smiled. "That's why we want to do this project, you know. Next year the company will have been in business for a century. Of course, the products we make have changed a great deal over that time, along with medicine itself. Now we're not only producing medical equipment but support machines. Take our automated gatekeeper, for instance. We designed it to control access to certain areas in hospitals, but it works equally well for other purposes."

"I was going to ask about that." Molly flicked a fingertip against the laminated badge she wore. "What's to prevent someone from typing in any employee's name, getting a badge and wandering freely all over the plant?"

"You don't think the machine's that simpleminded, do you? It doesn't issue a pass till it's made sure the employee's actually here and has authorized a visitor."

"And how does somebody get in if they don't know the name of the person they need to see? Or if they don't have an appointment?"

"Oh, that sets off an entirely different routine. And before you ask what happened to our human security guards, we didn't fire them. A couple of them retired and the rest moved into other jobs. Don't you think the badges are nice?"

"I don't think I'll be ordering reprints of the photo," Molly said wryly.

"That one's certainly not its best work. By the way, the machine keeps those on file, too, so next time you come, it'll compare the two and make sure you're really you."

"In that case, I'll have to remember to reproduce the grimace, or it'll kick me out entirely because I look so different. You were just starting to tell me about the

project you have in mind, Mr. Hudson. My father mentioned that you were looking for someone with
publications experience, but he didn't have many details.''

Warren settled deeper into his chair. ''We want to use
our hundred years of history to promote Meditronics.
There will be things like updated sales brochures and
new ads, of course, but we have an agency for that. What
you'll be doing is gathering and organizing the history
of the company so the advertising and promotions people can choose the bits that will be most useful.''

What you'll be doing. It sounded as if the job was
hers, and some of the tension drained from the muscles
in Molly's neck and shoulders. She cautioned herself,
though, about taking too much for granted. He hadn't
even asked to look at samples of her work.

''But what I'd really like to focus on is a book,''
Warren said. ''A nice, glossy hardcover—a complete
history of the company that we could send out to all our
customers.''

''A gift as we look forward to serving you for another
century,'' Molly mused.

''You've got the idea exactly—and it's not a bad slo-
gan. You're sure you're not an advertising specialist?
What do you think, Molly?''

She could see the eagerness in his eyes. He didn't look
his age at all. In fact, he reminded her a little of Bailey
when she'd just come up with a new scheme and was
plotting to win approval so she could try it out.

He was the boss, Molly told herself. All she had to
do was smile and agree, and the job would drop like a
plum into her lap. And it wasn't a bad idea.

Still…

She took a deep breath. ''Good, as far as it goes.''

The gleam in Warren Hudson's eyes diminished.

''Since books are solid and look valuable,'' Molly
went on quickly, ''most people hesitate to discard

them—so your book will hang around the customer's office and remind him of Meditronics every time he sees it. But I wonder if that's enough. A book may also lie there for years and never be read. If you were to create a video presentation, though—''

Warren shifted in his chair. ''Trying to work yourself out of a job?''

Molly smiled. ''Oh, no. I can do video, too—organize and write and supervise it, at least. And I'm not suggesting you do video instead of the book, but along with it. A video presentation would be more flexible. It could be carried around by your salesmen, used at conventions or sales expositions—and it could also be combined with the book into a slick gift package that nobody could throw away.'' She was on a roll. ''It wouldn't be inexpensive, of course, but…''

''But we're only old once,'' Warren said, and grinned. ''Now that's my kind of attitude, Molly—taking an idea and making it better. In fact, I think there's only one more thing to take care of before we make this deal official—''

He'd want to see examples of her work, of course. Molly reached for the portfolio at her feet.

From the outer office, through the half-open door, floated the sound of a masculine voice, and for a moment she felt as if every joint in her body had locked simultaneously.

But she couldn't be hearing what she thought, she told herself. It was—it had to be—purely a trick of the imagination.

She'd already discovered in the four short days since she'd come home that simply being back in Duluth—driving down London Road, gazing across the lake, walking on the beach—had given new life to old memories. It was only reasonable that sitting in Warren Hudson's office would make her think of his son. She should have expected that. And it was memory, not fact, that had made her think for an instant that Luke was just beyond that half-open door. He couldn't be. He was half a continent away.

The man in the outer office spoke again, and Molly's heartbeat slowed toward normal. This man's voice was deeper than Luke's, and richer somehow. The two weren't really alike at all.

She picked up the calfskin portfolio.

"Oh, good," Warren Hudson said. "I hoped Lucas would come in time to meet you."

Her fingers went numb, and the portfolio slipped from her grasp. It tipped flat, and a slim catalog slid halfway out onto the carpet.

But he's not even in Minnesota anymore, Molly thought. *He's a fully qualified doctor, and he's in California.* It had been two years ago at least that her mother had written that Lucas Hudson had gone to the West Coast for his internship, and Alix hadn't mentioned him again after that.

But that didn't mean there'd been no more news about him, Molly realized, just that Alix hadn't happened to think of it while she was writing her terse, dutiful, infrequent letters.

"Though surely you two knew each other," Warren said, "before you left Duluth?"

Molly told herself firmly that she had nothing to be embarrassed about now. She was grown up, and what had happened years ago didn't matter any more. So what if she'd had a crush on Lucas Hudson when she was a kid? So what if the way he'd told her to get over it had made her want to crawl under the nearest boulder and die? He'd probably believed he was doing her a favor.

In the long run, she thought, he probably had.

"He was more my sister's age," she said. Luke had been Megan's friend, not Molly's—that much was true. The fact that she was also being evasive was beside the point.

Warren didn't seem to hear, anyway. "Lucas, my boy," he called. "Come in here, if you've got a minute."

The door swung slowly, silently open. *It ought to creak,* Molly thought—although, as far as she was concerned, there was no need for any theatrics to heighten the suspense.

The doorway was large, but it couldn't dwarf the man who stood there with a herringbone tweed jacket slung over one shoulder, his other hand in his trouser pocket. Molly hadn't seen him in years, but she couldn't have missed him even in a crowd. She would never forget how tall he was, though he was broader of shoulder than she remembered. His hair was just as dark, just as thick, and it looked just as soft. He still resembled the athlete he'd been, his body perfectly balanced as if he might leap in any direction in the next moment.

And he was looking at her with casual interest in his hazel eyes. Eyes framed with lashes so long and dark and thick and curly that they were positively indecent.

Looking at her so casually that she wondered if he even remembered the day he'd lectured her about making a fool of herself over him.

Warren said, "Molly and I—you remember Molly Matthews, Lucas? I told you, didn't I, that Bernie was sending her in to see me?"

"You did, Dad." Luke came across the room. "And of course I remember Molly."

His voice *was* both deeper and richer, and Molly could detect nothing but friendliness in his tone. She willed herself not to tremble as she offered her hand, and she succeeded. But even after the brief contact was over, she could feel the warmth of his fingers against her palm.

"Molly," Warren said, "you haven't forgotten my son, Lucas? He's taken over the reins here at Meditronics, after that stroke I was telling you about."

She didn't flinch. She supposed she'd been preparing herself for that statement since she'd heard his voice in the outer office, knowing at some subconscious level that Luke wasn't simply home for a visit.

"In fact," Warren went on, "this whole history project is his idea—I've just agreed to oversee the process. Molly and I have been chatting about it, Lucas, and we've hit it off famously. So with your approval…"

Was Luke's approval the one more thing Warren had been talking of? And if the history project was his idea, did that mean she'd be answering to Luke instead of his father?

It doesn't matter, she told herself. The job hadn't changed in the last ten minutes, only the boss had. But there was something else that hadn't changed—she needed this job just as desperately as ever. If, in order to get it, she had to charm Lucas Hudson…

Then I'll charm him, she told herself grimly. *In fact, I'll be so charming he won't know what hit him.*

CHAPTER TWO

BEFORE MOLLY could embark on her campaign, however—or even decide on a plan of attack—Warren Hudson said, with a note of self-congratulation in his voice, "She's already come up with a much better idea than mine, too. Instead of just doing the book, Molly thinks—"

Hastily, Molly said, "Mr. Hudson, perhaps right now isn't a good time for—"

"Does she, now?" Luke said gently. "Perhaps I should hear all about this exotic idea. And I see you brought samples of your work, Molly? I wouldn't want to bore you, Dad, by making you sit through all this a second time. Why don't I take Molly on into the conference room for a few minutes?"

"It's no prob—" Warren began.

"You look tired, Dad, and I noticed Jason waiting with the car out front when I came in."

Warren pushed himself from his chair. "You might want to practice tossing out hints, Lucas. There's a knack to making them subtle, and you haven't acquired it." He closed the office door very firmly behind him.

Luke chuckled and sat on the arm of the chair Warren had occupied. "Now *that's* a subtle hint. Closing the door, I mean, so that he didn't actually have to say, 'If you want to have Molly all to yourself, all you need to do is ask.'"

She felt a tinge of color steal into her cheeks, and to conceal it she bent to gather the catalog that had spilled out of her portfolio. Of course there was nothing more personal in his comment than a desire to ask a few questions his father might object to. She wondered, for instance, if he guessed that Warren hadn't bothered to check out her work.

Be charming, she reminded herself. The trouble was she had no idea how to begin. In general, of course, being charming was no trouble at all, but this situation was like walking a tightrope. How much charm would be enough? Because if she applied too much, she'd look like…well, like a teenager with a bad crush. And that was an image she'd just as soon not bring into Luke's mind.

"I brought along several different examples of my work," she said. "Brochures, catalogs, an annual report to stockholders. Is there any type you'd like to see first?"

"Not particularly."

Molly frowned. It was odd that he didn't sound interested. "I didn't think to bring a sample of my video work, but I could drop one off—"

Luke shook his head. "No, thanks. I haven't time to sit and watch, and it wouldn't make any difference anyway."

But he'd said he wanted to see… *No,* she corrected herself. He'd implied—no doubt for his father's sake—that he wanted to look over her portfolio. He hadn't actually said anything definite.

And the fact that he didn't seem interested in the caliber of her work didn't necessarily mean he'd already made up his mind not to hire her, either. But Molly's throat grew tight, and she had to work to keep her fear from creeping into her voice. "Then do you want to hear about my idea?"

"The one my father thinks is so brilliant? It's not at the top of my list, no."

Molly stared at him. He seemed perfectly at ease as he sat on the arm of the chair. She couldn't detect so much as a twitch of nervousness, and he was obviously in no hurry to explain himself. His gaze was steady on her face, the hazel eyes narrowed slightly. She wondered for a moment if his eyes ever sparkled with delight any more, or if he always looked a bit suspicious.

She watched as he made up his mind, and she saw determination come into his face—jaw muscles tightening, eyes darkening—and she knew he was bracing himself for something he expected to be unpleasant.

Almost bitterly, she thought that Warren had been a long way off the mark. Luke could be very subtle indeed when he wanted to be—though Molly was having no trouble getting the hint.

She gathered her samples and slid them neatly into the portfolio, zipped it shut and stood up. ''I suppose the polite thing to do would be to thank you for the opportunity to prove my fitness for this job, but since you didn't give me that opportunity, Luke, I won't bother.''

His eyebrows arched slightly. ''Sit down, Molly.''

''So, since you're not going to have to waste your time telling me that I won't be working on your father's project, won't you at least take ten seconds to tell me why? Don't you think I've grown up enough to handle the job, is that it?''

''Have you?'' His voice was little more than a growl.

''I've certainly shed a number of idiotic illusions!''

''You had plenty of them to shed, as I recall. Now if you'll stop jumping to conclusions and sit down...''

She forced herself to take a slow, deep breath, but she didn't return to her chair. She clasped her portfolio in both hands and looked straight at him. ''Well?''

''It's interesting, however,'' Luke mused, ''that you picked up so quickly on the fact that I don't want to give you this job.'' He strolled to the window.

''Oh, that took great intuition.'' She couldn't quite keep the sarcasm out of her voice. ''Just because you had no interest in my ideas or my qualifications—''

Luke's voice cut across hers. "Because not examining your portfolio or questioning your plans could just as logically mean the exact opposite—that I'd already decided you were hired, so your credentials didn't matter a damn." He turned to face her. "Couldn't it?"

Molly felt as if she were choking. She'd really put her foot in her mouth this time. If there was a way to be more efficient at ruining her chances, she couldn't imagine what it would be.

But she couldn't have been so wrong, she thought frantically. The way Luke had looked at her *wasn't* the way an employer viewed a successful candidate.

"The truth is," Luke said, "I don't want to give anyone this job. But since I have to hire someone, and my father seems to have his mind made up, it might as well be you."

Molly stared at him, aghast. "Well, isn't that just terrific? Your enthusiasm overwhelms me, Luke. I've never before been offered employment under such welcoming circumstances. I'm absolutely honored, but if I didn't need this job—"

Her conscience whispered, *This is how you define 'charming'?* Too late Bailey's face flashed before her, creased in the silly grin her mother loved best, reminding Molly how important this was. No matter how reluctantly, he'd offered her the job. She told herself that was the only thing that should matter now—but she wasn't quite convinced.

"Cut out the sarcasm, Molly. It's nothing personal."

"Oh, now *that* makes me feel much better." Pure puzzlement crept in alongside her frustration. "Though if you actually didn't intend to insult me, I don't quite see why you even wanted a private conversation."

"I certainly didn't intend any insult. I was going to start by telling you the job was yours, but before I could say a word you got up and started to stamp out."

Molly thought about it for a moment and conceded

that he might have a point. Still… "You couldn't have told me the job was mine with your father in the room? If that was all you had to say—"

Luke shook his head. "I wanted to make sure you understand what's really going on here, and I could hardly explain in front of my father that you'll actually be working for me, not for him."

"Now *that* sounds interesting." Her head was spinning, her knees shaking, and she welcomed the excuse to sit down. "So what have you got in mind? And how do you propose to keep him from finding out you've stolen his employee?"

This time Luke settled on the edge of the chair, not the arm. At least, Molly thought, he wasn't looming over her at the moment, but the set of his jaw was threatening nonetheless.

"I'm not stealing anybody. I just have an extra set of job requirements that I don't want my father to know about."

"Oh, this I can't wait to hear," Molly muttered.

Luke leaned forward, elbows on knees and hands clasped. "After my father's stroke," he said, "he lost interest in things. Almost everything, in fact, except the past, which he talked about endlessly and morbidly until it seemed he was retreating into his memories altogether."

Molly frowned. "Then why are you encouraging him to think about the plant's history? He said this project was your idea."

"Oh, it's my idea, all right." Luke sounded almost grim. "You might even call this a last-ditch effort to focus him onto something positive. If he wants to dwell on the past, fine—I give up. But there's a difference between just pondering it over and over and finding ways to use that history to help the company in the future."

"The difference between looking back and looking forward."

There was a gleam in his eyes that might have been appreciation. Or more likely, Molly thought irritably, it was surprise that she'd actually understood.

"And you want me to help manipulate him," she went on.

"So far, it seems to be working. Today is the first time in weeks he's been in the office."

So that's why he was waiting for me with nothing better to do than read the newspaper, Molly thought. "I'm sure his reluctance to hang around Meditronics has nothing to do with your sunny presence and the fact that you've taken over his job since he got sick." She looked around the room. "In fact, is this office his or yours these days?"

"Mine." Luke's voice was stiff.

"No wonder he's been staying home."

"Look, Molly, he may have left you with the impression that I came charging in here two minutes after his stroke, riding my big white horse and determined to take over Meditronics—but the fact is I've been here for well over a year. I was already running things long before he got sick. But that doesn't mean he wasn't still involved. He's chairman of the board. He came to work every day. So when he stopped expressing opinions—or even having them, it seemed—of course I started to get worried."

"So the medical career didn't work out, after all," Molly mused.

"It's not a bad background for selling equipment to hospitals. But about my father—let's get this clear right now, Molly. The only thing that's important about this book idea is that Warren believes in it."

"And you're not really hiring me to help with the book, but to reawaken his interest in life."

"Something like that. You can start tomorrow. We'll find you an office down the hall."

"And if I'm successful," she mused, "just as soon as your father starts being more interested in Meditronics' future than its past, I suppose you'll cut the whole project loose and I'm out of a job, just like that." She shook her head. "You know, it may not have been very wise of you to tell me this, after all."

"Pull that miracle off, and I'll pay you for a book you don't even have to finish. I might even add a nice bonus."

Molly rested her chin on her tented fingertips and considered. "The bonus is a nice touch. Of course, all I have to do is tell your father what you're up to—"

"You said," he reminded, "that you need this job."

He didn't miss a trick, did he? "True enough. Throw in a good recommendation for me to every business you come into contact with, and you're on."

Luke countered, "The most I'll promise is an honest letter of introduction. And as for recommendations, I'll give you one right now—if you're headed for another business appointment, you might want to wipe the smudge off your face."

Before she could stop herself, Molly's hand flew to cover the bruise on her jaw. *Laugh it off,* she ordered herself. *Tell him the somersault story.*

But she couldn't force the words out. Instead, she said lamely, "It's nothing."

His eyes narrowed, and he tipped his head as if to study her more closely.

Molly picked up her portfolio and started toward the outer office. "I'll settle for your promise of a letter of introduction, Luke, but only because it will end up being the same thing as a recommendation, anyway."

"Will it?" He opened the door for her. "I certainly hope you're right."

Luke closed the office door behind Molly and settled into the deep leather chair behind his desk. He'd done all he could. Now it was simply a matter of waiting to see whether the treatment would be effective. If anybody could needle a man out of a state of apathy, he thought it would be Molly Matthews. He'd seen more liveliness in his father's eyes today than there'd been in months—and she'd certainly had Luke in the mood to wring her dainty little neck. *So the medical career didn't work out after all....* He was half-surprised she hadn't asked if the problem was that he fainted at the sight of blood.

But she knew her job now, and he supposed she'd set about it in her unique way. One thing was certain—there was no point in giving any more thought to Molly Matthews in the meantime.

He pulled a stack of correspondence from the in-basket, turned on the mini cassette recorder he used for dictation and leaned back to consider his answers.

But the tape spun uselessly, for his favorite thinking position, with his elbow propped on the arm of the black leather chair and his jaw leaning against his hand, reminded him of the discoloration on Molly's face.

It's nothing, she had said. But she'd given herself away by touching it like that. If it had been only a smudge, she wouldn't have known where it was.

Somebody had socked her in the jaw.

And it's none of your business who or why, Luke reminded himself. He'd hired her for a purpose, not for old times' sake. She was no longer the annoying kid whom he'd rescued now and then from treetops, undertows or merciless teasing. She was no longer the coltish adolescent whose pitifully adoring green eyes had made him so uncomfortable. She was no longer the naive girl who had tearfully insisted she would love him forever, no matter what....

In the last five years, Luke thought, Molly Matthews's body might have acquired soft curves in all the right places, but the rest of her had honed down to a knife's edge. She'd lost her illusions, all right.

A fist in the face will do that to you. Especially if it happens regularly.

Some women, he told himself, were hard to figure out.

Molly would have given anything to be able to drive past her parents' house and head north, up the old scenic highway toward Two Harbors. She longed for the freedom to drive until she'd left all her frustrations behind. Or perhaps she'd pull off the road and walk on the pebbly beach and listen to the lake until the timeless rhythm of the waves washed her tension away.

But she'd been gone much longer than she'd expected, and she didn't dare take extra advantage of her mother. Just because Alix had offered to baby-sit today didn't mean she ever would again.

Another thing for the list tomorrow, Molly thought. Now that she had her first client, she'd have to line up steady day care. And thanks to Luke, she was going to need more of it than she'd expected. She'd hoped to do most of her work at home, where she could keep one eye on Bailey. In fact, with access to the right archives, she could design and produce Warren Hudson's book almost anywhere. But if he wasn't involved on a daily basis, she could hardly spark his interests in once more taking up his real job—and that meant hanging around Meditronics a whole lot more than she'd planned on.

Obviously, by the time this was done she'd be able to put that bonus Luke had mentioned to good use. If she earned it.

But how hard could that be? She'd bet anything Warren Hudson was already starting to come out of his shell. With or without her—or the book, either, for that matter—she suspected he'd be plunging into the mainstream within a few weeks. Even without the bonus, Luke was paying good money for nothing.

And he can afford to, she told herself. *So don't feel*

sorry for him. He offered this deal, you didn't twist his arm.

Besides, he wouldn't be getting *nothing,* anyway. No matter what, he'd end up with something out of the deal—even if it was only a book of company history that he didn't want.

And considering the way he'd looked at her just before he'd offered her the job—like a man with a toothache facing the dentist's drill, knowing it was both unpleasant and unavoidable—Molly thought that was about what he deserved.

Alix was in the kitchen, chopping something that looked suspiciously like chicory. She looked up when Molly came in. "I'm making Chicken Crecy," she said. "I hope Bailey will eat it."

Molly hoped so, too. The dish smelled wonderful to her, but with a three-year-old one never quite knew. "Well, it's making me hungry, so if she doesn't like it she has no taste at all. Is she asleep?"

"No, your father came home and took her up to Knife River to hunt for agates." Alix's tone left no doubt as to her feelings about Bernie's choice of pastime.

"I don't suppose Megan went along." Molly's voice was droll. Megan in a white cashmere sweater, hunting agates on the beach, was the most unlikely picture she could think of.

"Of course not. She and Rand are going to a dinner party tonight."

In the four days Molly had been home, this must be the third party she'd heard about. She wondered when Megan and Rand ever had time to talk to each other. On the drive to the parties, perhaps? "Can I help with anything, Mom?"

"No, it's all done. Did you get the contract?"

Molly nodded. "It's not quite what I expected, though—it's going to be more like a regular job. I'd hoped to be able to bring a lot of the work home, but it looks like I'll be spending more time at Meditronics than I'd bargained for.'' She hung her jacket over the back of a chair and started to rinse the few dishes Alix had left in the sink. ''So I'll have to start looking for day care tomorrow.''

Alix frowned. ''If that's a hint that I should volunteer to keep Bailey every day—''

Molly's hand clenched on the scrubbing brush, and her voice was taut. ''Of course it wasn't, Mother. You're doing so much for me already, how could I possibly expect any more?''

A booming voice from the back door said, ''Don't be hasty about this, Alix.'' Bernie Matthews ducked through the doorway with Bailey perched on his shoulders, dipping just far enough so her head cleared the top of the casing.

The child giggled and clutched at his hair. ''Do it again, Grampa!''

Bernie obliged. ''She's the only granddaughter you've got, Alix. Now that you've got the chance to know her, grab it—or else don't be surprised, when she's old enough to interest you, that she doesn't want to come and visit.''

Molly saw the irritation in her mother's eyes and intervened. ''She's right, Dad. It's too much to expect her to do. And I'd better start looking, anyway. It'll get even tougher to find day care when the school year ends and everybody's scrambling to get kids settled for the summer.''

''I don't want to go to day care.'' Bailey sounded mutinous.

''You know, Molly, I hadn't thought of it that way,'' Bernie mused. ''Taking care of a child *is* awfully hard work.''

Molly opened her mouth to point out that wasn't quite what she'd said.

''Of course you haven't thought of it that way,'' Alix

snapped. "You take her out on the beach and let someone else clean up the mess!"

Bernie winked at Molly. "And Alix has been starting to slow down and lose some of the pep she had when she was young."

Alix's eyes flared. "Bern, if you're implying that I'm getting old—"

"If you're not, why are we celebrating thirty years of marriage the end of this month?"

"Because Megan thought we shouldn't let the occasion go by without a party."

Bernie snorted. "Megan considers a broken fingernail a good enough reason for a party. Hey, maybe she'd look after Bailey once in a while. Even if she's not ever going to settle down and have kids of her own, she ought to get a taste of what parenting's all about." He swung Bailey off his shoulders. "You'd behave yourself for Aunt Megan, wouldn't you, punkin?"

Bailey shook her head. "I'm not a punkin, Grampa."

"Well, that's a relief. I thought for a second you meant you wouldn't be good. Show your mother your agates."

Bailey held out a fist and slowly unfurled her fingers. She'd clutched the dozen tiny red-orange stones so tightly they'd left indentations in her palm. "I like going to the lake. Aren't they pretty, Mommy?"

"Indeed they are, dear. Let's go put them with your collection and wash all that sand off you before dinner."

Bailey had never liked having her face washed. It would be a lot easier, Molly thought, to just put her in the tub and start from scratch. But Alix wouldn't like to keep dinner waiting.

She handed Bailey a sliver of soap so the child's hands would be occupied while she tried to restore some order to her hair. One ponytail had disintegrated altogether, leaving a pink bow hanging by a couple of curls, and the other had slid so far it looked more like a cow-lick.

Bernie poked his head around the edge of the door. "I got sent to wash up, too."

Bailey generously handed over her soap.

Molly gave up on the ponytails and settled for combing the tangles out of Bailey's long, fine hair. "Dad, I know you were trying to help, but please don't make Mom feel guilty if she doesn't want to keep Bailey every day. It wouldn't be good for either of them if she feels she's stuck with the job."

"Oh, I don't know. A little guilt now and then's a good thing. But Meditronics has a day-care center right down the street from the administration building."

That would be absolutely ideal, Molly told herself. And yet…

"And if you start taking Bailey there every day," her father said slyly, "I'll bet before long your mother will be pouting and begging to keep her."

Reluctantly, Molly smiled. "Reverse psychology? I won't hold my breath. But if you can come up with as good a plan to get her to quit talking about this divorce business—"

Bernie shook his head. "I think that one's beyond me, sweetheart." He dried his hands, patted Bailey's cheek and headed toward the dining room.

"Mommy." Bailey smoothed the suds over her hands till it looked as if she was wearing white gloves. "What's divorced?"

At least she didn't ask my mother, Molly thought. "It's what happens when two people decide not to be married any more."

Bailey held out her hands to study the effect. "Is that what happened to you and my daddy?"

"Something like that, Bailey. Rinse the soap off now and we'll have dinner—and we'll talk about it later, all right?"

Bailey's lower lip crept out. Molly wasn't sure if the objection was to postponing the conversation or giving up her soap. At the moment, she didn't want to know.

Luke hadn't specified a time for her to come to work the next day, so Molly took her best guess and planned to be in the office by nine. She was almost on her way out of the house when Bailey realized belatedly that she was being left and began to shriek. It took Molly the better part of half an hour to get the child settled down enough to leave her.

By then Alix was tapping her foot and looking impatient, and Molly was not only feeling frazzled, she was longing to point out to her mother that there was an enormous difference between a three-year-old throwing a pure and simple temper tantrum and one who was genuinely miserable at being left behind. Obviously, she wasn't going to have the luxury of even a day to look around for someone to care for Bailey. If there was a spot in the Meditronics facility, she'd better grab it. At least with Bailey just down the street Molly could pop in from time to time.

She was only beginning to breathe freely again when she walked into the main office, but when the secretary who had greeted her the day before looked up with a smile, Molly relaxed.

"Good morning," the secretary said. "I've set up an office for you next door to the conference room, just around that corner. Mr. Luke had some things sent over from the warehouse, but if there's anything special you need—"

"Now that you mention it," Molly began.

The door of the inner office opened and Luke appeared, carrying an open file folder. He laid it on the secretary's desk and, eyes narrowed, studied Molly. "Quite a knack you have—showing up just in time to clock out for lunch."

He sounded genuinely admiring, but Molly wasn't fooled. "I have no plans to leave the building till the end of the day. And in any case, I'm not exactly an employee, remember? I'm a contractor, which means I don't have to punch a time card."

"I suppose not. However, Dad's been here for an hour already."

"Oh. I thought since he was still recuperating…"

"You seem to have inspired him into becoming a morning person." He pushed the folder toward the secretary, but his gaze was on Molly.

He was looking at her as if he couldn't believe his eyes, and Molly wondered if Bailey's tantrum had left her disheveled. By sheer willpower she kept herself from smoothing her palms over her tomato-red skirt. No matter what the reason for that stare, she wasn't going to give him the satisfaction of reacting.

"That's certainly a good indication, isn't it?" she mused. "That he's so eager to start, I mean."

"Don't start spending that bonus just yet," Luke recommended. "Wanda, make sure Ms. Matthews gets an employee badge before she leaves so she doesn't have to go through the routine at the gate every day."

"Yes, sir," the secretary murmured.

"You expect me to give up a daily portrait session?" Molly turned the little laminated card around. "I thought this was much better than yesterday's. And as long as we're on the subject, I was really unhappy when the automated gatekeeper made me give that one back last night before I could leave. What do you use them for, blackmail?"

The secretary, Molly noticed, was trying to fight off a smile.

"It's an idea—though I'll have to work on figuring out what you have that I want." He strode toward his office.

"Luke," Molly said quickly. "I do have a serious question. If I could have a minute in private…?"

"That's just about all I have." He pushed the door open and stood aside for her to precede him.

Molly stopped a few feet inside the door. "There's a little problem of a budget. In addition to the price of my time, putting together a book is going to cost some money. Even if you're assuming it'll never get to the publication stage, there will be certain expenses—"

"We set up a budget. Wanda can get you the precise figures."

"And if your father wants me to pursue my other idea?" She was deliberately nonspecific. He'd had his chance yesterday to explore that avenue, and he hadn't bothered. She wasn't about to make it easy for him. "It won't be inexpensive, either."

"You mean the video version?"

Molly's eyebrows lifted. She had to give him credit for that one. "Curious, were you?"

"Not especially. He rattled on about it all through dinner last night." He glanced at his watch and walked toward his desk. "You'd better hurry," he suggested, "before Dad gets all his joie de vivre back and I conclude you haven't earned anything at all."

Molly fought a sensation of breathlessness and said cheerfully, "Want me to go tell him you've already fired me because you don't care what happens to his book, and then wait and see how long his enthusiasm lasts?"

He tossed a sheaf of papers on the desk blotter. "Dammit, Molly, exactly what do you want?"

"Besides for you to admit you need me just now? Permission to spend some money on the video."

He glared at her. "Put a proposal in writing and have Wanda leave it on my desk."

"Happily," Molly murmured. "Especially the part

about Wanda as delivery person. Goodness knows I don't have any desire to come in here ever again.''

He was still standing by his desk when she walked out, staring after her. Molly knew, because his gaze felt like sandpaper running up and down her spine.

CHAPTER THREE

MOLLY'S nerves were still vibrating when she reached the office Wanda had indicated, and her first sight of it didn't help. The room was small and almost bare of furniture, but corrugated archival boxes—thirty of them, at least—had been stacked in a ragged half-circle around the desk, taking up most of the floor space. One had been opened. The papers inside were untidy, as if they'd been tossed in rather than filed in order. And the only hint of what the precise contents of each box might be was a date scribbled on the once-white cardboard lid.

Mr. Luke's had some things sent over from the warehouse, Wanda had said. Molly would bet he'd taken great delight in creating this mess. Though it would have been thoughtful of him to have given some consideration to how this sight might affect his father's mood. She'd waded through this kind of chaos before, but for someone who hadn't—someone who wasn't in top condition to start with—the confusion might be overwhelming.

Near the window Warren sat, leafing through what looked like a crumbling scrapbook. He'd shed his coat and tie and rolled up the sleeves of his white shirt. He looked a little overwhelmed, Molly thought, though perhaps that impression arose not so much from Warren himself as the fact that the wall of boxes seemed to be confining him like a prison fence.

"Look here," he said. "It's the original brochure listing products my great-grandfather sold." He held out the scrapbook.

The pages were crackly and the ink faded. The descriptions were fascinating, but the poor quality of the

etched illustrations would make them difficult to reproduce. "Somebody went to a lot of trouble to put this
scrapbook together."

"It's from the earliest box. Unfortunately, it looks as
if nobody had time to look after the later things, and
they're a mess." Warren looked perplexed. "I don't
know, Molly. This seemed like such a good idea, but
now that I see it all spread out…"

"You'll be surprised how quickly we'll be able to
make sense of it," Molly said cheerfully. She hoped he
didn't suspect that she had her fingers crossed behind
her back.

Even with all the clutter, however, and the dust that
had her sneezing fiercely and frequently, working with
Warren was a joy. The hours sped by, and Molly was
surprised when Luke tapped on the office door with a
uniformed chauffeur standing behind him.

"Jason was getting worried, Dad," Luke said mildly.
"He's been waiting since two o'clock—which is when
you told him to pick you up."

"What time is it?" Warren brushed off his fingertips
and rolled down his sleeves. Molly noted a streak of
grime on the once pristine shirt. "I hadn't noticed."

Molly cast what she intended to be a triumphant look
at Luke, and spoiled it with a sneeze.

"God bless you, Molly," Warren said punctiliously.
"Though now that you mention it, Lucas, I am feeling
a little hungry. What about you, my dear? You've
missed your lunch, too. If you'll come with me, I'm sure
the cook can find us something."

"Oh—thanks, Warren, it's very sweet of you. But I
have some errands to run."

"Of course. I'll see you in the morning, then." He set
his hat firmly in place and strolled out, leaning just a
little on the chauffeur's arm.

Luke's gaze was like ice. "You just ignored lunch?"

"I didn't intend to," Molly admitted. She felt a little

ashamed of herself for not paying more attention. She should have insisted Warren take a break. "But I'd say we made a good start, wouldn't you?"

Luke surveyed the boxes, now stacked along one wall in a semblance of order, and the desktop, lined with neatly sorted piles. "I told you to inspire him, not work him to death."

"I am sorry about that," she said frankly. "I really did lose track of the time, and I'll be more careful in the future." She took her handbag from the bottom drawer of her desk.

"Are you leaving, too? It's only the middle of the afternoon."

Molly paused in the doorway. "Remember? You said yourself the book isn't my job, Warren is." She smiled at him and snapped off the lights.

Molly was early the next morning—until the automatic gatekeeper refused to acknowledge that she existed. Somewhere inside that emotionless hunk of plastic and metal was the employee badge Wanda had issued her. She'd turned it in as commanded when she'd left the plant at the end of the day, and the machine wouldn't give it back.

She muttered under her breath and tried again, but with an almost threatening buzz the machine said, "Access is denied."

From her safety seat in the back of the car, Bailey commented, "That was a naughty word you said, Mommy."

"It certainly was. And it's a naughty machine, too." A car's horn beeped behind her, and Molly glanced into her mirror. Not only was she blocking traffic, but the black Jaguar waiting in line had pulled so close that she couldn't even get out of the way. It didn't take an Einstein to figure out who was behind the wheel of that sleek, expensive car. "Great," she muttered as she watched Luke get out of the Jaguar.

He strolled up and leaned into her car, his arms folded on the window ledge. "Having a problem?"

"That depends. Have you told the gatekeeper to lock me out?"

"Hadn't thought of it, no."

"Then I don't have a problem, the machine does. I keep typing in my name, but it won't spit out my badge or—more important—open the gate. Perhaps it's gone on strike. How long has it had to work without a day off?"

Luke turned to the keyboard, and moments later the gatekeeper docilely produced Molly's badge. Luke caught it and presented it to her with a tiny bow.

"Stupid machine," she muttered, and hooked the badge onto the collar of her sweater. "Thanks for making me look like a fool. The humans who used to do this job wouldn't have had a problem."

"Oh, I don't know. It seems to be confused about whether you're a regular employee—which puts it in pretty good company, I'd say. On the other hand, it might just not have recognized you with your hair pulled up like that."

Molly's fingertips went to the French braid at the back of her head. "If you think I'm taking my hair down because a machine doesn't approve of the style—"

From the back seat, Bailey piped up. "I need a badge, too."

Molly wanted to groan.

Luke raised his eyebrows, and leaned into the car once more. "Who's this?"

"A very short industrial spy," Molly muttered. "I was hoping to sneak her past you by pretending to enroll her in the day-care center, but of course now that she's blown her cover—"

Luke grinned, but it was Bailey he addressed. "A badge? I think that could be arranged, tyke."

"I'm not a tyke," the child announced with dignity. "I'm Bailey."

"We shouldn't hold up traffic," Molly said. "And whatever she thinks, she doesn't need a badge."

"Well, no—she doesn't. We haven't started labeling all the day-care kids yet. But why shouldn't she have one if she wants?" Luke looked over his shoulder. "There isn't anybody waiting, and it'll only take a minute, anyway. But you'll have to get out of the car, Miss Bailey, to have your picture taken."

Before Molly could object, he lifted the child out of her safety seat and held her up beside the gatekeeper. A couple of minutes later Bailey gleefully showed off her still-warm trophy. The camera had caught her almost in profile, looking at Luke instead of the lens, giggling, with her eyes squeezed almost shut. It was nearly as bad as Molly's first one had been.

"The resemblance between the two of you," Luke said solemnly, "is almost astounding."

"Thank you very much," Molly said. "I suppose when it's time to turn the badge in at the end of the day you'll meet us here and explain why she can't take it home? Because I don't think I can possibly—"

"But she can keep it. It's only a sample, missing all the important coding." He winked at Bailey. "Just in case you really are an industrial spy and intend to flood us with illicit copies." He set her in her seat and stepped away from the car, whistling as he walked to the Jaguar.

Molly shook her head and put the car in gear.

"He's a funny man, Mommy."

"Isn't he, though," Molly muttered. "A regular comedian."

And he'd been practically friendly, too. Which was enough all by itself to make her wonder what the man was up to.

*   *   *

Pure habit was all that guided the Jaguar up the curving main drive to the administration building. Luke pulled the keys from the ignition and sat tapping them on the steering wheel, staring at nothing.

So Molly Matthews had a little girl.

Three years old, maybe? He was no judge of kids' ages—not only did he lack first-hand experience, but he had no particular desire to acquire any. But if he had to take a guess…

So Molly had done exactly as he'd predicted she would. Despite his best efforts, she hadn't learned a thing from her infatuation with him. Angry, frustrated, hurt by what she saw as Luke's rejection, she'd turned to another man to soothe her wounded pride. Obviously not a prizewinner, either, or she wouldn't need this job so desperately. And now she had a child.

Luke carried no guilt for the choices Molly had made, of course. He'd done his best to warn her, to explain how vulnerable she was. But Molly had obviously not been able to see beyond her own nose.

And he certainly felt no satisfaction at being proved correct. He'd done what he thought—what he'd *known*—was right. If, instead, he'd taken advantage of what she'd so trustingly offered him all those years ago…

That little girl might have been mine.

The words were like a jab to his gut, a blow that reminded him of the bruise on Molly' jaw. But he had done what he had to, and apparently so had Molly. And this was no time to start regretting it.

Molly looked over Warren's shoulder at the invoice he'd discovered, folded into a tiny square in a corner of one of the archive boxes. One of the earliest dates they'd found yet, it hadn't been in the earliest of the boxes but with a number of things from a couple of decades later. Just sorting out the mess was shaping up to be a bigger job than Molly had anticipated. After nearly a week they still hadn't opened all the boxes.

Warren's eyes were aglow. "From the date, this must be the first delivery truck my great-grandfather ever owned, and just look what he paid for it. You couldn't buy a bicycle for that these days."

"Not much of a bike, at any rate. Though I'm sure it wasn't inexpensive then." Molly made a note to herself. "In order to compare, we'll need to calculate the average rate of pay in this area at that time. Then we can figure how many hours a person had to work in order to buy—" The phone on the desk rang. "That's probably for you, Warren."

He glanced at his watch. "No doubt it's Jason, and he's early. Tell him I'll be a few minutes yet, will you?"

Molly smiled at him. "You're still spoiled from all the years of having a private secretary." She reached for the phone.

But it wasn't the chauffeur's polite tones that greeted her but a woman's voice saying, "Molly, I need you desperately."

Megan, Molly thought. *Well, there's a first time for everything.* "What's wrong?"

"I'm having a dinner party tonight, and one of my guests called this minute and canceled. So of course I thought of you."

"Because you need an extra woman?" Of course, Molly thought, for Megan that *would* be an emergency. "It's really not a good night for me. By the time I finish here and pick up Bailey and find a sitter—"

"I've already called Mom, and she'll take care of her. Actually, she told me at lunch today that she misses Bailey, can you believe it?"

"Strange, isn't it?" Molly said dryly. *Daddy, the psychologist, was right,* she thought. Of course, he couldn't possibly have lived with Alix for thirty years without figuring out what made her tick.

"Molly, please come."

Molly had to admit to a tinge of curiosity. This might be the only opportunity she'd ever have to get a direct look at how the Bannisters lived. "All right. What time?"

"The guests are invited for seven, but come at six so we can find you a dress."

"I might be able to manage one of my own," Molly said dryly.

"I'm sorry." Megan's voice was small. "I just thought... I'm sorry, Mol."

"It's all right. If Daddy can take Bailey home, I'll come straight there. Otherwise I'll be just as quick as I can."

She thought she heard Megan whisper, "Thanks."

Molly put the phone down with a thoughtful frown. Only when Megan stopped being brittle was it apparent how far from normal she was most of the time.

Molly felt a sudden twinge of guilt because she hadn't tried harder to stay in touch with her sister through the years. But of course Megan hadn't made an effort to maintain contact, either. She hadn't seemed to care, and Molly had had far too much on her mind to worry about it.

Warren's voice brought her back. "Go on and get ready for your party, my dear. You deserve it. I'll sit here and sort a little longer."

"If you're sure... Just don't lift anything heavier than a paper clip, all right?"

Warren smiled. "Don't worry about that. I'm a bit too tired today to be flinging boxes around."

"I'll see you tomorrow, then." Molly picked up her handbag and started down the hall toward her father's office. If Bernie could pick up Bailey tonight...

It was odd, Molly thought, that she suddenly felt so anxious to reach Megan's side.

She popped around a corner and ran headlong into

Luke, who caught her, set her on her feet and stepped out of her way. "Sorry," he said. "If I'd realized what a hurry you were in I'd have gone the other way around."

Molly felt a rush of color in her face. That figured. She'd hardly caught a glimpse of the man since their encounter beside the automatic gatekeeper—so what did she do? Almost trample him, of course. The impact had left her almost breathless, and the muscles in her upper arms, where his hands had rested, were still tingling.

She ignored the sensation and hurried to fill the gap. "I haven't had a chance to tell you how much Bailey loves her badge. She wears it all the time and sleeps with it under her pillow."

"When it wears out let me know."

"You're kidding. Meditronics badges wear out sometimes?"

Luke didn't seem to be listening. His gaze slid from her face down the length of her body. "I know we changed the rules a while back to allow casual dress, but I hardly expected jeans and flannel shirts in the administrative offices."

"Sorry." Molly knew she didn't sound it. "I do try not to run all over the building dressed like this, but it's a purely practical move. That warehouse must not have been dusted since the Roaring Twenties. Come in anytime and dig through a few boxes, and you'll see what I mean. Just don't expect me to wash your shirts afterward." She saw light flare in his eyes, and too late wished she'd put a guard on her tongue.

"Once," he said quietly, "you seemed to want that job."

Molly's breath caught in her throat, and she had to force a smile. "Well, we all have crazy ideas when we're young, don't we? You were right, Luke. You told me that no matter what I thought I couldn't possibly love you, and—obviously—I didn't."

"You were too young and inexperienced to know what love was. That's why I warned you about repeating your mistakes. But you didn't listen, did you, Molly? You plunged straight in anyway. Another man, and then a child—"

She put her chin up a fraction. "If you're implying that Bailey was a mistake, let me assure you that you're dead wrong." She pushed past him.

"And her father?" Luke called after her.

Molly didn't turn around. "What about him?"

"Was he a mistake?"

The question hit her like a knife in the ribs. She clutched at her chest. The silence stretched like taffy.

"Sorry," Luke said. His voice was heavy. "It's not my business."

"It certainly isn't." Molly didn't look back, and she didn't hesitate till she was safely around the next corner. Then she leaned against the wall and sucked in one deep breath after another.

Was he a mistake? "You might say so," Molly muttered. In fact, he'd been the biggest one of her lifetime.

Molly's small car looked pathetically plebeian next to the Bannisters' glass and steel house, perched high atop the bluff overlooking Lake Superior. Molly had never visited the house, though she knew the neighborhood. And Alix had of course sent photographs throughout the two years it had taken to build and decorate the house— so many photographs, in fact, that Molly thought she could probably walk through the place blindfolded.

The pictures hadn't prepared her, though, for the sheer size of the soaring atrium foyer or the trim little blond maid who answered the door. "Mrs. Bannister is in her boudoir," she said. "I'll show you upstairs."

She led the way up a long curved flight of polished black marble steps, down a hallway hushed by the deepest carpet Molly had ever seen, to a closed door, and knocked. Inside, Megan, in an ivory lace peignoir, was taking dresses from a row of closets that lined one wall of the room. She looked distracted. "There's a tanger-ine-orange thing here somewhere that would look won-derful on you. I bought it before I lightened my hair and—"

"Megan," Molly said firmly. "What is it?"

For a moment, she thought her sister was teetering on the edge of telling her. Then Megan laughed, lightly and unconvincingly, and said, "Oh, you know, some times are better than others. And this is supposed to be one of the good ones." She pulled open another door. "Oh, here it is."

Molly's heart twisted with regret. How she wished they'd been the sort of sisters who could laugh over their triumphs, share their sorrows and be brutally frank with each other when necessary.

As it was, she couldn't force Megan to confide in her. And of course she had to admit that her older sister had never been her first choice of confidante, either.

Megan kept up a steady stream of chatter while Molly showered, then helped her into the silky tangerine dress and stood back for an inspection. "That looks good," she said. "Better than it ever did on me, as a matter of fact. Let's go downstairs, because the guests will be ar-riving soon. What are you going to wear to Mother and Daddy's anniversary party?"

"I haven't had time to think."

"It's only three weeks off. If you don't want to go shopping, come and rummage through my closets. Of course, if you'd rather go shopping I can tell you all the best places." She led the way down the great staircase and through the atrium and hesitated on the threshold of an enormous living room. She closed her eyes for an instant and took a deep breath, then forced a smile which Molly saw didn't reach her eyes.

"If you hate this so," Molly said, "why do you do it?"

Megan stared at her for an instant, wide-eyed, and then gave a little laugh. "Entertain, you mean? Oh, everybody's nervous right before a party."

Still puzzled, Molly followed her sister into an enormous salon. One end of the room was entirely glass, a dozen huge panes fitted together into a curved wall that provided a stunning panoramic view of the lake far below. Near a white marble fireplace Rand Bannister stood by a black lacquered cart on which a portable bar had been set up, pouring Scotch from a heavy crystal decanter.

Molly hadn't seen him since the wedding, and she regarded him with interest. The years had been kind to Rand, she thought. The young man who had been a bit pompous for Molly's taste seemed to have matured into dignity. His black hair was faintly touched with silver, but his dark good looks still formed a perfect foil for Megan's delicate beauty.

"Molly," he said. "What a surprise to see you."

"Catherine canceled at the last moment," Megan said. "Molly's being a sweetheart and filling in."

"Sweet of her, indeed," he agreed. He added a splash of soda to the glass and handed it to Megan. "Your usual, my dear. And what can I get for you, Molly?"

She accepted a glass of white wine and strolled toward the windows. But the floor-to-ceiling glass was so clear that it seemed nonexistent, and she had a sudden sensation of standing on the edge of a cliff with nothing between her and the lake but a sheer five-hundred-foot drop. Vertigo made her head spin, and she quickly backed away from the windows.

"An incredible view, isn't it?" Rand asked. "I could stand next to that window for hours on end."

Before Molly had to find an answer, the butler spoke

from almost directly behind her, announcing the first couple to arrive.

Molly moved hastily aside, out of the doorway, just as a blond woman in brilliant white swept through. Her flawless skin looked as if she'd been gilded, and Molly wasted a moment speculating how many hours a day she had to spend under a sunlamp to achieve that effect before she let her gaze drift to the woman's escort, standing half a step behind her with his hand resting gently at the small of her back.

Molly's eyes widened, and her heartbeat sped up.

Megan could have warned me, Molly thought, and a second later told herself not to be so silly. Why should she need a warning, after all? Or expect one? Megan had known Luke Hudson forever. Why shouldn't she invite him to dinner?

Luke said, "No wonder you were so anxious to get out of the office today." His gaze flicked over Molly from head to foot, and she saw a gleam in his eyes she thought might have been reluctant approval.

She felt a little glow of warmth and told herself tartly that Luke's evaluation was nothing to get excited about. He probably wasn't admiring her, just the cut of Megan's dress.

"Melinda," he said, "this is Molly Matthews."

The golden girl smiled and held out a hand. "Megan's little sister? What a pleasant surprise to meet you here."

Was there the faintest emphasis on the last word, Molly wondered, or was she only imagining it because she felt so out of place at Megan's party, among Megan's friends?

Melinda went on earnestly, "And may I tell you how much I've always liked that dress? Every time I've seen Megan wearing it, I've meant to tell her."

Well, that removes all doubt about her opinion of me, Molly thought. She manufactured a smile. "Megan has wonderful taste, doesn't she?'' *In everything but her friends,* she wanted to add.

Melinda looked vaguely disappointed at the calm reaction, which made Molly feel a little better—though she was still wondering what had prompted the woman to attack. If it was that casually appraising look Luke had given her... Well, Melinda would have a full-time job if she set out to claw every woman Luke ever glanced at.

The pair moved across the room. Melinda coolly offered her cheek for Rand to kiss, and Luke actually let go of the golden girl long enough to take both of Megan's hands. Molly wondered if he saw the tension she'd noticed in Megan. Was that the slightest trace of a frown on his face as he looked at her?

Another couple arrived a few minutes later, but the last of the guests—a married couple and the single man who was obviously Molly's counterpart—were what she supposed was considered fashionably late. In her opinion, they were just plain rude to keep everyone waiting for more than half an hour.

Of course, she admitted, her judgment was probably affected by the fact that until their arrival she'd felt more like a fifth wheel than an important cog in Megan's dinner party. Or perhaps she was just a bit vexed at the evident disappointment felt by the single man when he realized there'd been a substitution in the guest list. She was almost relieved when Megan asked him to take the golden girl in to dinner, until she realized that left her sitting next to Luke.

By the time they were all seated at Megan's steel and glass dining table, Molly was already eager to call it an evening. She shook out her napkin and tried not to shudder at the sight of the first course.

Luke, beside her, said under his breath, ''You don't need to glare at me. I'm not going to pursue the subject of Bailey and her father.''

"That's a relief," Molly retorted. "But I wasn't glaring at you. Though you needn't take it as a compliment, on my list of unpleasant things, you aren't anywhere near as low as oysters on the half shell." She poked at the offending mollusks. "I'd rather read *Green Eggs and Ham* twenty-three times in a row than have to sit here and look at these."

"Relax, they won't last long. What *are* you doing here, anyway?"

"I thought Megan told you."

He nodded. "Catherine canceled, I know. And now that I've met the moon-faced gentleman sitting opposite us I think I can guess why. But—"

"I'm sure he's perfectly nice," Molly said automatically. "So if you mean you're just surprised that Megan was desperate enough to ask me to fill in—"

He winced. "I wouldn't have put it so crudely, Molly."

"It hardly matters, it's the truth. And don't ask me why she called, because I don't know." She hesitated, half-tempted to ask him what he thought of Megan's mood tonight. But before she could, the butler returned to remove the crystal oyster plates and replace them with bowls of steaming clear broth, and she thought better of the question.

Across the table, Melinda picked up her soup spoon and said, "Do you like being back in Duluth, Molly? It seems a strange choice. But then, I don't suppose someone in your position had a lot of options after your divorce."

If it hadn't been for the earlier remark about Megan's dress, Molly would probably have ignored the condescension in Melinda's voice. But she'd had just a little too much of the golden girl tonight, and before she could stop herself she'd let a faint note of sarcasm creep into her voice. "Now that you mention it, Melinda, crawling home and pleading for pity did seem the best of my options.''

Megan hastily broke in and changed the subject, and Molly picked up her soup spoon, noting with detached interest that her fingertips trembled only slightly. She saw, from the corner of her eye, that Luke was frowning. But of course she shouldn't be too surprised at that. She'd have to apologize to Megan, of course.

''If you wouldn't mind, Luke,'' she said softly, ''I'd appreciate it if you'd take Melinda out on the terrace after dinner—'' *and drop her in the lake* ''—and assure her that she can safely stop taking potshots because she doesn't have a thing to fear from me.''

''You know,'' Luke said thoughtfully, ''I'm not so sure I agree with you.''

For a moment Molly wasn't certain she'd heard him correctly, and her breath caught painfully in her throat. Could he mean that he truly thought Melinda had a reason to run scared of her? Of plain old Molly Matthews? If so, that could only mean that Luke really had been…intrigued by her, perhaps? Impressed? Attracted? Every nerve in her body tingled. She felt half-frightened, half-excited, as if without thought she'd embarked on a new and scary carnival ride and it was now too late to get off.

''If cattiness was a world-class poker game,'' he mused, ''I'd say you beat her pair of insults with a very nicely played humiliation.''

The electrical thrumming of her nerves died till only an occasional spark jerked through her body. How stupid could she be, assuming that he thought she was any real competition for the glamorous Melinda! Of course he didn't.

And why should you care what he thinks? she asked herself.

She hardly noticed the rest of the dinner. Courses came and went, and the conversation shifted from art to politics to people Molly had never met. Eventually, however, the butler served chocolate mousse and started to pour coffee, and Molly tried to smother a sigh of relief. Just a little longer, she told herself, and she could make her escape.

The maid who had greeted Molly at the door that afternoon came into the dining room and whispered something to the butler. He frowned and leaned over Luke's shoulder, and Molly heard him murmur, "A telephone call for you, sir. It seems to be quite important."

Luke pushed his chair back. He was almost clumsy in his haste. His chest brushed Molly's bare shoulder as he rose, sending a quiver of heat through her. "Excuse me, please."

The golden girl said, "What is it, Lucas? In the middle of a dinner party, I should think you—"

Luke shook his head and followed the maid from the room. When he came back a couple of minutes later, he looked pale, and foreboding clutched at Molly's heart.

"It's my father," he said. "He's had a relapse, and they're taking him to the hospital. I'm sorry, Megan, but I'll have to go."

"Good heavens, Luke," Megan said, "don't you dare apologize!" Her voice was low and almost shaky, and fondness stirred in Molly's heart. Perhaps inside that fragile shell there was still a woman worth knowing, after all.

"Someone will make sure Melinda gets home," Rand said. "There's no need for her to go now and miss out on chocolate mousse."

After all, the mousse is so much more important than Warren being ill, Molly thought. But of course Rand hadn't meant it that way. He'd just been trying to reassure Luke.

She felt half sick. What was it Warren had said this afternoon as she was saying goodbye? *I'm a bit too tired today to be flinging boxes around,* that was it. Had he been feeling ill and refused to admit it?

And what, exactly, did "relapse" mean? She supposed it could be anything from a feeling of weakness to another stroke.

And she wondered—and felt disloyal for even thinking about it, when Warren might be fighting for his life—where this would leave his beloved book project…and Molly herself.

Her own words came back to her in a haunted echo. *The book's not my job,* she'd told Luke. *Warren is.*

So what would happen now?

CHAPTER FOUR

MOLLY noticed that Melinda daintily spooned up every bit of her chocolate mousse, but the rest of them didn't have much appetite, and the party broke up not long after Luke left.

Molly fought a losing battle with her conscience and finally offered Melinda a ride. But the golden girl flashed a smile at Rand and said, "Oh, can't I have a run in your new Mercedes instead, Rand? And I'm sure Molly and Megan are longing to have a good chat—they seem to find so few chances to talk."

Molly bit her tongue till after they were gone. "No doubt she would have picked up some sort of infection from my car.... I'm really sorry I snapped at her over dinner, though."

Megan shrugged. "Don't worry. I've done it myself."

Then why do you have her around? Molly wanted to ask.

"Some women are just like that." Megan's voice was flat. "Needing all the masculine attention in the room and with no time at all for other women."

Molly felt alarmed at the lifeless tone. "You're exhausted. Can I help you up to bed? Maybe call the maid?"

Megan shook her head. "Just sit with me a while, will you?"

"Well, I can't stay long. I have to go to work tomorrow." Until she heard otherwise... No, that was defeatist thinking—assuming the worst. She'd just pretend Warren was vacationing for a few days, and she'd work like fury so she'd have something wonderful to show him when he got back.

Unless Luke told her not to bother.

"Just when I thought I could see a light at the end of the tunnel," Molly mused, "this happens."

"Funny you should put it that way." Megan let her head drop against the brocade chair. "I was thinking just about the same thing myself."

Molly sat very still, afraid that if she moved her sister might once more dance away from the subject.

With a short and entirely humorless laugh, Megan said, "I'm pregnant."

Molly was stunned. There was no joy in her sister's voice, no glow in her eyes, no wonder in her face. *This is supposed to be one of the good times,* she had said.

"Do you want to be?" Molly asked bluntly.

"I don't know." Megan didn't meet her eyes. "Do me a favor, all right? Don't tell Mother."

"You haven't told *Mother?*" The words were out before Molly could stop herself. "Sorry. Not my business." When the silence became unbearable, she moved from her chair to kneel next to Megan's. Her sister's hands were cold and almost limp. Molly held them between hers. "I know how it feels to be pregnant and scared. And I'm here for you, Meg. Anytime you want me."

Megan's eyes pooled with tears. "Even though I wasn't there for you?"

"That was a long time ago."

Megan wet her lips. "Thanks, Mol. I'll remember. I think I can sleep now."

Molly waited till Megan had climbed the stairs before she let herself out the front door and went to her car.

Megan pregnant. And drinking Scotch and soda. She'd had a glass in her hand most of the evening. Though it had been a full glass, Molly recalled, so maybe she'd only been holding it, not drinking. But surely Rand wouldn't have poured alcohol for her if…

Had she even told Rand yet? Even if she hadn't, Molly reminded herself, it didn't mean there was anything sinister going on. Maybe there hadn't been an opportunity. However, if Megan hadn't insisted on Molly coming early, she'd have had plenty of time before dinner tonight.

Maybe that was what was wrong, she thought—if there was a reason Megan didn't want to tell him. Maybe he didn't want a child. Or maybe it wasn't his child.

"And you," Molly told herself rudely, "could start writing for the soap operas any day!"

Well, she'd done all she could for now. She couldn't turn Megan upside down and shake her till the truth fell out, no matter how much she'd like to.

She took the long way home so she could drive down London Road past Warren Hudson's house. It would be more accurate to call Oakwood an estate, she supposed, for the property stretched over several acres and to the lakefront. The house lay well back from the street, sheltered by so many trees that she could barely see the gleam of moonlight on brick walls and tile roof. The windows were dark except for a couple of lights toward the back, where the servants' quarters were. It looked like a house at peace, settled down for the night, but Molly knew better. It was a house waiting, breath held, for news.

She tried not to remember the set, drained look on Luke's face when he'd gotten the news. She'd seen him looking like that once, on the night before his mother had died.

But the similarity of expression didn't mean, necessarily, that Warren was in grave danger—only that Luke was afraid. As of course he would be, getting the news like that. Perhaps, by the time he'd reached his father's side, the medical report had been better than he'd expected it would be.

Molly wished she knew which hospital they'd taken Warren to. Not that she'd rush straight over to console Luke, of course. It was hardly her place to do that, though the thought of him sitting there alone made her heart shiver.

Wasn't it a bit odd that the golden girl hadn't insisted on rushing out with him? Of course, the fact that they'd arrived at the party together didn't mean they were seriously involved. And though Melinda hadn't hesitated to show her claws the instant Luke paid attention to Molly, she hadn't seemed to mind at all when he'd departed so suddenly. Maybe Megan was right and the golden girl would have reacted the same way if it had been another man—Rand, even—instead of Luke who'd dared to notice Molly. And Luke hadn't apologized to Melinda for stranding her, just to Megan for breaking up the party.

It was a shame, actually, if they weren't involved—because Molly would find great humor in the idea of Luke being spellbound by a woman who saw him as no more than a convenient accessory. That sort of treatment would be no more than he deserved. There had been a time, after all, when Molly would have been thrilled to have even that much notice from Luke. Instead, he'd viewed her as a damned nuisance.

At the Matthews house, lights blazed from the living room where her parents were playing bridge with another couple. George and Jessie, Molly recalled. She'd met them last week. Or was it Jesse and Georgia?

Molly's father tossed down his cards when he saw her. "Now I know why I'm fighting off yawns," he said. "If Megan's party has already broken up, it's past time for my old bones to be in bed."

"But it's not all that late," Alix said. Her gaze focused suspiciously on Molly.

I didn't disgrace myself, Mother, and I wasn't asked to leave, she wanted to say. Instead, she told them the little she knew about Warren's setback.

Bernie shook his head. Molly got the impression he wasn't shocked or even startled—just sad. She wondered if she was the only one who'd been convinced Warren was getting better by the day.

"Anyway," she went on, "nobody felt much like celebrating, and Megan was tired, so we all left."

"I've never known Megan to be worn out," Jessie said. "The girl's inexhaustible. Of course, we could all keep going forever if we had Rand's resources to draw on."

Molly said carefully, "She seemed to have something on her mind." She wouldn't tell her mother about Megan's secret—but surely, if Alix had a hint that all wasn't well, she would be more alert to Megan's needs.

"Trouble with her hairdresser, I suppose," Jessie said with a laugh. "It couldn't be much more. With the tub of money she fell into, Megan's got nothing to worry about for the rest of her life." She played her last card triumphantly. "Not like you, Molly, dear. And poor little Bailey—losing her father like that."

Molly shot a look at her mother.

"Bad enough that your marriage didn't work out," Jessie went on, "but then for him to die like that so you're not even getting child support—"

Alix had turned pink. She swept up the deck of cards and said, "Another drink, anyone? Hot cider?"

Molly said, "Sounds great. I'll help you, Mom." In the kitchen, she glanced over her shoulder to be certain they were alone. "And what was *that* all about?"

Alix shrugged. "Darling, the man never visits his daughter, he doesn't help you with money… I have to explain your situation somehow."

"You don't have to explain anything," Molly said grimly. "But I know better than to think you'll stop—

so in the future will you at least warn me of the twists in the plot?''

Alix bit her lip.

"I'm going to check on Bailey,'' Molly announced. ''Tell your friends good-night for me, will you?''

She tiptoed into the smallest bedroom, the one she had occupied as a child. Bailey was sprawled on top of the blankets, her neck bent at an awkward angle, her face smashed firmly into her pillow. Molly straightened and covered her, and marveled at the way the child was growing. Though she'd always been small for her age, Bailey was obviously starting into a growth spurt. She'd need an entirely new wardrobe before long.

Molly rubbed her temples. It was all very well to tell herself not to borrow trouble. But she hadn't sought out tonight's whole truckload of worries, it had been dumped on her. As if Warren's relapse wasn't enough, there was Megan's pregnancy. And just to top things off, her mother had blithely killed off her inconvenient ex-husband.

Something had to give. Molly just hoped it wouldn't be her.

As she climbed the front steps of the Hudson mansion a couple of days later, Molly squared her shoulders and tried to fight off a sense of déjà vu.

This visit wasn't truly a repetition, of course. The other time she'd found herself standing on Oakwood's doorstep on a visit of sympathy, it had been a chilly, damp October evening. Luke's mother had still been fighting her futile battle against the virulent cancer that had killed her, and Molly had been sent to deliver a basket of flowers from her parents.

This time it was full daylight, though the sun was dropping rapidly and was no longer producing much warmth. She'd tucked a gaily wrapped compact disk under her arm, and Bailey was tugging impatiently at her hand.

"This is a *big* house. Will we go in? Can I ring the doorbell, Mommy?"

"Yes, you may ring the bell, and no, I don't think we'll be going inside." But the child couldn't reach high enough, so Molly lifted her so she could press the ornate button, then stooped to make one last hopeless effort to brush the streaks of dirt off the child's pastel jacket. "At least your face is clean," she muttered. "But of all the days for the day-care center to take a field trip to the zoo…"

The door opened behind Molly, and Bailey leaned to one side of her mother so she could peer into the house. For an instant, as if in a dream, time seemed to fold back on itself. Molly half expected to turn around and look up at Watkins the butler and see, as she had that night so long ago, that his usually impassive face was tight with worry.

The change in him that October night had startled her out of her planned speech. Instead of the pretty words telling how sad her parents were about Isabel Hudson's struggle, she'd heard herself say in little more than a whisper, "Is Luke here?"

Watkins had stared at her for a long moment and then said, "Yes, miss. He went out to the garden some time ago to be by himself." His voice steadied. "But I'm not sure he should be alone right now. I believe he's sitting in the treehouse."

The treehouse…

Molly wondered if it was still there, perched in the huge old maple tree halfway between the house and the lake. Surely not, after all these years without a child around to use it.

Though Luke hadn't been a child when his mother lay dying and he'd looked for solace there.

A deep voice, very unlike Watkins's, said, ''If you want to see my father—''

Luke. She hadn't expected him to be answering the door. Hastily Molly straightened and faced him. ''No, I didn't intend to disturb him on his first day at home— or you, either. I just stopped by on my way from work to drop off a little gift. Perhaps you'd give him this?'' She held out the small square package.

Luke showed no inclination to take it.

''You don't need to act as if it's poisonous,'' Molly said impatiently. ''In fact, unlike candy, it's nonfattening and cholesterol-free, and unlike flowers, it's guaranteed not to set off hay fever. And it's not even depressing— I chose the music very carefully. I'd think you'd realize I'm the last person who'd want to do Warren any harm just now.''

Luke rubbed a hand across the back of his neck. ''Sorry. It's been a long couple of days.'' He reached for the package.

Molly was instantly contrite. She knew perfectly well he hadn't set foot in the office since Warren's relapse, and she wouldn't be surprised to find that he hadn't left the hospital at all. ''And I'm sure the nights were longer yet,'' she said gently.

''I don't know. Time all blurred together somehow— sort of like it used to in med school.''

Bailey took a step toward Luke, dug a small hand into the back pocket of her blue jeans and held up a plastic rectangle, its edges sadly frayed. ''I still have my badge,'' she announced.

''It looks a bit the worse for wear,'' Luke said.

''That's 'cause Joey took it at day care. The teacher made him give it back, but he bent it all up. He's mean sometimes.''

''Bailey, don't pester Mr. Hudson. He's very tired just now.''

Bailey studied him, her tiny nose wrinkled thoughtfully. "Then you have to take a nap."

"Life's so simple when you're not quite four," Molly said. "But it's not bad advice, anyway."

Luke smiled slowly. "Thanks, Molly. I'll give this to Dad and tell him—"

From the dim hallway behind him, Warren said, "You'll tell Dad what?" He came into view, moving slowly, leaning on a walker. "Hello, Molly. Did Lucas tell you I wanted to talk to you?"

She flashed a glance at Luke. He looked a little guilty, she thought as he stood aside for her to enter. But she couldn't exactly blame him—Warren looked like a pale shadow of the man he'd been just a few days ago, and hardly up to having visitors.

As she stepped across the threshold into Oakwood, Molly automatically reached for Bailey's hand. But the child slipped away from her and moved three steps into the hallway, with its parquet floor and linen-fold paneling, where she stood stockstill and stared up the long, wide, straight, golden oak staircase to the first landing, almost as large as a room. Her eyes had gone wide. Molly wasn't surprised. Lots of people had that sort of reaction to this house.

Certain that Bailey was too awed to move, she turned her attention once more to Warren. "You know," she said mildly, "if all you wanted to do is talk to me, it really wasn't necessary to create all this fuss. You could have just asked me to stick around and chat the other day."

Warren smiled weakly—about all the reaction the feeble joke was worth, Molly admitted—and sank down on the bench at the foot of the stairs. "Pardon me, but I think I'd better rest a bit before I go up."

Molly was horrified. "You aren't going to try to walk up, are you?"

"No, I'll just go as far as the elevator, for today."

Bailey had slowly turned a full circle, inspecting the hallway. Now she focused on Warren's walker. "What's that, Mommy?"

"It's to help Mr. Hudson get around the house, dear."

Bailey frowned. "Why did you call him Mr. Hudson?"

"Because that's his name." Molly saw the child's puzzled gaze shift from Warren to Luke, and added hastily, "Both of them are Mr. Hudson."

Bailey obviously thought that made no sense at all, but she politely turned her attention to the walker. "Did you break your leg?" she asked earnestly. "When my mommy fell down the stairs and broke her leg she used crutches."

Warren shook his head. "I'm sick in a different way, but it's still hard for me to walk."

"When I'm sick," Bailey confided, "I have to stay in bed."

Molly's patience had vanished. "Bailey, I don't think your contributions to the conversation are quite—"

Through a door at the shadowed back of the hall came a large dog, her red-gold coat gleaming, her head up, nose twitching, toenails clicking against the parquet floor. She trotted straight to Bailey and sniffed at the child's face, almost on the level with her own.

Bailey giggled and threw her arms around the dog's neck.

Before Molly could move, Luke had caught the animal's collar. "Lucky's pretty much kid-proof," he said, "but just in case…"

The dog swiped her tongue across Bailey's face, and the child shrieked with laughter.

Molly thought she saw the shadow of pain cross Warren's face at the noise. "I'm sorry," she said. "If you want to talk to me, Warren, I can stop in the morning after I've taken Bailey to day care. I shouldn't have brought her with me today."

Warren shook his head, but she thought it was no more than a polite protest.

Luke obviously thought so, too, for he released the dog's collar and stood up. "Bailey, let's take Lucky out for a bit. I'll show you how to make her do tricks."

As the door swung shut behind the trio, Molly said, "So much for asking permission." She sat beside Warren. "So what do the doctors say?"

"Just that I've been overdoing it."

"It wasn't another stroke, then?"

Warren shook his head. "My blood pressure went way up the other night, till they thought I was likely to have one. Then it dropped to the vanishing point, and that didn't make them happy, either. Damned doctors," he grumbled. "You can't please them no matter what you do."

Molly smothered a smile. "It isn't fair of them to keep changing the rules, is it?"

"So they tell me I have to slow down, and nobody has any idea how long it'll be before I can do anything productive again. If ever." His voice was heavy, almost lifeless. Then he cleared his throat and said with determination, "But the project must go on. You'll have to handle it by yourself, of course, but I want you to know that I have complete faith—"

The project must go on. *Fat chance of that,* Molly thought. As soon as Luke realized that his father couldn't be involved any more...

But it had been Warren's mental state Luke had seemed most interested in, not the physical work he'd been doing. And Warren was obviously still interested, so surely he could still play some part in the whole process.

It was not, however, the possibility of preserving her job which prompted her to say, "It wouldn't be the same without you. I need you to bounce ideas off, and to give me background and context. Could you spare energy for that if I stopped by now and then to show you the pieces I'm working on?''

A faint light sprang to life in Warren's eyes, but he shook his head. ''It'd be a lot of trouble for you—driving back and forth, dragging things over here.''

As a matter of fact, Molly admitted to herself, it would be a bit of a pain. But she'd put up with a lot more inconvenience than that if it would help Warren. ''It wouldn't even be out of my way. I could just stop by on my way home from work.''

With Bailey in tow? Hardly.

But, she reminded herself, the whole reason for working at the plant had been Warren. Now she could be much more flexible.

He seemed to have read her mind. ''Maybe you could work here instead. There's plenty of room. We could have all the archives moved, and set up a little office for you—''

And why not? Molly asked herself. Of course Warren's doctors didn't want him to overdo, but she suspected it wasn't the work that had exhausted him but the way he'd gone about it. She could see it as she looked over the week they'd worked together. He'd only missed lunch that one time—but though he'd never said so, Warren had obviously felt that if he'd gone to the effort to get dressed and have Jason drive him across Duluth to the plant he should stay half a day, at least.

But if she moved a minimal office into Oakwood, Warren could work precisely when he felt like it, in ten-minute stretches if he wanted. He wouldn't even have to get out of bed.

''I'll talk to Luke about the idea,'' she said.

Warren snorted. ''What's it got to do with him? This isn't Luke's house, it's still mine—and I can do what I please with it. Besides, you're working for me, so what's it to him where you put your desk? I'll expect you in

the morning.'' He pushed himself up from the bench.
''Watkins!''

The butler appeared silently. ''Yes, sir?''

''Help me up to my room, will you? And that small
bedroom next to mine—I want you to put a desk in
there, and a couple of tables.''

His voice faded as he trudged down the hallway.
Molly watched as the butler opened what appeared to be
a closet door and helped Warren step inside. A moment
later the elevator's whir emphasized that she'd been dismissed.

She shook her head and turned toward the back of the
house, the direction she figured Luke and Bailey and the
dog had gone.

The hallway led past a well-equipped butler's pantry
and into the kitchen where a woman with rosy, plump
cheeks was cleaning vegetables.

''Sorry to intrude,'' Molly said. ''But I'm looking for
my little girl, and I thought perhaps…''

''They went on out to the garden,'' the cook said.

The words echoed faintly in Molly's mind. *He went
out to the garden to be by himself,* Watkins had told her
on that long-ago night. And today, tired and worn, Luke
would probably have enjoyed the same sort of solitude.
Instead, she'd unintentionally saddled him with an active
three-year-old. ''Thanks,'' she said, and hurried to the
back door.

From the narrow porch she could hear Bailey, and she
followed the sound of high-pitched giggles through the
garden, where crocus and daffodils were just coming to
life, and down a winding path toward the lake.

She found Luke sitting on a wrought-iron bench at the
farthest corner of the formal garden, where between the
trees she could just catch the glimmer of water.

Bailey knelt nearby, her arms around the dog's neck.
''I like the lake,'' she announced as Molly came within
earshot. ''Can I go down by the water?''

"Not today," Luke said. "I might take you sometime, though."

"Not even if Lucky goes?"

Luke didn't answer. He started to rise when he saw Molly, but she shook her head and he sank onto the bench.

The dog pulled free and edged in front of Bailey, eyes intent on Molly.

"Lucky," Luke warned. "You don't need to protect the kid from her mother, so knock it off."

Molly sat next to him. "I see they've become the best of buddies."

Lucky settled onto her haunches, knocking Bailey off balance. The child sat down hard and rolled onto her back. "What's that?" she asked, pointing into a big tree beyond the edge of the formal garden.

Luke didn't even turn his head. "A treehouse," he said.

Molly's throat tightened. Despite her best intentions of ignoring the treehouse, the reminder made her look up.

The treehouse was no rustic boys' hideaway slapped together from odd boards. It was an actual tiny cabin, which happened to be located twenty feet above the ground in the spreading branches of an ancient maple. The dark green paint was chipping, and the windows looked as if they hadn't been cleaned in years. But the door was solid, the shingles all in place, the glass unbroken—so she was certain the inside would still be dry. Dusty, perhaps, and cold from long disuse, and smelling a bit stale...

Just as it had been that October night when she'd found Luke sitting there, staring at nothing.

Bailey was still sprawled on her back staring at the tree. "Who lives up there?"

"Nobody," Luke said.

"Why not?"

"Stop pestering, Bailey. Mr. Hudson's very tired."

"His name's Luke," Bailey informed her. "He told me so."

Molly asked, "You don't mind if she calls you that?" But she forgot her question as she took her first really good look at Luke. In the shadow of the front portico, in the dimness of the house, he'd looked tired. But now, in the sunlight, she could see that his eyes were red-rimmed and his face was haggard. "This is ridiculous," she said. "We're going home, and you're going to rest. In fact, come to think of it…have you bothered to eat?"

Luke rubbed a hand over his jaw. "Not lately, that I remember."

"At least we can do something about that. Don't move, I'll be right back. Bailey, come with me. You can charm the cook, and Mr. Hudson—Luke—doesn't need to look after you any more."

Lucky protested the abrupt loss of her playmate and only settled after a stern word from Luke.

A few minutes later, when they returned with a basket, Luke had leaned his head against the back of the bench and closed his eyes. *Sound asleep,* Molly thought, but it was too late to hush Bailey. She broke free and raced down the path, calling, "Treats! We brought treats!"

Luke opened his eyes. "Judging from the size of that basket, Molly, I'd say you were right about her being able to con the cook."

"I said charm, not con." Molly dug into the basket. "A cookie for Bailey—"

Bailey grinned and tried to hold the enormous round of chocolate-chip cookie safely above the dog's head.

Molly added hastily, "And a rawhide chew for Lucky." She tossed it to the dog and sat on the bench once more, the basket between her and Luke. "And the rest is for you. The cook was a bit defensive—she said she'd tried twice since you came home to feed you. So

I think you'd better eat every crumb if you expect her to speak to you ever again.''

He picked up a foil-wrapped sandwich. ''You seem to always be taking care of me, Molly. Not always the same way, but—''

Molly tried to will herself not to tense, but the effort was in vain. She stared straight ahead, but she wasn't seeing Oakwood's gardens but the inside of that cold, silent treehouse on a chilly night in October. The night she had asked Luke to make love to her.

He pressed two fingers to the center of his forehead. ''I'm sorry. That was…''

She forced herself to smile. ''You're worn out.''

''I'm a clumsy fool. But since the subject's been raised—and since you're all grown up now and obviously over that crush you had on me—''

''No question about that,'' Molly said crisply.

''I might as well confess that sending you away that night was one of the tougher things I've ever done.''

''Really? You sounded as if you enjoyed telling me to get lost.''

''I had to—or I couldn't have managed to pull it off. If you'd stayed another minute—''

Another minute, Molly thought, *and my life would be completely different today.*

His voice was little more than a whisper. ''You were so very, very sweet that night.…''

She knew he'd leaned closer, but she kept her gaze fixed on Bailey, who was quietly feeding the crumbs of her cookie to the dog. His fingertips came to rest on the nape of her neck, four small spots, which functioned like electrical connections, sending jolts of current through her skin, urging her to turn her head to look at him.

She closed her eyes and fixed her will on denying that impulse. The man was exhausted, she told herself. He hardly knew what he was saying, and as for kissing her…she knew very well they'd both regret that.

But why? a little voice whispered deep in her mind. *What's such a big deal about a kiss of gratitude? You're over him. You've been done with that stupid crush for years. He just wants to thank you....*

Luke's lips brushed the line of her jaw, precisely on the faded spot where the bruise had been. "So sweet," he whispered again, and raised his other hand to her chin and turned her face toward his.

She stared into his eyes, far darker than their usual hazel tones, and tried to tell herself that there would be nothing remarkable about this kiss. It was just a different way to say thanks....

She didn't remember moving, but an instant later she was standing on the path in front of the bench, holding out a hand to Bailey. "Come on, honey, and say good-bye to the dog. We need to get home."

"Running away?" Luke asked. His voice was low, almost husky.

Molly didn't look at him. "Avoiding unpleasantness."

But she knew she wasn't telling the truth. She had pulled away not because she expected his kiss to be distasteful—but because she hadn't wanted him to kiss her in gratitude.

And she also knew that if he had, she wouldn't have wanted him to stop.

CHAPTER FIVE

As THE butler set a steaming waffle before him and re-filled his coffee cup, Luke folded the newspaper and laid it aside. "Is my father awake yet, Watkins?"

"Yes, sir. He's having breakfast in his room, though. He said something about reserving his energy for later, when he might need it."

Luke frowned as he cut into the waffle. Warren was taking it easy, looking after himself—exactly as he should. *So why do I have such a negative feeling about it?*

And what did he mean, reserving energy in case he needed it later? It was perfectly fine to be cautious, but if Warren started treating himself like spun sugar candy...

That, Luke thought gloomily, was just about where the trouble had started before, right after the stroke. Uncertain of what he could safely do in the present, Warren had retreated to the past. But the cure Luke thought he'd found for that particular difficulty had turned out to be almost as bad as the problem. Now he not only had his father's frail health to be concerned about, but he was stuck with an expensive project to record the company's history....

Though in fact he *wasn't* boxed in. He could call a halt any time, for there'd been no contract signed between Molly Matthews and Meditronics.

Major oversight on her part, Luke thought, *not to insist on one.* Or perhaps it was just one more indication of how badly she'd needed this job...

Maybe Molly would have some insights on handling

73

Warren. He'd ask her as soon as he got to work. Not that there was any point in hurrying to the plant. He was already setting an all-time record for lateness after his first sleep in longer than he cared to think about. So he might as well enjoy his breakfast.

Automatically, he cut another bite from his waffle.

Molly. She'd been so gentle with Warren yesterday. Without minimizing the severity of his illness, she'd still managed to encourage him to find humor in the situation. And she'd been concerned about Luke, as well—distressed by his lack of sleep, worried about whether he ate.

Right up to the moment when, in response to that warmth, he'd tried to kiss her. Just a simple kiss, the sort of thing every other woman he knew exchanged at the drop of a greeting—but Molly had flash frozen.

Why hadn't she let him kiss her? She'd wanted to—he couldn't be wrong about that. When he'd first turned her face toward him, her eyes had been great dark pools flooded with desire. And then, within a millisecond, instead of a warm and willing woman, there'd been an iceberg in his arms. Or, rather, *not* in his arms. He still wasn't quite sure how she'd slipped away. Of course, he hadn't been holding her so tightly that she couldn't move. That had never been Luke's style. But his reflexes should have been fast enough to counter whatever it was that had so suddenly changed her mind and at least try to change it back.

The part that really annoyed him, he concluded, was not knowing what had caused that sudden transformation.

Nothing he'd done, that was sure. She hadn't shied from his touch. She'd known perfectly well he intended to kiss her, and at first she'd been more than willing. So what might she have seen, or thought, or remembered, which had prompted her behavior?

The fact that her daughter was there? Possible, he

thought, but not very likely. The child must have seen casual kisses before—and maybe not-so-casual ones, too.

And surely that sudden freeze hadn't been caused by a stray feeling of loyalty to the ex-husband, either. That marriage had obviously been over with long ago, so long that there wasn't even a hint of an indentation at the base of Molly's finger where a wedding ring would have rested. After so much time…

Wait a minute, he thought. If she'd been divorced long enough for all traces of a ring to vanish, who had put that bruise on her jaw just a couple of weeks ago?

But a divorce didn't put the ex-husband out of the running entirely, he realized. There would still have to be contact when there was a child involved. If the ex had come to see Bailey and gotten angry at her mother…

If he ever tries it again, he thought grimly, *I hope I'm there to make sure he finds out what it feels like to get a solid fist in his face.*

Whatever had happened between her parents, though, it hadn't seemed to leave a mark on Bailey. Molly was doing a good job there. He couldn't remember seeing a child take more pleasure in simple things than Bailey had yesterday, romping with Lucky, sharing her cookie, giggling in delight. She'd even given him an unprompted hug to say goodbye—a gesture of affection that had touched his heart—while her mother had refused even to look him in the eye because he'd tried to steal a kiss.

Which pretty much brought him right back to where he'd started. Except that now his waffle was cold.

He noted the sound of the doorbell, but when a moment later Watkins's footsteps sounded on the parquet floor of the hall he dismissed it from his mind. Another delivery of flowers, no doubt—it was a bit early for any of Warren's friends to be stopping by to visit.

It was only when he heard the muted sound of a feminine voice in the hall that he paid attention. At first he thought it was Megan Bannister, but Megan's husky tones were the product of years of practice. This voice was softer and even more sultry—and he'd bet his next set of stock options that its owner had no idea how sexy it was. But what was Molly doing here in the middle of the morning?

He didn't make a conscious decision to push his plate aside and investigate. He was in the hallway before he realized he'd moved.

She was just inside the front door, handing a brown suede jacket to Watkins. She certainly didn't dress like a woman in need of a job, Luke thought. No jeans today—which was something of a pity, actually. When a woman had legs as long and slim as Molly's were... Of course, she looked good in that narrow silky skirt, too, even though it covered up more than he'd like.

She stooped to retrieve her briefcase and spoke to the butler. "There are some boxes in my car. I'd appreciate it if someone could bring them in."

Luke stepped forward. "Thank you, Watkins. That's all."

He saw the instant flare of fear in Molly's eyes, and annoyance washed over him. What was the matter with the woman? It had only been a kiss, and he could take a hint. After the message he'd gotten yesterday, he was hardly likely to throw her on the floor and...what was that wonderful Victorian phrase? Oh, yes, have his way with her.

Even if the idea did sound inviting.

The door of the butler's pantry shut behind Watkins, and Luke said, "Boxes? What are you doing, moving in?"

"Didn't your father tell you?"

No wonder, he thought, that Warren was still in bed this morning, reserving his strength! "There wasn't much time," he admitted. "We were both pretty busy sleeping last night."

"I'm sorry, because I meant to tell you yesterday. What Warren and I talked about, I mean."

"I can't imagine," he drawled, "what would have made you forget."

She turned a delicious shade of pink. At least, Luke thought, fear wasn't the only emotion in her mind when she recalled that aborted kiss. He remembered the instant yesterday when she'd been looking forward to his caress, and he wondered how difficult it would be to make her look at him that way again.

"I've been to the plant this morning," she said, "and I brought a couple of boxes over to work on here."

"Determined, aren't you?"

"To keep my word, yes. Look, it wasn't my idea to move my office over here, but what difference does it make where I work?"

"Oh, it's just the *office* you're moving," he murmured.

"You can't honestly think Warren suggested I *live* here?"

"The place does have its advantages. Tennis court, swimming pool, full-time staff…"

"Well, he didn't. And since I intended in the first place to do the bulk of my work at home, what's the big deal about bringing it here? That way Warren can be as involved as he wants, do what he's able to and still get all the rest he needs."

Despite the way she'd raised her chin the fraction of an inch, Luke thought he could hear the slightest trace of a quaver in her voice. "I'm not going to argue with you about it, Molly." He took a step closer and realized that her lower lip was trembling slightly.

"Does that mean you've already made up your mind? Even with this setback, Warren hasn't given up. Why should you be in a hurry to sacrifice the whole idea?"

"Who said I was giving up?"

She hesitated. "Then I still have a job?"

Luke nodded. He watched the sleek line of her throat and saw the convulsive ripple of muscles as she swallowed hard.

And he wondered if that meant she was relieved, or if she understood he hadn't just been talking about her job.

Now that it was far too late, Molly knew she should have just let him kiss her in the garden yesterday, because that would have been the end of it. One quick, simple kiss. But no—she'd had to make a challenge out of it, and now his interest was piqued. Or at least he wanted her to think it was, just for the fun of keeping her off balance. Either way, she'd have to watch her step more closely than before.

She watched as he strolled across the hallway and went out the front door without a backward glance, and she released a tiny sigh of relief as the latch clicked. With any luck, she wouldn't catch another glimpse of him all day.

She looked up the long staircase with a frown. She could hardly start by wandering around upstairs looking from room to room for an office that might not even be set up yet.

A soft voice pulled her attention to the main floor, to a small woman dressed in black who had quietly approached. "Miss Matthews? I'm Hilda Ekberg, the housekeeper. Mr. Warren asked me to show you upstairs and to get you anything you might want."

Molly smiled. "He might regret giving me quite so much latitude."

The housekeeper's gaze was unexpectedly shrewd. Molly felt almost as if she was being turned inside out for inspection. "Oh, I'm sure he knows exactly what he's doing." She led the way up the long stairs and turned toward the back of the house.

"He mentioned the bedroom next to his," Molly said.

"I'll do my best to be quiet, of course, but if there's any chance that I'd disturb him—"

"With the way this house is built, if you set off a cherry bomb in that room he probably wouldn't hear it next door. It's supposed to be a sitting room for the master suite, actually." Mrs. Ekberg pushed open an arched door and stood back for Molly to enter. "It was turned into a bedroom for Mr. Warren at the time of Mrs. Hudson's last illness, and he's never bothered to put it back as it was."

Molly wondered why the words sounded almost like a warning—until she stepped across the threshold.

Every room had an identity entirely its own, she'd always thought, a character that was built into the structure. It could be influenced by the furnishings and the decorating scheme, but not completely changed. Some rooms were feminine. Some were brisk, some relaxing, some peaceful.

This one, she thought, had a multiple-personality disorder.

The carpet was moss green, thick and plush. The hangings on the tall French doors that looked onto a tiny balcony and the gardens below were pale pink satin, elegantly draped. The small fireplace was topped with a white marble mantel. The chandelier was a dainty creation of Austrian crystal.

But the furniture that should have been scattered around the room—except for one gilt chair with a velvet-covered seat—was nowhere to be seen. Instead, at one side of the room was a hospital bed with a metal frame and not even a basic headboard—one of Meditronics' older models, Molly knew from her study of the company's catalogs. The blankets were tucked in neatly and the pillows plumped, but there was no bedspread and not even a night table.

Nearby was a tubular metal laundry rack, which had obviously served as a makeshift closet. There were still a couple of shirts hanging on it. A very masculine—and very worn—brown leather recliner stood in a corner next to a reading lamp.

In front of the windows, nearly blocking the view, was a huge old desk, its battered top almost as big as the bed. The gilt chair standing next to it looked as delicate in comparison as if it was built of toothpicks. Close by were the boxes Molly had brought that morning. *Watkins is even more efficient than I thought,* she concluded. He must have spirited them up the back stairs while she'd been talking to Luke.

"Every time I ask Mr. Warren if he doesn't want the room straightened out and that awful bed sent back to the attic," the housekeeper said, "he tells me just to leave it alone."

"Next time," Molly recommended, "don't ask."

Mrs. Ekberg smiled. "I'll keep that in mind. I'm sure it's not the kind of surroundings you're used to—"

"You can say that again. I've never had an office with a chandelier." Molly walked to the desk.

"I thought perhaps new draperies—"

"Heavens, no." She could almost hear what Luke would say if she started to redecorate.

Mrs. Ekberg looked disappointed. "But these are terribly faded."

"That doesn't mean it's my privilege to replace them."

"Very well, miss. If there's anything you want, just let Watkins or me know."

Molly lifted the lid off a box. "Some coffee in an hour?"

"And leave you alone till then?" There was an apologetic twinkle in the housekeeper's eyes. "Of course, miss. It's been a very long time, you see, since there's been a lady in the house. I've almost forgotten how to behave."

She left Molly shaking her head in confusion. There

hadn't been anything improper or impolite about Mrs. Ekberg's actions, but she'd sounded almost as if Molly was Oakwood's new mistress, not a temporary worker. *New draperies…anything you want…*

She shook her head at her own nonsense and went to work. Mrs. Ekberg had been friendly—that was all. The rest was entirely her imagination.

Warren appeared nearly an hour later, almost simultaneously with the coffee, wrapped in a dark red watered-silk dressing gown. The sheer splendor made Molly wonder how the same man who chose such an exotic fabric could ignore the confused state of the sitting room for years on end. But perhaps he hadn't bought the robe himself, she concluded. It looked like the sort of thing that might have been a Christmas gift.

He looked shamefaced. "I dropped off to sleep again after my breakfast," he admitted.

"Nothing wrong with that—but I'm awfully glad you're here now. Look at the letter I've just found. The handwriting alone is a treasure, but I don't have a hint what it means." She passed the pages across the desk and delighted in the sparkle that sprang to life in Warren's eyes. He looked better today, she thought. And though he'd leaned on the furniture as he crossed the room, he wasn't using the walker.

After lunch, Warren retired for another nap, and it was late afternoon before he reappeared. Molly had started a small pile of documents for his inspection, but instead of picking up the first one he looked at her and frowned. "Is it my imagination, or is it awfully quiet around here? And the dog's lying under my chair. Why isn't she out playing with your little girl?"

"Bailey? She's at the plant—in the day-care center."

"You took her all the way down there?"

"I had to pick up these boxes anyway."

"But now you'll have to drive across town to pick her up. That's ridiculous."

"Well, I can't bring her here."

Warren scowled. "Why not?"

"I hardly think she belongs at—"

"I insist."

Molly leaned back in her chair—neither the gilt and velvet one nor the recliner, but a small armchair she'd discovered downstairs. "Autocratic old soul, aren't you?" she said politely.

Warren smiled. "I figure there have to be some privileges to age and illness."

"Among them having your every request treated as a command?"

"That would be a good start, don't you think?"

"Why am I so certain that wasn't really a question?"

"Then you'll bring her?"

"I'll think about it." Molly glanced at her wristwatch. The timing, she thought, couldn't have been worse. She set a stapler atop the documents she was working on to serve as a paperweight and stood up. "I have to go and get her now, I'm afraid. The center closes in half an hour."

His brows drew together. "That proves my point. I'm feeling refreshed and ready to work, and you're leaving."

Molly waggled a finger at him. "You don't fight fair."

"Of course I don't. Now are you going to bring her? There are always at least three adults in this house, any one of whom is capable of keeping an eye on a small child."

"And I'm sure they'll be delighted to have babysitting added to their duties." She walked around the desk to stand beside Warren. "But it's sweet of you, it really is." Impulsively, she leaned over him and pressed a kiss on his forehead.

A voice from the doorway said, "There's your mommy."

Molly jerked upright so fast she almost lost her balance. She had no doubt, from the coolness in Luke's eyes, that he'd seen just enough to make him think the very worst. A minute earlier and he'd have seen the whole episode and known it for the innocent gesture it was. A minute later and he'd have seen nothing at all.

Her whole history with Luke, she thought irritably, seemed to come down to a matter of minutes.

Bailey came running, waving a sheet of blue construction paper. "Look what I made in day care, Mommy!"

She took the collage Bailey held out, but she looked from the child—who'd flung herself down beside the dog—to Luke instead. "Thank you for picking her up. But—"

He shrugged. "I was driving past the center on my way home, and it seemed a waste for you to have to go all the way back."

"It was very thoughtful of you," Molly said. "But the people at the center aren't supposed to let Bailey go with just anyone."

Warren made a sound that resembled a strangled sneeze.

Molly caught herself. "I mean—of course you're not just anyone, you're the boss. But still…"

"They're on the lookout for her father, I suppose you mean? Well, since it's pretty apparent I'm not him, the director didn't have any problem with me checking her out. And Bailey didn't, either. But if you do—"

Molly swallowed hard. "Of course not."

"Well, now," Warren said smoothly. "Since you don't have to make the trek down to the plant after all, Molly, let's settle down and get some work done. Lucas won't mind watching out for little Miss B, I'm sure. After all, he volunteered. Didn't you, my boy?"

Molly's jaw dropped. Luke was obviously speechless.

Warren sat back in his chair and smiled.

* * *

Molly tucked in fresh sheets on the bed in the Matthews's guest room while her printer spit out the last few pages of the chapter she'd finished that morning. She glanced over them and dropped the bundle into her briefcase. This afternoon—in just a few minutes—she'd take it to Oakwood for Warren to critique.

She leaned out the kitchen door and called to Bailey, who was lining up her agate collection on the deck railing, just as Megan's dark red BMW pulled into the driveway.

Molly's heart gave a jolt. She shooed Bailey off to wash her hands and went to meet her sister.

She hadn't seen Megan since the night of the dinner party, and their few phone conversations had been brief and light, mostly over details of the anniversary celebration, less than two weeks away. She'd let Megan set the pace in those conversations, and the subject of her pregnancy hadn't come up again. Molly had concluded, finally, that her sister had come to regret her impulsive outburst and was pretending the whole conversation had never happened.

Of course, it was Megan's choice. If she wanted to play her hand alone, that was her right. *You didn't like it when people tried to interfere and tell you what to do,* Molly reminded herself. And she definitely had no right to instruct her sister.

''Come on in,'' she said as Megan stepped onto the deck. ''Mother's gone out to her card club, and I'll have to leave in a few minutes, but I think there's still some coffee.''

''Oh—I forgot this was her club day.'' Megan tugged off her sunglasses and rubbed the bridge of her nose. ''I didn't expect you to be here. I thought you were working down at Oakwood.''

''That's where I'm headed. We've gotten into a sort of routine. Bailey's enrolled in the preschool down the street, so I work here till she gets home, and—''

But she wasn't thinking about the pattern of her days but about how pale Megan looked. In the week since the dinner party, she'd turned into a ghostly wraith with faint blue shadows under her eyes, despite the expert hand that had applied her makeup. To say nothing of the fact that she didn't seem to remember what day it was.

Megan sat at the kitchen table. ''Do you like it? Oakwood, I mean?''

It was a throwaway question, Molly thought, asked more to keep the conversation going than because Megan really wanted to know. ''Who wouldn't like it? I work here every morning, so Warren can be as lazy as he likes. Then we go to Oakwood in the afternoons.'' She glanced at the clock. ''Bailey, it's time to get your things together. Are you going to take your dolls today, or the building blocks?''

''You take her with you?'' Megan sounded incredulous.

Molly didn't blame her. ''Warren insists. Just as he insists I come in time for lunch every day so we can talk over the progress we're making. I think he's just lonely, but—''

''So what do you do with the kid? I can't quite see her in that elegant dining room.''

''You'd be surprised,'' Molly said dryly. ''But usually she entertains the cook by playing with her food in the kitchen. Then she spends the rest of the time coloring, taking a nap, romping with the dog, fixing treats and exploring Oakwood—which the staff encourages her to regard as her private playhouse.''

Megan shivered.

''I know—all those lovely breakable things. I walked into the drawing room one day last week and found her having a pretend tea party with Mrs. Ekberg—using the Haviland china. And when I nearly had a heart attack and asked Mrs. Ekberg not to let Bailey have quite so much freedom, she looked at me blankly and said that the child was being very careful and she wasn't hurting anything. And she *is* careful and she *hasn't* hurt anything, so…''

Megan didn't seem to be listening.

''But at least there haven't been any more tea parties.'' Molly asked bluntly, ''Meg, are you all right? I mean—have you decided what to do about the baby?''

''What is there to do? Pregnancy's pretty much a one-way ticket, wouldn't you say?''

Relief percolated through Molly's veins. ''Absolutely, it is. But you don't have to take the flight alone.''

''I know. I just… I'm not ready to talk about it.''

Molly was sure that wasn't what Megan had started to say.

''Actually, I'm glad to catch you,'' Megan went on brightly. ''Would you ask Mrs. Ekberg if we can borrow a dozen small tables and about fifty chairs from Oakwood for Mother and Dad's anniversary party? I can rent them, of course, but the ones at Oakwood are so much nicer.''

''I'll ask today and let you know. Anything else I can do? I feel like a dead weight where this party's concerned, you know—especially now that you're not feeling well.''

Megan shook her head. ''I think it's all under control, and you have plenty to do, anyway. But I wondered… Well, there's a Waterford crystal bowl I know Mother would like as an anniversary gift. Should we go together to buy it?''

''Depends on how pricey it is.''

''It's pretty high,'' Megan said frankly. ''But I didn't mean we should go halves. I know you're on a tight budget these days.''

And you also know what it'll look like if Megan gives crystal and Molly can only afford plain glass.…

She didn't think Megan was acting out of snobbishness, however, but genuine concern for her—so Molly swallowed her pride. "Sure. It'd be great. But I'll pay my half—I just probably can't do it all at once."

Megan waved a hand. "Take your time. I'll go pick it up this afternoon."

Bailey came down the hall pushing a doll stroller piled with building blocks.

"That's quite the combination," Megan murmured.

Molly watched her sister's face and tried to decipher the emotions that played across it. Fear, she thought, was the principal one. "Being responsible for a child isn't as overwhelming as it looks," she said. "You and Rand will soon get used to it. When they put your own baby in your arms…" Megan didn't answer, but Molly saw the gleam of tears in her eyes, and she added quickly, "I'm sorry. I didn't mean to upset you."

Megan touched a tissue to her eyelids. "I know." She jumped up. "I've got to meet someone, and you need to get to work. Drop by tonight and take a look at the bowl if you like, before I wrap it. Rand's got some business thing, so it'll just be me." Her gaze came to rest on Bailey, waiting impatiently by the door. "Bailey can come, too, if she likes."

The invitation was surprisingly awkward from a woman of Megan's sophistication, but Molly was touched, for it was the first time Megan had indicated any real interest in the child.

She'll be all right, Molly told herself. *Megan will come around. And she'll be a good mom.*

By the time she filled her briefcase and touched up her lipstick, she was a good ten minutes behind Megan. But traffic was light for a change, and the day was perfect—so beautiful that if her car had been a convertible she'd have been tempted to put the top down. The move would be sheer foolishness, of course, since brilliant sunshine hardly corresponded with warmth. But she saw, as she stopped for a red light, that the drive-in ice cream shop on the corner was not only open, but there were a few cars around the building.

Bailey saw it, too. "I want ice cream," she announced.

"Another time. We're going to have lunch right now."

"But Luke's there."

Highly doubtful, Molly thought, until she noticed the black Jaguar tucked into a corner of the parking lot. There couldn't be many of those around Duluth. This one was half hidden by the building. *Bailey obviously doesn't need her vision tested,* she thought, *if she spotted that.*

Then she saw Luke. He was standing with his back to the street, but those broad shoulders and trim hips were unmistakable. As was the car he was standing next to—a dark red BMW with a woman behind the wheel.

I've got to meet someone, Megan had said. But... Luke?

And why shouldn't it be Luke? Molly asked herself. They'd been friends for years and years.

So why are they meeting at an obscure ice cream shop? asked a suspicious little voice in the back of her brain. *It's hardly Megan's sort of place.*

The light changed, and Molly drove almost automatically toward Oakwood. Was Megan turning to Luke for comfort and support? Why him and not her husband? Or was Luke the reason Megan was so plainly unhappy? Was it possible he was the father of the child Megan was carrying?

Molly felt sick.

Despite all the delays, she was still a few minutes early when she parked her car beside Oakwood and lifted out both Bailey and the stroller full of toys. "Let's walk in the garden for a minute before we go in," she said.

The crisp air cleared her head, and by the time she

turned toward the house Molly had regained her common sense.

Talk about making a mountain out of a molehill, she told herself. *Two people happen to meet at an ice cream shop in broad daylight, and you've turned it into a conspiracy!*

Warren made several suggestions which would improve the section of the book she was working on, and Molly listened carefully. His enthusiasm was so contagious that she didn't notice when he started to tire, and the sky was fading to dull gray before she realized that the zeal in his eyes was covering fatigue.

The instant she saw it, she stood up, cutting him off in the middle of a sentence. "Hold that thought," she said. "We'll start there tomorrow. But in the meantime, I'm not going to be responsible for you wearing yourself out."

"Trying to remember till tomorrow will be harder," Warren said, but she knew he was arguing more from habit than conviction, for the next minute he was trying to conceal a yawn.

She dropped a kiss on his forehead, as she had started to do every day when she said goodbye.

"Bring Miss B up to give me a hug before you go," he ordered.

"I will, unless she's asleep. Or you are."

"If it isn't nap time for one of us, it is for the other," Warren grumbled, and yawned again.

Molly was smiling as she ran down the stairs, briefcase in hand. There was no one in the drawing room—but she'd expected that. It was too late in the day for tea parties, even pretend ones.

Bailey was probably still in the kitchen. She'd helped bake cookies this afternoon, and she'd proudly carried a plate of them upstairs to her mother and Warren all by herself. A china plate, too. Molly thought Mrs. Ekberg needed her head examined to turn a three-year-old loose with anything so delicate.

The soft flicker of firelight from the library drew her close, and she paused by the door to peek in. Bailey had been known to snuggle up in one of the leather chairs by the fire as soon as it was lit and fall asleep waiting for Luke.

But tonight the chairs were empty. Luke was standing by the fireplace, however, with a glass in his hand. Was his brow creased with worry, Molly wondered, or was it only a trick of the firelight?

He'd been home a while, she noted, for he'd changed into jeans and a heavy pullover sweater that made his shoulders look even broader.

"Calling it a day, Molly?" he said. "Would you like a drink?"

She shook her head. "I told Megan I'd stop by tonight. She wanted to talk to me about something."

It was technically true—even if the something was a Waterford crystal bowl and not a baby. She watched him narrowly, wondering if he'd admit to having seen Megan. If she *had* confided in him...

"Have a good time," he said.

Which left her knowing precisely nothing. Of course, Molly hadn't really expected anything else.

The kitchen was warm and bright. The spicy fragrance of Bailey's cookies still hung in the air, mingling with the scents of wine and cream and herbs from the range, where the cook was stirring a sauce. "I thought you'd gone home an hour ago," she said cheerfully, and offered a spoon. "Would you taste this and see if it needs just a little more dill?"

Molly absently took the spoon. "Isn't Bailey here?"

"No. That's why I thought you'd gone home when she didn't come back after she took the cookies upstairs. You mean—"

"Then where is she?" Molly flung the spoon down and turned toward the hallway.

Mrs. Ekberg was in the dining room, shaking her head over a half-set table. "Miss Molly," she called. "Can you look at this tablecloth? I just don't think it's going to survive another laundering, and it's the only one left that fits the table when it's fully extended."

Molly hardly heard her. "Mrs. Ekberg, when was the last time you saw Bailey?"

"I don't remember. When she was taking your cookies upstairs, I suppose."

"But that was an hour ago!" Molly said frantically.

Mrs. Ekberg stared for an instant. "I'll check with Watkins," she said. Her voice was trembling. "She likes to help him polish silver. We had to give her a bath the other day, she was so covered with tarnish."

Luke appeared in the library door, glass still in hand, just as Mrs. Ekberg, looking grave, reappeared, with Watkins only half a step behind her.

"What's up?" Luke asked.

Molly tried, without success, to swallow the rock in her throat. Just speaking the fear out loud gave it more power, she thought. Made it more real. She had to force herself to say the words. "We can't seem to find Bailey."

CHAPTER SIX

THOUGH Molly's voice was little more than a whisper, the terror it held echoed through the hallway like a scream.

For one long instant Luke stared at her, and then he heard himself say, "She's three years old. What in the hell were you all thinking of to let her wander on her own?"

Watkins looked at his clenched hands. The cook flinched. Mrs. Ekberg seemed to shrink six inches.

Molly said, "Assigning blame isn't going to do any good now. It's my fault—I'm her mother, and it's my responsibility. Now do you suppose we could try finding her?"

"Sorry," Luke muttered. "Let's split up the house. She's got to be here somewhere."

"Probably curled up asleep in the most unlikely spot." But the quaver in Mrs. Ekberg's voice belied the comforting words.

They started to spread out through the lower floor. "Wait a minute," Molly said. "Does anybody know where the dog is?"

Because Bailey is apt to be nearby, Luke thought. "Probably with Dad." He was halfway up the stairs in two bounds.

Molly called, "Luke—wait a minute."

He looked over the railing at her. Her face was white, her eyes huge and dark. She looked very small and very fragile. "Warren must not find out that Bailey's missing."

"Then how do you expect me to—" But she was

right, he thought. The last thing his father needed was a shock. And the likelihood was that they'd find the child within minutes anyway, curled up with the dog in some out-of-the-way corner, and Warren would have been alarmed for nothing. "All right," he said, and went upstairs at a slightly slower pace.

When he tapped on the door of the master bedroom, there was no answer. Luke gently pushed the door open. Warren was stretched out on the velvet chaise longue in the bow window, eyes closed, his breathing steady.

The chaise had been Luke's mother's favorite resting place during her illness, looking out over the gardens she would never walk in again. He wondered if that was why Warren had adopted it.

Luke eased across the room, hoping the floor wouldn't creak. Lucky was nowhere in sight, but he thought she might be tucked away in the window nook behind the chaise.

Warren opened his eyes, but he didn't move. "What do you want, Lucas? Surely it's not time for dinner yet."

It was, as a matter of fact—but nobody was going to pay any attention to the time till Bailey was safe. Not that anyone would have an appetite anyway, except perhaps Warren.

"Not yet," Luke said. "There seems to be a problem in the kitchen that's holding things up."

"So why are you tiptoeing around my room?"

"Looking for Lucky."

Warren's eyebrows rose. "Feel the need for a good frolic, do you? Ask Miss B. She'll know."

I wish I could, Luke thought.

"She's a pretty little girl, isn't she?" Warren mused. He sat up and propped a pillow behind his back.

Please, Dad, Luke thought. *This is no time for a long chat.* If the dog wasn't here, then neither was Bailey, and he was frantic to get back to the search. But Molly's face flashed in his mind. Even in the midst of her pain,

she'd been determined to protect Warren as long as possible—and if Luke walked out right now, the old man
would know there was something going on. ''She's cute,
yeah.''

''And as well-behaved as she is pretty, too. Don't you
agree, Lucas?''

*Oh, yes…except for this little matter of wandering off
without permission.*

Unless, of course, Luke thought, Bailey hadn't wandered off. His gut knotted. Now *there* was a thought that
promised nightmares—and it came complete with a
whole lineup of suspects. Bailey's father, snatching his
daughter in violation of custody agreements. Some unknown monster who thought any kid who came from the
Hudson mansion would be the ticket to a big ransom…

Somebody needs to sit by the phone. Just in case.

''Lucas?'' Warren's voice had acquired a sardonic
edge. ''I didn't expect you to need a task-force study
before you answered that question.''

Luke blinked and tried to pull himself together. What
was the question? Oh, right—*whether Bailey's well-
behaved.* ''She's amazingly good. And funny, too.''

Warren nodded. ''Molly's done a terrific job. She's
had a tough time of it, you know. Being a single mom
with all the pressures and responsibilities and almost no
security… And she's got such a loving heart, too.''

*And right now her loving heart means I'm killing time
here instead of searching.* ''Lovely woman.''

''I've been thinking a lot about her lately, Lucas.
About what's in the future for Molly and Bailey.''

Luke felt as if he were standing off to the side of the
room, watching himself carry on this conversation, so
ridiculously lightweight in comparison to the reality
downstairs. That distance added a sardonic note to his
voice. ''So what are you going to do? Propose, just to
make it up to her?''

Warren's eyes closed for a moment, and when he

looked at his son again Luke saw a brilliance that startled him.

Warren said, "I'm so glad to know that you approve."

Now that was a smooth interpretation, Luke thought. One minute he'd been without a clue, the next his father had him practically walking Molly down the aisle. "I didn't say—"

"You used to tell us you wanted a sister," Warren murmured. "Though there is a bit of an age gap, of course."

Luke frowned. "Four years or so. That's—"

"Oh, no, I wasn't talking about Molly. She'd be your stepmother. I meant the age difference between you and Miss B. But that won't bother you, I'm sure—you play together so well."

I wouldn't mind anything he wants to do for Bailey, Luke thought. *Just as long as we can get her back here to enjoy it.*

He stood up, unable to stay still for another single instant. "Let me have a chance to think about all this, Dad."

Warren settled back on the chaise. "Don't take too long, my boy. I don't have all the time in the world, you know."

Luke felt as if he'd been gone forever, but Mrs. Ekberg was just coming out of the bedroom at the top of the stairs. She shook her head. "I've checked all the rooms up here. The attic door is locked, and—"

"Closets?"

"No sign of either Bailey or the dog. We could just call for Lucky, but Molly thought hearing that would upset Warren."

Damn Warren, Luke almost said. *He deserves a little upsetting—he's doing plenty of his own!*

Molly was standing at the library door. In her hands was a wad of bright pastel fabric. She looked at Luke, her face set and icy cold despite the fire's heat, and held the wad out to him. "It's her jacket. The cook found it in the kitchen."

Relief rocketed through him. "Then she's got to be somewhere in the house."

"Or else she's out there." She turned sightless eyes toward the glass panels beside the front door. "Without it."

With the wind picking up, and the temperature dropping. He had never felt so powerless in his life.

Luke reached for the telephone. "I'm calling the police."

Molly knew it was the next logical and necessary step. They needed help, and fast. But hearing Luke's voice as he summoned the authorities was like having her skin stripped away by inches.

My baby's gone, she thought helplessly.

Luke put the telephone down. "They'll have a car here in a few minutes. In the meantime, Watkins and I will start searching the grounds." His gaze flicked to Mrs. Ekberg and the cook. "You two, check right around the house. If she wandered outside—"

"She couldn't reach the doorbell," Molly said. "I had to lift her." She started for the door.

Luke caught her arm. "Somebody needs to stay by the phone."

His voice was gentle, but she heard the rough edge under it. He was afraid, she thought. Afraid of what they might find. And he didn't want her to be the one to stumble across—

She couldn't bear to think about it, and she cast her mind wildly for something else to hang onto. "I want Megan," she whispered. "I want my sister!" What she'd give right now to have that damned Waterford crystal bowl be her biggest problem...

"I'll call her," Luke said.

Megan must have had her hand on the phone, for in less than a minute he was back, easing Molly into a chair. "She's on her way." He crouched beside her, his gaze compelling her to look at him, to listen. "Perhaps you should call Bailey's father."

She shook her head.

"Molly, I really think—"

"No. And I'm not going to sit here beside a phone that isn't going to ring. I'm going out, right now, to look for her."

Luke bit his lip. "All right." He held her back from the door while he forced her arms into a thick, oversize wool jacket as if she were a child. He picked up a flannel-lined windbreaker for himself, and they went out together into the gathering dark.

Molly hadn't expected to need the coat. She'd pictured the scene so clearly in her mind, the moment she'd thought of the doorbell—Bailey wandering outside for some unknown reason, without her jacket because she didn't intend to stay out and play. Then the door blowing shut behind her. And, when she found she couldn't reach the bell, she wouldn't have thought of going round the house looking for a low window so she could get someone's attention. She was three, after all. She'd have sat down beside the front door, in the shelter of the juniper bush, to wait. And Molly would open the door and scoop her up—

She'd built the scene so well in her mind that she couldn't bring herself to believe, when she stood on the front steps, that there was no child huddled against the juniper bush. She stood absolutely still, staring at the place where she'd been so certain Bailey would be.

But there were all kinds of holes in the story she'd constructed. Unable to reach the bell, Bailey would have pounded on the door. And she'd have heard Luke's car come down the drive and run to meet him.

Molly gulped and braced herself and went into the

deep gray of evening. It wasn't as dark as she'd expected. Though in her mind time had stretched out like taffy, according to her watch barely twenty minutes had passed since she'd realized Bailey was gone.

But the shadows were almost worse than pitch blackness would have been, for they moved as the wind stirred the trees. And every movement made her heart jerk with hope, and then with disappointment.

The headlights of a car swept across the drive. Megan's BMW screeched to a halt in front of the house, and Molly ran toward it. Megan flung herself from the car, leaving the engine running and the door open, and swept Molly into her arms.

Molly let herself have the luxury of a fifteen-second-long hug. Megan kissed her cheek, patted her back and looked at Luke. "Mother and Dad are about two minutes behind me. I called them while I was driving down the hill. What else can I do?"

"Go sit with my father," he said promptly. "Whatever you do, don't tell him what's going on. Make some excuse for being here, and you might try to explain the screeching tires, too—"

Molly thought, *So he does know about Megan's condition. And he's assigning her a safe job.*

"And if the phone rings, grab it before he can."

"And still keep a lid on the story?" Megan said dryly. "Oh, that should be fun."

Another car pulled up behind the BMW, and Alix and Bernie got out. "My dear," Alix called. "This is horrible. How did it happen?"

"Doesn't matter, Mom," Megan said crisply. "Get your orders and save the explanations for later, okay?" She winked at Molly. "Keep your chin up. Bailey's a lucky kid. She'll be all right."

Lucky. For a moment, Molly had almost forgotten about the dog. The wind had risen, and it was hard to hear. Was that a dog's yelp, or a wild creature, or only her imagination?

As Molly's parents came up to them, Luke said, "I've been trying to convince Molly to call her ex-husband. I suppose he's got a right to know when Bailey's in danger—but we can also make sure he's where he's supposed to be and that he hasn't run off with her. But Molly doesn't—"

"He didn't snatch her," Molly said.

Luke stared at her. "And why, precisely, are you so certain of that?"

"Can't you take her word for it?" Alix asked.

"No."

"Then how about this?" Alix's voice dripped impatience. "We know he didn't do it because he's dead."

Luke drew back as if he'd been slapped.

Molly was too numb even to care. There were more important problems right now than trying to straighten out that complication.

Besides, Alix was absolutely correct, even if it was for all the wrong reasons.

Molly turned toward the side of Oakwood, where a narrow ravine edged between the trees. The woods were darker. In these conditions, she could walk within inches of Bailey and not see her.

Through the fogginess in her brain, she realized she'd come to accept the possibility that Bailey wasn't able to call for help.

Her parents took the strip between the front driveway and the street, and the staff moved around the far corner of the house. Luke, Molly noticed, stayed within yards of her, far enough away to search an additional strip of land, close enough that he could reach her in a few steps if...

She didn't want to think about that.

She thought instead about the pitifully slow progress they were making in covering the ground. "Strange," she said, "to send an able-bodied woman inside instead of putting her to work in the search."

Luke didn't look up from the leaf-strewn shadows he was inspecting. "Do you think you can cut out being jealous of your sister for one minute? You wanted her, she came, she's where she can do the most good right now. So lay off her, all right?"

Molly felt ashamed of herself, but not enough to admit it to him. "It's still odd."

"Would you rather I'd sent your mother up to soothe him? Look, you don't have to fuss about Megan being with Warren—it's clearly you he's got his eye on."

She thought she hadn't heard him right. "What?"

"You know, Molly, I intended for you to reawaken his interest in life in general, not in you specifically."

"I don't know what you mean."

"Oh, really? It hadn't occurred to you that he's planning wedding bells?"

She stood stock-still in the middle of a lighter patch of woods and stared at him. Suddenly it was all too much—the fear and the cold and the tension and the dread—and she started to laugh, bursts of giggles that quickly turned to sobs that shook her body like an aspen leaf.

In a moment, Luke was beside her, hands on her shoulders, shaking her. But the quaking only grew worse, and suddenly she couldn't get her breath.

Luke said something she didn't hear and dragged her against his body, and his mouth came down on hers, punishingly fierce.

Before she knew what she was doing, her hand had raised a red welt on his cheek, and her palm was stinging with the impact. "You just had to try it out, didn't you?"

Luke rubbed his cheek. "At least you're not hysterical any more. Now can we get down to business again?"

She was horrified to realize that for one instant Bailey

had been blanked out of her mind completely. She stumbled as she walked into the ravine that marked the edge of Oakwood's grounds.

They had worked down the ravine quite a way when the moon came out from behind a cloud, and she caught the glint of its light against something high above her head. "The treehouse," she said. "She was fascinated by the treehouse."

Luke shook his head. "I haven't been up there since…"

Since the night before his mother died. *Don't kid yourself, Molly—it's not you he's thinking about.*

He didn't finish. "Besides, it's locked up tight."

"To keep kids out. But Bailey wouldn't know that."

Molly waited at the base of the tree while he climbed, and when he shouted that there was no sign, she sagged against the rough bark and folded her arms across her chest as if to hug the child who wasn't there.

Bailey, you can't just have vanished. Where are you?

Luke was climbing down. She closed her eyes and listened to the rhythmic scrape of his shoes against the treehouse ladder. But between those sounds, there was something else, only once—a faint far-off cry that might have been the yelp of a dog.

Luke leaped the last two steps and stood dusting off his hands. "I think—"

"Listen!"

Luke tipped his head. The wind calmed, and they both heard. "Down by the lake," he said.

For a moment, they stared at each other, silently acknowledging what neither had dared to say before—that the lake was a last resort. If Bailey had fallen into that inland sea, the largest freshwater lake in the world, the graveyard of thousand-foot-long ships whose wreckage had yet to be located, she might never be found. So they had looked everywhere else first. Now there was only the lake left.

And if they found Lucky pacing the seawall, looking across the water in search of her small companion…

I might just throw myself in, too, Molly thought.

She jogged from time to time, but she was in no shape for this race. Her lungs were shrieking for relief when, a couple of yards behind Luke, she reached the concrete wall that protected the shore from the pounding waves.

And saw nothing but Luke poised atop the seawall, silhouetted against the moonlit water, and the six-foot drop beyond him to where waves sloshed over the rocky lake bottom and shattered in white foam against the concrete barricade.

Then the dog barked from out of nowhere. It seemed to Molly that Luke leaped off the wall into empty air, and she reached out to stop him an instant too late. Had his feet slipped on the wet concrete? Or had he really jumped?

She crept closer, cautious of her balance, and saw him, waves breaking around his knees as he sloshed toward a dark, wet lump huddled against the seawall twenty feet down the shore. She strained to see and recognized Lucky leaning against the concrete with her feet in the water, her claws scrabbling on the rocky bottom. And pressed between the dog's body and the wall, just above the water, was a sopping, bedraggled bundle.

"Good dog," Luke said, and reached over Lucky to drag Bailey into his arms.

Molly scrambled along the wall till she was directly above them and waited an eternity until he boosted his burden to her. "She's breathing," he said.

Bailey whimpered, "I want Mommy."

Hot tears streamed down Molly's face. "Mommy's here, love. Luke, she's so cold!"

"Of course she's cold. She's soaked. Get her clothes off."

Had he lost his mind? "What do you mean, *off?*" She stared at him in horror, then remembered his medical training and began to fumble with Bailey's dripping sweatshirt.

"I mean, strip her." He heaved the dog out of the water and pulled himself onto the wall. "The wind hitting her wet clothes is sucking the heat straight out of her body." He tore off his windbreaker, pulled his sweater over his head and put the jacket on.

Molly fought to get Bailey out of her sodden jeans. The moment the child was free, she reached for his sweater, but Luke scooped Bailey against his bare chest, draped his sweater across her back like a blanket and folded the windbreaker around both of them. "Body heat," he said. "Hurry."

"Mommy," Bailey said. It was a hopeless, helpless little murmur that nearly broke Molly's heart.

She didn't know how she managed to stay even with Luke's longer stride, even burdened as he was. Lucky bounded toward the house ahead of them, barking wildly.

"Too bad she couldn't do that before," Luke said. "But she was using all her strength to keep them both from going into the drink."

A siren shut off abruptly in the driveway as they came around the corner of the house. Why had it taken so long for the police to arrive, Molly wondered. Or was her mind fooling her again? Had they been out searching for only a few minutes, even though it felt like years?

Luke waved down a patrolman, and within a minute they were in a police car, headed for the hospital. Bailey was still snuggled close against Luke's body, and Molly was using the sleeve of her wool jacket to dry the child's straggly hair.

"My badge," Bailey murmured. "I want…badge."

Molly thought that weak little voice was the most beautiful sound in the world. "Later, honey. We'll get it for you later."

*   *   *

The emergency room crew shut the door of the treatment room in Molly's face. Very politely, of course, and with the best of explanations. She'd be in the way while they got Bailey stabilized and warm once more. And then she'd need X rays, to make sure she hadn't gotten water in her lungs. But after that… Just as soon as Molly could be with her daughter, they'd come and get her.

Luke coaxed her to a quiet corner of the waiting room, but Molly couldn't sit still. "She'll be okay, won't she?"

"Sure," he said. Then, as if he recognized how very unconvincing he'd sounded, he went on. "She was conscious when I pulled her out—that's a good sign. The dog's body broke the force of the waves and the wind, and because they were huddled together they didn't lose heat quite as quickly."

She looked at him, drew a deep, shaky breath and relaxed a tiny bit. "What about Lucky?"

"She looked all right. Maybe some frostbite on her paws. I don't know. Depends on how long they were in the water, I suppose. Watkins will make sure the dog's taken care of."

"I hope he makes sure she gets a couple of steaks. No, I don't—I want to do that myself, and feed them to her bite by bite." She tried to wipe the tears away.

"Molly." He was staring at his shoes and the puddle of lake water that had dripped from his jeans, and his voice was heavy. "That first day you brought her to Oakwood, I told Bailey I'd take her down to the lake. And I didn't do it. I never got around to it—"

"And you think that's why she went, so you're blaming yourself? Don't, Luke."

"You don't hold it against me?"

Molly shook her head. "I could just as easily blame my father. He's the one who taught her to love the lake. It's not your fault, Luke, any more than it's his."

He looked at her for a long moment. "Thanks,

Molly.'' He reached out to her, and his hand closed slowly around hers. Molly looked at their linked fingers, his tanned, hers much paler.

She had cared about him once—as a girl cares. And she knew he'd been right, all those years ago, that what she felt was far closer to infatuation than to love. When she had first come back to Duluth, she'd thought she was indifferent to him. She'd intended to do her job, live her life and pay no heed to Lucas Hudson.

But now… Now she felt confused.

She'd seen him in a different light tonight, that was certain. She'd known that Bailey thought he was pretty neat, for Bailey had told her. But Luke had been harder to read until tonight. He'd been stunned by the child's disappearance and determined to find her at any cost to himself—traits that would win him a place in any mother's heart.

She had to admit that she still got a lump in her throat whenever she closed her eyes and pictured the way he'd flung himself off the seawall, heedless of anything except the need to get Bailey out of the lake.

Bailey. That, of course, was the common thread. He'd fallen in love with her little girl—which wasn't much of a surprise. That sparkling child could walk off with almost anybody's heart—and it was clear she'd added Luke's to her collection.

What in the hell were you thinking of to let her wander on her own? he'd said in that first stunned moment when Molly had told him Bailey was gone. And he'd kissed her tonight not out of any fondness—she could never forget the bruising force of that kiss—but to shock her out of hysteria and back to the business of finding Bailey.

Even when he hadn't been a hundred percent focused on the child, he'd had nothing flattering to say to Molly. *Do you think you can cut out being jealous of your sister for one minute?* he'd asked. And that crack he'd made about Warren asking her to marry him… Luke obviously hadn't any personal feelings on the matter, except that he'd clearly thought his father had lost his mind.

Bailey was a different matter. It was Bailey who kept him sitting here, even though he was dripping and chilled, waiting to be certain she was all right. It was Bailey who occupied his mind. Bailey…

Ever so slowly, she pulled her hand away from his. Or had he purposely loosened his hold and let her slip away?

Luke sat up a little straighter. "So," he said. He was trying very hard, she thought, to sound completely normal. "As long as we've got time to kill, why don't you tell me how you got the bruise? If it wasn't the ex, who punched you in the face? And why wouldn't you tell me what happened?"

"You expected me to explain?" Molly countered. "It was a job interview. Questions about personal business have no place in—"

Luke snorted. "I suppose you're going to file sexual harassment charges for the way I treated your hysteria tonight?"

"Of course not. Assault would be more like it."

"That's a relief. And by the way, you haven't answered the question this time, either. Who punched you?"

A nurse—not the one who'd asked Molly to wait outside —came into the waiting room. "Are you Bailey's parents? You can come in now."

Molly watched the shadow settle across Luke's face, and the heaviness that had lain across her heart for more years than she wanted to remember translated itself into a new and different sort of pain.

She stood up and very deliberately stretched out her hand to him.

A trace of a frown flickered across his face. Then he

folded his fingers around hers and walked beside her to a cubicle.

Just outside the half-closed door, a young man was scribbling on a chart. He looked up and said, ''That's one fortunate kid, you know. We want to keep an eye on her for another few hours—keep a warm IV running, that sort of thing. But if she doesn't have any further problems you'll be able to take her home yet tonight.''

Molly didn't realize till then she'd been holding her breath.

Perched high atop a hospital bed, propped with a stack of pillows, Bailey sat with a tray table arranged across her lap and a mug in her tiny hands. She looked like a doll among the multitude of blankets folded around her.

The moment she saw Molly, Bailey held out her arm to display the IV drip. ''Mommy, they stuck a *needle* in me.'' She was obviously incensed. ''And it's *still there.*''

Luke chuckled. ''You go right ahead and complain, princess.''

She turned her big brown eyes to him. ''Will you make them take it out, Luke?''

''Later. They're pretty busy right now, so we'll have to wait our turn again.'' He laid a hand on her shoulder.

Was it only her imagination, Molly wondered, or were his fingers trembling? She moved to the other side of the bed and leaned on the railing. ''What are you drinking, Bailey?''

''Hot chocolate.'' The child looked a little guilty. ''I forgot about having to ask you first.''

''It's all right. I'm sure the doctor knows what he's doing.'' Molly pushed a lock of dark hair from the child's forehead. Her hair was dry but it felt sticky from the lake water.

Bailey pushed the cup away. ''Did you bring my badge?''

Molly had almost forgotten. ''No, honey. But it'll be

waiting for us. Was it in your pocket?'' She'd left the
sodden clothes on the seawall, but there'd be plenty of
time to get them later.

Bailey shook her head. ''It went down in the lake. It
blew away and went out in the water, so I climbed down
off the wall like I do off the jungle gym at the park. It
wasn't very far.''

Molly's heart was quaking. A six-foot wall, and
Bailey had simply hung by her hands and dropped off
it?

''But I couldn't reach it. And the wall was too slick
so I couldn't climb back up, and Lucky jumped down
and splashed me and got me all wet. And then I got
cold.'' She yawned.

''But now you're warm again.'' Molly tried to smile.

''The badge,'' Luke said. ''The damned badge. I'm
sorry, Molly. You didn't want her to have it in the first
place.''

''Put a plug in it, Luke, will you? No one could have
anticipated that she'd go in the lake...'' Molly couldn't
keep her voice from shaking.

Luke reached across the bed to squeeze her hand.

Bailey's second yawn was even bigger, and she let
her head drop on the pillow. ''I still like the lake, even
if it was all wet and nasty.''

They stood there till she was asleep. ''That's good,''
Luke said. ''That she still likes the lake, I mean. She
could have been so traumatized that she'd never go near
water again.''

Molly nodded and let her head sink down to rest on
the chrome rail of Bailey's bed.

''You're exhausted,'' Luke said.

''I'm not leaving.''

''Of course not. But surely I can find you a chair.''
But he didn't step away from the bed. ''Molly,'' he said
quietly. ''I know you probably didn't even hear what the
nurse was saying out there—about parents, plural. But

thanks for letting me come in. For letting them think I'm her father.''

She looked at him, and at their clasped hands, and then at the face of her sleeping daughter. ''Why not?'' she said. ''After all…it's true.''

CHAPTER SEVEN

FROM out in the hallway Molly could hear the clinking of stainless steel instruments as a cart was wheeled by. Above her head, one of the fluorescent lights hummed in a off-key pitch that grated on her nerves. But there was no other sound.

She watched her daughter's face and stroked the child's hair. Her fingertips, she noted with detached interest, weren't shaking at all. That was just as well, for now that she'd made her declaration it was too late to worry.

But she couldn't deny that the longer the silence lasted the more apprehension oozed through her veins until finally she could bear it no longer. Slowly, she raised her head until her gaze met Luke's.

If she'd suddenly sprouted horns, he couldn't have looked more flabbergasted. Almost dazed, she thought. As if he was staring straight through her.

Then, as she watched, his gaze focused on her face. "You've snapped," he said firmly. "It's been a terrible few hours, and now that the stress is finally off—"

Of course, she hadn't really expected anything else. Nevertheless, Molly's shoulders drooped as the weight of fatigue settled onto them once more. But this exhaustion wasn't from the evening's strain. it was a tiredness born years ago. "Fine," she said. "I've snapped. Call the men in the little white coats."

"You're not…" He paused. "You haven't mistaken me for someone else?"

"Like who? Santa Claus? Come off it, Luke. I'm not having hallucinations."

He relaxed. She watched the taut muscles of his face ease. "Well, in that case... This is actually pretty funny, Molly. Haven't you overlooked one minor detail?"

"You mean the fact that we never quite made love?"

"Well, it does seem—"

"The key word, of course, is *quite*. Remember, Luke? You said yourself that another minute and it would have been too late. Well, it *was* too late. Making love is a process—and even though we didn't finish, we'd certainly started."

"That's impossible."

"It wouldn't be the first time it's happened—two kids fooling around, never quite going the whole way but getting plenty excited. I actually thought once of going on the speaking circuit—talking to teenagers as a living example of why keeping all their clothes on and both feet on the floor is such a good idea. Showing them the impossible baby." Molly knew she sounded bitter, and she was afraid he'd misunderstand the source of that feeling. "Bailey's a blessing, the best thing that ever happened to me. But coming to terms with how it happened was a different matter altogether."

Luke shook his head.

She had known, of course, that he wasn't likely to believe her. She'd had enough trouble in the beginning accepting it herself. But seeing his doubt, feeling the waves of disbelief, infuriated her. "If you want blood tests, Luke, we're all right here in the hospital—and they already have plenty of Bailey's, no doubt."

He seemed not to have heard her. "What about your husband?"

Molly sighed. "There never was one. Mother couldn't bear the idea of me having a baby without a wedding ring, so when I was in Chicago she kept up the fiction of a marriage, and after a while a divorce. Then when I came home and her friends started wondering rather loudly why Bailey's father didn't help support her—as if it was any of their business—she killed him off.''

"And you played along with it."

"I didn't even know she'd manufactured a story till I got home. And then what was I supposed to do about it? Announce to the world that my mother had created the whole scenario in order to save face with her friends? Call her a liar while my daughter and I are living in her house, eating her food, wearing clothes she laundered? Besides, that's hardly the point just now, is it?''

"No," he agreed. "It's the other incredible story that's the problem."

Molly faced him squarely. "Suit yourself." Her voice was almost lifeless. "Forget it. I never said a word, all right?"

"Molly—"

"Now just go away," she said, "and leave me and *my* daughter alone."

Once, when he'd been just a kid and learning to ride, Luke had been kicked squarely in the stomach by a horse. It was the only time in his life he'd felt anything like the blow Molly had dealt him tonight.

She looked like an angry Madonna as she bent over the hospital bed, tucking the blankets closer around...

His daughter?

No, he told himself. It was completely, absolutely impossible. For some incomprehensible reason, she'd decided to try out an incredible scam.

As he walked down the long hallway toward the emergency room exit, he stumbled over nothing but air. An aide coming toward him gave him a suspicious look. *She probably thinks I'm intoxicated,* Luke thought. *And she's right—only the poison in my system is accusations, not alcohol.*

He walked unseeing through the waiting room, and he was at the door when a woman approached. He turned away, unwilling to attempt to be polite to a stranger wanting the time, much less a staff member wanting information.

"Luke!" Megan Bannister grabbed his arm. "You look awful. Is she… Has she—?"

He shook his head to clear it. "Bailey's fine. She's asleep, and Molly's with her."

Megan's face had gone ashen, and she swayed. Quickly, Luke guided her to the nearest chair. "Put your head down," he ordered.

"I'm not going to faint. I just thought for a moment…" She shuddered. "If I had to go tell my parents that their granddaughter was gone…"

Luke put his arm around her. "Don't torment yourself, Meg. She's all right. She can probably go home in a few hours."

She turned her face against his shoulder. "Oh, Luke, what would I do without you?"

"A better question is what you're doing here when you should be home with your feet up."

Megan shook her head. "If I hadn't come, Mother would have—and I think Molly would much rather have me. That's not saying a whole lot, as I'm sure my little sister can function quite well without me. But after some of the run-ins they've had over—" She stopped awkwardly, and her color came back in a embarrassed flood.

"Over the late and not lamented ex-husband?"

Megan wouldn't look at him. "That's part of it. Look, I don't know what happened to my presence of mind, but I shouldn't have said—"

"Why not? Friends tell friends what they need to know."

"And you need to know about Molly's ex?"

He nodded. He felt almost as if he was going behind Molly's back to ask. But that was stupid. He had every right in the world to check out her story in any way he could. "And Bailey's father." The words tasted funny on his tongue.

Megan laughed. "You sound as if they were two different people."

"Weren't they?" There was no amusement in his voice.

She bit her lip. "Okay, Luke—I'll tell you what I know. But it isn't much, all right? So don't expect the encyclopedia. There never was a husband. And Molly would never tell anyone who Bailey's father was."

Molly would never tell. That wasn't the same as saying Megan didn't know. "You must have an idea."

"How? I went away to college, Molly stayed here. And we never did confide much in each other. We certainly didn't share insights on our men of the moment. She could have been dating every man at the university."

"Or somebody else altogether."

Megan nodded. "All I know is, she was fighting morning sickness at my wedding."

The wedding had been at Christmastime, Luke remembered. He'd been an usher, Molly the maid of honor. She'd been very pale that day in her dark green velvet gown, and just a little shaky. The guests had probably thought it was nerves. Luke had assumed—a bit vainly, perhaps—it was because she was seeing him for the first time since he'd given her the lecture of her life.

But if she'd been ill at Megan's wedding...

"She didn't tell anyone," Megan went on. "In fact, she waited till after my honeymoon was over, and then she called a family meeting and announced that she was expecting a baby."

"I bet that went over well," Luke said dryly.

Megan rolled her eyes. "Mother exploded and demanded a name...and Molly refused. I've never seen anyone with so much dignity. Little Molly—who would have believed it?"

I would, he thought. *Because she displayed it for me, too.*

"It was like she was sealed inside a plastic cube," Megan said, "where nothing could reach her. I don't think she'd have talked under torture because—let's face it—my mother tried. So Molly went off to Chicago to finish school and make a life for herself and her baby. The whole thing makes my problems look kind of small, doesn't it?"

Luke gave her a hug. "Feeling any better?"

"No. But I've resigned myself. There's no reason my baby shouldn't be all right, and that's the important thing."

"You're important, too," he reminded.

She smiled at that, but he didn't think she really believed it. "Where's Bailey's room? Which way do I go?"

"How about home?"

Megan shook her head. "You all got here without a car, and if Bailey's released how are you going to get her home?"

"Taxis are a wonderful invention." But he relented and gave her the room number. "I'll see you tomorrow, probably."

"You're leaving? Oh, of course—you're still squishing around in wet shoes yourself."

He waited till Megan was out of sight down the long hall before he called a cab, and he went into the bracing cold of the evening to wait, hardly feeling the wind against his damp jeans.

A chilly evening. It had been cold that October night in the treehouse, too. He'd been miserable, shattered at the news that his mother, who two weeks before had seemed perfectly healthy, had—at most—days to live. He didn't remember climbing the tree. He'd automatically fled to the security of his childhood. And he'd sat there in the dark and cold, feeling the finality of the darkness and coldness that was creeping over his mother.

That was when Molly had appeared.

She hadn't asked his permission to join him. She'd seemed to know he'd tell her to go away. She'd let herself into the treehouse, turned on the electric heater and sat beside him on the bunk. Without a word she reached for his hands and held them between hers, rubbing gently till the chill was gone.

And then she'd talked—not in the platitudes so many others had tried to feed him, but with gentle understanding. And she'd listened while he poured out his feelings, spilled fears that were so deeply entrenched he'd been almost incoherent. And yet she had understood.

He'd been spent, finally, and relaxed for the first time in days, and he'd turned to her in silent gratitude.

But she was as generous in her kisses as she'd been in her compassionate silence, and he hadn't wanted to stop. Neither had she. There was no question in his mind that Molly wanted him as much as he wanted her. And so they'd lain together on the bunk and explored each other and taken comfort in their closeness…

We didn't finish, Molly had said, *but we'd certainly started.*

She was right. He'd told her once that another minute and he wouldn't have been able to send her away. But it would be more accurate to say that it had been a matter of seconds.

At the last possible moment, his mother's face had flashed before him. He saw her eyes, racked with pain not only from her illness but from his conduct. He was disgusted with himself, and in his guilt he'd lashed out at Molly.

His mother was dying. And here he was…

He didn't realize he'd said it aloud until the crudeness of the words had sent ugly color flaring into Molly's face. But even then she hadn't struck back. She'd looked at him levelly, and then she'd slid off the bunk and reached for her clothes, and before he'd found his voice she'd dressed and left.

His mother had died the next day. After the funeral services, when the Hudsons' friends, relatives and employees gathered at Oakwood, Molly had been among them, standing with her parents, holding an untouched cup of punch. He'd managed to get her alone without drawing anyone's attention in the small sun room at the back of the house.

He'd intended to apologize both for his words and for his conduct. But she didn't seem to hear anything he said. She looked at him like a zombie—what was the comparison Megan had made tonight? *Like she was sealed inside a plastic cube.*

He'd been afraid for her. Unintentionally, he had taken advantage of her warmth, her inexperience, her willingness. She didn't seem to understand the danger she'd put herself in—or that another man might not hesitate to use her. She didn't seem to see that her innocence invited that very sort of man.

She'd let him talk, and then she'd said, "I only wanted you to feel better."

Luke had exploded. "That's exactly what I'm talking about! And you can stop looking at me like that. It isn't going to happen again—not ever. And for heaven's sake don't be stupid enough to take up with some jerk just because you're trying to prove something to me."

She had said, "I love you, Luke. I'll always love you."

"You aren't old enough to know what love is," he'd snapped. "You're only infatuated, and you'd better get over it." And in frustration, Luke had turned away. He'd done all he could. If she was naive enough to get herself involved in something worse, it wasn't his fault.

But he'd been wrong about what she might do. She hadn't bounced straight to another man—there hadn't been time. If she'd been suffering from morning sickness at Megan's wedding, just two months later…

"Hey, buddy," the taxi driver called. "You the one that wants a ride? 'Cause I'm leaving one way or the other."

Luke directed the cabby to stop in front of Oakwood, paid his fare and walked slowly down the drive. But instead of the long rows of pine trees, he was seeing the wide aisle of the church where Megan and Rand had been married. Megan, excited and happy in her white satin with the marabou trim and the huge bouquet of white roses.

And Molly, paler than ever against the forest green of her dress, clutching the dark fur muff that she carried instead of flowers. Pale, he'd thought, because she had to face him for the first time since he'd made it clear her infatuation wasn't going to lead anywhere.

But it had led somewhere—and Molly had known it. She'd known when she walked down that aisle in her dark green velvet, no doubt praying that she wouldn't be sick in public, that she was carrying his child.

And she hadn't told him. Not till tonight, when he'd almost lost the daughter he'd never known he had.

He'd expected that after their painful confrontation she'd try to get even with him for rejecting her. He'd just hoped she wouldn't hurt herself in the process. She hadn't done what he'd anticipated—but she'd gotten even, all right.

She had deliberately cheated him of his daughter.

For a long time after he walked out, Molly stood very still beside Bailey's bed, elbows propped on the railing, face in her hands.

What had she expected, anyway? That he'd throw his arms around her in delight at the news that he'd suddenly acquired a daughter? Rush straight out and buy cigars?

Run through the hospital corridors shouting, "It's a girl!"?

You just blasted the man's whole life, she told herself. Or at least, that was what she'd done if he believed her. And if he didn't believe her... Well, she'd decided long ago that self-pity was a waste of time.

If Luke wanted to pursue the blood tests she'd mentioned, of course she'd cooperate. She could understand if he needed to be certain. It *was* a quaint little story, after all.

As a matter of fact, in order to prove she was telling the truth, she could demand that he go through with the tests. But she wouldn't force the issue. Under the circumstances, being dubious—feeling doubts—was a sensible sort of reaction. But to flatly deny the possibility...

A man who had to be coerced even to admit that he might have fathered a child wasn't much of a father. Bailey deserved better than that. In fact, having no father at all would be worlds better than having a reluctant one.

You should have kept your mouth shut, Molly told herself.

Two scalding tears rolled down her cheeks just as a tap sounded on the door, and she turned away to wipe her face.

"Hi," Megan said. "I ran into Luke in the lobby, and he filled me in."

Luke had filled her in? In the frame of mind he'd been in, he might have said anything. Just short of panic, Molly faced her sister. But there seemed to be nothing in Megan's expression except concern for Molly and tenderness when she moved to the side of the bed and looked at Bailey.

Molly breathed a little easier.

"So I stopped to phone Mother and Dad with a report before I came on back here. I hope you don't mind me interfering?"

Molly shook her head. "Of course not. I hadn't even

thought about calling. I wonder if anyone's talked to Warren?''

''I broke the news to him as gently as I could after you found her, and Mrs. Ekberg was sitting with him when I left. Besides, Luke's going straight home, isn't he? He'll take care of the rest, I'm sure.''

Molly wouldn't bet any money on Luke's destination. And she wondered, even if he did go to Oakwood, exactly what he would tell his father. Part of her would love to be a mouse in that corner. The rest of her shuddered away from the very idea.

''You haven't actually been here that long, anyway,'' Megan pointed out. ''Even though I'll bet it feels like all night.''

No, Molly thought. *It feels more like a whole lifetime.*

''So give me all the details. Remember, I was stuck on the sidelines with Warren while all the excitement was going on. I couldn't even shout downstairs for an update.''

Briefly, Molly told her. Her voice shook when she relived the brief space between Luke's leap off the seawall and the moment she once more had her baby—frighteningly cold, but breathing and conscious enough to want her mother—in her arms.

''Luke was quite the hero tonight, wasn't he?'' Megan said. Her tone was careless, but Molly knew better than to take it at face value.

''Straight out of legend,'' she said dryly. ''Silver armor and all.''

Bailey stirred, and Megan looked at her. ''I got the notion—foolish, I suppose—that he's thinking of trying out for a new role.'' She glanced at Molly. ''As Bailey's stepfather.''

She sounded amused, Molly thought, and bewilderment tugged at her. Megan didn't know the truth, that was plain, for her comment would have been deliberately cruel, and that wasn't like Megan. So was she using humor as a shield to feel out an unwelcome suspicion that Luke might be developing an interest in someone else? Or was she being absolutely straightforward? Totally wrong, of course—but with good intentions nonetheless?

Molly decided that a comment as ambiguous as that deserved a painfully direct question in return. ''Do you object?''

''Me?'' Megan's eyebrows arched. ''Of course not. Go for it, darling.''

Too late, Molly realized that she'd snared herself in the trap she'd set for Megan. ''No,'' she said hastily. ''That's not at all what I meant. He's not…and I wouldn't… It's just that…'' She stammered to a halt; she could hardly say, *I only wanted to know if you're having an affair with him.*

Megan's smile was tolerant. ''Of course,'' she said gently. ''I'll forget the whole thing, I promise, now that you've assured me there's nothing to it. Oh, did I mention that Mother wants to talk to you? I told her you were pretty busy at the moment and you'd probably just wait till you got home.''

Molly managed a smile. ''Thanks, Meg.''

''No trouble at all. I'll accept applause later for my role in keeping her away from the hospital.'' Megan reached across the narrow bed to touch Molly's arm. ''Mother means well, you know.''

''If you tell me she's just eager to help, I will bite you.''

Megan frowned. ''I'm not defending her, you understand, just explaining. But I'm surprised I have to, Molly. With the way she was raised, of course she does whatever she has to in order to save face, to appear as good as the rest of the crowd. She was tormented by other kids all through her childhood, you know, because she didn't fit in. She didn't speak properly because her parents didn't know how, and her clothes weren't just out of fashion, they were patched and faded and all the wrong size. She didn't own a winter coat till she went to work and earned it.''

Molly's eyes were wide.

"She scrabbled herself up from something so far below poverty there isn't even a word to describe it. She remade herself. Did you know her name was Alice originally? But the abuse of those early years left scars. She can't stand the thought that someone might be pointing at her, criticizing her, making fun of her—because she lived with cruelty for too many years to forget it. I thought surely you'd understand how inadequate she feels, Molly. You're the brains in this outfit, not me.''

"She's never told me any of that! I think you're wrong that I'm the brains—but you're certainly the favorite.''

Megan shrugged. "If so, it's because I went along. I was a good girl. I complied. And I fulfilled her dreams—acquiring the wealthy husband, the blue-blooded relatives, the perfect house. And becoming the social leader that even the social leaders look up to.'' Her voice was full of irony.

"I knew those things were important to her," Molly said softly. "I didn't know why. No wonder, when I announced that I was pregnant and there was no chance I'd marry the father of my baby, she went up in smoke.''

"And she told a whole lot of very silly stories that I'm sure she regrets. But now, of course, to admit what she's done would set off the old cycle again, make her the focus of criticism and gossip. So she's stuck between wanting to preserve her image and wanting to make everything right with you again.'' Her gaze rested thoughtfully on Bailey. "She doesn't know how to bridge that gap, Molly. She's afraid to get too attached to either of you. Afraid you'll leave again.''

"She seems to be doing her best to drive me away.''

Molly shook her head. "Between the advice and the criticism—"

"Probably that's exactly what she's doing. Not on purpose, of course." Megan hesitated, then said more softly, "I think I can understand how she feels, Molly. I had time to think tonight, too, when Bailey was missing. I realized what I was giving up by not getting to know her." There was pain in her voice. "And I faced up to why I've been so distant and so rude."

Molly held her breath, afraid that the slightest sound would break the mood.

"I was jealous of you because you had what I wanted—a healthy baby. And I didn't want to get close to Bailey because it hurts too much to be reminded of the child I lost."

Molly's chest felt like a boa constrictor had seized her. "I didn't know. I'm sorry, Meg. There's so much I didn't know."

"Don't blame yourself. No one knew at the time. I miscarried so early in the pregnancy that we hadn't even told Mother and Dad about the baby."

Molly remembered something her father had said about Megan not wanting to have children. It would have been a horribly insensitive remark if he knew what had happened. So obviously he didn't know.

But it was equally apparent that Luke did. No wonder he'd sent Megan upstairs to sit with Warren instead of out in the cold to search! He'd wanted to protect her in this second possibly delicate pregnancy.

And no wonder Megan had been of two minds about being pregnant—pleased about the baby, frightened of the possibility of another miscarriage.

"And then, afterward, Rand didn't want to tell anybody what had happened," Megan went on. "He said they'd just ask nosy questions and offer awkward sympathy. And there'd soon be another pregnancy, anyway,

so there was no sense in talking about the one that had
gone wrong.''

Molly had her own opinions about that, but she decided it would be prudent to keep them to herself just
now.

"Only there wasn't. It's been more than two years.''

"But you have another chance,'' Molly said. "And
this time will be different. Lots of women miscarry for
all sorts of reasons. It doesn't mean you will again.''

She would do anything in her power to be able to
wipe the haunted look from Megan's eyes. But Molly
knew only one thing would accomplish that—holding
her baby in her arms.

And Megan would have the additional joy of having
a loving husband, a happy father, at her side in that
moment.

Bailey stirred and opened her eyes and cried out, confused by the unfamiliar surroundings, and Molly
scooped her up.

It's you and me, honey, she thought as she held her
daughter. *That's all there's going to be. And that's all
we need.*

When her head finally touched her own pillow, Molly
dropped like a rock into sleep. She woke knowing it was
late and heard Bailey's cheerful chatter coming from the
kitchen. She wrapped herself in a bathrobe and followed
the sound.

Bailey was daintily nibbling a doughnut and in the
process showering powdered sugar over table, chair,
floor and pajamas. Another doughnut lay on her plate
awaiting attention. A mug full of hot chocolate, with a
marshmallow on top, stood at her elbow.

Molly eyed the breakfast and raised an eyebrow at
Alix, who took a deep breath. "I'm just so glad... If
she'd wanted caviar for breakfast I'd have gotten it for
her.'' There was a trace of defiance in her tone.

"Gramma was nice to give me doughnuts," Bailey added. Her voice was thick with powdered sugar.

So we have a new alliance forming, Molly thought. But that was as it should be. A grandparent and a grandchild teaming up against the generation in the middle could be healthy once in a while.

Alix's gaze wavered, and that small sign of uncertainty tugged at Molly. Maybe Megan was right, she thought. Her mother was trying, but didn't know how to break the ice.

Molly reached into the doughnut box. "Oh, why not? Everybody needs to be hyperactive once in a while, and I'll need all the energy I can muster to work today. Put another spoonful of sugar in your coffee, Mom, and join us."

Alix sat down, her spine straight and her body stiff. "Surely you're not taking Bailey to Oakwood today?"

"Why not? She'll have to learn the rules, so why not do it while the memories are still strong? Besides, the longer you just think about things the worse they get."

That philosophy, she thought, applied to her every bit as well as it did to Bailey. She couldn't avoid Luke, so her best move was to face him as soon as possible, act just as she normally would and wait to see how he intended to approach the problem.

Alix was studying Bailey's face. The child was intent on her hot chocolate, repeatedly submerging the marshmallow in an effort to melt it. "I expect you're right."

Molly dropped her doughnut.

"And I suppose the less everybody makes of this incident," Alix said thoughtfully, "the more likely she is to be all right and not turn into a spoiled brat."

"Precisely." Molly could hardly get the word out.

"In other words," Alix said, "no more doughnuts for breakfast, Bailey."

Molly hadn't recovered from the shock of having her mother agree with her by the time Watkins opened

Oakwood's front door for them. She'd never seen such a sunny look as the one he fixed on Bailey or seen a dog go into ecstasy as Lucky did when she spotted her playmate. Bailey, calmly taking the homage as her due, peeled off her jacket, dropped it in the precise center of the floor and held out her arm for Watkins to inspect the faint mark—already starting to bruise—where the intravenous needle had been.

Upstairs in the makeshift office, Warren listened patiently to Bailey's fractured account of her hospital experience. And when she went off with Mrs. Ekberg to be delivered to the kitchen, he leaned back in his chair with a sigh and said, "I'm so thankful that she's safe."

But that was all. So, Molly thought, whatever Luke might have told his father about the episode, he hadn't dropped the biggest bombshell.

But why should she have expected any other result? She should have known he'd react this way—with cynicism and disbelief.

In fact, she admitted, she *had* known it. That was why she'd sworn, long before Bailey was born, never to tell him. Only shock had made her break her vow of silence last night, with results she could have—should have—predicted. He was going to take her at her word and convince himself that the whole thing had been a nightmare woven in her overwrought mind.

At mid-afternoon, after the third time she'd had to ask Warren to repeat himself, he pointed across the room at the out-of-place hospital bed and said sternly, "It's your nap time, young woman."

Molly was too strung out to argue even if she could have mustered a logical line of reasoning. As she collapsed on the bed, she heard Warren mutter in satisfaction, "And Mrs. Ekberg wanted me to send this back to the attic. Ha!"

He was nowhere to be seen when she woke, and the room was dim. Molly stretched and sat up. The day had been a complete loss, she thought. She might as well get Bailey and go home.

She found Mrs. Ekberg dusting in the drawing room. "I'm going to call it a day," Molly said. "Where's Bailey?"

The housekeeper's duster paused. "She's not here."

Dread gnawed at Molly's stomach.

"Mr. Luke took her with him," Mrs. Ekberg said. "I assumed he'd told you because he went upstairs before he left, and when he came down he just announced that they were going out."

Molly raised her voice. "And did he happen to announce where he was going, or when he'd be back?"

From the hallway, Luke said, "As a matter of fact, I didn't."

Bailey bounded across the hallway with Lucky at her heels. "Look, Mommy! Luke made me a new badge! It's ever so much better than the one I lost!"

"It's lovely, dear. Would you go out to the kitchen for a minute with Mrs. Ekberg, please?"

They stood in silence till the childish voice and the click of the dog's claws were muffled by the kitchen door.

"That's quite the air of authority you have," Luke said, "dismissing not only the child but the staff. I didn't realize you'd been given free rein to issue orders around here."

Molly ignored him. "I'd like an explanation."

"Of what? When I thought about it, I realized you were right—the badge wasn't really the problem. So I took her down to the plant to make a new one. End of story."

"I'd decided that was to be one of the consequences of her disobedience yesterday. It was Bailey's doing that she lost her badge, and she wasn't going to get a new one for a long while."

"And I happen to think having a new one might

lessen the chances that she'll wander off toward the lake again looking for the one she lost. Do you want to make a federal case of it?''

''You had no right, Luke—''

''Oh, but I do.'' His voice was low, but there was an edge to it like polished steel. ''I have it on the best authority that I'm her father. And that gives me all the rights I choose to take.''

Molly closed her eyes in pain. She had no one to blame but herself. She had cut the ground from under her own feet with that ill-advised confidence last night.

''Molly, why didn't you tell me long ago?'' The edge was still in his voice, but it was marginally less threatening.

She didn't answer right away. She was remembering the day in his office when she'd seen him for the first time since Megan's wedding. She had looked at him— elegant, professional, calm, self-assured, without so much as a shadow in his eyes to show that he remembered the night they had reached out to each other. She had looked at the man who was Bailey's father and she had known that she could stand there in his office and tell him about his daughter and he wouldn't believe her. So she hadn't.

She wet her lips and admitted, ''I never intended to tell you at all. Last night was a mistake.''

''A very big mistake, Molly, from your point of view.''

''Can't you see? I was doing my best to be fair!''

''What about four and a half years ago? Did you give any thought to fairness then? No—you never even gave me a chance to know her. You deliberately kept her away from me. Well, now that I know, I want my daughter, Molly. And I am going to keep her.''

CHAPTER EIGHT

LUKE'S words, low and fierce, seemed to bounce off the drawing room walls like billiard balls. *I am going to keep her....*

"Closing your eyes and covering up your ears isn't going to change the situation," he said. "Stop acting like an ostrich."

Molly realized he was right. She was standing in the middle of the room with her hands cupped over her ears as if to shut out what she didn't want to hear. And not only was that kind of reaction not going to alter the facts, the display of fear was only going to encourage him to renew—maybe even expand—his demands.

Except, she thought, it was impossible to expand this particular threat. There was nothing larger, nothing worse than taking her daughter away.

She folded her hands on the back of a Chippendale side chair and tried to regain the ground she'd lost. "You can't have her," she said. Her voice shook, and she had to stop and swallow hard. "You can't take her away from me. You'd have to prove I was an unfit mother—and you can't do it."

"Sure of that, are you? You don't even have a home of your own."

"You don't, either. Warren told me himself he still owns this house. You're living on the goodwill of your father just the same way I am right now. The difference is, I'm planning to move out just as soon as I can."

"As soon as you can afford it? That's another interesting point. The matter of your job—"

"What does that mean?" she asked angrily. "Are you

planning to get rid of me just to improve your case? And on what grounds? How are you going to explain to your father that I've suddenly become inadequate to do my work?''

''I'm not planning anything of the sort. But you must admit your new business—with its one client—isn't going to look terribly promising to a judge.''

She wasn't listening. ''And as long as we're on the subject, what about your father, Luke? You haven't even told him, have you? He has no idea the little girl he was holding on his lap today is his grandchild. Which means that your threat is a pretty empty one.''

''I should think with the interest you have in keeping your job that you wouldn't want him to have another shock just now. You were the one who insisted he not even know Bailey was missing—''

''He'll have to face the shock sometime, won't he? Unless, of course, you just forget about this wild idea of yours altogether.''

''You'd like that, wouldn't you? Well, you're not going to get your wish.'' Luke turned on his heel. ''Just to satisfy you, I'll go drop the news on him right now. Perhaps you'd like to come along in case he needs soothing. I'm sure you'd be happy to play the angel of mercy.''

He didn't wait for an answer before he stalked out of the room.

In the sudden silence, Molly's hands clenched on the back of the chair as if she was trying to squeeze it into pieces. Once again, she thought, he had turned things against her—though this time, she admitted, she'd handed him the opportunity on a platter. She'd incited him. And if, when Warren heard this announcement, he had another relapse, it would be as much her fault as Luke's.

Luke tapped once at the door of the temporary office next to Warren's bedroom and went in. The lights were off and the room was silent.

He stood there for a moment, letting his eyes adjust to the dimness. Despite the incongruous furnishings and the passage of years, the sitting room was still permeated with his mother's presence, and gradually, under the influence of that gentle atmosphere, he felt his anger seep away.

It hadn't truly been anger, anyway, he admitted. Yes, he'd been furious with Molly, but mostly he'd been apprehensive about Warren. He wasn't afraid of how his father would react, exactly. Luke was a grown man, and he was taking full responsibility for his actions. Warren couldn't ask any more than that.

But he dreaded seeing the hurt in Warren's eyes and knowing that his carelessness had caused that pain. And so, without even understanding why, he had almost gone to his father in defiance, with something like adolescent bravado—which would have made it all so much harder for Warren.

"Thanks, Mom," he said under his breath, and stepped into the hall.

Through the stair railing he could see Mrs. Ekberg, just closing the front door. *Molly didn't waste any time in getting clear,* he thought. Though he didn't exactly blame her. Warren wasn't likely to be too pleased with her, either. Luke wondered if she'd considered how that might affect her job.

Mrs. Ekberg started up the stairs. Luke waited till she reached the top and asked, "Do you happen to know where my father is?"

"In the sun room, I believe." She looked past him and clicked her tongue. "I do wish he'd let me straighten up this room."

"It doesn't really matter, does it, Mrs. Ekberg? There are plenty of other rooms." *And putting the old furniture in place won't bring Mother back,* he thought, *it'll only make the memories stronger.* Which, he suspected, was why Warren was so stubborn about it. He moved to the top of the stairs.

"I know. It's my pride that stings, I suppose, at seeing it look so ratty. It was such a pretty room once, and your mother loved it so." She pulled the door closed with an air of finality. "Though of course as long as Miss Molly needs it for an office… It's worth any amount of injury to my pride to have her here. She's so good for Mr. Warren. He laughs again, you know."

"I know." *But he may not be laughing after I give him this news.*

He wondered what had drawn Warren to the sun room at this hour. It wasn't at its best in the afternoon. It was a room for mornings, when sunshine spilled through the long windows and emphasized the brilliant colors of flowers and birds in the gardens.

Of course, it was a fittingly ironic place for this talk, Luke thought, for it was to the sun room that he'd taken Molly the day of his mother's funeral for the chat that had been intended as apology but ended as lecture, instead.

Warren was sitting in a wicker chair so large that it made him look even more frail, his back to the windows, a book open on his lap and the dog sprawled at his feet.

Luke stopped in the doorway. "May I have a minute, Dad?"

Warren put his finger between the pages to mark his place and closed the book. "Of course. Minnesota history's been around a long time. It can wait for me a bit longer."

Luke settled on the arm of a sofa. "I have something to tell you that I'm afraid may come as a shock."

Warren looked at him, his expression politely inquiring.

As gently as he could, Luke said, "Little Bailey…

Well, she can't be my stepsister. Because she's my daughter.''

Warren didn't even blink.

The silence stretched painfully. *Didn't he understand?* ''Did you hear me, Dad?''

''I'm not deaf, Lucas.'' Warren sounded testy. ''But you said I might be shocked. I was waiting for you to get to the shocking part.''

Luke's head was reeling. ''That... that was it.''

''Well, I hate to question your judgment, but if you truly expected me to be surprised, I'm very disappointed in you. Hadn't you noticed how much Bailey looks like your mother? It's mostly the shape of her face, I think— and perhaps the eyes, as well. I caught it the first time I saw her.''

Luke hit the heel of his hand against his temple. ''Let me get this straight.'' He couldn't keep the sarcasm out of his voice. ''Do you go around checking out every kid you see in case there might be a resemblance?''

''Oh, no. Under the circumstances, I was looking for it.''

Luke felt as if he'd regrouped from the first sucker punch just in time to be hit with another. Why would his father have considered the possibility when Luke himself hadn't even been suspicious?

''That day I interviewed Molly,'' Warren went on, sounding pleased with himself, ''she was very nervous when you showed up. And she didn't answer the question when I asked if you and she had been friends. I just...wondered.'' His voice picked up a tart edge. ''Of course as time's gone on, I wondered even more whether anyone was going to admit it.''

''I didn't know, Dad. Believe me. If I had—''

If I had known, what would I have done? He'd have shouldered his responsibility for his child, of course. But beyond that...

It was easy to look back through rose-colored glasses

and create some happy-ever-after scenario. But the fact was they'd been a couple of careless kids caught in a passionate moment. Molly had been suffering from a massive infatuation. Luke had never before seen her as anything but the kid who tagged along and too often had to be rescued. It was hardly a blueprint for any kind of long-term relationship.

How long would it have been before her infatuation burned itself out in day-to-day contact and left her bitterly blaming him? How long would it have been before he grew to resent that she'd had to be rescued once more?

Not that any of those things mattered, of course. Trying to figure out what might have happened in the past if things had been different was pure fiction. It was the present that had to be dealt with.

Luke said, softly, "I don't know what to do, Dad."

Nothing interrupted the silence except the scrape of a stray branch against the glass.

Finally Warren leaned forward and patted Luke's arm. "I'm not worried about that," he said. "You'll do the right thing, I'm certain." He smiled reassuringly and pushed himself up from his chair, and left Luke sitting there alone.

Even with the fits and starts of the last few days, the book was progressing nicely. Warren was obviously pleased with the project. He read the new section Molly had finished that morning and set it aside with a contented sigh. "I can't think of a single way to improve it," he said. "We seem to be on exactly the same wavelength, Molly."

Hardly, Molly thought. *Because if you knew what I was thinking…*

She'd had to force herself to walk into Oakwood that afternoon for her first encounter with Warren since Luke had talked to him. He'd been waiting for her in the dining room. She sent Bailey straight to the kitchen, squared her shoulders and went in to face him. But Warren's demeanor hadn't changed at all. Over lunch he told her about the volume of history he'd been reading with the same gentle, self-deprecating humor he'd shown so many times before.

She'd been seriously off balance until she realized that he wouldn't mention such a sensitive subject where some of the staff might overhear. He'd wait till they were alone.

But even when they'd gone up to the sitting room where no one could intrude, he said nothing.

Luke lost his nerve, Molly thought, and told herself it was stupid to feel disappointed—for wasn't that exactly what she wanted?

She pushed the question aside. She'd have the rest of her life to sort out the answer. "Now that we've got an overview of all of Meditronics' history," she said, "I think we should start playing with the video idea. What do we want it to look like?"

Warren's brow wrinkled. "I thought it would just follow along the same path as the book."

"It could. That way it would be something like a fast-paced slide show. Or we could present it as—"

She was interrupted by a soft knock, and a moment later Bailey's face appeared around the edge of the door. She clutched a basket piled high with aromatic golden-brown scones, and two steps behind her was Mrs. Ekberg with a tea tray.

"Cook made scones so Bailey could practice her measuring," the housekeeper explained, "and we decided to share the wealth. I hope we're not interrupting, but they're best when they're fresh and hot. And you two need a break now and then, anyway."

Bailey set the basket squarely atop her mother's papers and bounded across the room to fling herself at Warren. "I didn't get to show you my ouch today," she told him and held out her arm to display the bruised spot where the IV needle had been. But as soon as he'd sympathized, she slid off his lap and tugged at Mrs. Ekberg's sleeve. "I'm ready to go. Come play tea with me."

As the door closed behind them, Molly shook her head in wonder. "She made scones just so Bailey could measure the ingredients? Your staff is the limit, Warren. Furthermore, I'll bet Bailey decided to use the silver tea service today, and that's the only reason we got the Haviland one."

Warren didn't answer.

Molly glanced at him and was startled to see the brilliance of tears in his eyes.

He wiped them away and said, "Thank you, my dear. I'm so glad to have the chance to know my beautiful granddaughter."

Molly felt as if she was being choked. "He told you, then," she managed to say.

Warren nodded. "My only regret is how long it took."

"I'm sorry," Molly said. Conscience, shrieking that she must be fair, pushed her on. "That isn't Luke's fault. He didn't know." She bit her lip and added under her breath, "And now that he does, he's plenty angry about it."

Warren split a scone and spread jam across the steaming surface. "Lucas is generally pretty levelheaded. Give him a little time, and I expect he'll come around." He looked up and smiled. "Now, tell me what Miss B was like as a baby."

The reminiscences, and Warren's reaction to them, left Molly feeling almost buoyant when she came downstairs to collect Bailey an hour later. There was no doubt where to find her. The child was sitting on the bottom step next to Luke, holding a new doll and surrounded by heaps of tiny, exquisite doll clothes—a wardrobe that made Molly's look sparse.

Suddenly she wasn't flying high any more. She felt like a week-old helium balloon. Yesterday it had been the badge. Today he'd escalated to a doll. At the rate he was going, Luke's little princess was very quickly going to become a spoiled brat whining for a present every time she saw him.

Bailey looked blissful. "Look, Mommy, what Luke brought me."

"I see," Molly said. She stepped across the sea of doll clothes and faced Luke squarely. "I believe I need to talk to you."

"And I have a few things to bring to your attention, too." He stood up, and Molly thought of a rattlesnake uncoiling just enough to strike. "I've made arrangements with Mrs. Ekberg for Bailey to stay with her so we can go out for an early dinner."

"I'd sooner eat grass."

"We could stay here, of course. But this conversation is likely to take a while, and unless you'd enjoy having my father's input into the discussion—"

Molly glared at him. "Obviously I don't have a choice. So yes, I'd love to have dinner with you."

"That's what I thought," Luke murmured. "Mrs. Ekberg will put Bailey to bed here, and she can stay the night."

Molly didn't need a guidebook to see the logic behind that suggestion. He was starting to lay the foundations for his custody case. It would look good to a judge for Bailey to already be spending nights at Oakwood.

"Absolutely not," Molly said. "She can put her to bed—if we're gone that long, which I doubt will be the case. But I'll take her home with me. I won't leave her alone."

"She won't be alone. And we might as well start making the transition."

She could hardly believe her ears. "*What* transition?

If that's what you want to talk to me about, don't get the idea that a steak will change my mind."

"I'm of the opinion," he said gently, "that nothing short of a stick of dynamite would change your mind."

And what exactly does that mean? Before Molly had a chance to dissect the statement, he'd picked Bailey up for a hug. "I'm taking your mother out on a dinner date, princess. Be good for Mrs. Ekberg, all right?"

Bailey's lower lip crept out. "I want to go."

"Do you? Maybe I'll take you next time." He held her while she leaned out of his arms to give her mother a kiss, then turned her over to Mrs. Ekberg.

"Don't think I missed that," Molly said acidly as he swept her out the front door to the Jaguar. "The little maneuver where you didn't even let me hold her to kiss her goodbye."

Luke raised his eyebrows, but didn't comment, just opened the passenger door for her.

Molly settled herself and folded her arms tightly. "You are not taking her away from me," she said as Luke slid behind the wheel.

"Molly, sometimes you sound like a broken record."

"And I'll keep right on until you understand what I'm saying. Another thing, Luke—the incredible toys have to stop."

"One doll," he said. "This is hardly a crime."

"It looked like Christmas in that hallway."

He glanced at her. "Obviously you've never experienced an Oakwood Christmas."

"Your family traditions are beside the point. If you try to buy her, you'll destroy her, Luke."

He didn't comment, and in a few minutes the Jaguar stopped in front of one of the most elegant restaurants in the city.

Great, Molly thought. *My one chance to come here, and not only does it have to be with Luke, but I didn't even have a minute to freshen my lipstick.*

Luke helped her out, a valet took charge of the car, and a uniformed doorman ushered them inside.

It was early, and the dining room, which looked over the deep blue water of Lake Superior, was almost empty. The maître d' showed them to a table in an isolated corner and fussed over seating Molly so she had the best view of the lake.

Perhaps his idea of going out for dinner hadn't been so crazy after all, Molly thought. On a weeknight, in this quiet place, they were not likely to be disturbed. On the other hand, anything she tried to eat was apt to choke her. Luke seemed to understand that. He didn't ask what she'd like for an appetizer, he simply ordered.

"I don't intend to drown her in gifts," Luke said, "just provide a few things—"

"A few things?"

"That will make her feel…comfortable at Oakwood."

She knew he'd almost said *at home* but had thought better of it at the last moment.

Luke leaned forward. His eyes were so dark and intense she couldn't meet his gaze any longer. "Molly, I want to tell her I'm her father."

She stared at her menu as if it was the most interesting piece of literature in the world. "I'm sure you don't need my permission."

"I'd like to have your help."

She slapped the menu shut and flung it on the table. "You're threatening to take my daughter away from me, and you want me to help you do it?"

"Not exactly." Luke looked past Molly and nodded, and the wine steward approached the table.

By the time Luke had approved the wine, Molly had managed to regain her self-control.

"The wine's very good," he said. "Try some, it'll help you relax."

"I don't want to relax. To answer your question, Luke—"

"She's going to be told. Would you rather be there to answer her questions and help her adjust or not?"

Molly bit her lip. He knew perfectly well she couldn't deliberately hurt Bailey. He'd neatly boxed her in. She had no real choice.

Obviously he knew it, but instead of closing in for the kill as she'd expected, Luke sat back in his chair. The only sign of nerves she could see was that he held his wineglass by the stem and was endlessly turning it, staring at the deep red liquid as it sloshed in rhythm with the movement of his fingers. "I talked to my attorney today."

She hadn't expected him to move quite so fast—or, having done so, to give her warning. "And?" she asked cautiously.

"He feels my chances of getting custody aren't very good."

His voice was very quiet, and it took Molly an instant to register the importance of the words. "But that's—"

Before hope could rush over her, he snatched it away. "Except, of course, that I have far more resources than you do, and I can wear you down until you can't afford to fight me any more, and I'll win by default."

She drew a long, slow, shaky breath, which burned her throat worse than raw alcohol would. "That's not fair."

The waiter set a tray between them. Luke picked up his wineglass and looked at her over the rim. "And you have been fair to me?"

Molly put her face into her cupped hands. She had made a very big mistake. He'd told her so. She suspected she was only beginning to understand how huge her miscalculation had been.

"Do try the pâté," Luke murmured. "I think you'll enjoy it. I've found it to be the best anywhere in the city."

The only way she would enjoy the pâté, Molly

thought, was if she pushed his face into it. But surely she didn't have to sit still for this torture. "I'm sure it's lovely," she said icily. "But I don't seem to be hungry, after all. If you'll excuse me—"

"Sit down."

"Why?"

"Because we've only started. You're quite right—bankrupting you wouldn't be fair. More to the point, it would take longer than I care to wait."

If he knew the state of her resources, Molly thought, he might change his mind about that. She sank into her chair.

Luke spread pâté on a toast point and held it out to her. "So I'm offering you a compromise."

"I'm listening." Absentmindedly, she took the tidbit.

"Joint custody."

"Which means precisely what? Half her time with you, half with me? I'm not agreeing to that, you understand, just asking."

"Some families handle it that way. It wouldn't be my first choice. In legal terms, joint custody means we both retain full parental rights to the child. What it comes down to is that neither of us makes decisions about her without the approval of the other."

"And judging by the way we've agreed on everything so far," Molly said sweetly, "that ought to be positively enjoyable. Do you mean major decisions or any at all? If I'd have to consult you before I get her hair cut—"

"Major decisions." He looked at her approvingly. "I'm glad you're enjoying the pâté. Would you care for another?"

Molly hadn't been aware that she'd eaten it, but her hand was empty.

He carefully created another tidbit and passed it to her. "For instance, you couldn't move back to Chicago with her unless I agreed to it."

Molly hadn't even considered the idea. Suddenly it looked horribly attractive.

"In practical terms," Luke went on, "it would mean Bailey will continue to live with you, at least for now—but I'd have unrestricted contact. None of this every-other-weekend-and-three-hours-on-Wednesdays sort of nonsense."

"*At least for now?* And what precisely does that mean?"

"It means," Luke said levelly, "when she's a few years older, she can make up her own mind where she lives."

"And you'll no doubt make sure she has all the goodies in the meantime, so she'll choose you."

"I don't happen to think she's quite that easily manipulated, Molly, and I know I'm not that stupid. In any case, you aren't going to be hard-pressed for cash yourself. My attorney also told me what I could expect a court to order in child support under a joint custody arrangement. So I'll start writing you a check every month." He held out another toast point.

"No." She reached across the table and pushed his hand back. Her palm felt as if it had been scalded by the brief contact. "I will not live on your money."

He ignored her. "I've also started an account into which I'll deposit the amount I'd have paid over the last four years."

Molly gritted her teeth and fought a battle with her pride. She had supported her daughter for nearly four years and she could continue to do so. But was it fair to Bailey to turn down the sort of security his nest egg would represent? "All right," she said reluctantly. "But I want you to know right now that I won't draw a dollar out of it. It'll be Bailey's college fund."

Luke shrugged. "Dad's already taken care of that. He made the arrangements this morning. Those are my terms, Molly. My name goes on her birth certificate. We agree to joint custody. We have an equal voice in what happens to her. I have free access to her any time. And of course I pay child support.''

''And if I don't agree, you take me to court.''

Luke said genially, ''And wear you down until you can't afford to fight any more.''

''That's blackmail, Luke.''

''I prefer to think of it as the stick of dynamite it takes to change your mind.'' He picked up his wineglass. ''It's reality, Molly. Make your choice.''

But she had none, and both of them knew it. Molly took a deep breath and nodded.

Luke raised his wineglass. ''To our daughter. When shall we tell her, do you think?''

Luke was more nervous about facing a three-year-old than he'd been in any other situation in his life. Being called on the carpet during his teenage years, watching his first autopsy in medical school, committing himself to a ten-million-dollar deal—none of them could compare.

It didn't help that their conversation with Bailey had to be put off till the next day. She'd been asleep when they got back to Oakwood, and Molly said, ''It won't do any good to try to wake her, because she wouldn't remember a thing.''

So he had reluctantly carried his drowsy daughter to Molly's car and spent the night rehearsing what he'd say to her.

They'd agreed to take her for a drive up the lakeshore late the following afternoon, to a beach where there would be complete privacy and no interruptions. That had been Molly's suggestion. Luke suspected it was because she had no more idea how Bailey might react than he did. She'd never admit it, though. He was certain of that.

He went home early and changed into jeans and running shoes, but when he went to the makeshift office to see when Molly would be free, he was startled to find the door open, the enormous desk in pieces in the hallway and Mrs. Ekberg stripping the sheets off the hospital bed. "What happened?" he asked.

The housekeeper shrugged. "Don't ask me. He called a crew in to move most of the boxes to the storage room and told me he was well enough now to work in the library, so I could do what I liked in here. I thought I'd better leap at the chance."

"I can see that," Luke said.

"*And* he told me to make up the green bedroom at the far end of the hall for him because he's moving down there."

"What? Why's he giving up his bedroom?"

"That's what I asked him. He just gave me that look of his that tells you to mind your own business and went off. He was whistling," Mrs. Ekberg added darkly. "Miss Molly said to tell you she'd be with you in a few minutes."

"Thanks," Luke said absently.

He found his father in the library with a legal document spread out on the desk blotter.

"Molly's changing her clothes," Warren said.

"I heard. Mrs. Ekberg thinks you've flipped."

"Why?"

"Because the master of the house is moving out of the master suite, that's why."

"Oh, that." He tapped the document. "I'm deeding the house over to you."

Luke's heart plunged to his toes. "Dad—you're not that sick. Are you?"

"Doesn't matter, it's time. So since I'm not going to be the owner anymore, I'm vacating the main bedroom." He added airily, "You'll notice, however, that before I sign the papers I'm settling myself firmly in a room just down the hall.'' He grinned and laid the document aside. ''So what are you and Molly up to today?''

You and Molly. So that was the way the wind had shifted. Well, Warren would get the message sooner or later that Luke and Molly weren't a combination and weren't ever going to be.

''Luke!'' Bailey called, and flung herself on him. He tossed her over his shoulder like a sack of grain and let his gaze roam over her mother. He'd been right about the jeans, he decided. With her long, slim legs Molly looked great in them. Though there might be other outfits that would do as well…

''Don't get any ideas, Warren.'' Molly's voice was crisp.

Luke frowned. Did she need to be quite so curt? Surely there was no need to fuss about Warren's crazy notions right now.

''Haven't had an idea in years,'' Warren murmured. ''Have a good time—whatever you have planned.''

They drove a few miles up the scenic highway toward Two Harbors and pulled off to walk along a deserted pebbly beach to look for agates. A little later, Molly sat on a driftwood log, cuddled Bailey close beside her and told the child that she now had the father she'd asked for.

Bailey looked from her mother to Luke. Her face was solemn, her forehead wrinkled as if she didn't quite understand. ''You're going to be my daddy?''

Luke nodded. He felt as if he was taking a vow. As carefully as if she were a bubble, he stretched out a forefinger to touch his daughter's hand. ''I'm very proud to be your daddy, Bailey.''

Bailey's face cleared. ''Okay.'' She bounced from her seat on the log, opened her sweaty little hand and dumped her trove of agates into Luke's palm. ''I'm ready to go,'' she announced. ''I want a date supper.''

''Dinner date,'' Molly corrected, but Bailey was gone,

plunging across the sand toward where they'd left the car.

Bewildered, Luke looked at Molly. "That's it?" he murmured. "That's all she's got to say about it?"

"What else is there?" She stood up and dusted off the seat of her jeans. "Congratulations, Mr. Hudson. You're a father."

He knew she'd meant the words to be ironic, but somewhere in the middle her voice caught. He spotted tears as she turned away.

He didn't know how to comfort her. He didn't even know if he wanted to try. After all, it wasn't as if he'd robbed her of her child. The whole point was that he didn't intend to.

Still, she'd been incredibly generous, handling the situation as she had. She could have made it all very difficult.

"Molly." He put his arm around her shoulders and was startled at how small and fragile she felt.

For a moment she stood still, her head bent, her face turned but pressed against his arm. Then she stepped away from him and walked to the car. She looked very much alone.

Luke lifted Bailey into her safety seat. "Now, how about that dinner date? Where are we going?"

She looked at him as if he'd sprung a cog and said, "KidzPlace."

Luke raised an eyebrow and turned to Molly. "She sounds as if there's nowhere else."

"There isn't, in her mind." Molly fastened her seat belt.

He was mildly annoyed that she hadn't looked at him even once since she'd sat with Bailey on the driftwood log.

"If you'll just drop me at Oakwood before you go to the restaurant, Luke—"

Bailey said, "I want Mommy, too."

He saw a flicker of pain cross Molly's face. "Honey, sometimes… Sometimes Daddy wants to just be with you."

It hurt her to say that, he thought. But she'd done it anyway. For Bailey's sake, of course, but still…

Bailey thrust lower lip out.

"But this isn't one of those times," Luke said. "Of course your mommy's going too, princess."

"Please don't, Luke." Her voice was so low he had to lean toward her to hear. "Don't encourage her to believe that we're a family—because we're not."

"We're going to have a hamburger, Molly," he said dryly. "Not a major life-style change."

She didn't say any more. But she still didn't look at him.

Between her rubbery chicken bits and KidzPlace's enormous indoor playground, Bailey was in heaven. She climbed over, under and around, now and then calling, "Look at me!" and beaming when they applauded.

"Little daredevil," Luke said. "She's really something, isn't she? I wish—" He stopped abruptly. "I wish I could be more than a part-time dad."

Molly stared at him. "Don't try it," she said harshly. "You made an agreement and you have no choice but to follow through with it."

"Do I?" he asked, almost to himself. "What if there's a different way? A better way?"

He saw the fear that filled her eyes—the fear that she would lose her daughter. And he felt the same fear deep in his gut.

Warren's words rang in his ears. *You'll do the right thing,* he'd said. *I'm sure of it.* And he'd moved out of the master bedroom and restored the room next door, as if he expected…

Don't encourage her to believe that we're a family, Molly had said a little while ago.

But why not?

Luke looked into his empty coffee cup, then across the table at the mother of his child. And he heard himself say, as if from a great distance, "Will you marry me?"

CHAPTER NINE

MOLLY'S hand went numb with shock, and almost in slow motion, her coffee cup tipped onto its side. She didn't realize it till the barely warm dregs dripped on her jeans and soaked through to her skin. She reached for a napkin to blot the spill, but the action was automatic. She was incapable of thinking.

Will you marry me?

What in heaven's name was the man up to now? He couldn't actually mean it, could he? Just a few minutes ago he'd said he had no intention of embarking on a major life-style change.

Her paper napkin turned brown and soggy, and Luke went after another handful from the service counter. As Molly finished mopping the mess he picked up his own empty cup and said, ''Would you like some more coffee?''

He sounded, Molly thought, as if the question was just as important as the last one he'd asked. ''No, thanks.''

Luke sat down. ''You're right. It tastes pretty bad, doesn't it?''

She watched his long fingers as he fiddled with the paper cup. He folded the handles and unrolled the rim. She looked on in fascination, wondering if he realized what he was doing.

''As nervous as you are about it,'' she said finally, ''perhaps you'd like to pretend you didn't ask that question. And I don't mean the one about the coffee.''

Luke didn't answer. He seemed to be thinking it over.

Time stood still. Molly waited, trying not to hold her breath, trying to tell herself that it really didn't matter whether he was thinking better of a few rash words. But she knew it did matter. She didn't want him to withdraw the question because—despite the years and the pain—she still cared for him.

No, that wasn't quite accurate. She didn't care for him *still*. She'd learned to care for him *again*.

Once, as a girl, she had worshipped him and thought it was the same as being in love. Now she knew the difference, and now she knew it wasn't infatuation she felt.

Because she had left behind that schoolgirl crush, she had foolishly believed she had gotten over Luke. Instead, in the past weeks, as she had come to know the man he had become, something far more lasting had awakened deep inside her.

She had fallen in love with him. She had done so blindly, heedlessly, foolishly—but no less certainly.

Looking back, she had no trouble at all diagnosing what had happened to her. She even knew the moment it had started—that very first day in his office, when she'd seen how worried Luke was about his father and the lengths he was willing to go to reawaken Warren's interest in life. And then there was the way he'd treated Bailey from the very beginning. How many men would have postponed the start of a business day to make a silly badge for a three-year-old? Or put aside exhaustion to teach her how to play with a dog as large as she was?

Molly had been tiptoeing along a precipice long before the night Bailey had been lost—but that was no doubt when she'd gone over the edge for good. She'd been so horribly upset, and Luke had been there like a rock, holding her steady and keeping her safe as surely as the dog had protected Bailey.

Even in the midst of her distress, how could she have failed to recognize that her reaction to him wasn't simple gratitude but something a great deal more complicated?

Subconsciously, she must have known—and she had

not wanted to let go of him even when the danger was past. So she'd blurted out the truth about his daughter—not only because it wouldn't have been fair not to tell him but because she wanted to hold onto Luke.

She had wanted…this.

"A little nervous yourself, aren't you?" Luke said.

Molly realized she'd turned the last dry napkin into infinitesimal shreds. Awkwardly, she bundled the evidence inside the coffee-logged wad of paper, propped her elbows on the table and folded her hands.

Luke said, "We aren't going to pretend I didn't ask, because I did. And the question stands."

It didn't only stand, Molly thought, it positively resounded. She was surprised Bailey hadn't heard it all the way up at the top of the playground.

Will you marry me?

But that wasn't truly what he was asking, she knew. At its heart, the question really had nothing to do with her. If it wasn't for Bailey, the thought of marrying Molly would never have crossed Luke's mind, and they both knew it.

All she had to do was say yes and she would have achieved exactly what she'd subconsciously set out to do. But only now did Molly realize how hollow the accomplishment would be. He didn't want to marry her, but he'd go through the motions. To have his child all the time, to be more than a makeshift dad, to give Bailey the semblance of a normal family, he would make the sacrifice of marrying her mother.

"For Bailey." Molly managed to keep her voice level.

Luke glanced at the playground. Molly followed his gaze and watched Bailey come down the plastic-tube slide headfirst.

He sounded impatient. "Of course it's for Bailey. I never said this would be the love match of the century."

His tone, as much as the words, scraped Molly's soul

raw. "I certainly can't argue with that." *Because even though I love you, you don't love me.*

He shrugged. "I thought we were actually getting along fairly well for a while until this little difficulty came up."

"This little difficulty?"

"Deciding who gets Bailey. If we don't have to argue about that, I don't see any reason we couldn't deal reasonably well together."

It was a chilly assessment of what would undoubtedly be an even cooler relationship.

I have to say no, Molly told herself. *It will only hurt worse, and longer, if I don't.* But even though she knew it would be a disaster if she agreed, she couldn't force herself to turn down what she wanted so badly. Not directly. She did the best she could. "Luke, listen to yourself. It's crazy."

"Is it? If you'd told me at Megan's wedding about the baby, and I'd proposed, you'd have married me in a minute."

"I thought I loved you, then." *And now I know I do— and it doesn't make a bit of difference, because you don't care about me.* "What sort of odds would you have given that marriage?"

He didn't hesitate. "Slim to none. But we're not kids anymore, Molly. We're not blinded by infatuation."

"We're not foolish enough to think that love solves everything," she said wryly.

"Exactly—love doesn't come into it at all. And we both want what's best for Bailey."

Bailey. They'd come around in a circle. Was he right, that this alliance—she could hardly call it a marriage— was in Bailey's best interests?

Instead of being shuffled between two people, two houses, never quite knowing where she fit in, Bailey would have two full-time parents, a fairly normal family life, one home. And what a home. Not that material things could be allowed to matter in a decision as important as this.

Molly had sworn on the day Bailey was born that she would put her child's welfare above everything else, that she would never again make a decision without first considering its impact on Bailey.

But how far did that go? Was it her duty to accept Luke's proposal—for Bailey's sake?

Or would she simply be using Bailey as an excuse for doing precisely what she wanted? And fooling herself all the while not only about her motives but their chances of success?

She was certain of only one thing—that she was too confused to make a rational decision. "I need some time to think about it, Luke."

"Molly, there have been peace treaties that were negotiated faster than this."

Under different circumstances, Molly thought, the edge in his voice might have sounded like the desperation of a young man deeply in love and afraid he was going to be turned down. At least he'd been honest. She was glad of that.

Bailey appeared at her elbow, her face flushed from exercise and her hair damp with perspiration. "Mommy, I want something to drink."

Molly reached across the table for her plastic milk glass.

"How long do you want?" Luke asked.

"Everything's changed so fast, Luke. Surely it isn't asking too much to take a few days to think it over."

"All right. But I'm not going to accept some vague I'll-let-you-know-whenever-I've-decided nonsense, so set a time."

"You really think I want to leave something like this hanging over my head indefinitely?" She sighed. "My parents' anniversary party is a week from Saturday. How's that?"

"I suppose it'll do. And if you make up your mind before then—"

"Believe me," Molly said, "you'll be the first to know."

Bailey fell asleep in her car seat on the drive home, worn out by her antics at the beach and on the playground, and she hardly stirred when Luke lifted her, seat and all, from the Jaguar and strapped her into Molly's car. Her overwhelming innocence tugged Molly's heart. *If only I could look into the future and see the best way to keep her from being hurt.*

Molly opened her car door, but she didn't get in. "We only talked about Bailey," she said, without looking at Luke. "What about…us?"

"Do you mean, am I suggesting a real marriage or something that only appears to be?"

"I guess that's what I'm asking, yes." She knew when he moved closer, for the back of her neck tingled.

His voice was very low. "I think separate bedrooms would be a little hypocritical, don't you, considering that we already have a daughter?"

Molly tried in vain to swallow the lump in her throat.

Luke's hands came to rest on her shoulders, and he turned her to face him. "Perhaps we should try a little experiment."

There was no doubt what he had in mind. The husky note in his voice would have told her even if there'd been no other signals.

Molly could hardly out-and-out refuse to let him kiss her when she'd brought up the subject herself. If she balked or didn't cooperate, he'd only ask why she was afraid of the very answers she'd asked for.

And in any case, she wanted to know.

She looked at him and closed her eyes and told herself that this would be basically the same as all the other good-night kisses she'd taken part in over the last few years. She wasn't so foolish—or so inexperienced—as to think that one kiss was exactly like another, but at the heart of the matter Luke's technique probably wasn't so very different than that of any of the men she'd dated.

The fact that he'd given her the first real kisses of her life, and the fact that the circumstances surrounding those kisses had been extremely emotional, had no doubt colored her perceptions and made each caress seem better than it had really been. There probably wasn't a man on earth who could live up to the memories she'd constructed from that long-ago night. It wasn't fair of her even to compare…

Her carefully crafted illusion lasted less than three seconds.

Luke cupped her face in his hands, ran his thumb gently across her lower lip and bent his head. He tasted her slowly and thoughtfully, his mouth barely brushing hers. She shivered uncontrollably, and she wondered how such a gentle touch could cause such violent darts of pleasure throughout her body.

He drew back slightly. "You don't like that approach? Then perhaps—in the name of experimentation—we should try another."

She wanted to say, *No, I like this one just fine.* But her vocal cords were paralyzed. That had never happened before.

Luke obviously took her silence for agreement, and his hands slid firmly over her shoulders and down her back, drawing her close until her body seemed to meld with his. Off balance, she could do nothing but cling to him while his kisses turned ravenous. He commanded her response, and when she obeyed, he demanded more and more. He took her breath, her strength, her willpower…but he gave, as well, until every nerve in her body was vibrating to his touch like the strings of a cello.

When he let her go, Molly sagged against the driver's door and tried not to gasp for air. She realized that Luke, too, was leaning against the car. Was he relying on it for support, she wondered, or simply striking a casual pose to show how unaffected he was?

"I'd consider that a success," he said. His voice was low and a little rough. "What about you, Molly?"

She gave up the struggle to regain control of her knees and sank into her seat. "Good night, Luke."

He leaned across her and solicitously fastened her seat belt. It was the first time Molly had ever considered such a utilitarian action in the light of a seduction technique, for though he didn't lay a finger on her body, his careful attention to the straps made her terribly aware that her breasts still tingled from his embrace and her stomach was simply gone.

He started to withdraw from the car and paused just long enough to press another brief butterfly of a kiss on her lips.

"Give it a chance," he murmured, "and you might get to like that one, too. Drive carefully, Molly."

The ripples of pleasure were diminishing, like the waves left behind by a rock tossed into still water, and reality was once more intruding.

She glanced in the driving mirror at Bailey, her face nestled into the cushioned car seat, sublimely unaware of a scene that would no doubt have fascinated her.

Bailey, who was the only reason he'd kissed her.

"I will," she said tightly. "I have precious cargo."

Luke raised his eyebrows a fraction. "But of course you do."

And she told herself, as she turned onto London Road, that a wise woman wouldn't forget that the entire episode had been only an investigation of whether they could stand each other well enough to form an alliance for Bailey.

Megan's maid opened the Bannisters' massive front door and stepped aside for Molly to enter. "Mrs. Bannister is in her boudoir."

"Thanks. I can find my way." Molly stopped halfway up the elegant staircase and looked over the huge atrium where a week from tomorrow her parents would celebrate their anniversary.

The day she must give Luke his answer.

But that was utter nonsense, of course. She'd lain awake half the night, and she'd concluded that she'd have to be completely mad to accept his proposal. Having made up her mind, there was no point in postponing. She'd tell him today and have it done with.

She tapped on the boudoir door and followed Megan's summons to the bedroom beyond.

Megan was lying on an enormous four-poster bed, her back propped against a stack of peach satin pillows, wearing a negligee that was more lace than anything else and holding a paperback in her hand. Molly thought she looked terribly fragile. Even her hair, brushed but left loose around her shoulders, seemed to have lost its healthy sheen.

"How was the trip yesterday?" Molly leaned over to kiss her sister's cheek.

"Dull, like most of Rand's business things. And it was a very long day, which is why I'm still in bed. When you called this morning I started to get up, but I just couldn't."

"You need to take care of yourself just now." Molly sat at the foot of the bed.

Megan's face brightened. "Anyway, I sneaked away for a couple of hours yesterday to shop. I brought home a couple of dresses for the anniversary party."

"How many are you planning to wear?"

Megan pulled her knees up and folded her arms around them. "Silly—they're for you. Obviously you haven't had time to shop. If you like what I chose— well, I missed your birthday last winter. And if you don't, I'll ship them back." She shrugged. "So please don't make a big deal of it. Looking for clothes for you was the most fun I had all day.''

If Molly had ever felt guiltier, she couldn't remember it. She had to reply to Megan's generosity with a piece of news that might cut her sister to the heart.

"Would you like some coffee or something?" Megan asked. "And you wanted to see the Waterford bowl, too.''

"Can we do that later? And no coffee, thanks.'' Molly braced herself. "I didn't really come to see the bowl, anyway.''

"Oh? This sounds promising.''

Molly asked, as delicately as she could, "You haven't talked to Luke lately?''

"Not since that night in the hospital. Why?''

"Nothing, really.'' She'd procrastinated long enough. There was no easy way to say this, so she might as well stop hoping one would drop into her lap. "I wanted to tell you about a sort of family meeting I had with Mother and Dad the night before last. I called to see if you could come, but Rand said you'd gone to bed already to rest for the trip.'' She couldn't look at Megan, so her gaze wandered. She noted almost absently that the other side of the big bed had obviously not been used last night. Had Rand thoughtfully left his wife alone so he wouldn't disturb her rest? Or was this a regular thing?

And Luke didn't want separate rooms. Maybe she should tell him—with only a hint of sarcasm, of course—that all the best people had them.

Megan's fingers plucked at the hem of the peach satin sheet. "He must have forgotten to tell me you'd called.'' She forced a smile. "So what was so weighty it needed a family meeting? And how does Luke come into it?''

"Luke—'' Molly bit her lip and looked at her hands, white-knuckled in her lap "—is Bailey's father.''

Megan couldn't have looked more stunned if Molly

had picked up the marble base of the bedside lamp and hit her over the head.

Molly's stomach tied itself into a half-dozen knots. ''I'm sorry,'' she said miserably. ''I know he's very important to you.'' *I just hoped he wasn't quite this important.* She fumbled, trying to think of anything that might lessen Megan's shock. ''Anyway, all this happened years ago, so it really doesn't affect—''

Except for the part about getting married, her conscience reminded her, and it looked as if that would affect Megan plenty. But since Molly wasn't going to marry him, after all…

''I thought maybe he'd have told you.'' Molly's voice trailed off.

Megan shook her head as if to clear it. ''No. He's never even dropped a hint to me. That night at the hospital he even asked me about Bailey's father.'' Delicate color rose in her cheeks as she admitted, ''I told him the little I knew and felt absolutely delinquent for talking about your secrets. When I get my hands on him—''

Molly frowned. Megan didn't sound quite as she would have expected for a woman whose world had been turned on its axis.

''I'm surprised you didn't brain me when I started talking about stepfathers,'' Megan muttered. ''I deserved it. Here I was feeling out whether you even knew you were falling for him without so much as a suspicion that you'd already… Well!''

Molly's head was swimming. ''You don't…mind?''

''Mind what? That one of my best friends doesn't tell me a teensy detail like the fact that he's my niece's father, or that my little sister didn't trust me any more than that?''

''Luke didn't know. I told him at the hospital.''

''Oh, in that case, no wonder he looked as if he'd been hit by a tree.''

Or a treehouse, Molly thought. She was giddy. If

Megan really didn't feel romantic about Luke... The whole thing would have been so much more unpleasant if Megan's heart was at stake, too.

Megan was sitting up straight, and there was more sparkle in her eyes than Molly had seen there in weeks. "How did Mother take it? With fireworks, or was she thrilled to pieces that her granddaughter's a Hudson? I wish I'd been there."

Molly shook her head. "Neither. It was weird, Meg. Almost scary. She looked at me and blinked twice and said something about how that might account for the graceful way Bailey moves, since Luke's mother was a dancer. That was it."

"Now I *really* wish I'd been there," Megan said. "So...what's next? With you and Luke, I mean."

"Nothing's next. The arrangements won't be any different than the ordinary divorced couple makes, really."

Megan raised her delicately plucked eyebrows. "Whatever you say, dear. But you look pretty guilty to me."

Molly felt herself color. But she was *not* going to tell Megan about Luke's proposal. What was the point in asking for trouble? Or leaving herself open to well-meant advice, which might be even worse?

She'd decided to turn him down, anyway.

Hadn't she?

Lucky was outside Oakwood that afternoon, sniffing through a flower bed, when Molly parked her car. Bailey bounced in her seat, so eager to join the dog that she made it hard to release her safety harness. But finally she was free to race off. Molly got her briefcase and the stack of books she was returning to Warren and called to the child. "Come on, Bailey, you know the rule. You can't be outside without an adult, and Lucky doesn't count."

"I'll be good," Bailey pleaded.

"I'm just making sure you remember not to wander off again."

Bailey pouted for a few seconds until she concluded her mother wasn't paying any attention, then obeyed. Three-year-olds were so delightfully transparent, Molly thought.

The child bounded to the front door, knocked confidently and swept past the butler with a cheerful, "Good afternoon, Watkins!"

Where had she picked up that one, Molly wondered.

Watkins made the required daily inspection of Bailey's yellowing bruise, then she hopped on one foot to the kitchen to greet the cook.

Bailey was so obviously happy at Oakwood, Molly thought. For the first time she considered what would happen after her work was done. The book was moving along. Most of the work on the video couldn't be done from Oakwood.

When Molly no longer came to Oakwood every afternoon, there would be no reason for Bailey to do so. Of course, come autumn she'd be spending more time in preschool, anyway—but unless Luke made it a point to take her home with him, there might be whole weeks when she didn't see her pals at Oakwood.

She would miss them. Unless…

Molly bit her lip. *Unless I marry Luke,* she thought, and all her uncertainty swirled once more.

Could she live without love? There would unquestionably be passion. After last night, there could be no doubt of that. Would it be an adequate substitute? Could she be contented knowing Bailey was happy? Would that satisfaction be enough?

And could she manage all of that…for a lifetime?

Not a day went by without a fresh jolt for Molly, and an additional argument to add to the ongoing battle in her head.

On Monday afternoon when she arrived at Oakwood, Mrs. Ekberg told her that Luke wanted her to choose a bedroom for Bailey and decide how it should be decorated. Molly nearly dropped her briefcase. Was he so certain of her answer he'd announced to the staff that there would be a wedding? Mrs. Ekberg was matter-of-fact.

Then Molly realized that whether Bailey moved in or simply came for visits, she'd feel more comfortable if she had her own room. Molly couldn't fault Luke for that. In fact, she had to give him grudging credit for asking her advice—since no one knew better than she what Bailey liked or needed.

The next day was one of the rare ones when Warren felt up to visiting friends, and Luke invited Molly—and Bailey, of course—to stay and have dinner with him. As the three of them sat together in the dining room, Molly thought, *He's showing me what I'll be missing if I turn him down.*

And she found herself thinking, as they spent the evening like a family, that perhaps she could marry him, after all.

The following evening, when she was leaving very late, she ran into Luke on his way out of the house. She hadn't seen him wearing a tux since Megan's wedding, and to tell the truth she hadn't really seen much of anything that day—so the impact was stronger than it would otherwise have been.

Even Bailey was impressed by the tux. She stood absolutely still for an unusually long time while she looked at him, and then said, ''You're pretty, Daddy,'' and he'd laughed and swept her up for a kiss.

But it wasn't only his faultless tailoring that made him look so good, Molly thought. There was something about his expression that spoke of exhilaration and eagerness. She couldn't help but wonder where he was going, and with whom.

The next day she found out, when Melinda the golden girl stopped by Oakwood. ''I'm returning the bow tie he left at my house last night,'' she told Watkins. ''Do tell him what a memorable evening I had, won't you?'' Then she'd flashed a superior smile at Molly, who'd had the bad luck to walk through the hall just then, and departed.

Molly, a bit depressed, remembered that while Luke had said he expected their marriage would be a real one, he hadn't uttered a word about limiting himself to his wife—and she concluded that if she had any sense she'd immediately tell him no.

Shortly afterward he called her aside to tell her that his attorney had finished all the paperwork for the custody agreement, parental rights and child support—but it was up to Molly, of course, whether they signed the documents or tore them up. And—faced with the legal realities—she wavered once more.

The day after that he asked Bailey if she'd like to stay at Oakwood overnight, and she eagerly agreed, excited at the adventure. Molly's heart twisted at the thought of how easily Bailey was breaking away from her. She gritted her teeth, however, and told herself it was just as well, for this was what Bailey's future would be—moving back and forth between households. Unless, of course...

But when the time came for her mother to leave her, Bailey burst into a storm of tears, and finally Luke took her out to Molly's car. And then, to Molly's dismay, she sobbed all the way home—because she didn't have her daddy.

Molly couldn't blame the poor child for being confused when she herself hardly knew up from down. The trouble was, time was growing short. The anniversary party was tomorrow, and she still didn't know what her answer would be.

Molly hadn't known her parents had so many friends, for the guest list—like so much of the party—had been

Megan's work. The nicest part about the horde, Molly thought, was that by the time she'd greeted each guest the evening would be at least half over. And with the sheer number of people—enough to make even the Bannisters' enormous house seem crowded—avoiding Luke would probably be no trick at all.

She crossed the atrium and ran into Megan in the dining room doorway. "I'm heartily ashamed of myself," she said. "All the work you put into this party, and I haven't helped at all."

Megan shrugged. "It's what I do best—and heaven knows I have plenty of time."

"Well, tell me what I can do right now, and go sit down."

"Do I look that bad?"

Yes, Molly wanted to say. Megan's face looked pinched, her eyes were shadowed, and even the rich apricot of her dress couldn't seem to reflect color to her cheeks. "You look a little tired," she said tactfully.

A matron fluttered up and kissed Megan's cheek. "Delightful party, darling. Where's that delicious husband of yours?"

"Rand had a business emergency. He's so sorry he couldn't be here."

Molly had heard her utter exactly the same words, with precisely the same inflection, at least a dozen times since the party began. Was Rand's absence the reason Megan seemed so drained and tired? A party this size would be stress enough, of course, even without a missing host.

The band switched from background music to dance numbers, the crowd fell back to leave the center of the atrium free, and Alix and Bernie took the floor for their anniversary waltz.

Thirty years, Molly thought. Three long decades of

living together, raising children, building a home. How had they done it?

What I really want to know is how much it mattered whether or not they loved each other. Had love been like the extra touch of spice which made a dish extraordinary, even though it tasted perfectly good without that last ingredient? Or had it been like the lubricant in an engine that kept the pieces from grating intolerably against each other, eventually to overheat and destroy the whole mechanism?

And how about a one-sided love? Would that be better or worse for a marriage than having none at all?

"I believe," Luke said behind her, "this is my dance."

With a sense of unreality, Molly stepped into his arms.

They hadn't danced together since their dutiful single turn around the floor at Megan's wedding. And he hadn't held her since that incendiary kiss in Oakwood's drive more than a week ago. She tried not to remember what that had felt like, for if she ever needed all her wits about her, it was now. But the warmth of his fingers clasping hers, the weight of his other hand at the small of her back, the brush of his cheek against her hair awakened every sensual memory from that night.

She was startled to realize, however, that in some ways this embrace was even more erotic. The ebb and flow of the music, the movement of their bodies in a rhythmic pattern sent her pulse racing. And the restraint imposed by the crowd added a piquant edge. There were so many things they couldn't do with all the world watching—and that made her want them all the more.

He whispered, "Molly, what—"

She said hastily, "Was Bailey all right? She didn't give you any trouble about staying at Oakwood, I mean? After that scene last night—"

"She was fine as soon as Watkins promised to take

her and Lucky for a walk. You're procrastinating, Molly.''

Breathlessly she plunged on. ''She wanted so badly to come to the party, but it's not the sort of thing for children, is it?''

''Megan's parties never are. Molly, you told me you'd answer at your parents' party. I'm waiting.''

The time for analyzing was over. Molly had argued the question over and over and reached no firm conclusion. The answer would have to come from her heart.

She closed her eyes and looked deep within herself and said, ''Yes.''

As if on cue, the music shifted to a slower tempo, and with increased assurance Luke drew her closer. ''Shall we tell everyone right now?''

He didn't sound happy about it, she thought with a trickle of uneasiness, or even particularly pleased. He sounded triumphant.

As if he'd won a battle...or maybe the whole war.

CHAPTER TEN

ANNOUNCE their engagement—when the prospective bride was already half-regretting her answer and really wanted nothing more than to climb into a damp cave and pretend to be a mushroom?

"No," Molly said hastily. "I mean… This is my parents' special night."

"Don't you think our announcement would make it even more special?"

"I think it would be very rude not to tell our families first. And what about Bailey? Surely she shouldn't be the last to know."

"I doubt she'll file a complaint with the etiquette department," Luke said dryly.

"What's the rush, anyway?" But Molly knew, of course. He wanted her to make a public commitment. The expectations of friends and family would assure she wouldn't change her mind. Luke was no fool. He understood a decision that had taken a week to form wasn't more solid than a snap decision but a whole lot more fluid.

From the corner of her eye she caught rapid movement at the far side of the atrium—people hurrying toward a patch of brilliant apricot which lay on the floor.

"It's Megan," she said. "Something's very wrong."

She pulled away from him and hurried across the room. By the time she reached the edge of the confusion, Megan was sitting up, leaning against a male guest who'd knelt beside her and trying to smile. "I felt a little faint, that's all," she said, but there was no substance to her voice. Molly could hardly hear her. "Please, go on

and enjoy the party.'' She caught Molly's eye. Her gaze
was a desperate plea.

Molly pushed through the crowd and sank to the floor.
Her skirt formed a pool of teal-blue silk against the cold
marble. ''Meg, what is it?''

''It's happening again,'' Megan whispered. ''Come
with me...please?''

Another miscarriage? Oh, no... ''Try to keep me
away. Will you all move back and give her some air?''
Molly looked around wildly, but she couldn't see Luke.
Her mother was there, though. Alix promptly began
shooing people off to the dance floor, the dining room,
the terrace.

Luke appeared out of nowhere. Molly didn't want to
admit the rush of relief she felt at knowing he was there
beside her.

He bent over Megan. ''It's the hospital for you, my
dear. I told the valet to bring my car around.''

She managed a feeble smile. ''You have something
against ambulances, Hudson?''

In the Jaguar's back seat, Molly blotted perspiration
from Megan's forehead. She'd thought her colorless before. Now she was pasty white.

Luke was frowning. ''How long's this been going on,
Meg?''

''A couple of days. Last time it took a whole week,
so I thought surely I could get through the party. And
don't look at me that way, Luke. Just because I didn't
want to ruin Mother and Dad's special day—''

Molly muttered, ''You should have been in bed instead of giving a party.''

''It wasn't the party that caused this. Believe me, I
know the signs. And my doctor said bed rest wouldn't
change a thing, so I might as well go about my normal
activities.''

Much later, as Molly paced the waiting room and
Luke flipped through a magazine, she said, with a trace

of acid, ''I wonder if Megan's doctor knows she includes a party for three hundred in her definition of normal activities.''

Luke didn't look up from the pages of *Fortune*. ''He's probably right that it wouldn't have made a difference.''

''Shouldn't somebody try to find Rand?''

''Why? If Megan wants him, she'll ask for him.''

''That's pretty hard-hearted of you. He has a right....'' Molly's voice trailed off. *And a responsibility. If Megan knew two days ago that this was happening, and Rand went off on business anyway...*

''I see you're finally getting around to wondering why we're the ones sitting in the waiting room,'' Luke murmured. ''If we keep making visits of this frequency and duration, you know, they're going to have to put up a bronze plaque in our honor.''

''At least we're better dressed this time.''

''Speak for yourself. Given a choice between wet running shoes and a bow tie...'' He tugged the tie loose and stuffed it in his pocket. ''But as long as we're sitting here, we might as well accomplish something. There's the matter of setting a wedding date, for one thing.''

Molly's stomach tightened. ''I suppose you want to make it soon.''

''Any reason not to? A big white wedding would be in rather poor taste, so there's no real reason to delay, is there?''

I wish there was, Molly thought. But slowly, she shook her head.

Near midnight, when the worst was over, Luke left to break the news to Bernie and Alix, and Molly stayed at Megan's bedside, stroking her hair and talking softly.

''You're treating me the same way you did Bailey when she was here,'' Megan said finally.

Was the reminder of the child like salt in the wound? ''I'm sorry.''

"No—I meant it's nice to be pampered." She closed her eyes. "It's for the best, I know."

"Maybe so, though it doesn't hurt any less." Molly added carefully, "Perhaps, when you've had time to heal, you'll think about adopting. Once a baby's in your arms, it doesn't matter whether you carried him or not—"

"I know that. But Rand would never agree to giving his name to a child who wasn't of his blood, one who might have tainted genes. As if the two I've lost didn't... But of course, he's certain that's my fault. My blue-collar ancestry."

Molly was horrified at the matter-of-fact note in Megan's voice.

"I guess he thought his own blood would be rich enough to make the difference. But when I miscarried his heir... And then I couldn't seem to get pregnant again. Well, of course I was to blame. You wondered, didn't you, why I was so unhappy about what should be wonderful news?"

Molly said wryly, "I'm beginning to understand."

"I was working up my nerve to tell Rand I wanted out when I realized I was pregnant again. And I knew that if I carried the baby to term, he would consider that child his personal property—and if I divorced him, I'd lose my child just as surely as I had the first one. So I decided to keep quiet."

"You didn't even tell him?"

Megan shook her head. "If I got through the dangerous time, then of course he'd have to know. And if so, my only option would be to make the best of it. Keep a stiff upper lip and all that." She shrugged. "In a horrible way, I feel almost relieved. I'll grieve my baby, of course. But I'm not facing a life sentence any more, tied to a man who doesn't love me."

Her voice trailed off, and for a moment, Molly thought she'd drifted into sleep.

A life sentence…tied to a man who doesn't love me.

"Mother will probably never speak to me again," Megan said. "Giving up all that lovely money and my social position. It's ironic, isn't it? In the space of a couple of weeks we've changed places entirely, in her estimation. You're in the bosom of the Hudson family, and I'm an outcast."

"I don't think I'd go quite that far about either of us."

Megan didn't seem to hear. "Well, she's just going to have to lump it. As soon as Rand gets back from his business trip…"

Something about her inflection warned Molly. "It isn't a business trip?"

"Of course it isn't. He only married me because he wanted a son to carry on the dynasty and because he liked the idea of a wife who was so dependent that she could never walk out no matter how many other women he had. That part backfired, though, because if he was the one who wanted a divorce it would cost him more in a settlement. So he stayed. And I grew more miserable, until I couldn't take it any more…"

Eventually she dozed, but Molly stood for a long time beside the bed, still holding Megan's hand and listening to the chilling echo of her words.

Facing a life sentence. Tied to a man who doesn't love me. He only married me because he wanted a son.

There was an eerie familiarity to the phrases.

Luke's not Rand, Molly told herself. It wasn't fair to compare them. Nevertheless…

Megan had loved Rand once. Molly would never forget the radiance in her sister's face on her wedding day. But her love hadn't been enough to hold the marriage together. Weighed in the balance against a man who didn't love her, a man who only wanted his child, Megan's love hadn't stood a chance. Her love hadn't changed Rand, and in the end it had been crushed to death under the weight of her resentment and pain.

And what about Molly and her love for Luke? Would her case be any different? Luke had been straightforward from the beginning, as she suspected Rand hadn't. He'd admitted he didn't love her, admitted that his main motivation was his daughter. But was honesty a substitute for caring?

Could she afford to take the chance—with herself and with Bailey?

Molly was lying in a lounge chair behind the house, basking in the sunlight and catching up on her rest, when Luke came through the sliding doors onto the deck.

He had never looked better, Molly thought. His worn jeans hugged trim hips, and his lightweight coffee-brown sweater made his eyes look even bigger and more inviting. As she caught his gaze he smiled at her, a slow smile that reached straight through her and turned her heart upside down.

But she couldn't let a smile outweigh what she knew was right. She sat up a little straighter. "Hi. There's some lemonade on the table."

He shook his head and pulled a chair around. "Your mother told me Megan's here."

"She and Bailey are curled up together having a nap. Meg didn't want to go back to that house." Molly deliberately didn't say *home,* but it was apparent Luke knew what she meant. "And since Mother didn't disown her, after all—"

"Megan told you everything, then?"

Molly nodded. "At least, I hope she isn't still leaving something out. I understand why she kept quiet. The fewer people who knew, the easier to maintain her dignity if she had to stay in the situation. But—" *But she told you,* Molly thought. *And I want to know why.*

"It's going to be close quarters with all of you here."

''We'll make room. It probably won't be for long, anyway.''

''Is that why you wanted to talk to me? We can move the wedding date up.''

Molly stared at her fingernails. *Tell him. You have to tell him.*

''Remember?'' Luke prompted. ''You left a message for me that you wanted to talk to me about the wedding.''

''I didn't put it quite that way.''

''No, you were very discreet. Watkins didn't quite lose his professional demeanor, but it was plain that he was dying to know what you were talking about.'' He reached into his pocket. ''I thought you should have this right away.''

He tossed a small white velvet box into her lap. Molly picked it up, but she didn't open it. She didn't need to. The only question was what diamond cut he'd chosen and how it was set. Even the stone's size, she thought, was fairly predictable. For Luke Hudson's bride, only large would do.

If Molly hadn't already been certain of what she must do, that simple action of his would have clarified her thinking. A man in love didn't toss a diamond ring, he put it on his beloved's finger. She gave Luke some credit for not pretending a sentiment he didn't feel. But the missing tenderness was just one more piece of evidence in the chain that had brought her to this moment.

She threw the box back, and he fielded it easily. ''I'm not moving the wedding up, Luke. I'm calling it off.''

''You can't.'' He stood and dropped the box into her lap. ''You gave your word.''

''Well, I've changed my mind.''

''No, Molly. You had more than a week to think about it. And you can't say I pestered you. I never said a thing.''

No, he hadn't, she admitted. After their initial discussion, his efforts to influence her decision had been strictly nonverbal.

She followed him to the deck rail, where he stood with hands braced, and set the box carefully between his thumbs. "I'm a rat," she said. "I can't be trusted. I've led you on once. I could do it again. I've lost my mind altogether. You've had a lucky escape. Take your pick, Luke, I don't care. But let this be the end of it—so it doesn't hurt Bailey."

He picked up the velvet box and tossed it gently from one hand to the other as if he was toying with a hard-boiled egg.

"Why?"

"I told you—"

"No. I mean the reason, not the string of excuses." He didn't sound hurt or offended or resentful—only curious.

She hesitated. He'd been honest with her, she reminded herself, all the way through. Out of simple respect, she couldn't reciprocate with a lie.

But she certainly couldn't tell the truth.

She didn't look at him but at the lake, shimmering blue under the brilliant sun. "I don't think it's any of your business," she said honestly. "I've given you my decision, and it stands."

"That's what you implied last night, too—that you meant what you said." His voice was too calm, she thought, and she felt a shiver of fear. "But if your decisions are so very flexible, perhaps a little persuasion is in order."

Molly tried to move away, but his arm clamped around her and pulled her tight against him. His first kiss was demanding, almost violent—but she still couldn't keep herself entirely aloof, and with the first hint of her response his entire attitude changed. He caressed instead of attacked, asked rather than commanded. And where continued ferocity would have hardened her resolve, his gentleness seized her soul and shook it and made it even more fully his. By the time he let her go, every cell of Molly's body was trembling.

"Well, now," he drawled. "We've once more established that you're not indifferent to me."

Not that it seemed to make any real difference to him.

Shaken to the core, Molly had to take a second to compose herself before she could answer. "You're right, Luke. I'm not indifferent. Offended is more like it." She stalked across the deck and turned at the door for one last look at the man she loved. After today, he would be the father of her daughter, and nothing more.

Luke was in the midst of his mail on Wednesday morning when his secretary came in. "Excuse me, sir," she said. "But Ms. Matthews would like to speak with you. She said she'd wait."

Luke's hand clenched on the mini recorder. Molly had said she wanted to talk to him on Sunday, too—but instead she'd made her grandstand announcement and refused to discuss it. What was going on now? Yet another change of mind? "Tell her I'll be a few minutes, Wanda."

The secretary nodded and withdrew, and Luke toyed with his correspondence for a little longer, accomplishing nothing. He went to the door.

She stood the moment she saw him, and he let his gaze drift over her jade green suit. He'd thought she had the best set of legs in Minnesota, but he'd been wrong—it was more like the North American continent. With regret he stopped looking and said, "Come in, Molly."

Deliberately, he didn't indicate where she should sit. But without hesitation she chose one of the straight-backed chairs across from his desk and settled herself with a leather portfolio on her lap. "I'd like you to look over my proposals for the video portion of the history project, Luke."

Business as usual, he thought, and told himself he was neither surprised nor disappointed. Molly was obviously having no trouble separating business from personal affairs—and there was no reason he should, either.

"I actually overestimated the costs," she said, "so we can do a no-frills package and use the rest of the cash for something else, or add some extras. I've put some suggestions together to give you an idea of what I'd like to do. When you've had a chance to review this, perhaps we can discuss it." She took a neatly bound document from her portfolio and set it on his desk.

He reached for the folder and flipped through it slowly.

She didn't move, and he wondered if she was waiting for some sort of dismissal or if the video been only an excuse after all.

"There's one more thing," Molly said finally.

A curl of anticipation ran through him.

"When you hired me, Luke, we talked about recommendations to other firms. The book project is well underway and the video soon will be, so I'm starting to look for additional clients. It would be very helpful if I could use Meditronics as a reference."

Meditronics. *Not you, Luke, just your company.*

"Of course."

Molly slid to the edge of her chair.

There seemed nothing else to say, and he called himself foolish for groping for a subject, not wanting to let her go. "Megan called me last night. She said Rand finally showed up and they'd reached an agreement."

"That's one way of putting it." Molly's voice held a dry note. "It turns out the golden girl had her eyes on Rand all along. He's planning to marry Melinda."

She was watching him very closely, he thought. Was she hoping that Melinda's plans would upset him? Or hoping that they wouldn't?

"After that, it got pretty funny," Molly went on.

"Mother told Rand she didn't think he was being cheap at all, just very wise to choose a second wife with the same first initial so he didn't have to change the monograms on the towels." She stood. "But I shouldn't take up your time with gossip. You'll let me know, won't you, when you've had a chance to review my suggestions?"

She crossed the office so quickly that there was no point in going after her to hold the door. Instead, he stood by his desk and watched the enticing sway of that slim skirt. "Molly—"

She turned, eyebrows raised.

He hadn't meant to call her name. He wasn't certain why he'd done so, and he was embarrassingly tongue-tied.

"Is there something else, Luke?"

"No. I mean… If you don't have plans this evening, I'd like to take Bailey home with me."

"Of course. Do you want to pick her up from day care?"

He nodded, and she was gone with a friendly little wave.

She was as casual, he thought, as if there had never been anything between them. No evening of passion years ago. No sultry, seductive kisses. No less-than-a-day-long engagement.

Why had she changed her mind? It was none of his business, she'd said. An absolutely foolish statement, of course. If her reasons for rejecting him weren't his business, what in hell was?

What was it she hadn't been able to stomach?

Of course, it was a terrible sacrifice he'd asked her to make, he thought sardonically. To live at Oakwood with its elegance and its devoted staff. To work only if she wanted to, not because she had to put food in her daughter's mouth. To have every day with her child. To wear his ring…

He took the velvet box from his desk drawer and watched the stones flash fire as he turned the ring.

There was certainly nothing wrong with the ring. She hadn't even bothered to look at it.

To marry me. That, of course, was the crux of it.

He put the ring on the desk blotter and rubbed his temples.

And he wondered if someday he'd be able to forget the taste of her.

Bailey had crept into bed with Molly in the middle of the night, and still sound asleep, she was taking up far more than her fair share of space. *What a way to start Mother's Day,* Molly thought as she yawned and got up.

Her father was in the kitchen, stirring his special pancakes. "Be a good girl and take your mother coffee, will you?" he asked.

Molly got a bone china mug from the cabinet and carried the steaming coffee down the hall to the master bedroom where Alix was sitting up in bed, propped with pillows, reading *Vogue.*

"Your coffee, madam," Molly said. "Happy Mother's Day."

Alix laid the magazine aside. "I suppose Bernie's being silly about pancakes?"

"Well, please don't stop him. I love his pancakes." Molly sat on the edge of the bed. "Mother, I just wanted to tell you I'm sorry. I know I've been a huge disappointment." *And now that I'm not going to marry Luke, I'm no doubt shaming you all over again.*

Alix sipped her coffee and stared across the room until Molly wondered if she was going to ignore the apology altogether.

"I wasn't disappointed with you," Alix said slowly, "but with myself. You frightened me—your depth, your independence, your intelligence…"

"My stubbornness?"

Alix smiled. "Maybe that, too. Megan was so easy as a teenager, so open. She had to wait till now to turn into a mystery. No doubt the struggle she's having is because of the way I raised her—to be too sensitive to what others would think. But you—even when you faced the worst time of your life, you wouldn't let me in. I know I didn't go about it very well—"

"You did what you thought was best, Mom."

Alix shook her head. "No. I'm sorry, Molly, for the stories I told. I even managed to convince myself that I honestly intended them for your protection, when all the time... Now I don't know if I should correct all my lies, or if that would only make things worse for you."

"Leave it alone, Mom." Molly leaned over to give Alix a hug, and her mother held her tightly for a very long time.

Bailey came in, dragging a stuffed lion by the tail, and climbed into Alix's lap. "Gramma, I drew you a picture for Mother's Day."

"Did you, darling? I'll frame it." Alix nestled her close. "I am so very proud of you, Molly—and of my granddaughter."

Bailey snuggled into Alix's arms and yawned.

At least, Molly thought, something was turning out right.

After breakfast Molly took Bailey for a drive and pulled her car off the road near the child's favorite beach. *You're asking for heartache,* she told herself. Coming here, where she'd told Bailey about her father, was guaranteed to be painful—but if she lived in Duluth she couldn't stay away from this stretch of shoreline forever. And it was hardly the lake's fault.

"Daddy lets me bring Lucky," Bailey pointed out. But she took off down the beach, tromping along the edge of the water and now and then sending up a giant splash when a bigger-than-usual wave surprised her.

Molly sat on the driftwood log where she'd broken the news and started drawing patterns in the pebbly beach. She didn't know how long she'd been sitting there when a red-gold streak flashed past her and toward the water, barking wildly. She jumped up, panicked, helpless to get between Bailey and the dog that threatened her—until she realized it was Lucky.

Which meant, of course, that Luke was very near. She closed her eyes to try to gather strength.

His jeans and running shoes contrasted oddly with the gold foil wrapping and enormous ribbons on the box he carried under one arm. "Hi," he said. "Your dad told me you'd come up this way, and then I saw the car." He held out the box. "Happy Mother's Day."

She didn't want to open it. But he meant well, and she could hardly fling his gift back in his face. So she sat on the driftwood log once more and slowly began to pull the tape loose.

Luke sat beside her, a careful foot away. He leaned forward to scoop up a handful of pebbles and let them sift slowly through his fingers.

As soon as she saw the box, Molly's stomach churned in protest. It wasn't only unfair and manipulative, she thought, it was absolutely tasteless of him to buy her a gift at Milady Lingerie. Even if he'd chosen something innocuous, just the suggestive simplicity of the box sent a message that she didn't want to hear.

The gift inside was far from innocent. She folded back the gold tissue paper to reveal a satin and lace teddy in a soft shade of emerald green—exactly the color to make her skin glow and her eyes shine. It was even, she noted, precisely the right size.

She stared at it for a moment and gritted her teeth against the pain. As if she was shallow enough to let a sexy bit of lingerie affect her judgment! Didn't he even begin to understand that physical attraction wasn't enough, that feelings were overwhelmingly important?

"This isn't funny, Luke." She folded the tissue in place, her hands trembling. "It's inappropriate and insulting."

As soon as I can keep my voice from shaking, she thought, *I'll call for Bailey, and we'll leave. Only a moment more…*

"I'm sorry," he said.

She didn't look at him, but she nodded, in acceptance though not agreement. He'd never truly understand, she knew. So she might as well not break her heart over it—or waste her time trying to explain.

"Not for the lingerie," he said. "For…a long time ago."

Molly sat very still.

"My mother," Luke said slowly. "I adored her, you know. Two weeks before she died, I came home for her birthday and she was—appeared to be—in perfect health. Then in a moment, she collapsed. They told us she was dying. And I couldn't do anything to save her. My time in med school had been worse than useless—I only knew enough to understand how bad it was."

Molly put out a hand to him, but he seemed too enclosed in his mind to see it.

"That night in the treehouse was the worst as I struggled to accept that I was losing her. Then suddenly you were there, only trying to help.… Molly, I felt so guilty for taking advantage of you."

"You didn't. I threw myself at you." Bitterness crept into her voice. "That was painfully clear when you couldn't bring yourself to go through with it, to actually make love to me.…"

"That was never the problem. What terrified me was how much I wanted you—when I knew you had no idea what you were doing."

A cool breeze stirred Molly's hair and made the gold foil paper rustle. "I was already embarrassed and ashamed, and when you took me aside a few days later and made it clear what you thought of me…'' She bit her lip. "When I found out the impossible had happened and I was going to have your child…''

"I understand why you didn't tell me."

"Oh, you've finally figured it out! What was I supposed to do, Luke? You'd made it absolutely plain that you didn't want to see me ever again, that there was nothing about me you found attractive—''

"There were lots of things even then. Now…'' He drew a deep breath. "Your dignity in the face of uncertainty and trouble. Bailey—and the fact that you brought her into the world with the situation you were in. There were easier ways.''

Molly shook her head. "Not for me.''

"Then there's my father—I wouldn't be surprised if he proposes to you yet when he discovers that you've turned me down. The staff would lie on the floor and let you clean your shoes on them. In fact, the only living creature at Oakwood who isn't totally in love with you—''

Is the one I care most about, she thought sadly.

"Is the dog, and that's only because you scold her adored playmate once in a while.''

Every muscle in Molly's body tightened like an overwound spring. Did he realize what he'd said? And if so, did he—could he—actually mean it?

"And then there's me.'' Luke cleared his throat. "I said all those years ago that you were too young to know what love was. And I still think I was right. But I didn't recognize love, either. When you refused me last week, I was furious. To throw aside an opportunity like the one I'd offered you…''

Molly wanted to say, *And what an opportunity! All the material things and nothing that really mattered.*

"I tried to be logical, to figure it out. Obviously, it wasn't Oakwood that you disliked. And though you weren't greedy when it came to money, I didn't think you hated the stuff enough to refuse me on the grounds that I had too much of it. And it was apparent there was very little you wouldn't do for Bailey. So that left marriage itself—or rather, marriage to me—that you found so distasteful.''

She wanted to say, *Not if it could be a real marriage.* But she had lost control of her voice.

''And that was when I realized I wasn't angry, after all. I was hurt, and terribly sad that you didn't care about me. That even for Bailey's sake you couldn't face sharing a life with me. And yet when you kissed me…''

''There's more to being married than sharing a bed, Luke.''

''Yeah.'' He picked up the lingerie box. ''This was really a bad idea, wasn't it?''

''I don't know,'' Molly said carefully. ''It depends on why you did it.''

''To tell you that the reason I want you isn't that you're Bailey's mother. But I miscalculated, didn't I? Because I don't just want you to be my wife in the bedroom, either, but everywhere. All the time. Forever. I love you, Molly.''

Her hands were squeezed so tightly together that her knuckles were white.

''Yes, I want Bailey,'' he said. ''I don't want to be a part-time father to my little girl. That's fact, and there's no sense dodging it. But it wasn't Bailey I thought of last Sunday when you so much as told me to go jump off the aerial lift bridge. I thought of myself—and how empty my life was going to be. Not because I wouldn't have Bailey…but because I wouldn't have you.'' He fitted the top on the lingerie box. ''I'm sorry, Molly. For everything.''

He was ten feet away before she found her voice. ''What are you going to do with my Mother's Day gift, Luke?''

He didn't look back. ''Probably start by ripping it

apart with my bare hands. Then I might— Do you mean you want it?''

''I didn't turn you down because I found you distasteful, Luke. I did it because I knew it would tear me apart to live with a man who didn't love me when I loved you so much I drove myself crazy trying to find any reason to believe we could make it work.''

The box went spinning to the ground. Luke seized Molly's hands and pulled her into his arms, and she discovered that kisses were even better when there were no secrets left between them.

''You were so casual.'' Luke sounded a little breathless. Molly wasn't surprised. ''So cool—in the office. As if you'd forgotten…everything.''

Molly shrugged. ''Acting that way wasn't the most fun I've ever had, that's sure. But we were going to have to deal with each other for years to come—till Bailey grew up, at least. And I knew if I slipped and let you see what I was going through, and if you felt sorry for me—''

''I wouldn't have had time to feel sorry for you, I was too busy staring at a ring you wouldn't wear and feeling sorry for myself.'' He pulled the velvet box from his pocket. ''Want it?''

The box looked dingy and a bit the worse for wear, Molly thought, as if he'd been carrying it for days. ''Yes.'' She reached for the box, but Luke held it out of her reach while he extracted the ring and used one hand to shield it from view till he'd slipped it into place on her finger.

Molly held out her hand. She'd never seen an emerald so brilliant, so richly colored, so perfect.

''It's the color of your eyes,'' he said. ''Only I was too deluded when I bought it to know why that was so important.'' She started to cry, and he kissed her tears away. After a while, he said, ''Now are we going to set a wedding date, or shall I call Rand for his preferred list of love nests and carry you off to one of them and make love to you so often you can't remember your name, much less your objections?''

"I'll bet your choice would be better than his.''

"Is that a challenge, Ms. Matthews? I'll see what I can do.''

"You weren't surprised about Melinda, were you?''

"Of course not. I'd thought for a long time that she and Rand were just a little too formal with each other to be real.''

"But you were dating her anyway?'' Molly sounded doubtful.

"Only in the spirit of collecting information for Megan. It wasn't difficult, because Melinda always had an eye out for an extra man, and she must have thought I'd make especially good cover since I was Megan's friend.''

"And that's why you and Megan were meeting in out-of-the-way ice cream shops? You were reporting?''

"I wasn't going to go into detail where her maid might be able to hear. But how'd you know that?''

"Bailey spotted you.'' Molly shook her head. "Next time you try to go undercover, Luke, you might drive something besides a Jaguar.''

"I'll keep it in mind. The final confirmation was that Rand made the reservations for their little weekend in Melinda's name and sent the tickets to her with a very juicy note.''

"And I suppose she told you all about it?''

"I snooped,'' Luke said cheerfully. "But I didn't have to work very hard at it. She'd left the package right on her desk, and I had plenty of time to browse while I was waiting for her to finish dressing for the opera.''

The night, Molly thought, that he'd left Oakwood looking eager and full of anticipation—not because he was going to see Melinda, but because he was hoping to catch her red-handed. ''Just don't get in the habit of leaving your bow ties in other women's houses.''

''And you think she took it off me in a passionate interlude? Sorry to disappoint you, darling, but I never wear those things any longer than necessary.''

She remembered him tugging his tie off in the hospital while they were waiting out Megan's miscarriage and stuffing it in his pocket.

''I must have dropped it. I'm only surprised she didn't deliver it to Megan as a smoke screen.''

''She probably figured the message would get passed along,'' Molly said dryly. ''There is one more thing, Luke. About that teddy—how'd you know what size to buy?''

''Would you believe I walked into the shop and told the clerk that you were just about this shape—'' He demonstrated.

''No.''

''I didn't think so. The truth, unfortunately, is much less romantic. You were still in their computer from the last time you bought something in the Chicago store. So not only did I know what size to buy, but exactly the kind of thing you like—and if you think *that* didn't start affecting my dreams…''

He bent once more to kiss her and paused to stroke her cheek. ''That bruise on your jaw. You never did tell me how you got it.''

''I told you it was nothing. Bailey was demonstrating her new gymnastic tricks for me, but somehow she stretched out instead of tucking in, and she kicked me. Almost knocked me down.''

''Why didn't you tell me that in the beginning?''

''Because the first time you asked, you didn't even know about her, and the last thing I wanted to do was explain.''

He considered and nodded. ''And your broken leg? Bailey said you fell down the stairs.''

Molly frowned. "And you thought I'd been pushed? No, I slipped on a patch of ice at the top of a flight of concrete steps."

"I'm glad."

"That I broke my leg?"

"That you weren't battered. Every time I thought about that bruise, I felt guilty, because if my clumsiness had made you turn to a man like that…"

She turned her head away so he couldn't see her face and admitted, "Luke, I know this sounds crazy. My daughter's almost four. But that time—with you—was the only…" She paused. "I've never…"

He was silent and still for so long that she began to regret her confession. "Surely there were other men."

"I dated. But there was nobody like you."

"At times," Luke said dryly, "that must have seemed a blessing. My darling… I'll make it up to you. All of it—I swear."

He kissed her again, long and deeply, and Molly came back to earth only when a little hand tugged firmly at her sweater. "Mommy," Bailey said indignantly. "Daddy. I want a hug, too!"

So they picked up their daughter and held her between them, and Bailey put an arm around each neck and drew them closer yet.

ONE MUM TOO MANY
by
Vicki Lewis Thompson

Vicki Lewis Thompson says of herself, "I'm probably a writer because my parents couldn't afford music or dance lessons. Pencils are cheap, and all that emotional intensity had to escape somehow! I've scribbled poetry and stories ever since I learned how to arrange the alphabet into words, and I even published some pieces here and there, but nothing compares to the thrilling ride that began in 1983 when I sold my first book. Nearly forty books later, with a few awards thrown in, I can't imagine ballet roles or piano solos making me the least bit happier. Thanks Mom and Dad."

1

"JUST SUPPOSE YOUR sperm loses motility," Maureen O'Malley called to her son from the kitchen where she was tending a pot of Irish stew.

"*What?*" Daniel almost dropped the picture frame in his hand as he whirled from his examination of the family photos on the mantel. Surely the noise of Brooklyn traffic outside the apartment window had made him misunderstand his mother. She couldn't have been talking about his sperm.

"Motility. How fast the little buggers can swim." His mother came to the kitchen doorway, a flowered apron over her expansive middle and a ladle in one hand. Other than the shocking shade of red she dyed her hair, she looked like a middle-aged matron out of a Hallmark commercial, but she sure as hell wasn't talking like one. "Did you know you could lose that, Daniel?"

He eased a finger around the back of his collar. The room was way too warm all of a sudden. "Look, Mom, I don't think—"

"Happens with age, it does." She pointed the ladle at him. "I read it in *Prevention* magazine. If you don't watch out, it could happen to you, Mr. I-don't-want-to-get-married-yet.''

Daniel clenched his jaw. Ever since his father died his mother had been on this kick, and he'd about had it. In his more sympathetic moments, he understood her need to enlarge the family that suddenly seemed too small, and he'd vowed months ago to remain patient even as he refused to fall in with her timetable. Patience was getting harder to come by.

Discussing his sperm count was a new tactic, and he definitely didn't want her going any farther down that road. He took refuge in the first thing at hand. He held up the picture frame. ''What's up with this, Mom?''

''You're changing the subject.''

''It needed changing. How come you have this on the mantel when nothing's in it but the picture stuck in there by the frame company?''

His mother looked uncomfortable and her Irish brogue grew more prominent. ''Reminded me of Bridget Hogan, is all. So I bought it.''

''Bridget? Wasn't she your bitter enemy?''

''Well, she was, indeed. But before that, she was my best friend. Never had another. That woman in the frame is the spitting image of her.''

''Is she, now?'' Daniel held the picture up and looked more closely at the model in the photograph. Ringlets of soft auburn hair fell gracefully around delicate shoulders. Kissable red lips framed even white teeth, and the sparkle in the woman's green gaze gave new meaning to the clichéd words of the old song

"When Irish Eyes are Smiling." For if she wasn't Irish, she could certainly pass.

Daniel was touched by his mother's impulse to buy the frame just because of the picture in it. Probably just another example of how lonely she'd become in her widowhood. He walked over and positioned the photograph exactly as she'd had it before, right next to the one of him after he'd graduated from the New York City Police Academy.

His mother came over to study the two adjacent pictures. "You look good with that model."

"Of course I do. She's a professional beauty. She'd make any guy look good."

His mother swatted his arm. "'Twas not what I meant. I meant you two would make a nice couple."

Daniel blew out his breath in exasperation. "Could we agree not to talk about that anymore tonight? I just turned thirty-three, for God's sake. Dad didn't marry you until he was thirty-five."

"And you see what happened. We were only blessed once."

Daniel put an arm around her shoulders, hoping to kid her out of her preoccupation. "What's the matter, aren't you happy with the one you've got?"

"I think you're lovely, and well you know it. But I'd thought to have a nursery full of babes." She sighed. "I realize now your dear, departed father probably had slow sperm."

Daniel snorted. Slow sperm was obviously Maureen O'Malley's current health-news preoccupation.

Last week it had been the carcinogens from aluminum cooking pots.

"Laugh all you like. 'Tis a fact of life, and time is running out for you. Just remember that a man with no wife and children is like a boot with no laces."

He gave her a quick hug. "Exactly. Free to be loose and comfortable."

She pulled away and glared at him. "Daniel Patrick O'Malley, I did not raise you to toy with the hearts of young girls. 'Tis past time for you to pick out some lucky lass and ask her to be your wife. Surely there's someone you fancy."

This was one stubborn woman, Daniel thought wearily. He'd gained new respect for his father's patience in dealing with her all those years. "Well, come to think of it, there is someone," he said, guiding her back toward the kitchen.

"I knew you'd been holding out on me! Who is she? The one you took to the Policemen's Ball? No, wait. I'll wager 'tis the one you met at that New Year's Eve party."

"Nope." He grinned at her, quite sure his answer was a safe one. "That girl in the picture frame. She's exactly what I'm looking for."

"WHAT DO YOU THINK, St. Paddy? Shall I call Maureen O'Malley or not?" Rose Kingsford lifted the cloth muzzle of her Irish wolfhound, a stuffed animal version of the dog she hoped someday to own. St. Paddy, created slightly smaller than a live wolfhound, stared back at her with soulful brown eyes. "Can't resist a mystery, can you, pup? Okay, I'll call her. It's safe enough to do that, I think.''

The stuffed animal draped over her shoulder, Rose went in search of her portable phone. She longed for a real dog, but as long as she lived in a New York City high-rise, keeping an animal the size of a wolfhound seemed criminally selfish.

But Rose didn't intend to spend the rest of her life in an apartment. An apartment was no place for a big dog or a growing child, and she intended to have both. At one point she'd thought a husband would be part of the mix, but she'd finally abandoned that dream. Most men focused so exclusively on her looks that she'd never trust them to stick around when gray hair and wrinkles showed up.

Aside from that, she'd dated fun-loving men with no maturity, and serious types with no gift for play. A combination of mature self-confidence and playfulness seemed nonexistent, and after the way her parents' marriage had turned out, she'd decided to settle for just having a child. She'd always longed for the creative role of parenting a son or daughter, and she was afraid of becoming too set in her solitary ways if she didn't act soon.

If necessary she'd go to a sperm bank, but she'd rather ask a willing donor she'd met and screened herself—someone with no interest in a commitment, someone with intelligence and reasonably good looks, someone with no life-threatening genetic flaws. So far, no good candidate had presented himself, but

Rose had trusted in her instincts for most of her thirty years. When the right man came along, she'd know.

She located the phone on her drafting table under a stack of Sunday comic pages from all over the country. "Guard my stuff, Paddy," she instructed, plopping the dog on her stool as she picked up the phone and returned to the living room.

After switching on a lamp against the twilight, Rose pulled up the antenna on the phone and dialed the number. Then she stretched out on her chintz sofa and propped her long legs over the back cushions. Probably some creative sales scheme, she thought as the phone rang. Balancing the phone between her cheek and her shoulder, she pulled her long red hair into a ponytail and wound it with a scrunchy.

"Hello?" said a musical, feminine voice.

Rose sat up straighter. No answering machine at the O'Malley residence, which was unusual in today's world. And Maureen O'Malley's voice, if that was the woman who'd answered, contained the same lilt as Rose's mother's. Perhaps Maureen had been born in Ireland. Rose was always on the lookout for material for her fledgling comic strip, her ticket out of the modeling business. "May I speak to Maureen O'Malley, please?" she asked.

"'Tis her you have."

Rose warmed to the soft brogue. Maureen sounded even more Irish than Rose's mother, who had been coached by her English husband to give up some of her native inflections.

She adjusted the phone against her ear. "This is

Rose Kingsford. You contacted the modeling agency about me, I believe.''

"Oh! I did indeed! So 'tis Rose, then? What a lovely name. An Irish name, for sure. Do you have Irish in your background, then?''

"On my mother's side.'' Upon hearing the familiar cadence of an Irish-born woman's speech, Rose instinctively let down her guard. "My father's English.'' And her mother now referred to him as "that Brit bastard I married.''

"I knew you must be Irish! I saw that face and said to myself, 'That's an Irish lass for sure.' And I was right.''

Rose reached for a pen and pad of paper she kept handy on the coffee table. This conversation could yield some homespun expressions she might be able to use in the comic strip. "Is there something I can do for you, Mrs. O'Malley?'' She took a guess at the woman's marital status because she didn't feel comfortable calling someone from her mother's generation by her first name.

"Oh, Rose, there is. There most certainly is. 'Twould do me so much good to lay eyes on you. Some tea, perhaps. I know you're very busy, but it would mean so much.''

Rose stopped doodling on the pad as warnings sounded in her head. This was why she guarded her privacy so carefully. Her face and figure might be out there for public consumption, but she remained personally elusive, unreachable. Crazies were everywhere, and more than one of her modeling friends had attracted a stalker. Rose cleared her throat. ''I am very busy, Mrs. O'Malley, and I'm afraid that I can't—''

''But you see, you're the exact likeness of my dear friend Bridget, who threw herself off the Cliffs of Moher and drowned herself. I've been missing her for thirty-seven years, come this summer.''

Rose's mouth dropped open. Her mother's name was Bridget. And her mother had once told Rose a story about a long-lost friend who had thrown herself in front of a train some thirty-seven years ago. A friend by the name of…Maureen. This had to be more than coincidence. Feeling as if she'd entered some twilight zone, Rose chose her words carefully. ''I'll have to, uh, check my schedule, Mrs. O'Malley. Could I get back to you on this in, say, twenty-four hours?''

''Oh, 'twould be grand, Rose. I'll be waiting for your call, I will.''

''Right. Goodbye, now.'' Rose pushed the disconnect button on her phone, got the dial tone back and punched in her mother's number. Her mother's machine came on, and Bridget Kingsford's intonations were very similar to Maureen O'Malley's. Rose knew her mother was probably home and screening her calls. ''Put the kettle on, Mom,'' she instructed. ''I'm on my way.''

BRIDGET HOGAN KINGSFORD'S third-floor apartment looked out on Central Park. The apartment and a generous monthly allowance had been part of the settlement from Cecil Kingsford when he'd dumped his wife of twenty-five years for a younger, better-educated, smoother-skinned trophy wife. The divorce had presented Rose with a harsh example of what could happen when a man married a woman primarily for her beauty.

Rose used her key and called out a greeting as she opened the door to the apartment. The muffled, muted response told her to look for her mother in the bedroom. She walked into the Victorian room of lace and flowers and found her mother, dressed in a pale blue jogging suit, lying on the floor with her feet propped vertically against the pink-striped wall. Her face was covered with a hardening lime-green mask.

"Well, if it isn't Freddy Krueger," Rose said, plopping to the floor next to her.

"Don't make me laugh," her mother said, barely moving her lips.

"I have some news that just might crack that thing right off your face. How much longer before you can wash it off?"

Bridget picked up the egg timer from the floor beside her and looked at it. "Eight minutes."

"Have you eaten?"

"Nope."

"Me neither." Rose pushed herself to her feet. "I'll go nuke a couple of Lean Cuisines and put on some tea."

Ten minutes later when Bridget appeared in the kitchen with her face scrubbed clean and her short auburn hair brushed softly around her face, Rose thought she looked at least twenty years younger than her actual age of fifty-six. Cecil Kingsford was a fool for sure.

"So what's this news?" her mother said as she got out Wedgwood cups and saucers for the tea.

Rose scraped the second Lean Cuisine onto a plate and carried both servings to the linen-covered table in the small dining area just beyond the kitchen. "You might want to come and sit down first."

The cups rattled in their saucers as her mother set them quickly on the counter. "My God, you've gotten yourself pregnant!"

"No, no. That's not it. Nothing to do with that."

Abandoning the serving of tea, Bridget stomped into the dining area, her hands on her hips. A frown creased the forehead she'd been working so hard to smooth with the clay mask. "Then I suppose you've found a 'candidate' for this unholy plan of yours. Rose Erin Kingsford, I don't know how I failed, that you would even consider having a babe out of wedlock. Your grandmother Hogan would turn over in her grave."

"Mom, this has nothing to do with me getting pregnant. I'm not sure I'm going to do that, anyway," she hedged, regretting once again that she'd ever confided her plan to her mother. "Please, bring the tea and I'll tell you all about my news."

Bridget brought the tea on a little tray along with the Wedgwood teapot, creamer and sugar bowl. Had her mother not always served tea with such ceremony, Rose might have thought the formality was designed to remind her daughter of the proprieties. Deep down, Bridget Kingsford, despite her apparently modern attitudes, was an Irish country girl who believed in chastity before marriage, not to mention legitimate offspring.

Bridget settled herself in her chair, placed her napkin in her lap and poured the tea. Then she carefully doctored hers with cream and sugar before glancing up. "Well? Am I sufficiently calm now, do you suppose? Or would you prefer me lying down?"

Rose laughed. Thank goodness her mother was so feisty. Otherwise, the divorce would have broken her. Rose picked up her tea and took a sip, which was wonderful, as always. Nobody could make a pot of tea like Bridget Kingsford. "I returned a call today from a woman named Maureen O'Malley. She contacted the agency because she was attracted by my picture, the one the frame company's using."

"I'm not surprised. That's a lovely shot of you."

"So she said. Reminded her of a girlhood friend who'd thrown herself off the Cliffs of Moher." Rose took a bite of her dinner, watching her mother's face.

"Good heavens!"

Rose chewed and swallowed. "She said her friend's name was Bridget." Her mother's green eyes widened and two spots of color appeared on her cheeks. "Tell me again what the woman's name was who called the agency."

"Maureen."

Her mother threw her napkin to the table and leaped up. "It's her! She should have the Blarney

Stone welded to her lips!'' Bridget paced the dining area and waved both arms. ''How dare she go around saying I leaped off the Cliffs of Moher! But what else could I expect from the likes of her?''

Rose refrained from mentioning that the woman whom her mother had claimed had thrown herself in front of a speeding train was alive and living in Brooklyn.

Bridget spun to face her daughter. ''Does she know who you are?''

''I'm not sure. She didn't sound as if she had the slightest clue. She wants to meet me, though.''

Bridget clutched her head with both hands. ''Let me think, let me think. Mark my words, she has something up her sleeve. You can't trust that one farther than you can toss a haywagon. Why would she want to meet you if she doesn't know you're my daughter?''

''I really don't know. Just exactly what happened between you two, Mom?''

''What happened? She ruined the biggest chance of my life. Kept me from winning the Rose of Tralee crown. May her children have warts on their hindmost parts.''

Rose smothered a grin. When her mother became agitated she slipped into the most wonderfully colorful language. ''You never told me exactly how she kept you from winning the crown.''

Her mother threw up an arm in a dramatic gesture. ''*She* had the brilliant idea that we were too white-skinned, that we needed a kiss of sun on our cheeks before the judging. She rented a tanning lamp and I bought the suntan oil. But at the last minute my sainted mother, may she rest in peace, talked me out of it. I took the tanning oil over to Maureen, because she insisted on doing it, anyway. And she burned her face something terrible. Had to drop out of the contest altogether.''

''So how did that stop you from winning?''

''I will tell you.'' Bridget lifted her chin, a picture of wronged innocence. ''Personality counts as much as beauty in that contest, and Maureen spread the word that I'd deliberately sabotaged her because I was afraid of the competition! As if that sheep-faced woman ever had a chance. But those fools of judges must have believed her, because I didn't win.''

Rose shook her head. It seemed that thirty-seven years hadn't dimmed her mother's memory, or her fury. She couldn't help but ask now, ''How come each of you claimed the other committed suicide?''

Her mother had the good grace to look uncomfortable at being caught in an outright lie. ''The last time we saw each other, she shouted at me 'You might as well be dead, Bridget Mary Hogan!' So I shouted back 'Same to you, Maureen Fiona Keegan!' She took a position as a nanny here in New York, and about a year later I came over to work as a model. I didn't like thinking of her in the same city as me, so I made up a story about her throwing herself in front of a train.''

''And she had you taking a swan dive off the Cliffs of Moher.''

"Which is ridiculous! She knows I'm terribly afraid of high places." Bridget continued to pace. "She *must* suspect who you are."

"I don't think so, Mom. But it doesn't matter. I have no intention of meeting her."

Bridget faced her. "Oh, but you must! I want to know how she turned out!"

"You *want* me to meet this woman you hate?"

"I do, indeed." Bridget gazed out the window and tapped her finger against her lips. "That little tearoom on Forty-sixth is perfect. You can sit on one side of that planter and I'll sit on the other. She'll never see me through the dieffenbachia."

Rose nearly lost it. "You're going to hide in the greenery and spy on her? Tell me you're not."

Her mother crossed her arms and gave Rose a look that might have come from a nineteen-year-old. "If I know Maureen Keegan, and I certainly do know that bag of wind, she's up to something. I intend to find out exactly what it is."

SOMEWHERE ALONG the line, Rose thought as she headed for the tearoom two days later, she'd switched roles with her mother. Rose was now expected to be the responsible one while her mother cavorted around like some giddy teenager concocting elaborate schemes to thwart her girlhood rival. An episode of "Mission: Impossible" hadn't been given this much thought or preparation. Everything had been planned down to the last detail, including a hat and sunglasses for her mother, in case somehow Maureen might recognize her.

According to the timetable Bridget was already in the tearoom, and whichever side of the planter she'd managed to secure for herself, Rose was supposed to get a table on the other side. Maureen wasn't scheduled to arrive for another fifteen minutes, so Rose and Bridget would have time to jockey for position in case other patrons had seated themselves in ways that would louse up the Plan.

Rose stepped into the warmth of the tearoom and unbuttoned her trench coat as she approached the hostess. "I have a reservation for two. The name is Kingsford."

"Right this way." Carrying menus, the hostess led her into the delicately appointed room featuring antiques from the turn of the century.

Rose spotted her mother with her back to the door, looking like Mata Hari in her broad-brimmed hat of navy wool pulled low over her dark glasses. The hostess was heading for the table right behind her, on the same side of the planter. On the other side, the tables were filled. Rose sighed. Then she touched the hostess on the shoulder. "I'm afraid this will be a terrible bother, but I have a strange request regarding my table."

Rose's mother stiffened at the sound of her daughter's voice.

The hostess turned with a smile that looked totally insincere. "What can I do for you?"

"The person I'm meeting is very sentimental, and

she has fond memories of that table over there.'' Rose
pointed to a table on the opposite side of the planter
and directly across from where her mother was sip-
ping a cup of tea.

''Customers are occupying that table.''

''I can see that, but if they could possibly be persuaded to move…'' Rose gave the hostess her most
soulful look, something approximating the expression
of her stuffed dog St. Paddy. Then she slipped a
folded twenty into the hostess's hand.

The hostess glanced at the denomination of the bill.
''Perhaps that can be arranged,'' she murmured. ''Just
give me a moment.''

Rose glanced at her watch and hoped a moment
wasn't very long with this chick. The hostess had less
than ten moments to get Rose seated or the whole
program would collapse. Rose hoped Maureen wasn't
the sort of woman who arrived early.

The two women who'd been asked to relocate
didn't look very pleased, but Rose finally took possession of the table and sat facing the entry to the
tearoom, so Maureen O'Malley would be able to spot
her easily.

''Nice work,'' her mother said through the leaves.
She sounded as if she was talking out of the corner
of her mouth.

''I'm ignoring you,'' Rose replied, barely moving
her lips. ''The hostess already thinks I have a screw
loose. I won't let her catch me talking to the planter.''

''The tea here isn't as good as I remembered.''

''Ignoring you,'' Rose sang under her breath. Just

then a stout woman in a green wool coat bustled into
the tearoom and homed right in on Rose. Perched on
her dyed red hair was a green derby with a feather in
the band. Rose knew instantly that Maureen Fiona
Keegan O'Malley had come upon the scene. As a kid,
Rose had played around with ventriloquism, and she
managed to smile and say "She's here" to her mother
at the same time.

"Jesus, Mary and Joseph." Her mother sounded
totally freaked out.

Maureen brushed the hostess aside and made
straight for Rose's table. "If you aren't lovelier than
your picture," she crooned. "Would you mind taking
the other chair? The light's so much better over there
and I want to get a really good look at you."

"It's a trick," whispered Bridget through the dieffenbachia.

Maureen looked startled. "Did you say something,
Rose?"

"Just a little sneeze." Rose faked one and tried to
make it sound like a whisper as she got up to trade
chairs with Maureen.

"Must be my hearing. My Daniel told me to get it
checked, but I've been putting it off, I have." Maureen took off her coat and draped it over the back of
her chair before sitting down. She wore black stretch
pants and an oversize flowered tunic containing every
color in the rainbow.

"Daniel's your husband?" Rose asked, knowing
her mother wanted every little detail. Personally, Rose
was captivated by this sweet woman. Far from being

"sheep-faced," she had expressive blue eyes and a wonderfully kind expression. Rose was beginning to feel guilty about the subterfuge.

"No, my husband was Patrick, bless his soul. Died in the line of duty, he did, two years ago in June."

"I'm sorry." A lonely widow. Rose felt worse and worse.

"Aye, 'twas a black day for sure, but at least I have Daniel, and he's a great comfort to me. Daniel's my son."

"I see." A slight uneasiness replaced Rose's goodwill.

"And speak of the devil, there he is, coming through the door!" Maureen waved enthusiastically.

Trapped. All Rose's kindly thoughts about Maureen O'Malley vanished.

"Come on over here, Daniel, my boy," said Maureen. "I have someone I want you to meet."

Rose closed her eyes in dismay.

Through the dieffenbachia came her mother's terse whisper: "Told you."

2

ROSE FELT the movement of air as Daniel paused right behind her.

"I can't believe this, Mom," he said in a deep baritone. "You've gone too far this time."

The voice was intriguing enough that Rose turned to face Maureen's son, although she thoroughly expected some nerdy guy who had to depend on his mother to arrange his dates.

Wrong. Daniel O'Malley towered above her, six feet of magnificent Irish manhood. With his leather jacket unzipped and his hands propped on his hips, he gave Rose an up-close-and-personal view of a tantalizingly broad chest tapering to a narrow waist. The wind had tousled his dark hair, making him look rumpled and sexy. All he needed was a passionate gaze to complete the picture. Although his deep brown eyes looked capable of melting the heart of any woman, they were currently snapping with anger as he confronted his mother.

Maureen seemed unfazed by his attitude. "Daniel O'Malley, where are your manners? Please say hello to Rose Kingsford. As I suspected, she's Irish. Gets it from her mother's side."

Rose heard violent coughing through the dieffen-bachia. She ignored it, and held out her hand to this Celtic god. "Glad to meet you." A truer statement she'd never made.

Daniel's gaze moved down to connect with hers and his angry stare gave way to a flush of embar-rassment. "I apologize for the inconvenience," he said, his hand closing over hers. "I—I can't remem-ber ever being so uncomfortable in my life."

"Don't give it another thought." Rose looked into his eyes as she returned the firm pressure of his hand-shake. The moment was brief, because he soon re-leased her hand and concentrated on his mother again, but Rose reacted as if he'd suddenly swept her into his arms. Her heart was beating at a furious pace and she struggled for breath, but the turmoil within her made perfect sense. After all, she'd just met the man she would ask to father her child.

A waitress came up, gave Daniel an admiring glance and inquired if she should set another place at the table.

"Yes," Maureen said.

"No, that won't be necessary," Daniel said. "I'm not staying."

Rose had expected that and wasn't perturbed. She still had the mother in tow, and the mother wanted to matchmake.

"Daniel, for heaven's sake," Maureen protested. "You can sit down and have a cup of tea, at least."

"I'm afraid not," he said with a quiet authority that prompted the waitress to retreat and tend to another customer. Then he turned toward Rose. "But it was nice meeting you." With that, he left the tearoom.

"Daniel!" Maureen called, but she might as well have saved the effort. He didn't even break stride. "Well, I guess I know what that's all about," Maureen said, glancing back at Rose. "His scar has made him dreadfully shy with the ladies."

"Scar?" Rose searched the vivid picture she now carried of Maureen's son. "I didn't notice any scar."

"That's because 'tis in a very…delicate spot, you see."

"Oh?" Rose could hear muffled noises coming from the other side of the planter where her mother was undoubtedly struggling to contain herself.

"'Tis on his, er, on his bum. Bullet wound."

"*Bullet* wound?"

"Well, naturally. He's a police officer with the mounted unit. Many of the lads he works with have been shot, one time or another. My Patrick had three bullet wounds. Got them before we were married, fortunately. The saints be praised he made detective right after we got married, so the work wasn't so dangerous."

"But didn't you say he died in the line of duty?"

Maureen nodded. "And so he did. Keeled over while he was at his desk making out a report. Fell face down into a box of donuts. Raised glazed."

The waitress's return saved Rose from trying to come up with a response to that detailed revelation. She decided to stick with just tea, but Maureen ordered a basket of muffins.

"You can share the muffins," Maureen said after the waitress left. "You could use a little more weight on your bones. Not that you aren't perfectly lovely the way you are. I know models are supposed to stay very thin. My best friend Bridget, the one you look so much like, was thin, too. She thought to go into modeling. 'Twas before she came to such a tragic end, you see."

The entire teapot on the other side of the planter hit the floor, judging from the splintering crash. The waitress hurried over and Rose pretended to cough into her napkin.

"Goodness, but that woman seems to be having a terrible lot of trouble over there," Maureen commented as she attempted to peer through the green barricade to the table next to them.

"Don't look," Rose cautioned, her voice low and choked with laughter. "I saw her when I came in, and she's…not right, if you know what I mean. I'm sure we'd embarrass her by commenting on her struggles."

"Oh, dear." Maureen glanced away from the planter immediately. "Poor soul. Trying to get herself a little cheer, I expect. I'm surprised the tearoom let her in."

"They probably won't let her come back after this episode," Rose said. "Ah, here's our order."

After the waitress left them a steaming pot of tea and a basket of fragrant muffins, Rose settled in to gather information. "Tell me more about your son, Daniel."

"Well, he's not usually so abrupt, I promise you. Unless he's dealing with the criminal element, of course. He and his da were the same when it came to keeping the peace. The uniform seems to give him a harder edge, somehow."

"Interesting." Rose found the concept sexy.

"You should have seen him as a wee lad. Loved to run through the house buck naked."

"Really?" Rose figured Daniel would die a thousand deaths if he knew what stories his mother was telling about him.

"And smart as a whip." Maureen's blue eyes shone. "The sisters said he could be anything he wanted, but he chose police work, like his father. 'Tis a long-standing O'Malley tradition."

Intelligence, Rose thought, was very important for the purpose she had in mind. "Sisters? You have daughters?"

"No, the nuns, where he went to school. He played pranks, like most lads, but the sisters said 'twas probably because he got bored and needed to amuse himself." Maureen became incandescent with pride. "He ranked first in his class at the police academy."

"Remarkable." Rose moved to the next item on her mental list. "You have to be in pretty good shape to get on the police force, don't you?" The table on the other side of the planter had become totally silent, and Rose could almost hear her mother listening to every syllable. Bridget was no dummy. She'd figured out why her daughter was taking this tack with Maureen. And she hated it.

"Indeed, you must be in good shape to get on the force," Maureen said. "But 'tis no problem for my Daniel. He inherited my good eyesight and he can do those push-ups like nobody's business. He's in grand condition."

I would say so, Rose thought with admiration.

A warning hiss of breath came from beyond the leaves.

"Daniel is everything I would want in a son, except for one thing," Maureen said.

Rose set down her teacup and waited to hear the worst. Some inherited family disease, perhaps. Or maybe Daniel was gay and Maureen hoped Rose could turn him around.

The words came out in a rush. "He's thirty-three, and I say 'tis high time for him to settle down with some nice girl, but he says he won't do that until he makes detective, like my Patrick did, and when I ask him when that will be, he says not while he's having such a grand time riding with the mounted patrol unit." Maureen heaved a sigh and took a large bite of a muffin.

The litany sounded familiar to Rose. Her own mother's lectures ran along similar lines, except that Rose hadn't held out any hope to her mother about a day in the future when she'd get married. She just couldn't see the likelihood of it.

"'Tis the scar," Maureen said, regarding Rose with a hopeful expression. "Some lass needs to teach him not to be self-conscious about it. That would do the trick."

Rose doubted the scar had anything to do with Daniel being marriage-shy. He probably just wasn't ready to settle down, which made him a perfect candidate for her plan. But Maureen deserved a measure of honesty. "If you're looking for someone with marriage on her mind, I'm the wrong person, Mrs. O'Malley."

"You don't fancy Daniel?"

"I didn't say that. I'm just not interested in marriage."

"Then you *do* fancy him!"

"My goodness, what woman in her right mind wouldn't, Mrs. O'Malley?"

Maureen smiled with motherly satisfaction. "Lovely. That's a start." Pulling a stubby pencil and a scrap of paper from her purse, she scribbled on it and shoved it across the table toward Rose. "'Tis his phone number, if you'd like to call him. I'm willing to take my chances on the rest."

"Thank you. I will call him."

The groan through the dieffenbachia was barely muffled, as if Rose's mother was truly beside herself and no longer cared about detection.

Maureen shot a glance at the planter before leaning closer to Rose. "Should we do something? She sounds as if she's in mortal pain, she does. We could—"

"No, I don't think we should do anything," Rose said quickly. The last thing she wanted was for Maureen to discover Bridget and ruin everything. "From what I've read on the subject, you will only make them worse if you comment on their mental state.''

"I think I'll just visit the Ladies, then, and take a look at her on the way, just to make sure she's not foaming at the mouth.''

Figuratively, she probably was, Rose thought. "Just take care not to disturb her further,'' she cautioned Maureen.

"Right.''

Rose held her breath as Maureen made her way through the tearoom, but there was no surprised exclamation of recognition. The secret was safe for another few minutes.

"I know what you're up to!'' Bridget said in a stage whisper. "Don't think I don't, Rose Erin Kingsford!''

Rose spoke in an undertone. "Mom, what's wrong with me wanting to go out with someone as cute as Daniel? Did you see him?''

"I saw him, all right. And you looking him up and down, like a mouse eyeing a wheel of cheese. And those questions you were asking, like he was on the auction block.''

"He probably won't even go out with me after this incident with his mother.''

"I have half a mind to reveal myself to Maureen. That would put the brakes on your little scheme, now, wouldn't it?''

Rose decided to call her bluff. "Go ahead. So I won't get a date with a cute guy. So what else is new?''

"I should. I really should. Here she comes, back from the Ladies."

"Then you have your chance, don't you?"

"Mutton dressed as lamb," Bridget muttered.

Rose braced herself, but nothing happened.

Maureen sat down again and leaned toward Rose before pointing toward the planter. "I've figured out her problem," she whispered. "You know that old movie *Breakfast at Tiffany's?*"

Rose nodded.

"That poor woman over there, who must be my age if she's a day, thinks she's playing the part in that picture. She thinks she's Audrey Hepburn."

Rose bit her lip to keep from laughing. Her mother wouldn't reveal herself in a million years after a remark like that. Maybe, just maybe, the date with Daniel O'Malley wasn't out of the question, after all.

UNLIKE HIS MOTHER, Daniel believed in answering machines. The next day when he arrived at his apartment after his shift, the message light on his answering machine was blinking, and he had a very good idea why. His mother had already told him that Rose Kingsford planned to call. They'd had quite a row about it, in fact. He winced as he remembered telling his own dear mother in no uncertain terms to get the hell out of his love life.

She'd promised to do that, but it was like closing the barn door after the horse escaped.

After changing into jeans and a sweatshirt, he made himself a corned-beef sandwich and opened a beer.

He switched on the news and began to eat, all the while keeping an eye on that blinking red light and trying to imagine why Rose Kingsford was bothering with him. According to his mother, Rose "fancied" him, but then he didn't put much stock in anything his mother said about Rose.

He still couldn't believe that his mother had tracked down the model in the picture frame, arranged a meeting and then lured him there by pretending she wanted to have a cozy teatime chat, mother-and-son. Daniel hadn't realized how much of a rein his father must have kept on his mother. She would never have tried such a stunt while Patrick O'Malley was around. But lately she was acting like some…some *teenager*.

Finishing his sandwich and beer, Daniel wandered over to the living-room window of his small flat and stared out at the evening traffic below him. Moments such as this were somewhat lonely, but he was willing to pay that price. The first time he'd had to notify an officer's wife of the death of her husband, he'd vowed to do everything he could to avoid putting a woman through that. In a couple of years he'd seriously pursue a promotion that would take him out of the line of fire, and then maybe he'd consider finding a wife. On his own, without his mother's interference.

Her subdued reaction to his tirade told him she'd finally understood the line she must not cross again. But she'd left a loose end dangling, and he might as well deal with it now.

Turning from the window, he walked over to the answering machine and pushed the playback button.

Rose Kingsford's voice came dancing from the speaker, with a lilt he would have recognized as hers even without her first identifying statement.

"Hi, Daniel. This is Rose Kingsford."

Rose Kingsford. Rose—a perfect name for a woman with laughing eyes, an upturned nose, a dusting of freckles, fiery hair and a smile that could swell a man's heart or rip it to shreds. Amazing how indelibly her image remained in his mind after more than twenty-four hours, when he'd only seen her for a few moments. Two armed robberies, an attempted rape and a four-car pileup should have erased the face of Rose Kingsford from his memory. But he could close his eyes and she was right in front of him, her hand so soft and delicate as she placed it in his....

"We got off to rather an unfortunate start. Perhaps if we met for dinner, we could repair the damage. I'm free on Tuesday night at seven." Then she named a little Italian restaurant in the Village.

Tuesday night was his first night off next week, and he was particularly fond of good Italian food— pieces of information his mother must have passed on. But the idea of Rose and his mother conspiring to rob him of his bachelor status just didn't make sense. Daniel had asked a couple of people today, and the consensus seemed to be that a successful model pulled down at least a hundred grand a year, most likely more. Somebody who looked like Rose and made that kind of money wouldn't be interested in the matchmaking schemes of some little Irish woman from Brooklyn.

So what did Rose want of Daniel O'Malley? Or worse yet, what outrageous stories had his mother told that had convinced Rose to take pity on him and invite him to dinner? He could let the whole thing go, of course, and leave the questions unanswered.

Like hell he could.

IN A SECLUDED BOOTH on a rainy Tuesday night Rose watched the flame flicker in the small oil lamp centered on the checkered tablecloth. Her stomach was in knots, although she'd certainly asked men out on dates before. After all, this was the nineties, and she wasn't the sort of shrinking violet who hung back and waited for some man to make the first move. But this was different. The outcome of this meeting could change her entire life.

She'd decided that no man would react well to a frank statement that she considered him the perfect candidate to father her child. Some men might be flattered, but they wouldn't be the type she'd want. Others would be pleased at the idea of a one-night stand, but she also didn't want that kind. She didn't think Daniel fit in either category. Therefore, she'd have to handle the matter with great delicacy.

The timing couldn't have been better. Renovations were complete on her little cottage upstate, and two rural New York papers had agreed to carry her comic strip, ''St. Paddy and Flynn.'' She figured she was less than a year from ending her modeling career and working full-time on the strip, less than a year from settling into the country life she'd yearned for nearly all her life, it seemed. Pregnancy would push her into the decision to turn down future modeling jobs, and she would welcome the shove.

Of course Daniel might not show up tonight. She'd left the invitation on his answering machine without requiring an R.S.V.P. It was a calculated risk, but one that gave him the kind of leeway she'd thought necessary. It was the sort of gesture she'd have appreciated, in his shoes.

She glanced at her watch. Five minutes past seven. Her stomach lurched at the thought that he really might not come. Somehow her instincts had told her he would. She caught the eye of a waiter and ordered a glass of Chianti.

By seven-thirty she'd finished the wine, even though she'd sipped it very slowly. On an empty stomach, it had made her light-headed. And more than a little irritated. Sure, she hadn't forced him to respond to her invitation, but if he really hadn't meant to show he might have had the courtesy to notify her. Maybe a man who looked like Daniel had so many invitations he could afford to stand up several women a week. Maybe her precious instincts had been off somewhere napping when Daniel had arrived on the scene and simple lust had blinded her to his arrogant nature.

Well, she was sick of the pitying looks she kept getting from the waiter, who'd stopped by several times to inquire about whether she'd like to go ahead and order a meal. She was sick of sitting here waiting for some fellow who was so full of himself he took women's dinner invitations for granted. She was, finally and completely, sick of men in general. Maybe a sperm bank was the answer, after all.

Leaving money on the table for her wine and the time she'd spent in the booth, she gathered her trench coat and purse from the seat beside her. After shoving her arms angrily into the sleeves, she pushed her way out the restaurant door into the rain, where she started searching for a cab. Every one that sailed past her was occupied.

"Perfect. Just perfect," she muttered.

"Rose!"

When she heard her name, her heartbeat clicked into high gear. She turned and saw Daniel running toward her, his feet splashing through puddles in total abandon, as if he cared nothing for getting soaked so long as he reached her before she left. Instantly her anger evaporated, but she thought it prudent to retain some show of indignation.

"Rose, I'm so sorry." His breath came out in great clouds as he loped up beside her. "The cab got in a wreck about four blocks from here. Tourists in a Ford Tempo ran into him. Then when they discovered I was a cop…well, I had a devil of a time getting out of there." He paused. "I suppose you've eaten and are ready to go home."

She'd meant to chastise him for making her wait, but she was mesmerized with the way raindrops clung to his dark lashes. Then he blinked and one drop shook loose to run down the side of his nose and over to the corner of his mouth. She reached up and brushed it away. Then she glanced up into his eyes. There was the look she'd wished for when she'd seen him in the tearoom, the look that could melt a woman's heart.

Gently he pushed a damp tendril from her cheek and tucked it behind her ear. "You're getting wet."

"So are you."

His gaze caressed her face as he slid his hand over the nape of her neck. "It's only rain."

Her pulse pounded in her ears as she recognized the touch of a man who understood how to arouse a woman. What he was about to do was audacious, and all the more thrilling because of that. "I guess you're used to…the elements," she said.

"I'll tell you something, Rose." He leaned closer, his brown eyes warm with intent. "The elements never looked quite like this." Then, as the rain pattered all around them, he kissed her.

3

IN FOR A PENNY, in for a pound, Daniel thought as he took possession of Rose's moist, completely irresistible mouth. As a fact-finding mission, it wasn't a bad move. As he explored her velvet lips he learned several things—she tasted of honey and wine, she had the most responsive mouth he'd ever been fortunate enough to kiss, and he was trembling like a sapling in the wind from the excitement they generated together.

He had no idea how long he might have stood there enjoying the heated pleasure of kissing Rose, indifferent to the drizzle falling steadily on them, if a car hadn't whizzed through a puddle in the street beside them. The water hit them with enough velocity to awaken them from their daze. They broke apart and stared at each other in shock, as though just now realizing what had happened between them.

Rose started laughing first, and the sound filled the rain-soaked air with such delight that before Daniel realized it, he was laughing, too. His shoes, relatively new, were ruined, and God knew if he'd ever get the mud stains out of his slacks. He didn't care.

"Let's go inside and get some pasta," she said.

"And more of that wine."

"Wine?"

"I could taste it."

"Oh." Her cheeks grew even pinker.

A maidenly blush. He was enchanted out of his mind. He took her elbow and propelled her toward the restaurant to keep himself from making an indecent proposal and luring her back to his flat this very minute. He still didn't know what Rose Kingsford wanted with him, but he was getting some idea of what he wanted with her.

The restaurant was almost deserted as they dripped their way back to a booth. A teenaged boy appeared from the kitchen to follow them with a rag mop, and Daniel turned and gave him a tip. Then he took off his jacket and handed it to the waiter who appeared at their table. He suggested Rose do the same. "Can you find a place to hang these where they can dry?" he asked the waiter.

"Sure thing."

"And bring a bottle of wine, the same kind she had before."

"You couldn't tell what kind it was?" Rose teased as the waiter left.

"It was Chianti, but I didn't want to show off." Then he adjusted the little oil lamp so he could look at her. He had a feeling the activity could absorb his attention for some time.

She leaned her chin on her fist and seemed to be copying his behavior. "So you decided to come, after all."

''Can't resist a good Italian meal, but then I guess you know that.''

She smiled.

He pretended to shield his eyes from the brilliance. ''You know, you should have that thing registered. Could cause blindness.''

Her smile broadened into a chuckle.

He grinned back, inordinately pleased with himself. Even though he knew rationally that she smiled for a living, he decided he would kid himself that this one had been for him and him alone. ''Besides my fondness for Italian food and what nights I'm off duty, what did my mother tell you about me?''

A secret sparkle lurked in her green eyes.

''Come on, let's have it.''

''Am I being interrogated?''

''You bet your sweet shamrocks. No telling what that woman's been spreading around town in hopes of getting me to the altar.'' He regarded her intently and took a deep breath. Honesty was called for. ''In spite of what just happened outside, I'm not in the market for a wife, Rose.''

''She told me that.''

''No doubt she had some twisted version of why that is.''

She remained silent, but the dancing light in her eyes told him that Maureen had indeed made up some woolly tale that explained his single status.

''Whatever it is, it's not true,'' he said. ''I'm single because that's what I choose to be right now.''

''Same here.''

He fell backward against the booth in feigned shock. "What? No arguments about the blissful wedded state?"

"I have no interest in getting married, either."

"Does my sainted mother know this singular fact about you?"

"I told her. She gave me your phone number and said she'd take her chances."

Daniel considered this as the bottle of Chianti arrived and they both ordered dinner. After the waiter left, Daniel sipped his wine until their sense of intimacy had reasserted itself. Then he leaned both arms on the table and fixed Rose with a steady gaze. "So you don't want a husband."

"No. Have no interest in that, thank you."

"Then what do you want, Rose Kingsford?" He watched her eyes and knew before she opened her mouth that he wasn't about to get the whole truth. Twelve years in police work had taught him that much.

"Believe it or not, I find it difficult to meet men," she began.

"I don't believe it."

"Well, it's true." She took a long, graceful sip of her wine. "First, there are the male models. Chuck, the best of that bunch, is gay. Then there are the photographers. Some are great, usually the married ones, and some are sleazeballs—grope city."

"Sounds unpleasant."

Rose sighed. "I don't know if it's just the nature of what I do, putting my body out there for everyone to see, but most men seem to be focused on that body and not the person, which turns me off. Besides that, I work very hard and put in a lot of hours. When I have time off I don't feel like making the effort to hit the nightclubs, so the result is…not much chance to meet regular guys.''

''That's how you'd classify me?''

''I'd classify you as the deluxe model.''

He nearly choked on his wine. ''Isn't that a little extravagant, considering we've known each other less than an hour?''

''I trust my instincts. In your line of work, I'm sure you do, too.''

''That's why I'm here.'' *And why I kissed you.*

She gazed at him over the rim of her goblet. ''Do you know how many men concentrate on my eyes when we meet?''

''I have no idea.''

''Almost none. But you did.''

''I was embarrassed. I don't know if you can give me much credit for the way I behaved, considering that my mother had just put me in one of the most awkward situations any man can imagine. Maybe if we'd met at a cocktail party I'd have given you the full-body once-over, like all the others.''

''I don't think so, Daniel O'Malley.'' She turned on that million-dollar smile again. ''I don't think so at all.''

''Talk about hamstringing a guy. I'm going to be afraid to look below the level of your nose from now on, for fear you'll bump my classification down to sleazeball, fourth class.''

''Wrong. You passed the test, so you can relax.''

''Hey, that's great. Would you mind standing up, then?''

She blinked. ''Excuse me?''

He stifled a grin and motioned her up. ''Ogling time. I figure I'm behind on my quota.''

She gazed at him for a full thirty seconds and he figured that was the end of that. She couldn't take a joke, and it was good that he'd found it out now before things progressed beyond that sizzling kiss.

Then she slowly eased out of the booth. ''Pay attention,'' she said. ''I only intend to do this once.'' She stood and smoothed her damp clothes, a leather miniskirt, knee-high boots, a form-fitting knit top and a funky little vest with tiny gold chains all over it. Lifting her chin and squaring her shoulders, she threw him a look of haughty confidence before moving sinuously down the aisle beside the booths.

Daniel realized she'd mentally placed herself on a runway. In total awe, he sank back against the booth and watched the provocative sway of her slender hips as she walked away from him on those terrific legs. No wonder guys skipped looking into her eyes, he thought. The message coming from the rest of her was too potent for mere mortals to ignore.

Just before she reached the kitchen door she pivoted and started back. Her breasts were small, but she thrust them forward so seductively that Daniel's mouth went dry as the little chains on her vest danced invitingly. Thank God he had a table to cover the effect she was having on him. Usually attracted to more well-endowed women, he would never have imagined someone as willowy as Rose would inspire such lust. Carriage was everything, apparently, and Rose had that in spades.

He decided to concentrate on her face to keep himself from starting to drool. No help there. She'd turned the heat up from warm and sweet to hot and smoldering. He took a deep breath and gripped the table as she drew nearer. It was either that or throw her down on top of it once she came close enough.

She reached their table and glanced down at him as if he were one of her subjects. Which he was, now. She had only to command him.

"Well?" she asked.

He cleared his throat. "Thanks," he managed.

She slid into the booth and the arrogance slipped from her like a cloak. "Now we're even."

He didn't think they were on the same playing field, let alone even. "What do you mean?"

"I've been watching you for days."

"What?"

"As luck would have it, I was working this past week quite close to your…beat, I guess you call it. I'm a sucker for a guy in a uniform, and then, when you climb up on that magnificent horse…" The corners of her mouth twitched in amusement. "Let's just say I did my share of ogling, too."

Heat crept up from his damp collar. "I didn't see you."

"I was using binoculars."

"Good grief."

She chuckled. "I've embarrassed you. But that's a good sign. You're not vain, at any rate."

Daniel was speechless. When the waiter showed up with their dinner he'd never been so glad to see a plate of pasta in his life. "Thank God. I'm starved," he said. As he picked up his fork he glanced at Rose and caught her smiling at him. "Binoculars? Really?"

"Don't sound so surprised. You cut quite a figure, as my mother would say."

"Your Irish mother," he said, remembering his own mother's comment that afternoon in the tearoom. "Where's she from?"

"Tralee."

He finished a bite of the most succulent linguine he'd ever tasted. He liked Rose's choice in restaurants, among other things. "That's quite a coincidence, considering that my mother comes from Tralee. You don't suppose that they knew each—"

"I'm sure not," she said quickly.

Too quickly, he thought. The plot was thickening. "Does your mother live in New York?"

"Oh, yes."

There was a world of meaning in that phrase, he thought. "Sounds like your mother's somewhat of a trial to you, too."

"Let's just say we don't agree on how I should live my life."

"Let me guess. She'd like you to find some nice guy and settle down."

Rose paused with a forkful of fettucine halfway to her mouth. "Bingo."

"And your father?"

"He doesn't get much say in the matter. They're divorced."

"His idea?"

She took a long swallow of Chianti. "Yep."

That could explain her aversion to marriage, he thought, and decided to risk finding out. "Look, I don't really know you well enough to ask this—"

"Yes, you do." She met his gaze across the subtle flame of the oil lamp.

Those green eyes. He was helpless, going down for the count. Green was supposed to be a cool color, but there was nothing even remotely cool about the way she was looking at him.

"What did you want to ask?" she murmured.

He hadn't the slightest idea. More important questions had begun to shove out whatever inane thing he'd been about to say. Questions that began with *when* and *where*. Then his pager vibrated against his thigh. He extracted it from his pocket and reluctantly broke eye contact with Rose in order to check the number. Damn. The station.

"I have to make a quick phone call," he said. "Be right back."

"That would be nice."

He slid from the booth with a silent prayer that this wasn't a call asking him to go in to work. The prayer went unanswered. On his way back from using the pay phone in the back of the restaurant he found the waiter and told him to bring the check and his jacket.

"Problems?" Rose asked as he returned to the booth.

"A guy called in sick. I have to leave, but I hope you'll stay and finish your meal."

"Don't worry. I will. Maybe yours, too." She glanced up as the waiter approached with the check and Daniel's jacket. She held out her hand to the waiter. "This one's on me."

The waiter started toward her.

"I'm afraid not." Daniel motioned for the check.

The waiter sighed and looked at the ceiling. "Oh, boy."

"Daniel, I invited you to dinner. It's as simple as that."

The waiter gritted his teeth and stepped toward her again.

Daniel interceded and took the bill from him. "No, it's even simpler. When I have dinner with a woman, I pay for it. End of discussion." He reached in his back pocket for his wallet.

"I won't let you do this."

"Let him," the waiter said.

"Yeah, let me." Daniel glanced at the total and pulled some bills from his wallet. "Thanks," he said to the waiter, putting both the check and money in the guy's hand. Then he shrugged into his jacket. "I'll call you," he said as he started out of the restaurant.

"That's what they all say," the waiter commented to Rose.

Daniel turned and backed toward the door as he zipped his jacket. "In this case, it happens to be true." Then he gave Rose a salute and went outside to look for a cab. The rain had stopped, but a chill wind had picked up. Daniel had just whistled a cab over when Rose came out of the restaurant, coatless.

"Daniel, I'm paying for dinner!" she said, shoving the money at him.

"No, you're not." He took her by the shoulders and turned her around. "Now go back inside. It's cold out here."

"You want a cab or not?" the cabbie called from the window.

"Yeah," Daniel said over his shoulder.

"Meter's running, then."

"Come on, Daniel." She twisted in his grip. "Don't be so old-fashioned."

"But you see, that's exactly what I am." He turned her to face him again. "Look, I know you could buy and sell me. Let me preserve some of my pride by taking care of dinner."

She gazed at him. "I don't care how much money you make or don't make. That's not the point."

"It is for me."

She closed her eyes in apparent frustration. "You know, I really—"

He interrupted her protest by pulling her close.

Her eyes flew open.

"Forgot something," he murmured. "Dessert."

Then he gave himself up to the richness of her mouth. Oh, the promise of those ripe lips. He cursed Tom Peterson, who had had the poor judgment to call in sick tonight. Otherwise, this evening might have ended quite differently.

The cabbie beeped the horn and Daniel lifted his head with regret. "Gotta go."

Rose's lashes drifted upward and she reached to stroke his cheek with the tip of her finger. "I'll accept your generosity tonight on one condition."

"What's that?"

"Next time, I'll cook."

It took only a fraction of a second for the implication of that to sink in, and his body tightened in anticipation. "All right."

She eased out of his embrace. "Next Tuesday, same time?"

"You've got it."

She backed toward the restaurant. "I'll leave my address on your machine."

"Fine."

"Good night, Daniel."

"Good night." He remained standing there long after the door closed behind her.

The cab window creaked down again. "It's your business, buddy, but holding down the sidewalk is getting pretty expensive, don't you think?"

Daniel turned and climbed into the cab.

"However—" The cabbie pronounced it "how-evah." "I completely understand being distracted with a woman who looks like that."

MAUREEN DIDN'T ABUSE the privilege of having a key to her son's apartment. He'd given it to her for the times she came into Manhattan from Brooklyn to shop and wanted someplace to freshen up, someplace she could trust would be clean and safe.

Maureen never snooped through Daniel's dresser drawers or his mail. Daniel always laughed and told her to go ahead. There weren't any secrets in his apartment. Up until now she'd believed him, but in the past week he'd become more secretive. 'Twas pure luck that she discovered why.

She'd taken the subway into the city for a sale at Macy's and stopped at Daniel's afterward, as usual. While she was making herself a restorative cup of tea, Daniel's telephone rang. She hurried to pick up the receiver, but just then Daniel's voice came on and she remembered about the answering machine. The contraption confused her something awful, and she wasn't about to fool with it.

Instead she stood there and listened to Daniel's brisk message. He sounded so businesslike on that recording that whenever she got the machine she just hung up. Probably this person would, too. Daniel's social life would pick up considerably if he got rid of this machine, in Maureen's humble opinion.

But the person on the other end didn't hang up. Instead, Maureen listened in wonder as Rose Kingsford gave Daniel directions to her apartment and reminded him that they'd settled on Tuesday at seven. Maureen clapped a hand over her mouth as if afraid that Rose could hear her giggle of delight. Dinner at

Rose's apartment! That little devil Daniel had never let on that matters had progressed to this stage. If a woman cooked a man dinner, then she meant to demonstrate her domestic skills for him.

After Rose hung up, Maureen picked up her skirts and danced a jig around the apartment. Oh, this was grand news! She'd had a feeling about this girl from the moment she'd laid eyes on her, and now, the romance was getting under way! The jig didn't last very long before she was out of breath, but as she plopped to the couch and put a hand over her beating heart, she continued to smile.

Then she bounced up again, hurried to the bookcase and found the street map. Digging in her purse for her reading glasses, Maureen located the spot where the apartment house must be. Rose lived in a swanky part of town, all right. Maureen would dearly love to see Daniel walk into that place. She wondered if he'd take flowers. 'Twould be a good sign, if he took flowers.

As closemouthed as Daniel had become lately, he probably wouldn't tell her whether he went over to Rose's, let alone whether he took flowers. Maureen picked up a pad of paper beside the phone and wrote down Rose's address. 'Twould be quite dark at seven. She'd take a cab, never mind the expense. The sight of Daniel walking into that apartment building with a bouquet of flowers would be a picture she'd carry to her grave. Her Daniel was going courting.

SOMETHING WAS GOING ON. Bridget Kingsford was sure of it. Tuesday was the night Rose always came over to watch their favorite television shows, unless she was out of town on a shoot. When she'd cancelled out for the second Tuesday in a row, and offered no explanation, Bridget feared it had something to do with Daniel O'Malley.

It was a long shot, but maybe if she just dropped in on Rose Tuesday night, she'd find out something. A chat with the doorman might work almost as well. Bridget didn't intend to stand by while her daughter conceived a child out of wedlock, most especially if the prospective father was the son of her age-old rival. She'd sooner dance with the devil on the steps of St. Patrick's Cathedral than allow that to take place.

4

ROSE HAD FIGURED on learning to cook someday. For one thing, she couldn't imagine being a mother and not knowing how to bake chocolate chip cookies. It was one of her favorite fantasies of motherhood—a warm kitchen filled with the aroma of baking dough as a little child perched on a stool, her fat fingers making chip-filled balls and arranging them carefully on a cookie sheet.

Rose's mother had always made cooking seem easy enough, although her recent obsession with her figure had ended some of her enthusiasm for baking. Rose would have loved to ask for some motherly advice on the meal she planned to serve Daniel on Tuesday night. But her mother wasn't supposed to know about that meal, or any of the activities that might follow.

As luck would have it, the Donna Karan shoot on Tuesday afternoon had run overtime, which had screwed up her cooking schedule and stressed her out. That probably explained why she'd cut her finger trying to machete some celery stalks into submission while keeping one eye on the clock. She stuck her finger in her mouth and ran for the bathroom cabinet where she hoped at least one bandage remained in the box she kept there.

Daniel was scheduled to arrive in forty minutes. According to the recipe, the stew needed nearly two hours to cook, and she had yet to brown the meat. Thank God she'd bought a decent bottle of cabernet to fill the extra hour the stew would require to cook. That was assuming she got everything in the pot within the next five minutes.

The bandage box was empty, so she fastened a tissue around her bleeding finger with masking tape from her drafting supplies and headed back to the kitchen. Ten minutes later, her knit top and jeans were coated in flour from rolling the cubed lamb in it, her forearm was taped with more tissue where hot grease had splattered while she browned the meat, and her eyes watered madly from chopping an onion. When she wiped her streaming eyes with the back of her hands, she got flour all over her face, too.

"Jesus, Mary and Joseph," she muttered, using one of her mother's favorite angry expressions. She finished chopping the onion and sighed. If she could get the stew in the oven, then shower and change, she'd decant the wine before Daniel arrived. With wine and intimate conversation, perhaps he'd never notice that dinner was delayed. She continued reading the recipe aloud.

"Tie parsley, celery, bay leaves and thyme in small bag," she murmured. *A small bag?* It made no sense. She had a couple of small paper bags, but they'd disintegrate in the stew. A plastic bag would melt. She left the kitchen and roamed the apartment, seeking inspiration. Twice she reached for the phone to call her mother before remembering she couldn't do that.

Finally she wandered into her bedroom where a dresser drawer hung open, its contents spilling out from her rush to find clean underwear that morning. A nylon stocking dangled nearly to the floor.

She pounced on the drawer as she remembered getting a run in a pair of Dark Seduction panty hose just yesterday. They had little spangles all over them, but so what? The stew wouldn't know the difference if the spices were encased in spangles or not. Moments later she'd amputated the foot from the panty hose. She washed and rinsed the bit of nylon, dumped the spices in the toe, knotted the ankle, and plopped the whole thing into the stew.

''Cook fast,'' she instructed the stew as she slid it into the oven and glanced at the clock. She twisted the oven dial up a few extra notches, figuring a higher temperature would make the stew cook faster.

She had nine minutes to make herself presentable. As she hurried toward her bedroom, the intercom buzzed. She walked to the intercom with a feeling of inevitability and pushed the button. ''Yes?''

''Daniel O'Malley's here to see you,'' said Jimmy, who monitored the desk in the lobby most evenings. ''Shall I send him up?''

Rose glanced down at her flour-covered clothes, then touched a flour-covered hand to her tangle of hair caught up in a clip. She'd need at least fifteen minutes to transform herself. Daniel was a good eight minutes early, but if she made him wait downstairs, he'd think he had a vain woman on his hands. Considering her career choice, she already had to fight that image with most people, and she didn't want to fight it with Daniel. For all she knew, he'd arrived early as a sort of test.

"Sure, send him up," she said.

Then she raced for a pad of paper, scribbled a note that invited him to come in, and unlocked the door to tape it on the outside. *The wine.* She should have it uncorked and a goblet sitting beside the bottle on the coffee table so he could help himself while she showered and changed. That would be a classy gesture and show she had his comfort in mind even though he'd have to wait.

Dashing into the kitchen, she wrenched open the drawer where she usually kept the corkscrew—the drawer where she also kept the scissors, the coupons for microwave dinners, the corks she saved from memorable wine tastings with friends, the dried remnants of a rose her mother had given her on her last birthday, toothpicks, and matches from every restaurant she'd ever been to in New York.

The corkscrew refused to show itself as she pawed through the jumbled contents of the drawer. Finally she glanced on the counter and saw the corkscrew lying where she'd left it for convenience, right next to the wine bottle. "Aha! Now I've got you, my pretty!"

She picked up the knife she'd used to cut both the celery and her finger, pared away the seal and twisted the corkscrew in. Then she tugged, but the cork wouldn't budge.

"Open up, you son of a cheap jug wine!" She stuck the bottle between her legs for leverage and started to yank the cork out.

"You shouldn't leave your door unlocked."

Rose shrieked in alarm. Pulling out the cork at the same time as she yelled was pure reflex. Without Daniel diving to catch it, the bottle would have hit the floor. As it was, it merely disgorged a couple of ounces on his brown leather boots as the weight of the bottle crushed the bouquet of violets he held in one hand.

Rose grabbed a dishcloth from the sink and dropped to her knees in front of him. "Don't move!" she instructed as she dabbed at the wine staining the soft leather.

"Hey, don't bother. It's okay."

"This is nice leather. I don't want to ruin—" She forgot what she'd meant to say as he crouched down and set the wine bottle and mangled flowers on the floor.

"It's okay," he said again, taking her by her arms and drawing her gently to her feet.

"No, it's not." She imagined how she must look to him with flour all over her, including in her hair, and not a speck of makeup on. "In fact, the disasters that have happened in this kitchen recently make *Twister* look like a comedy."

A smile flitted across his face, but his brown eyes

were grave. ''If you leave your door unlocked again, things could get a whole lot worse.''

''I thought I'd be in the shower when you arrived.'' His firm grip on her arms was interfering with clear thinking. Old Spice. She'd forgotten he used it. No designer cologne for this guy. ''I'm…running a little late.''

''So you left a note on the door inviting me and any wacko who happened along to walk right in and make himself at home? Not good, Rose.''

She'd about come to the end of her tether. Nothing was turning out the way she'd planned, and now she was getting a lecture from the man she'd hoped to seduce. Tears threatened, but she blinked them back and lifted her chin in defiance. ''Gonna arrest me for gross negligence, officer?''

''I—hey, don't cry. Aw, hell.'' He pulled her into his arms, flour and all.

''Daniel, don't! I'm covered with—''

''So I noticed.'' His mouth came down on hers.

With the first pressure of his lips, her luck began to change. Whoever had coined the phrase ''kiss it and make it better'' must have had Daniel O'Malley in mind for the job. All her anxiety over the meal and her appearance dissolved before the tender onslaught of his mouth on hers. Tension slipped from her body until she felt as liquid as the wine in the bottle she'd been trying to open.

He ended the kiss slowly, with exquisite timing. She lifted suddenly heavy eyelids to gaze up at him.

''I'm sorry I barked at you,'' he murmured.

The belligerence had been kissed right out of her. "I suppose you had a point about the unlocked door."

"I did, but I could also see how much trouble you were taking to cook me a meal." He rubbed the flat of his hand up and down her spine in a caress that soothed, yet stimulated at the same time. "I could have mentioned that before delivering my standard cop safety lecture."

She let out a long sigh. "I'm not much of a cook, Daniel. My mother's a great cook. I should have learned more from her, but I just haven't taken the time."

The corners of his mouth turned up. "You sound as if you're in a confessional relating a string of murders. It's not a sin, you know."

"The way I was raised, it is. And the way you were raised, I'd imagine. You said you were an old-fashioned guy."

"If you mean that my mother's a traditional house-wife, you'd be right. If you mean that I expect that role of all women, that I'm *that* kind of old-fashioned guy, you'd be wrong. I may be an Irish cop, but that's where the stereotype ends."

"But you insisted on paying for dinner."

He grinned. "Well, now, that's another whole is-sue. I had to establish my status."

"Status?"

"I don't want to be your boy toy."

"Oh, for heaven's sake! I would never—"

"Maybe not." He stopped rubbing her back and gazed at her intently. "But let's not kid ourselves that you're not one up on me in the fame-and-fortune department. I want it clearly understood from the beginning that I pay my own way. Don't invite me to St. Thomas for the weekend. I can't afford it.''

She chuckled and leaned back in his arms. "You can relax on that score. I have no intention of inviting you to St. Thomas for the weekend.''

"Oh.''

He looked so deflated she took pity on him. "*I* don't go to St. Thomas for the weekend.''

"Okay, so I got the destination wrong. I'm not sure what tropical vacation spots are trendy these days.''

"I don't take tropical vacations. The only way I get to those places is if my job sends me there.'' She stepped out of his arms and took his hand. "Come on. I'll show you what I spend my free time and money on.''

"If it's illegal, I don't want to know about it.''

She laughed as she led him toward her office. "You have a very jaded view of what people do with big salaries, bucko.''

"I'm a New York City cop.''

"Well, you'll find nothing to confiscate here.'' At her office door she became nervous about watching him study the work spread on her drafting table. "Give me your jacket and I'll hang it up while you're searching the place.''

As he shrugged out of his leather jacket and handed it to her, she took a moment to admire the way his knit Henley defined the muscled breadth of his chest. Her fingers itched to undo the buttons and explore what lay beneath. Talk about chemistry. Every move he made brought a flush of anticipation to her skin.

She waved her hand toward her office. ''Go ahead. I'll be right back.'' The decision to show him her cartooning work had been made impulsively, but as she hung his jacket in the hall closet she decided it was the right decision. The more he understood about her, the more likely he'd be to grant her ultimate request. She was encouraged by his statement that he wasn't a stereotypical Irish male who expected women to conform to a certain standard.

After hanging up the jacket, she returned to her office and paused in the doorway. Daniel stood in front of the drafting table, his back to her, his hands braced on his hips as he studied her cartoons. He chuckled, then laughed outright. She smiled with pleasure. Feeling far more confident than she had five minutes ago, she walked up beside him.

He glanced at her with a look of admiration. ''These are great, Rose. Better than the ones in the *Times*.''

''So far nobody at the *Times* agrees with you, but I've sold the strip to a couple of small papers upstate.''

''No kidding? Congratulations.'' He returned his attention to the drafting table. ''I don't have to ask you where you get your ideas. You've been listening in on a lot of Irish conversations.''

''Then you think I have the tone right?''

''It's uncanny. St. Paddy sounds just like my dad, and the little leprechaun's comebacks are exactly what my mother used to say to him. If I didn't know better I'd think you'd been eavesdropping all these years."

"Well, my grandmother, who spent one summer with us, talked that way, and I was in Ireland last year while we photographed the shots for my calendar."

He looked at her. "Calendar? I don't remember seeing one."

"You keep up with calendars?"

"In the past week I've done a study of magazines and calendars. My version of your routine with the binoculars."

She lifted her eyebrows. "I see. Well, this one's in production for next year. I'm hoping the royalties on it will cushion the loss of income when I retire from modeling in the next year or so."

"Now I'm really intimidated. You've saved enough money to retire already?"

"Not retire the way you're thinking. But I can last a few years while I work on getting the strip going."

"Whew." He gazed at her and shook his head. "And here I thought you were a free spirit whose top priority was—" he paused "—a relationship."

"That isn't what you were about to say."

"What I was about to say was uncalled for."

She moved closer to him. "Maybe it was correct."

"I doubt it. A woman with your sort of self-direction is a hell of a lot deeper than I was going to give you credit for."

"That doesn't mean I don't have...needs."

"I'm sure you do. But you'd never let them get in the way of your master plan."

She allowed herself to become lost in the power of his dark eyes. "Is that so bad?"

"I can't say it is. I'm the same way."

The impulse to unfasten the first button on his shirt became too strong to resist. "Then I guess we have a perfect situation," she murmured.

"It seems that way." His voice had taken on a huskier tone.

She moved to the second button and her fingers brushed against a tendril of dark chest hair. Her breathing quickened.

"What about dinner?" he asked softly.

She undid another button and looked up at him. "Dinner will take a while longer to cook."

He slid a hand along her jawline and tipped her mouth up to his. "That's the best news I've heard all night."

MAUREEN HAD MEANT to watch from the cab as Daniel walked into the apartment-building lobby, and then take the cab back home. But once he'd disappeared from sight she couldn't seem to leave. All her dreams could be coming true in that apartment building, and she wanted to savor the moment. Taking the cab to this spot had been terribly expensive, but justified. Sitting there with the meter running was pure extravagance, however.

"Pull up in front of the apartment," she instructed the driver. "I'm getting out."

"You want me to wait for you?" the driver asked.

"No, thank you." She dug out the proper amount from her purse and added a tip before putting it in the money chute set into the sheet of plastic that divided the front and back seats. "I'll call another cab when I need one."

"Suit yourself."

Maureen climbed out onto the sidewalk. She'd just stand here a moment, she thought, looking up at the rows of lighted windows above her. If only she knew for certain that one of those lighted windows belonged to Rose Kingsford. But perhaps Rose didn't have an apartment that looked out on the street.

A cold raindrop hit her in the eye, and then another. She opened her purse and fished around until she found the accordian-folded rain bonnet she carried everywhere. She tied it securely over her hair and hoped the rain would let up.

It started coming down harder, pelting her plastic bonnet as if the good Lord had got it into his head to drown her on the spot. New York raindrops seemed to hit a body harder than Irish rain, Maureen thought. Or at least the way she remembered Irish rain. Someday she'd love to go back and find out if she remembered right.

Soon she was standing in a puddle. No help for it, she'd have to head into the apartment lobby.

She scurried through the revolving door and stood blinking in the brightness of the interior. But she certainly approved of the atmosphere. A crystal chandelier sparkled above her, and what looked like very fine paintings hung on the wallpapered walls. Two wing chairs in a burgundy-and-gray print sat on either side of a small table with a lovely flower arrangement on it. Maureen wondered if she dared sit in one of the chairs for a wee bit.

"Can I help you, ma'am?" asked a nice-looking young man from behind an antique desk that had a computer on it.

"I was…uh…meeting someone, I was." She untied her rain bonnet. "But I think she must have been held up. I needed a place to get in out of the weather, you see. What is your name, young man?"

"I'm Jimmy, ma'am. Would you like me to call a cab for you?"

Maureen thought about that. She did so hate to leave the scene, but parking herself in the lobby might get awkward. "I'll wait a little longer, Jimmy," she said. "And then, if she doesn't come, I would be most obliged if you would call for a cab."

Jimmy smiled. "All right."

Maureen decided to talk with Jimmy, which might keep him from thinking she was some sort of bag lady. She noticed a textbook lying open on the desk and walked over toward where he sat. "Looks like you're studying for something, Jimmy."

"Yep. Economics exam tomorrow."

"Economics. 'Tis a good field. My son Daniel decided to go to the police academy. He's with the mounted patrol."

Jimmy nodded. "That sounds—" He paused and

glanced past her toward the door. "Why, hello there, Mrs. Kingsford."

"Hello, Jimmy," said a woman who had apparently just entered the lobby.

Mrs. Kingsford, Maureen thought with a thrill of excitement. It had to be Rose's mother, Daniel's future mother-in-law! The luck of the Irish was with Maureen tonight for sure. You could tell a lot about how a girl would turn out by looking at her mother, in Maureen's opinion, and here was a chance to find out about Rose's mother early on, without revealing that she was Daniel's mother. Putting on her best smile, Maureen turned.

The woman named Mrs. Kingsford stared at Maureen, and Maureen stared back. The poor demented bag lady from the tearoom!

A look of horror contorted the woman's face. "You!" she screamed.

5

DANIEL'S HEART galloped faster as Rose nestled her lithe body seductively close and opened her mouth beneath his. He'd never received such a delicious invitation in his life, and he was more than ready to accept it.

Holding Rose was like holding an arc of electricity. She galvanized every inch of him until he fairly hummed with the need to touch, to stroke, to possess her in the most intimate way possible. He didn't remember pulling her knit top from the waistband of her jeans, yet he must have, for soon his hands were gliding over warm, silken skin.

She wore nothing beneath the top, and the sweet weight of her breast filled his hand as if he'd been born to caress her this way. She trembled and gasped against his mouth, and fierce, almost frightening needs surged through him. He wondered if they'd make it into her bedroom or be forced by their driving passion to satisfy themselves on the floor of her office.

She kissed him as if she couldn't get enough, while her busy hands pulled his shirt out and lightly raked his back with her nails. As his breathing grew labored, his senses filled with her floral cologne and the intoxicating scent of thoroughly aroused woman.

He also smelled something burning.

He tried not to acknowledge it. Her lips tasted like heaven and he eagerly anticipated tasting the rest of her willing body. He didn't want something to be burning.

But it sure as hell was. Cursing the training that refused to let him ignore even the slightest hint of danger, he lifted his mouth from hers. "I think—" He stopped to clear the huskiness of desire from his throat. "There could be a problem in the kitchen."

She moaned softly.

He steeled himself not to return to lips blushing from his enthusiastic kisses. Reluctantly he removed his hand from her breast. "Rose, something's burning."

Her eyelids lifted, revealing green eyes sultry with desire.

One look into those eyes and he became as unconcerned as Nero when Rome was torched. "Never mind," he said as he lowered his head again.

Her nose wrinkled. "Something *is* burning!" She wiggled out of his embrace and rushed from the room.

He followed as best he could, considering his jeans had become way too tight in the past ten minutes.

Rose stood coughing in front of an open oven door, and the kitchen was enveloped in smoke. "It's our dinner!" she wailed, pulling on oven mitts before hauling out a smoking roaster and banging it onto the top of the stove. "It's ruined."

He took refuge in the timeworn male response to this sort of disaster. ''We'll go out.''

''I don't want to go out. I want to fix you a nice, home-cooked meal!'' She lifted the roaster lid and more smoke billowed out. ''Look at this! It's—it's—'' She peered into the roaster and her eyes widened. ''It's *sparkling*.''

''Sparkling?'' Daniel had witnessed a few kitchen disasters in his time, but none of them had sparkled. He stepped forward and surveyed the charred mess in the pan. Sure enough, sprinkled throughout the glop were tiny stars that winked in the kitchen's overhead light. He glanced at Rose in confusion.

''I'm not even going to tell you.'' She slammed the lid back on the roaster.

He chuckled and grabbed her by the arms. ''What do you mean, you're not going to tell me? I deserve to know why there are stars in the stew.''

She blushed and averted her gaze. ''I doubt it would have affected the taste.''

''What wouldn't?''

''My Dark Seduction panty hose.''

He couldn't stop the laughter that rolled out. ''You put panty hose in our dinner? Where'd you get the recipe, from an episode of 'The Addams Family'?''

She twisted out of his grip. ''Go ahead and make fun of me. I told you I'm not a very good cook, but at least I tried.''

He composed himself with difficulty. ''I can see that. I apologize for laughing. But if you don't explain what the panty hose were doing in that stew, I'll go crazy trying to imagine what your reasoning was. Have some pity on me, Rose.''

''You have to promise not to laugh if I tell you.''

''I promise.''

''I used the panty hose to hold the spices.''

''The spices?'' His lips twitched. ''You must have used a bay leaf the size of a Buick.''

''Daniel! You promised!''

''Right.'' He pressed his lips together and looked up at the ceiling. ''I take it your panty hose had little stars on them.''

''I didn't think they'd come *off*.''

''Of course not.'' He looked at her, his eyes brimming with the effort not to laugh. He'd never seen anything so cute in his life. Here was one of New York's top models, a talented cartoonist, an astute businesswoman, a passionate lover...and clueless in the kitchen. Yet she'd attempted to cook him what appeared to have once been an Irish stew. She flattered him more than she knew.

She took off her oven mitts and tossed them on the counter. ''Well, I've certainly botched everything, haven't I?''

''Not at all.'' He closed the distance between them and drew her back into his arms. ''This is turning out to be one terrific night.''

She gazed up at him. ''Daniel, be serious.''

''I'm absolutely serious.''

''You can't be. I was covered in flour when you arrived. I mashed your bouquet, spilled wine on your boots, put spangles in your stew and then laminated it to the bottom of the pan.''

''All because you, a woman of many talents, a woman with a fair measure of fame and a considerable measure of beauty, tried to impress an average guy like me. You want to know how that makes me feel, Rose? That makes me feel pretty special.''

The frown slowly disappeared from her face. ''Yeah?''

''Yeah.''

Gradually the spark returned to her eyes and the corners of her mouth tipped up into an endearing smile. ''It's all pretty funny, when you think of it.''

''You won't hear that from me.''

She chuckled. ''It's okay. I'm beginning to see the humor in it.'' She gave him an impish look. ''Seems like dinner's ruined.''

''Yep.''

''And that *is* what I invited you up here for.''

He guided her hips until they brushed against his. ''Is it?''

Her eyes grew sultry again. ''Maybe not entirely.''

''Then let me be brutally honest. I don't give a damn about eating dinner. It wasn't your home-cooked dinner I was looking forward to when I walked in your front door.''

She wound her arms around his neck and leaned into him. ''Is that right?''

''That's right.'' His voice had a raw edge, brought on by the press of her body against his. Nobody could lean quite so sensuously as Rose, he decided.

"Well, I certainly want to be a good hostess." Her seductive glance fired his blood.

Maybe she'd practiced that look a million times for the camera, but that didn't mute its effect on him. With a groan he took possession of her saucy mouth.

She kissed him back, even as she began maneuvering them out of the kitchen. Kissing and caressing each other as they went, they made their way through the living room. She kicked off her shoes; he stripped off his belt. By the time they reached her bedroom door, he had both hands on the hem of her shirt, ready to pull it over her head.

The intercom buzzed.

"Ignore it," she said breathlessly as she raised her arms over her head.

"Thank God for a secure building." He pulled off her shirt and tossed it aside as the buzzer sounded again.

Then the phone rang.

"The machine will get it," she said, pulling him into the bedroom.

"Thank God for machines. Ah, Rose," he murmured. "You're like a piece of fine sculpture."

"Sculpture for you to mold," she said, gliding into his arms as the answering machine beeped and prepared to accept a message.

"Miss Kingsford, I think you'd better get down here," said a male voice.

Daniel paused and looked at Rose, who had gone completely still.

"Your mother is wrestling in the lobby with a woman called Maureen," Jimmy said distinctly.

"OH, MY GOD." Rose looked around frantically for her shirt. She scooped it off the floor and pulled it over her head as she started for the apartment door.

"Rose?" Daniel seemed a little dazed.

"Put your belt on and come with me," she said, tucking her shirt into her jeans. "And button your shirt."

"You don't have any shoes on."

"Oh." She glanced down at her feet, then ran to find her shoes. After shoving her feet into them, she grabbed her keys from the table by the door and took hold of the doorknob. "Coming?" she said, looking back at Daniel.

He finished buckling his belt and started forward. "Why do I have the feeling you know what this is all about?"

"I'll tell you in the elevator. There's no time to waste. My mother works out in a gym, and she could do your mother serious damage."

"My mother?" He hurried after her. "What makes you think the Maureen wrestling with your mother downstairs is my Maureen?"

She slammed her hand against the elevator button. "Move, you geriatric machine!" Then she turned to him. "I was hoping none of this would have anything to do with us, but it seems your mother and mine knew each other back in Ireland."

He stared at her for a long moment. "You're not

going to tell me that your mother is Bridget Mary Hogan. I refuse to believe that.''

''Maybe the battling colleens in the lobby will convince you. Where is that blasted elevator? We should have taken the stairs. We—''

''Bridget Mary Hogan, the two-faced piece of baggage who cheated Maureen Fiona Keegan out of the Rose of Tralee crown?''

Rose glared at him. ''Watch your language or I'll be forced to mention that Maureen Fiona Keegan was the gossip-mongering, sheep-faced ne'er-do-well who cheated Bridget Mary Hogan out of the Rose of Tralee crown.'' The elevator arrived and she stepped inside, but when she turned around Daniel was still rooted to the spot.

''No. This isn't happening,'' he said in a disbelieving tone. ''Any minute I'm going to wake up.''

''You'd better wake up now and get in this blasted elevator,'' she said. ''I'll need your muscles downstairs.''

He followed her into the elevator. ''But Bridget Hogan is dead! My mother said she threw herself off the Cliffs of Moher in agony over what she'd done.''

''Yeah, well, your mother was supposed to have jumped in front of a speeding train, according to my mother.''

''Good God.'' He gazed at her as if he still couldn't comprehend the truth.

''Please button your shirt, Daniel. My mother likes to kid herself that I'm still a virgin.''

He complied, but his movements were the jerky motions of a robot. "What else don't I know?"

That I want you to father my child, Rose thought. Now wasn't a very propitious moment to bring that up, however. "My mother was hiding behind the planter in the tearoom when you and I first met. She was the one who insisted I go to the rendezvous with your mother. She wanted to discover how Maureen turned out."

Daniel groaned. "Did my mother know whose daughter you were?"

"No." Rose took a deep breath as the elevator clunked to a stop. "But I suspect she does now."

The elevator doors slid back like the curtains on a stage play. A violent stage play, Rose amended to herself. Maureen and Bridget rolled on the floor, screeching unintelligible things to each other. The match seemed to be more equal than Rose had expected. Her mother had agility, but Maureen had heft on her side, although she was hampered by the dress she wore, while Bridget's pantsuit allowed more freedom of movement.

Jimmy circled them like a referee. Every once in a while he'd dart in and make a tentative effort to stop the fighting, but he was obviously intimidated by the thought of accidentally grabbing some part of middle-aged female anatomy he was too well brought up to touch. One wing chair had been upset and the artificial-flower display was smashed into a million pieces on the floor.

Rose heard Daniel's horrified gasp, but he apparently had command of himself almost immediately.

"I'll get them apart," he said. "Then we'll each take our own. Get the kid to help you if you can't hold your mother yourself."

"Got it." Rose watched in admiration as Daniel waded into the fray. She winced as Bridget's foot connected with his stomach. If the kick had been a little lower, he might have been rendered out of action.

"Okay, ladies," he said in a voice that rang with authority. "Let's break it up now, shall we?"

"It's my Daniel!" screeched Maureen. "Daniel, get this madwoman off me!"

"I think technically you're on top of her." He pulled both women to their feet and wedged his body between them. "Rose? Jimmy? Can I get a hand, here?"

Rose bolted forward and clutched her mother's arm. "Come over here, Mom." She tugged, but Bridget planted both feet. She was stronger than Rose had expected.

"Maureen Fiona, you're no better than a pimp!" she shouted across Daniel.

"Hah!" Maureen shouted back. "I'd rather see my Daniel marry a duck in Central Park than any daughter of yours, Bridget Mary!"

"Okay, ladies, let's each go to our respective corners," Daniel said, putting both arms around his mother and maneuvering her a few feet away.

Rose felt her mother wriggling out of her grasp. "Jimmy, could you help me?"

Jimmy approached nervously. "Excuse me, Mrs. Kingsford," he said apologetically as he put a hammerlock on her neck.

"Very good, Jimmy," Rose said.

"He's choking the life out of me!" Bridget yelped.

"What a lovely idea," Rose muttered in her mother's ear. "What in hell are you doing here?"

"Don't you dare accuse me of wrongdoing, young lady! There's razor burn on your cheek!"

Rose struggled not to feel like a teenager caught coming home late from a torrid date with her steady. She lowered her voice. "I'm thirty years old, for heaven's sake!"

"Old enough to know better than to fool around with the likes of Maureen Keegan's son!"

"I heard that!" shouted Maureen from across the room. "Nobody insults my Daniel. I'll—"

"Not now, Mom," Daniel said. "Rose, I think we need a couple of cabs."

"I'll call," Rose offered. She marveled at his even tone of voice. She glanced across the room where he held his disheveled mother in a bear hug. When he was alone with his mother he'd probably chew her up one side and down the other, as Rose planned to do with her own mother. At the moment, however, he was reacting like a perfectly trained cop. Rose admired his self-possession.

Rose glanced at Jimmy. "Got her?"

"I've got her," Jimmy said, looking very determined. ''Miss Kingsford, I don't know what the owners are going to say about this mess.''

''Don't worry, Jimmy. I'll testify that it wasn't your fault that things got out of hand.'' She walked to the phone and dialed the number for the cab company she used. ''My mother will pay for the damage.''

''Me?'' Bridget shrieked. ''What about herself over there? None of this would have happened if she hadn't spread those terrible lies about me to the contest judges!''

Rose covered the ear that wasn't against the phone and ordered two cabs.

''You *deliberately* burned my face, you did!'' Maureen tried to struggle out of Daniel's grip. ''Daniel, are you going to let her speak to your mother like that?''

''Actually, I'm tempted to let you go and then call for the SWAT team,'' Daniel said.

Rose caught the barely leashed anger in his words. ''Cabs are on the way,'' she said.

''Good. I think we'll wait outside.''

''But 'tis raining cats and dogs out there,'' his mother protested.

''Sounds perfect. I'd also contemplated turning a fire hose on both of you.''

''Daniel, your jacket,'' Rose said, realizing it was still up in her apartment.

''I'll get it later.'' With one brief glance at Rose, Daniel escorted his mother out the revolving door.

Rose took some comfort from his last remark, but

not much. Retrieving his jacket at some future date wasn't exactly the same as continuing a relationship. She couldn't imagine he'd want that now. After all, the idea had been for them to enjoy an uncomplicated, sexy time together. This was turning out to be unbelievably complicated.

"She's gone. You can turn me loose, Jimmy," Bridget said.

"Don't you do it, Jimmy." Rose faced the source of all her troubles with renewed anger. "What were you doing here, spying on me?"

Even with a rip in the sleeve of her London Fog raincoat, a big black smudge on the knee of her designer slacks, and wildly tangled hair—and despite the fact that Jimmy held her in an uncompromising hammerlock—Bridget managed to look haughty. "I was merely checking to see if you were home. I'd just managed to get some tickets to a concert at the Kennedy Center, the tribute to that jazz musician you like, and I wanted to tell you right away. I was in the neighborhood, so naturally—"

"Bull."

"Rose, your language is shocking."

"I'm using restraint, Mom. Believe me, I could come up with several expressions that are a lot more crude, and they all apply."

"Looks like the cabs are outside, Miss Kingsford," Jimmy said, his voice charged with relief.

"Tell me when one has left with Daniel and his mother in it."

"He's shoving her—uh, I mean *helping* her into one now. There it goes."

"Okay. Mom, if Jimmy lets you go, do you promise to walk with me out to the cab?"

"There's no need to take that tone with me, Rose Erin Kingsford. Your grandmother would turn over in her—"

"No doubt Granny's spinning like a top in her grave," Rose said. "And I'm not taking any of the credit for it, either. You're the one who was brawling in the lobby of the apartment building. Now do you promise to get in the cab with me?"

"I promise."

Rose nodded to Jimmy and he relaxed his hammerlock and stepped back.

Bridget brushed at her clothes and patted her tangled hair. It looked as if Maureen had wound her fingers through it several times. "You don't need to ride in the cab, Rose," Bridget said as she started toward the door. "I'll go straight home."

"I think I'll just tag along, anyway." Rose fell into step beside her. "We have a few things to straighten out."

"You don't have a coat."

"As hot under the collar as I am at the moment, I don't need one, Mom. Let's just go."

"Take mine." Bridget started to pull off her London Fog.

"No, thanks." Rose helped her mother back on with the coat as she guided her toward the door. "I'm furious with you, but I wouldn't forgive myself if you caught a chill.''

''What you're going to give me is a heart attack.''

''Nonsense.'' The cold, wet air felt great as they walked outside and Rose took a deep breath. ''Your heart is fine. Anybody who can wrestle Maureen Keegan to the ground is in pretty good shape, if you ask me.''

Her mother stooped to climb into the back seat of the cab. Then she glanced over her shoulder. ''I would have had her begging for mercy in another five minutes.''

Rose rolled her eyes. ''I've decided you must be related to Hulk Hogan. I'm signing you up for the World Wrestling Federation Championships tomorrow.'' As she climbed in the cab she heard the strangest snorting sounds coming from her mother. Finally she figured out what it was. Her mother was trying to control an uncontrollable belly laugh. Rose leaned her head against the cracked upholstery and sighed. ''Go ahead, Mom. Let it out.''

Bridget laughed until the tears streamed down her face. ''You should have seen her expression when I told her who I was,'' she gasped. ''You'd have thought somebody had whacked her between the eyes with a sledgehammer. Jesus, Mary and Joseph, but it was a great moment. I'd have given anything for a camera.''

''Actually, I imagine we have footage of the whole episode,'' Rose said, smiling in spite of herself.

"There's that little closed-circuit camera mounted above Jimmy's desk."

Still laughing, Bridget clutched Rose's arm. "You simply *must* get me that tape. It will carry me happily into my old age. I just wish I'd had another five minutes to pin her to the floor."

Rose turned her head to look at her mother. "You're really sorry we interrupted you?"

"I've been waiting to get into a donnybrook with that woman my whole life. When we were girls we thought we were much too dignified for physical violence."

"Thank God you don't have your dignity to protect anymore."

"Rose, are you being sarcastic?"

"Who, me?"

"Well, at least we interrupted you two," Bridget said, "which was probably more important than finishing the fight good and proper. I don't suppose you'll be getting involved with Maureen Keegan O'Malley's son. She'll threaten him with everything, including excommunication, if he continues to see you."

Rose sighed. "I doubt if she'll need to threaten him at all, Mom. After this display tonight, he'll probably want to stay as far away from me as possible."

Bridget patted her hand. "That's for the best, Rose. Especially if you had in mind what I think you did." She shivered. "Talk about a fate worse than death. If I thought Maureen Keegan and I would be grandmothers to the same child, I'd have to throw myself off the Empire State Building.''

"Have you forgotten you have a fear of heights?"

Bridget gave her a long look. "I'd overcome it."

6

IT WAS A LONG cab ride to Brooklyn, but Daniel figured he'd let his mother pay for every mile. Still, furious as he was, he hoped she hadn't done herself any physical damage wrestling with Rose's mother. Wrestling in a public lobby. Sweet Jesus. And he'd thought she couldn't embarrass him any more than she had in the tearoom. At this rate he'd have to reduce his hours on the force just so he could keep an eye on her.

"Are you all right?" he asked after several moments of tense silence.

"She scared the life out of me, she did!" His mother fiddled with a button on her wool coat. "Tore the armhole seam of my coat, too."

"I don't give a damn about the coat. I just want to know if you pulled a muscle or broke anything."

His mother made a sound of disgust. "'Twould be a fine day when Bridget Hogan could overtake me in a fight. Did you see that I had the best of her, Daniel? She would have been begging for mercy in another two minutes."

From the vehemence and spirit of his mother's reply, Daniel decided only her dignity was damaged.

And he obviously cared about that more than she did. "Bridget has a pretty good kick for somebody who's been dead for thirty-seven years," he said.

"'Tis just like you to bring that little matter up to me at a time like this. 'Twas nothing but an innocent pretense."

"Innocent? Lying to Dad and me in great detail about how she flung herself off the cliffs because she couldn't live with the way she'd treated you in that beauty contest? What's so innocent about that?"

"Well, she should have done it."

Daniel turned sideways on the seat so he could confront her more directly. "Don't tell me you still hold a grudge."

His mother glared at him defiantly. In the dim light of the cab he could almost believe she'd transformed herself into a rebellious teenager. "She never said she was sorry, did she, now?"

Daniel closed his eyes. "Unbelievable."

"And it's not enough that she ruined the years when I was a tender bud ready to blossom forth in all my glory. Now she's ruined my golden years, too!"

"And how did she do that?" Daniel was having trouble following the tortured reasoning of this woman he thought he knew.

His mother shook her head. "At times I wonder if the sisters mixed up your test scores with some other lad's. You're not quick on the uptake sometimes, Daniel."

"Then I guess you'll just have to lay it out for me."

"Well, 'tis perfectly plain. Just how are you and Rose supposed to get married, now that Rose has turned out to be the daughter of that back-stabbing conniver? Answer me that!"

He stared at her. Then finally he began to laugh. He laughed so hard he almost choked.

His mother looked alarmed. "Are you having a fit, Daniel?"

"No." He took a long, steadying breath. "Just enjoying the irony of the situation. Maybe this will put an end to this wife-hunting you've been so hell-bent on. I couldn't have planned this better if I'd tried."

"'Tis fine for you to laugh, but you're not thinking of your poor mother at all. No grandchildren to gather around me in my declining years, no young woman I can teach the ways of an Irish housewife—the knitting, the cooking, the gardening."

"Since when did you have a garden?"

"Never mind. I know how to garden. You don't forget those things, once you learn them. But it doesn't matter, you see, because there'll be no garden, no family pictures, no sweet little birthday parties, no Christmas carols around the tree, no—"

"I think you're getting a little carried away, Mom." He paused. "Not that it's anything new with you these days."

"You think you're so smart. Just wait until you're fifty-six, with no family to comfort you!"

Daniel decided to shift the subject a little. "So I

take it you don't want me to see Rose Kingsford after all?''

''Well, of course I don't!'' She clasped a hand to her chest and looked at him in horror. ''Bridget Hogan weaseling her way into *our* family, pinching the dear little cheek of *my* grandchild? I can just see the shameless hussy, spoiling the dear thing with too many toys, too many sweets. She'd probably make up some sickening pet name for the babe, like Nana's wee elf, and I'd have to listen to her calling my little darling that awful name. She'd—''

''I take it that's a no?''

''I'd sooner be struck down by a bolt of lightning than have you marry Rose Kingsford!''

''Well, you can put your mind at rest, because I'm not going to marry Rose.'' He leaned back against the seat and folded his arms over his chest.

''Thank heavens you've come to your senses.''

''We'll just fool around.''

His mother gasped and clutched her chest again. ''Oh, no, you wouldn't be doin' *that* now, would you?''

Daniel faced her again, his expression grim. ''If it hadn't been for your interference, I wouldn't have met Rose. But I have met her, and if I decide to continue seeing her, I most definitely will. In fact, if I decided to marry her, I'd do that, too. But it's your good luck that I'm not looking for a wife, and Rose, coincidentally, is not looking for a husband.''

''Oh, Daniel, please don't say that you two will—''

''Don't worry. I won't say it. That's not the sort

of topic I want to discuss with you. I want this to be the very last time we talk about who I date and who I do or don't marry. This has gone on long enough.''

''I just can't bear to think of it.''

''Then don't think of it.'' Daniel leaned back and closed his eyes. ''Butt out of my business, Mom.''

ROSE WAS EXTREMELY grateful to be working with her buddy Chuck the following day. The modeling assignment involved shots of a honeymooning couple, alias Rose and Chuck, enjoying the wonders of a Gold Card. Tall, blond and muscled in all the right places, Chuck looked iike every woman's dream of the perfect guy to have on a honeymoon. And he'd just moved in with Pete, his lover of several months.

Rose cherished that she wouldn't be pawed during the shooting, and that she'd have an intelligent companion during breaks. Besides, she needed advice, and Chuck was well versed in the ways of the heart. It took all of the first break just to fill him in on the bizarre situation with her mother and Daniel's mother, so they didn't get down to the advice session until lunch.

Over a catered meal of deli sandwiches and mineral water consumed in a corner of the photography studio's deserted conference room, Rose asked Chuck what she should do next.

''Meaning you want to see him again?'' Chuck asked. ''In spite of the fact it will throw these two middle-aged ladies into fits, and they in turn could make your life miserable beyond words?''

"Yes."

"And that would be because…?"

"Well, I still have his jacket."

"You could courier that to him. Next reason."

"He's very sweet, and sexy, and he has more than two brain cells to rub together."

"That's a rare combination. Are you sure he's straight?"

"Chuck, believe it or not, there are a few heterosexual men out there who aren't jerks."

Chuck smiled. "Yeah, and a few gay guys who are. I'm happy for you, Rose."

"You can't be happy for me yet. He may have sworn off Rose Kingsford for life after last night. He wanted an uncomplicated relationship, and this is turning out to be anything but."

"And what do you want, Rose?"

"The same thing." She couldn't admit, not even to Chuck, that she harbored a dream of finding someone to father her child. Her mother had been the only one she'd told, and that had brought on a storm of judgment.

Chuck swallowed a bite of sandwich. "There's no such thing as an uncomplicated relationship unless you're talking about a dog."

"Okay, I'll admit that." Rose took a drink from the bottle of mineral water. "But neither of us wants a commitment. No rings, no march down the aisle. We got that settled right away."

"So it's just about sex, then?"

"You are so hard on me! Of course not! It's about companionship, and mutual interests, and—"

"Such as?"

"Well, we—" She gave him a sheepish look. "So far it's about sex."

Chuck nodded. "Just so you're not confused about that."

"Actually, let me amend my statement a little bit. It's about mutual respect, too. We've already weathered a few awkward situations, and he's good under fire."

"I sure as hell hope so. I like that in a member of the NYPD."

"I know, but more than that. He saw me at my worst and didn't get upset at all. I sense that he's a kind person."

"That's good. So are you."

"I don't think he'd blame me for what happened between our mothers, but I don't know if he wants the hassle of risking it again."

Chuck wadded up his deli sack and tossed a perfect basket into the nearby trash can. "Want Uncle Chuck to suggest something?"

"Please."

"Invite him up to your little place in the country for a few days. And don't tell the mothers."

Rose swirled the remaining mineral water and stared at the miniature whirlpool she'd created. "I don't know. He made a point of the difference in our income, and how he didn't want to be included in plans that were out of his financial league."

"Well, I don't see that a visit to your little house would fall into that category, but if you think he'll balk, tell him a friend offered the place. His stance will probably soften some if you two have a great time together. Pete gave me the same garbage at first, and I thought we'd have to live in a rat-infested walk-up because that was all he could afford in the city. We've finally worked it out."

"I guess that attitude's better than linking up with a gold digger, huh?"

"You know it. We'd better get back, kiddo."

"Yeah. Thanks, Chuck."

He stood. "Ready for the honeymoon?"

She blinked. "I said neither of us is interested in marriage."

Chuck gazed at her, a glint in his blue eyes. "I meant yours and mine, courtesy of a Gold Card. But it's rather interesting that you misunderstood."

"Don't you dare make something Freudian out of it. I do not have some subliminal desire to settle down with a man and be his devoted helpmate."

"If you say so."

ON WEDNESDAY, Daniel took an early shift, switching with a buddy. During the day, whenever there was a lag in the action, Daniel thought of Rose. When he got home that afternoon he reached for the phone a hundred times. Each time he pulled his hand back before committing to the call. No matter what he'd said to his mother, he wasn't sure he wanted to pursue a relationship with such a problematic woman. Their two mothers were only part of his reluctance.

The sizzle of chemistry between them had blocked out his surroundings for the most part the previous night, but enough had registered to make him decide that this woman had money. A *lot* of money, compared to him. He realized now that he'd dated only women who were approximately his economic equals. He'd never thought it would bother him to go out with someone financially better off than he was, but…it did. He wasn't proud to find out he was so hidebound, but there it was. He sensed a bedrock of prejudice that might take a nuclear blast to dislodge.

He'd finally decided to head out for a movie, when the phone rang. He stepped back into the apartment and answered it to discover Rose on the other end. She might have thought she'd get the answering machine, he realized when she seemed startled to hear his voice. She was probably calling about his jacket.

"I can hang up and let the machine get the message if you'd rather make this less personal," he said.

"Don't tempt me," she said. "You wouldn't believe how difficult it was for me to pick up the phone in the first place."

"I might."

"Listen, you can just send the jacket—"

"Oh, the jacket. I forgot. Do you need it?"

He was glad to know that wasn't why she'd called. "No rush."

"Because I can courier it over."

"It's not important, Rose. So if you didn't call about the jacket, why did you call?"

She took a deep breath. "Daniel, we've run into a bad patch right at the start."

"Yep."

"I probably should have told you all about our mothers from the beginning."

"Probably."

"Come on, Daniel, work with me, here. Don't leave me out on this limb all by myself."

He blew out a breath. "Okay. I've thought about calling you about a million times since last night."

"But you didn't."

"I had a lot to think about."

"I realize that. Discovering that I was the daughter of your mother's dearest enemy must have come as a shock."

He couldn't help laughing. "Dearest enemy is right. She's positively devoted to this thirty-seven-year-old grudge."

"So's my mother. And she's determined I won't have anything more to do with you."

He hesitated. "That's not why you're calling, is it? To show her who's boss?"

"No. I hope I've gotten past that kind of adolescent behavior."

"Which is more than they have."

"True," Rose said. "They're acting like a couple of naughty children, which is why I don't want to be ruled by their lunacy. I'd...I'd like to see you again," she finished in a rush.

He knew she needed an answer, but he wasn't sure which one he wanted to give her.

"Your silence is eloquent," she said. "I don't blame you for wanting to end the relationship. Goodbye, Daniel."

"Wait!"

"Yes?"

His heart pounded, as if he'd had to physically chase her down. "I'd like to see you again, too."

"You would?"

Her question lacked the bubbling confidence he'd become so fond of, and it was his fault. "Yes, I would. Forgive me for making you doubt it, or yourself. It's my problem, not yours."

"Your mother?"

"No, not my mother. It's—" He swallowed and forced himself to admit it. "It's your success. But it just occurred to me that only a fool would turn his back on someone like you because of stupid macho pride."

"You didn't seem too concerned about my success last night," she said gently.

"Exactly. I don't think our income levels will have much to do with anything when we make love."

She greeted that statement with a quick intake of breath. "And will we make love, Daniel?"

"If I haven't completely turned you off with my idiot attitudes, we will."

"You, um, haven't turned me off." She sounded a little breathless.

Just like that, he was becoming aroused. "Are you free tonight?"

"No. I promised my mother we'd go to a ballet. I could—"

"Don't chance it. I've told my mother to stay out of my business, but I'm not sure I trust her to do it."

"I've given my mother the same orders, but she's acting like a crazy woman over this. Which is why I thought perhaps, if we could go away somewhere...."

Daniel felt his defenses go up immediately. Was she planning on jetting them both to a lovers' hide-away? Despite his resolve not to let her money bother him, he couldn't be treated like some gigolo and retain his sense of himself. "Where?" he asked with deceptive calmness.

"A...person I know has a little cottage upstate. We're welcome to use it. If you'll tell me when you're off duty, I'll try to arrange my schedule around that. We can drive there in a couple of hours."

"It just so happens I have Friday through Sunday off, one of those rare weekends." He suspected there was more to this cottage business than she was telling him, but the way she'd phrased everything, he could deal with it. And there was no denying he was eager to spend time alone with her.

"That's perfect! I don't have any assignments this weekend, either. I have a tentative thing on Friday, but I can probably reschedule it for Monday."

He realized they were talking about leaving in less than two days. His blood began to heat at the prospect of all that delicious time alone with Rose. If, in fact, they could be alone. "Does your mother know where this cottage is?"

"I know what you're thinking, but we don't have to worry about her bursting in on us. She's been there, but I doubt she could find it by herself. Besides, she doesn't drive. We'd be safe."

"She could hire a car."

"I suppose, but she'd never be able to direct them to the place, which would embarrass her, so I can't believe she'd try it. It's very rural and there's no address. The owner picks up her mail at the post office in town. Not many people in town know she has the place."

He was pretty sure the owner was Rose Kingsford, but he decided not to press her. She was trying to find a way for them to be alone together, and her solution was better than any he could come up with. His apartment wouldn't work because his mother had a key. He should probably change that, although he didn't look forward to her tearful reaction, and then she wouldn't have a haven when she came into the city to go shopping.

"Well?" Rose asked.

He'd kept her waiting—again. "Sorry. I was thinking."

"Look, if you have doubts, I'll just hang up and that will be the end of it. I said I wouldn't blame you, and I won't."

"I'd like to go up to the cottage with you, Rose. I'd like that very much."

She gave a relieved little sigh. "Good."

"And I'll drive."

"You have a car? I mean, not that you couldn't afford one," she amended quickly. "It's just that lots of people in the city—"

"I have a car." He didn't even want to know what kind she had. "And why don't I bring some food along, too?"

"Food?"

He smiled to himself. "Just in case we find the time to eat."

"Oh!"

He could almost see her cheeks turning the color of her name, and his smile broadened. "Then again, maybe we could just pop a few vitamin pills and save time. I'm not picky."

"Well, of course we'll eat," she said, sounding out of breath. "But there's stuff up there, I'm sure."

The comment about the food clinched it for him. It was her house, no doubt about it. She'd called it a cottage but it could be a country mansion for all he knew. He kept up the pretense because it allowed him to contribute more to the weekend. "You wouldn't want to eat your friend's food supply, would you?"

"I guess that wouldn't be a good idea. Sure, bring whatever you like. That'll be fine."

He couldn't resist. "And whatever I know how to cook?"

"Hey."

He chuckled. "Sorry. The devil made me say it. I'll make sure whatever I bring is a no-brainer." He paused. "I see no reason to spend lots of time in the kitchen."

Another quick intake of breath told him she'd begun to envision where they would spend most of their time. He was envisioning it, too, and his whole body was beginning to hum in anticipation of holding her again. "I'll pick you up about nine, so we'll miss the rush-hour traffic."

"Sounds great. By the way, I'll probably make up some story to tell my mother about where I'll be this weekend, but I travel a lot, so it shouldn't be too difficult. How about you?"

"I've told my mother to stay out of my business."

She hesitated. "I see."

"You don't sound convinced that she will."

"I can only judge by my mother, who doesn't exactly take orders well. But maybe your mother is different. Maybe that authoritarian cop voice had an impact."

He laughed. "What authoritarian cop voice?"

"The one you used when you waded into the wrestling match. If somebody spoke to me in that tone of voice, I'd probably pay attention."

"Remind me to try it sometime."

"I said probably. I'm also my mother's daughter."

"Which is why we're sneaking around like this. Okay, in the interests of securing an uninterrupted weekend I'll tell my mother I'm attending an intensive three-day course on riot control. We have St. Patrick's Day coming up, so that's a logical story."

"This feels so illicit."

"I hope to hell that's not what's motivating you, because if it is, then maybe we shouldn't—"

"Hey, Daniel, remember how we reacted to each other last night?"

"Yeah." He took a shaky breath. "I do."

"That's what's motivating me. See you Friday morning. I'll bring your jacket."

"As if I'll be needing it."

7

On an impulse, Rose brought along some tapes of Irish folk songs for the drive to her cottage. She'd bought copies for herself and her mother during her recent trip to Ireland, and they'd become her favorite music. To her surprise, Daniel enjoyed them as much as she did, and even knew the words to a few of the more familiar ones.

"You have a great voice!" she announced after the first song they did together.

"But it's a baritone. I was supposed to be an Irish tenor. My grandfather was a tenor and my uncle was a tenor. When my voice changed and it became obvious I wouldn't be a tenor, my mother went into mourning."

Rose laughed. "Tradition is a blessing and a curse, isn't it?"

"Especially for the Irish."

"Oh, listen. It's 'The Titanic.' I used to sing that at camp when I was a kid."

Daniel grinned at her. "Didn't everybody?"

They belted out the song about the great ship going down, and followed it with a schmaltzy rendition of "Danny Boy," while a light snow fell all around them. Traffic was about as heavy as usual on 87 for a Friday, but Daniel drove his Toyota Supra with practiced ease. Rose couldn't remember the last time she'd felt so safe and secure.

They sang ''When Irish Eyes Are Smiling,'' and laughed when they stumbled over the words.

''My mother would kill me for not knowing that one better,'' Daniel said when the song ended. ''It's one of her favorites.''

''One of my mother's, too.''

''That figures.'' Daniel pulled around a slow-moving truck. ''It's too bad they can't give up this stupid grudge and be friends. They have so many things in common.''

''That's true.'' Rose contemplated what would happen if her mother and Maureen O'Malley became friends. Considering that Daniel was Rose's prime candidate for fathering a child, a chummy relationship between Maureen and Bridget wouldn't be such a great idea. In some ways the feud contributed to the overall plan. Yet she pictured vividly how a friendship with Maureen could enrich Bridget's life. An unselfish daughter would foster that friendship, not discourage it for her own reasons. Life became more complicated every minute, thought Rose as she listened to the opening chords of ''My Wild Irish Rose'' on the tape player.

She'd opened her mouth to sing along—she certainly knew that one after having her mother sing it to her all the time—but instinct told her to remain silent.

Daniel glanced at her with a half smile and launched into the song in his rich baritone.

No man had ever sung to her before, let alone a song that spoke of such tender love. She tried to tell herself that the words meant nothing, that Daniel was simply singing lyrics he knew well because of his Irish upbringing. Her heart was unconvinced by logic. And when he reached over and interlaced his fingers with hers, her heart believed every word.

By the time he'd finished the song, Rose had lapsed into a dreamy state that hadn't captured her in a very long time. Snuggled back against the bucket seat, she gazed at Daniel with pleasure. She would have this beautiful man all to herself for the next two days.

"What was that exit again?" he asked.

Rose jerked out of her trance and looked at a highway sign right at the moment they zoomed beyond the turnoff to her little hideaway. "We, uh, just passed it. I'm sorry, Daniel. There's another exit in three miles."

He grinned. "Hey, don't apologize. When a woman misses the highway exit because she's staring adoringly at me, how can I be upset?"

She bolted to an upright position. "I was not staring adoringly!"

"Were too. Admit it—that song made you all dewy-eyed."

"So the song has some meaning for me. Just because you happened to be the one singing it doesn't mean that I—"

"You don't have to get so defensive." He winked at her. "I enjoyed the admiration."

"Is this my reward for complimenting you on your singing voice? Are you now going to become insufferably vain and think that all you have to do is warble a few notes and I'll become hypnotized and do whatever you want?"

"I call 'em like I see 'em. You looked totally captivated to me."

She rolled her eyes. "With an ego that huge, I'm surprised you had room in this car for me and the luggage."

Daniel just smiled at her, and when "Peg O' My Heart" started playing, he sang while giving her soulful looks.

"You're impossible!" But she couldn't help laughing as he continued to clown around for her benefit.

They turned off at the next exit. As Daniel flicked on the car's turn signal in preparation for driving beneath the underpass and back onto the highway, Rose spotted a hand-lettered sign nailed to a fencepost about a hundred feet to the right. The Gentle Giants—Irish Wolfhound Puppies For Sale, announced the sign, and an arrow pointed down a country road.

"Wait." Rose put a hand on Daniel's arm. "See that sign?"

He hunched down and peered out the windshield. "Puppies?"

"I think we should go look at them."

"At puppies?"

A driver behind them honked his car's horn in obvious impatience.

"It won't take long. I promise."

Daniel shrugged and flipped on the right-turn signal. "I don't care about that. I just wonder why you want to go see puppies." He headed the car down the country road.

"I've wanted an Irish wolfhound for years. And here's somebody right in my area who raises them."

"In your area, you say?"

She could tell from the penetrating look in those brown eyes of his that he'd guessed the truth. She sighed. "Okay, the cottage belongs to me. But it's not all paid for," she added quickly. She didn't tell him that the renovations were the part still being paid off. She'd paid cash for the original building and land.

"How big is it?" he asked as they followed another sign that pointed down a narrow lane bordered by a white fence.

"Small. Very small." That much was true—three tiny bedrooms, a small kitchen only big enough for a table for two, one bathroom and a cozy living-dining room combination. But the custom thatched roof and leaded-glass windows had cost her a fortune.

"I guess a small house in the country isn't quite the same as a villa in the south of France." He pulled up in front of a two-story farmhouse with a deep red hay barn to the rear of the property. "This must be where your puppy lives."

"I'm not getting one right now," she said. "I just want to make the contact and find out when they'll have another litter ready to sell."

Daniel grabbed his leather jacket and her trench coat from the back seat. "Then we're not going inside?" he asked, handing her the coat.

"Of course we're going inside. I want to see the puppies, even if I'm not getting one today."

He reached for the door handle. "I can tell you're not an experienced puppy shopper."

"What do you mean?"

He paused and gazed at her. "If you were, you'd get the information at the front door, then leave."

"That's crazy! Why wouldn't I want to see what sort of puppies they breed?"

"Because you'll leave with one."

"I certainly will not. This is a preliminary visit, for heaven's sake. Don't you credit me with any will-power?"

He leaned toward her. "Nobody has any willpower when it comes to puppies."

"Well, I do."

"We'll see." He gave her a quick kiss and climbed out of the car.

AN HOUR LATER they pulled back onto the highway, a pet carrier in the back seat and a sheepish grin on Rose's face.

Daniel didn't have the heart to rub it in. He'd damn near picked out a puppy himself, although the price tag would have stopped him from doing something that stupid. The breeder had taken them back to the hay barn where ten puppies played happily among the chickens. Although at thirty-five pounds the eight-week-old puppies were big enough to kill a hen, they showed no desire to do that. Daniel had never seen such gentle animals.

When Rose crouched down, all the puppies had headed for her, but a tan male had put his front paws on her knee and reached up to give her a kiss on the cheek. Daniel had watched with indulgence and a trace of jealousy as Rose fell in love.

The breeder had loaned them the pet carrier and given them a few cans of dog food. She'd cautioned them about letting the puppy sleep in their bed to-night.

"You won't be able to bear the pitiful crying," she'd said, "but you'll start that habit at your peril. This dog will gain a half pound a day and eventually weigh around two-fifty. He'll own that bed."

Daniel was grateful for the tip. No matter how cute the puppy, Daniel didn't want him in bed with them tonight. He had other plans.

As if on cue, the little guy began to whimper as the car picked up speed.

Rose twisted in her seat so she could peer through the wire grate of the carrier. "It's okay, St. Paddy. You're going to be fine," she crooned. "Just fine."

St. Paddy stopped whimpering at the sound of her voice, but the minute she stopped talking to him he started up again.

"Easy, my little love," she murmured. "We'll be home before you know it."

Daniel was enchanted by her tone of voice as she comforted the puppy. Enchanted and somewhat worried. He wondered how much attention he'd get this weekend, now that St. Paddy was in the picture. Yet, realizing what joy having the puppy gave Rose, he wouldn't have dreamed of protesting.

"It was fate that we missed the exit," Rose said.

"Then I guess it was my fantastic singing that provided you with this dog."

"All right. I'll confess," she began, "if you promise to be just as truthful to me."

"I'm always truthful."

"Okay, it *was* your singing that…distracted me."

"In a good way or a bad way?"

"A good way. There, there, little Paddy," she reassured the puppy as he began crying again.

"That's what I figured." Actually he hadn't been sure. He'd surprised himself, getting all sentimental with that song, but it fit Rose so perfectly that he'd gotten a little carried away. It was nice to know he'd carried her away, too.

"Now it's my turn," she said. "How many women named Rose have you worked that little number on?"

"None."

She murmured a few soothing words to the puppy before turning back to him. "None? An Irish stud like you?"

He grinned. "If you think you're going to goad me into admitting something, you're wrong. I've never met anybody else named Rose except Rose Conners, a sweet but very old lady who was the church organist when I was a kid in the choir."

"Ha. Rose Conners was probably twenty-five and you seduced her in the choir loft."

He took the exit they'd missed before. "Where are you getting this idea that I'm some sort of Don Juan?"

"You didn't kiss me after our first date. You kissed me *before* our first date. I suppose you'll tell me that doesn't happen all the time, either."

"Not often." He decided not to tell her he'd never kissed a woman so soon after meeting her. But the night he came upon Rose standing outside the restaurant she'd looked like some heavenly being temporarily touching down to dazzle earthbound men. The streetlight had transformed the rain falling all around her into a shower of diamonds, and he'd had to kiss her to convince himself that she was real.

"It happens often enough, I'll bet. That was a very

experienced kind of kiss,'' she said. ''Okay, turn right
at the stop sign and slow down as we go through the
town. They put speeders in the stocks around here.''

''What do you mean by *experienced?*''

She smiled. ''Worried about your technique, are
you?''

''No, I—oh, hell.'' Red and blue lights flashed in
the rearview mirror.

''I warned you.''

So she had, and he'd been thinking about kissing
her and hadn't paid attention. ''This is damned embarrassing.'' He pulled off to the side of the road and
extracted his wallet from his hip pocket.

''I think it's kind of funny, a cop running afoul of
the law.''

''This isn't running afoul of the law. I was just
keeping up with traffic.''

''What traffic? The road was practically deserted.''

''Which made it difficult to judge my speed.''

''Tell it to the judge,'' Rose said, grinning.

Daniel scowled at her before rolling down the window and glancing up at the patrolman approaching
the driver's side of the car.

The patrolman asked for Daniel's license and registration, which Daniel handed out the window to
him. After glancing at it, the officer started to laugh.
''Daniel Patrick O'Malley.''

Daniel gritted his teeth and gave the officer his
most intimidating cop stare. Then his eyes widened
as he recognized Tim Bettencourt from his graduating
class at the police academy. ''Tim?''

The patrolman took off his dark glasses and held

out his hand. "Hey, bro. It's been a few years. How're you doin'?"

"A lot better than I was two minutes ago. I'd forgotten you took a job up here after you left the NYPD." Daniel shook his former classmate's hand and introduced him to Rose.

"We've met," Rose said.

"Nice to see you again, Rose."

Daniel opened the car door. "Let's discuss this little matter out there," he said, grabbing his jacket. "I'll only be a minute," he said in an undertone to Rose as he rolled up the car window. "Old Tim's not gonna give me a ticket, but he might not want to say so in front of you."

WHEN DANIEL CLOSED the car door, St. Paddy began to whine and paw at the wire door to his carrier.

"Soon you'll be out of there, little guy," Rose said. "Right after Daniel gets his ticket fixed we'll be heading down the road toward home. Or what will be home by the time you're too big for my apartment." She'd made some rapid calculations after she'd realized she couldn't leave the hay barn without this particular puppy with the big brown eyes. Her lease was up in three months, so by the time St. Paddy became too huge for apartment living, she'd be moved permanently to the country. In the meantime, she'd ask her mother to dog-sit during the day once in a while.

St. Paddy kept pawing at the wire and whining.

Rose leaned down to peer through the window and couldn't see much sign of the party breaking up outside. St. Paddy sounded as if he'd lost his best friend, which, in fact, he had. All his friends were gone, replaced by two strangers.

"Okay, I'll let you out, but you'd better be good," she instructed as she slowly unlatched the door.

St. Paddy came wriggling out with surprising speed. She made a grab for him but he squirmed out of her arms and leaped neatly onto Daniel's seat. Then he squatted and a growing stain appeared on the seat cover.

"St. Paddy, no!" Rose pulled him back into her lap just as Daniel opened the car door and tossed his jacket in the back.

"Daniel! Don't—"

He sat. And lifted up again immediately. "What the…?"

She held tight to the struggling puppy. "I'm afraid that St. Paddy…"

Holding on to the steering wheel so he could elevate his behind away from the wet seat, Daniel gazed over at her. "Lady, your dog leaks."

"I'm really sorry." She bit her lip against the awful urge to laugh. "You were taking so long, and he wanted so much to get out of the carrier."

"I can see why. He had business to take care of."

"Do you have a towel or anything in the trunk?"

"I think so. You'd better get him back in the carrier before I open this door, though."

"You're right." Rose leaned over the back of the seat and tried to maneuver the puppy inside the carrier. It was like putting toothpaste back in the tube. "Sorry. He doesn't want to go in."

"Take your time. I'll just hang out here."

"Daniel, I don't know if I can do this. He's stronger than I thought."

"Try grabbing him by the scruff of the neck. Like his mother would do if she wanted to move him. Then maybe you can back him in."

"Easier said than done." But she managed it. "Coast is clear," she said, snapping the door shut.

Daniel got out of the car with some difficulty, but he returned quickly with a blanket which he folded several times before placing it on the seat.

"You don't have anything more ratty than that?" Rose asked.

"Nope." He eased onto the seat, closed the door and fastened his seat belt.

"That looks too good for the purpose."

"It is." He started the engine. "There are all kinds of sentimental memories attached to it."

"Oh, dear. I'll bet your mother gave it to you."

He grinned at her. "Nope. Picked this baby out myself when I was about seventeen. It was carefully selected for durability, washability, and a soft, fluffy nap."

"You went through all that trouble for a blanket for your bed?"

"No, a blanket for my car. And it's been transferred to each car I've owned. It's my make-out blanket."

She groaned. "I should have guessed. And here you were pretending that you're not hell on wheels with women."

"I'm not hell on wheels, Rose." He winked at her. "But I've been told I'm heaven on a blanket."

8

DANIEL'S COMMENT about being heaven on a blanket set off a predictable reaction in Rose. She couldn't remember ever having such an intense response to a man as she had to Daniel. She expected to enjoy their lovemaking very much. What she hadn't expected, or even counted on, was that he'd be great company during the times when they weren't involved in the physical side of the relationship.

She'd experienced that sort of comradeship with Chuck to some extent and had assumed you could have either friendship or sex with a man, but not both. Daniel was demonstrating that she was wrong.

"Cute little town," Daniel said as they moved along Main Street at a snail's pace.

"You should see it at Christmas, with the white clapboard houses trimmed in evergreen and red bows, and little white lights everywhere." She was glad the slow pace had calmed St. Paddy. Or maybe emptying his bladder had done the trick. For whatever reason, he wasn't whining anymore.

"I'll bet it's also nice in the summer, when everything's in bloom," Daniel said.

"It is. And the best thing about it is the weekly paper."

"Because it carries your strip?"

"That's right."

Daniel nodded. "Sounds as if the people here have good sense and a scenic location. Too bad they also run a speed trap."

"Luckily you're friends with the local gendarme."

"I guess you could say that. If we hadn't been friends, maybe he would have locked me up in addition to fining me."

"He wrote you a ticket?"

"Sure did. Apologized all over the place while he was doing it, too. Touching as hell. Just let old Timmy set foot in *my* town, though. I'll bust him for jaywalking."

Rose gazed at him. "I'd hoped once we got away from the city and our mothers that life would go a little smoother for us."

Daniel lapsed into a heavy brogue. "And so it has, lass. We're headed down the road to your wee cottage, and me mither's nowhere about creatin' a brouhaha, and neither is yours. Sure and 'tis a fine day, Rose Erin Kingsford."

She laughed, relieved to discover he wasn't really upset. Many men she'd known would have let a speeding ticket ruin their whole day. "How did you know my middle name?"

"Called a buddy in motor vehicles."

"Oh. Then you know about my—"

"Speeding tickets? My friend Timmy is an equal-opportunity ticketer, apparently. He told me you'd tried to show a little leg and get the fine reduced the first time around, but an upstanding officer such as himself can't be bought.''

"I did not! Your *friend* has some nerve, saying that.'' She was all geared up to defend her integrity when she noticed the wide smile on his face. "He didn't say that at all. You made it up.''

"Just so you know, you can try that sort of bribery with me anytime.'' He turned to her and waggled his eyebrows.

"So you can be had.''

"Absolutely.''

Warmth coursed through her. They were getting closer to her cottage, closer to being alone—truly, deliciously alone. Except for St. Paddy, of course.

"Time for you to navigate again,'' Daniel said. "We're almost through town.''

Rose kept forgetting that Daniel hadn't been here before. She felt so comfortable with him that it seemed strange he hadn't been part of her life for a long time. "Take a right at the next stop sign, go over the bridge and take a left, then a right down the first lane. It's not marked.''

"You weren't kidding about it being tucked away.''

"That's what I looked for.''

"You're planning to live here someday, aren't you?''

"Yes.''

Daniel was silent for a while. "How soon?''

"My apartment lease expires in three months."

He stretched his arms against the wheel of the car. "Is that the time frame for us? Three months?"

The question hit her like a blow to the chest. "I...no, of course not. I wasn't thinking in those terms."

"What terms were you thinking in?"

"Daniel, I thought we weren't going to question the status of our relationship. I thought we were going to keep things loose, go with the feelings of the moment."

"That made a lot more sense when I thought you'd be living on the same island with me."

"My moving up here doesn't have to change anything. Not really. I can still drive down to the city. You can come up here."

He turned down the lane that wound its way to her cottage. "I guess you're right." He glanced at the pet carrier. "I was wondering how you'd fit a full-grown Irish wolfhound in your apartment. You weren't planning to try."

Guilt assailed her. He'd already made her feel as if she'd been hiding things from him, and she hadn't even broached the fatherhood issue. Her plan had seemed fine when it was on the drawing board, but now that she was trying to implement it, it seemed hopeless. Yet she couldn't bear to give up the idea of having a child. The urge had something to do with a strong mothering instinct and a lot to do with continuity. She was the only child of an only child. If she didn't carry on the line, no one else would. She blamed her Irish heritage for making that important to her.

But she'd begun to question the wisdom of asking Daniel to provide her with a baby. She'd only known him a short time, but she already suspected it might upset him. He had an ability to care deeply about people, and he might well hate the idea of fatherhood without all the usual connections. The same would probably be true of any man she considered worthy of the task. That was the fatal flaw in her reasoning, which she hadn't recognized until now.

They rounded a bend in the road and her little house came into view.

Daniel braked the car and stared. "It's an Irish cottage. Or at least it's the way I picture them. I've never actually been to Ireland."

"It's as close to an Irish cottage as I could get. I had the lace for the curtains shipped over, as well as one of those little fireplaces they use for burning peat, although I use wood."

"But that's a thatched roof. Nobody around here knows how to do that, do they?"

"It took me a long time, but I finally found somebody who'd emigrated just a few years ago. This was the first one he'd done in this country, but now he's gone into the business. He hadn't thought anybody would want to try it, but he's finding out it's turning into quite the rage."

Daniel put his foot on the brake as the car rolled into the driveway beside the cottage. Then he shut off the motor and studied the cottage a moment. At last he hooked an arm across the steering wheel and turned toward her. "It's perfect for you, Rose. If I hadn't guessed before that the place belonged to you, I would have once I'd seen it. This is where the creator of St. Paddy and Flynn should live."

"Thank you."

"I appreciate your bringing me up here. I can already tell it's a special place for you."

"You sound as if this will be the one and only time. I'm sure that we'll have many—"

He looked doubtful, a sad smile on his face.

"What?"

"I can see that you have a whole game plan mapped out, which you should, because you're loaded with talent. You're already somewhat rich and famous from your modeling. This next career will likely take you even further down that road."

"You don't know that's how it will go, and what if it does? We could still—"

"I may fit in your life all right now, Rose. But sooner or later, we'll move in different circles. Even if you don't realize it, I do."

"You're wrong. Very wrong."

St. Paddy began to whimper.

"We'd better get him in," Daniel said, reaching for his jacket.

As Rose opened the car door, she wondered why she should feel so bereft. Daniel had just outlined the course she'd hoped her life would take. Her strip would become famous, make her a lot of money, and she'd live quietly in this little cottage with her child.

And without Daniel. The fame and fortune might not separate them, but her decision to have a baby out of wedlock would. What had seemed like the most idyllic existence she could imagine suddenly no longer held the same appeal.

Daniel took the pet carrier out of the car. "Come on, St. Paddy. You were born to live in this little thatched cottage."

Rose grabbed her coat and purse from the back seat and followed Daniel up the curved cobblestone walk. The flower beds lining the walk were covered in mulch, but in less than two months daffodils would trim the cobblestones in bands of yellow.

"I'll bet your mother loves this place," Daniel said as they approached the front door.

Rose dug her keys out of her purse. "She does. She helped me with everything—the landscaping, the antiques inside, the choice of colors. She said it was a bit like taking a trip back home." Rose stuck the key in the lock and turned.

"Has she ever been back to Ireland?"

"No. When she was married to my dad, he never seemed to have the time, and now that she's divorced, she doesn't want to go back and have to explain…everything." She paused before opening the door and glanced at him. "I suppose that sounds silly."

"Not to me. I grew up with that kind of conservative thinking, don't forget."

"I guess you did." She opened the door and motioned him inside. "Welcome to Rose of Tralee cottage." She followed him inside.

She'd wondered if he'd look out of place in the small cottage. To her surprise, he looked as if he belonged there, an Irish man who'd finally come home.

Perhaps it was because the antiques she'd chosen were rugged country pieces rather than delicate, spindly things. A hutch held pottery plates and bowls, and the trestle table in one corner was solid oak. The couch and rocking chair grouped in front of the stone hearth both looked plenty big enough to hold a man of Daniel's size. She'd chosen them with an active child and a big dog in mind. But the man standing in the middle of the room hadn't been part of the picture. Nevertheless, he fit it perfectly.

Daniel set down the pet carrier on the pine floor and surveyed the room.

"Do you like it?" she asked with some nervousness.

"I don't know a damn thing about decorating, but if I tried to imagine the perfect room, this would be it."

She couldn't keep the grin of satisfaction off her face. "I think so, too. When I'm in Manhattan and the pace is getting to me, I just close my eyes and picture myself here. It takes away all my stress."

St. Paddy pawed at the gate of his carrier.

"I guess we should let him out." Rose started over toward the carrier.

"I have a suggestion. Have you ever had a puppy before?"

"No. I wasn't allowed."

"Then I'm the voice of experience in this crowd. I've had two. And what I remember is that we confined them pretty much to the kitchen until they were paper trained. Otherwise…"

"I get the picture. But we can't close the door and keep him in there, away from us, all the time. That would be mean."

"If I remember right, we used a piece of board high enough that he couldn't get over it but low enough that we could step over it. We can make him a bed in the corner of the kitchen, and if you have a ticking alarm clock and a hot-water bottle, which sort of substitutes for the other puppies' warmth and heartbeat, we're in business."

"I've heard about those things before. Do they really work?"

He grinned. "Sometimes. Sometimes the dog drives you crazy, like the breeder said."

"I'm really glad you're here to help me with this puppy, Daniel. I might make a mess of things by myself."

"I'm glad I'm here, too." His gaze caught and held hers for a moment. Then he looked away. "Do you have any scrap wood around?"

"There should be some in back left over from the renovations. If you'll go look, I'll get the windup clock out of the bedroom. I don't have a hot-water bottle, but I have one of those microwavable gel packs."

"That'll work."

She walked toward the bedroom and Daniel headed for the back door, which meant they had to pass each other.

As they did, he reached out an arm and spun her around to face him. "One for the road," he murmured, pulling her close.

Daniel's kiss, she discovered, could make her forget everything else. The velvet persuasion of his lips reminded her of all they had yet to share, and desire sluiced through her.

He ended the kiss just as she was getting started. She looked up at him, her knees weak, her brain fuzzy.

"Don't lose your place," he said, releasing her gently. "Right now we have to settle that puppy in."

"What if he needs…lots of attention?" For the first time she regretted her impulse.

"He's a baby. Babies sleep a lot, and he's definitely due for a nap."

"Oh."

"And so am I." With a wink he was out the door.

Rose stood there for a full ten seconds before she was able to remember the errand she'd been about to run when he'd pulled her into his arms.

AN HOUR LATER Daniel had created the barrier across the kitchen doorway and unloaded the groceries from the car. Rose had found a cardboard box to serve as a dog bed and lined it with an old blanket from the linen closet. The clock and microwave pouch were tucked into the blanket. St. Paddy roamed the kitchen sniffing everything while Rose and Daniel watched him get acquainted with his new surroundings.

"How about newspapers?" Daniel asked.

"I'll get them." She stepped over the barrier and scooped up an armful from a basket next to the fireplace. Then she recrossed the barrier and started spreading the papers around the kitchen.

Daniel stooped down to help. "Are these local?"

"Yes." She laughed as St. Paddy tried to climb in her lap and nearly knocked her over.

"Did you take out the comic page?"

"Yes, but you just gave me an idea. I've got several extras." She handed him the rest of the newspapers. "I'm going to get one for St. Paddy."

"He may be big for his age, but I doubt he can read yet."

"It's symbolic. Be right back." Soon she returned with the comic page from a recent paper and laid it ceremoniously down in front of the puppy. "For you, m'lord."

St. Paddy looked down at the paper and back up at her, his tail wagging vigorously.

"See? He likes it," Rose said.

Daniel rolled his eyes. "He sure does. I think he wants you to read it to him."

"Why not?" She got down on her hands and knees, which the puppy acknowledged by licking her face. "Come on, Daniel. You read St. Paddy's speeches, and I'll be Flynn."

"Are you sure I'm right for the part? Don't you want me to audition first?"

"Just get down here and read, smart aleck. It was your idea."

Daniel sank to his knees beside her. "Here we have Daniel O'Malley, supercop, reading a comic strip to a dog." He placed both hands on the floor and went nose-to-nose with St. Paddy. "Do you realize what this could do to my tough-guy image if anybody found out, pup?"

St. Paddy responded by swiping a tongue over Daniel's nose.

"Tough guy, huh?" Rose chuckled.

"Criminals tremble at the mention of my name. Come here, you," Daniel said, wrapping one arm around the wriggling puppy. He adopted a thick brogue and started to read. St. Paddy grew still and cocked his head.

"Daniel, he's really listening," Rose whispered.

"Of course he is. Are you going to read your part or do I have to do everything around here?"

Rose read the words of the little leprechaun in a lilting, teasing voice.

Daniel glanced at her and grinned. "That's so cute."

She blushed, suddenly self-conscious. "It's just how I hear him in my head."

"I can tell." Still smiling, he returned his attention to the strip and read the next St. Paddy line.

She sensed he was watching her with that same smile on his face as she started to read her next line. She stopped halfway through. "Don't look at me. You're making me nervous."

"Nervous? With what you do for a living?"

"This is different."

"But you look so adorable when you start talking like Flynn."

"Don't look."

"Okay." He shielded St. Paddy's eyes. "Don't look, pup. She's shy."

Her color high, Rose continued reading in tandem with Daniel. When his rich laughter greeted her final line, she didn't think she'd ever felt so validated in her life. She gazed at him. "Thanks."

"I wouldn't have missed it for the world." He regarded her with an appreciative light in his eyes. "Ready to try and settle him in now?"

"Sure."

But Paddy didn't seem to want to stay in the box.

"Just sit on the floor by the box and keep petting him while he's in there. I'll bet he goes to sleep eventually," Daniel said. "In the meantime I'll make us a couple of sandwiches."

"I didn't even remember about lunch!"

"I'll bet you don't eat as much as I do, anyway. You're probably not very hungry."

"No, I'm not, but it still doesn't say much for my hostessing skills that I didn't even bring up the subject."

Daniel opened the refrigerator and pulled out lunch meat and lettuce. "I thought we agreed that I'd think about the food this weekend."

"And what am I supposed to think about?"

He shot her a quick grin. "Me."

As if she could help it. It might have seemed she had all her attention focused on the puppy curled up in the box, but she recorded every nuance as Daniel moved around the kitchen. She watched the way a lock of his dark hair fell on his forehead as he leaned over the counter to spread mustard on the bread. She noticed the way his jeans fit in the back as he walked over to pull a bag of chips out of the cupboard. When he came toward her, she noticed how they fit in the front, too.

If St. Paddy would only drift off to sleep, she'd suggest they refrigerate the sandwiches until later. But the puppy continued to gaze up at her with his soulful brown eyes. And she had, after all, just deprived him of his nine brothers and sisters. Getting this puppy right now might not have been the brightest move she'd ever made.

Daniel handed her half a sandwich. "Eat this. You'll need your strength."

"Is that right?" Remarks like that made her heart race, but she felt uncertain about letting him know just how far gone she was when it came to his considerable sex appeal. She took a bite of sandwich, which was very good.

He squatted down in front of her, part of a sandwich in his hand. "Yeah. I'm known as a regular love machine. Ask anybody."

"Hmm. A supercop and now a love machine." She took another bite, chewed and swallowed before addressing St. Paddy. "Tell me, my good man, have you heard the news of this man's prowess in the sack?''

St. Paddy looked up at her and opened his mouth in an enormous yawn.

Rose glanced at Daniel. ''St. Paddy's unimpressed.''

''He's a guy. Guys never want to admit someone is better at it than they are.''

''And just how good are you?''

''Keep petting that puppy, who is definitely getting sleepy, and in about five minutes you'll find out.''

''Oh, the experience lasts for that long, does it? The women must go wild over you.''

''I meant in five minutes you'd *begin* to find out. I think I can manage a little more than five minutes' worth.''

''I see.'' She took another bite of the sandwich, but it was merely for show. She couldn't taste it as she looked into his eyes.

''He's asleep,'' he murmured, taking the rest of her sandwich from her and putting it on the counter with his. ''Take your hand away very, very slowly.''

She eased her fingers away from the puppy's fur.

''I'm going to pull you to your feet. Just let me do the guiding, and you won't bump the box.'' He stood slowly and held out both hands.

Her gaze locked with his. She put her hands into his larger ones and he drew her slowly to her feet. By the time he'd pulled her upright, her heart was hammering with excitement.

''I'll back out of here. Just follow me.''

With that glow of sensuality in his eyes, she would have followed him to Outer Mongolia. They moved cautiously over the barrier across the doorway of the kitchen.

Rose remembered the edge of the rag rug at the moment Daniel tripped on it and lost his balance. She tried to hold him upright, but he was far too heavy. They toppled backward, somehow managing to avoid the furniture, and landed on the floor with a heavy thud, Rose on top and Daniel on the bottom.

"Are you okay?" she asked, raising herself up to look down at him.

"Shh." He pulled her back to his chest. "Be still. Let's see if we woke him up."

"Oh, no doubt. Daniel, you probably hurt yourself. Let's—"

"I'm fine. Now be quiet. I think he's still asleep."

She rested her cheek against his chest and listened to the rapid thump of his heart through the fabric of his knit shirt. Slowly she reached up and unfastened a button on the placket at the neck.

"What do you think you're doing?"

"Checking to see if anything's broken." She slipped her hand inside his shirt.

His breathing quickened. "I've changed my mind. No telling what's wrong with me after that fall. I think you'd better check everything. Thoroughly."

9

DANIEL DIDN'T KID himself that this moment was the beginning of a long and glorious love affair. Rose needed someone right now, and thanks to his mother, he'd shown up. She was in transition between careers, between homes, between life-styles. Having someone to hold during a time like that could be a great comfort.

He'd hurt like hell when she no longer required his company. Yet knowing their time together was finite, he still gathered her close as they lay together on the braided rug and opened his heart. It was the only way he could make love to a woman, and Rose needed everything he could give her.

As Rose's hands crept beneath his shirt, he rolled her to her side and began kissing every freckle on her lovely Irish face. As he moved his lips over her warm skin, he hooked a finger in the tie holding her hair and pulled it down and away. He wanted her hair loose and wild, with its heady fragrance surrounding him as he nuzzled behind her ear.

He was glad he'd been interrupted back in her apartment. This was the place to make love to Rose, in this whitewashed cottage with its thatched roof and drifts of snowy lace at the leaded-glass windows. She tasted like the country, smelled like the country— fresh cream, wild honey, sparkling streams and grassy meadows. For a city boy, that was quite a treat. And Daniel feasted.

Her clothes came away with surprising ease as he uncovered more and more of the wonder that was Rose. Her skin seemed almost translucent, and her bones were so delicate that he was reminded of a Lladro porcelain figurine he'd broken as a child. Yet the heat pouring from her and the urgency of her touch told him she didn't want him to be gentle. He was gentle anyway. She had no idea of the brute strength in the hands of a well-trained cop, and she'd never find out from him.

Briefly, he thought of taking her into the bedroom so she'd have the softness of the mattress at her back, but then she unbuttoned the fly of his jeans and stroked him. He gave up the idea of moving anywhere as he became hard as a nightstick and crazy with the urge to bury himself inside her.

Gasping, he lifted his head to see if anything was handy that he could place beneath her. Two toss pillows were on the couch within arm's reach, and he grabbed them both. He tucked one under her head as he rolled her to her back and leaned down to explore her mouth once more. She'd worked her hand inside his briefs by this time, and he groaned with the intense pleasure. He would have to have her soon...very soon.

But first he wanted to take those saucy little breasts

in his mouth. Their pert upward thrust enticed him far more than abundance would have, and the obvious sensitivity of her nipples as she whimpered and writhed beneath his ministrations converted him forever to the magic of small breasts.

He moved between her slender thighs and lifted her hips for the second pillow. As slight as she was, he might drive her right into the floor with the force of the desire building in him. He'd never before felt the blood roaring in his ears like this, or his hands trembling so much when he dug into his pocket for the condom he'd put there this morning.

It wasn't easy finding the condom and putting it on while he continued to kiss her mouth and caress her passion-slicked body. And her eyes—how he loved to slide his hand down between her thighs and watch the turbulent reaction in her green, green eyes. The way she lifted into his caress when he probed her moist channel told him he could bring her to climax that way, but he was too selfish. He wanted to be inside her when she felt the first explosion. He wanted those spasms to set off his own.

At last he managed to get the condom on. Braced above her, he fastened his gaze on hers and eased forward, stopping when he was just barely inside her. She made a sound low in her throat and grasped his hips, her whole body radiating impatience.

He resisted her urging. "We'll only have this moment once in our lives," he said.

Her voice was ragged with passion. "So you want it to take forever?"

He laughed. He didn't think he could laugh when he was worked up like this, but it turned out he could. "Yes." He leaned down and kissed her.

She nipped at his lower lip.

He lifted his head and gazed down at her. "You're a handful, Rose Kingsford."

"Then use both hands, Officer O'Malley."

So he did. He slipped one arm under her shoulders, holding her a little off the floor, and slid his other hand under her firm behind. Then, when he was quite sure he wouldn't slam her against the hard floor, he pushed deep.

She gasped.

He withdrew in concern. "Rose?"

"That was lovely," she said in a breathless whisper. "You come right back here, Daniel."

With a soft moan he came back, back to paradise, back to the place it seemed he'd been seeking all his life. Nothing had ever seemed so right as locking his body tightly with hers, moving only enough to increase the delicious pressure for both of them. He'd wondered if he'd ever feel this perfection or if it was an impossible dream.

"Oh, Daniel," she murmured, her eyes closed and her voice full of awe. "Daniel."

"I'm here. Open your eyes, Rose."

Slowly her eyelids fluttered upward.

He looked into those green depths and saw more than momentary pleasure. In that moment he knew that Rose had opened her heart, as well. Perhaps she, like he, couldn't help herself.

"We're in trouble now," he whispered, gently increasing the rhythm.

"I know."

As the motion carried them both beyond reason, her body grew taut beneath his and her breathing came quick and fast. He focused on her face, suffused with desire and something more lasting than desire, and knew that he never wanted any other man to touch her like this, to possess either her body or her heart. Her violent climax triggered his, and at the moment of truth, her name was wrenched from him in an involuntary plea.

He *was* in trouble. Big trouble.

ROSE LAY in the tangle of clothes and wondered how in the heck she'd gotten herself in such a mess. For the first time in years she'd allowed a man to get under her skin. Daniel's sweetness and sense of humor had her questioning all her assumptions about marriage and happily-ever-afters. But this wasn't a very good time to be doing that now that she'd finally figured out what she wanted from life—a child, a new career and a charming country place to live in. A mounted policeman with the NYPD didn't fit in with any of that.

And as for Daniel, he'd been quite plain about his need for freedom. What it amounted to was that she'd picked a hell of a time to fall in love, and the worst person in the world to fall in love with.

Daniel's face was buried in her hair, but his weight didn't rest fully on her, so she knew he wasn't asleep.

She ran her finger up his spine and felt the quiver of response. "I respect a man who can back up his boast," she murmured. "I haven't experienced the blanket, but you're heaven on a rug."

He stirred and nuzzled the side of her neck. "It helps to be holding paradise in my arms."

"Spoken like a true Irishman."

He raised up on one elbow and gazed down at her. "Go ahead. Make fun of what we just shared. Make fun of me. But I saw your eyes, and I know you're making jokes because you're scared to death."

She swallowed. "Okay, I'm scared. I've never felt anything quite like this."

He leaned down and brushed his lips against hers. "Doesn't fit into your scheme, does it?"

"Does it fit into yours?"

He hesitated. "No."

"What are we going to do?"

He lifted his head to look into her eyes. "I'm not sure yet. When the whole world shifts, a wise man gets his balance before he goes off in any direction."

She smiled. "Now that really sounds Irish."

"Must be the influence of this little cottage. I feel like John Wayne in *The Quiet Man.*"

Rose wondered just how deeply he felt that role. John Wayne had played the part of a man who marries in that film. As she gazed into Daniel's dark eyes, she gradually became aware of another pair of brown eyes staring down at her in solemn wonder. She started to giggle.

Daniel looked puzzled and turned his head to follow the direction of her gaze.

St. Paddy licked his face.

"Yikes! Prison break."

"So much for your barrier theory."

"Keep an eye on him while I go wash up. We'll figure out something." He eased away from her, stood and walked unself-consciously into the bathroom.

Rose gazed after him. Sure enough, he had a small purple scar on his left buttock. He didn't seem the least worried about showing it off, either. She smiled to herself as she sat up to locate her underpants. While putting them on, she turned to St. Paddy, who was having a great time investigating the clothing scattered around the area. "Be a good dog," she said. "Don't—uh-oh."

St. Paddy scampered a short distance away with Daniel's briefs between his teeth.

"Come here," Rose coaxed.

The puppy edged forward, ready for a game.

"Just give them back." Easing forward, she made a grab for them and was instantly in a tug-of-war. "St. Paddy! Let go!"

The puppy tugged harder, his hind end in the air and his tail wagging madly.

Daniel walked in. "I need my—" he paused at the sound of ripping cotton "—duffel bag," he finished, going back to the bedroom.

"Daniel, I'm sorry," Rose called after him. "I'll buy you a new pair."

''Not on your life,'' he called back from the bedroom. ''Those are my insurance policy against you telling anybody I read a comic strip to a dog. If you ever do, I'm telling the world you ripped my underwear in a fit of passion.''

''You wouldn't!''

''Just try me.'' He came back into the room wearing only a low-slung pair of navy briefs.

Rose looked him up and down and ran the tip of her tongue over her lips. ''Is that an invitation, Officer O'Malley?''

He paused in the act of reaching for his jeans and glanced at her. Then he gave her a long, assessing look. ''This is going to be some weekend,'' he said quietly.

Her heart beat faster. ''I hope so.''

''But first we'd better give that puppy some exercise so he'll sleep a long, long time.''

''Good idea.'' She reveled in the promise contained in Daniel's intent gaze. ''We'll take him for a walk.''

THE WOODS surrounding the little cottage were soggy with the wet snowfall that had turned to rain at midday, so Rose decided to keep to the road when she and Daniel took St. Paddy for his first walk. She fashioned a makeshift collar out of a bandanna and found a length of clothesline for a temporary leash.

They stepped outside into the water-color light of a New England afternoon and Rose zipped up the ski jacket she kept at the cottage just for such walks in the woods. The pale sun touched oak and maple trees nubby with the promise of spring, and pine branches tipped light green with new growth.

Rose took a deep breath. "I love the way it smells here."

Daniel made a great show of filling his lungs. Then he began to cough.

Rose clapped him on the back. "Are you okay?"

"Sure." He cleared his throat and grinned at her. "I guess fresh air takes some getting used to, after a lifetime of car exhaust and rotting garbage."

Rose started down the road, with St. Paddy scampering around at the end of the clothesline. "Have you ever wanted to live in the country?" Instantly she regretted the impulsive question. Far too leading. And she didn't really want to lead anywhere.

"I guess *living* in the country never occurred to me, but I like the idea of vacations here." Daniel fell into step beside her on the asphalt lane. "I'm trained as a city cop, and I love the work."

It was the response she'd expected, yet still she felt disappointed. "I love the country. My mom says I have the heart of an Irish milkmaid."

"Don't tell me you're going to keep a cow in the backyard."

She laughed. "I've thought of it. Or a horse."

"Good God."

"What? You ride a horse on the job."

"Yeah, but he doesn't live in my apartment."

"Listen, don't pull that sophisticated-city-slicker routine with me, Daniel. I watched you with that animal, and you're crazy about him."

''Dan Foley's okay, I guess.''

''Excuse me? What's his name?''

''Our horses are often named after an officer killed in the line of duty, and Lieutenant Dan Foley died during a drug bust about ten years ago. So that's my horse's name. It's a nice way of memorializing some of our heroes.''

''How lovely and sentimental.''

''Cops can be more sentimental than you might— uh-oh. Wildlife at two o'clock. Better hold that puppy.''

Rose gripped the clothesline as a rabbit hopped across the road in front of them and St. Paddy leaped after it, pulling Rose slightly off balance. The rabbit disappeared into the underbrush as Rose coaxed St. Paddy back and got him headed in the same direction she and Daniel were walking.

''Judging from the size of those paws, you won't be able to haul him around like that much longer,'' Daniel said. ''What did the breeder say? He'll gain a half pound a day?''

''Something like that.''

''At that rate he'll outweigh you in no time.''

''I suppose. But these dogs are bred for their good disposition. He'll just naturally want to please me.''

''He's not the only one with that urge.''

''Oh, really?'' A shiver of pleasure travelled up her spine as she paused to glance at him. He looked as irresistibly masculine silhouetted against the darkening woods as he had inside her Irish cottage.

"Isn't it obvious?" A breeze ruffled his dark hair. "I figure I must look as eager as that pup."

"Think I could teach you to beg?"

"I think you already have." His gaze smoldered as he slipped a hand around her waist and drew her slowly toward him. "Kiss me, Rose."

"That's not begging." Her breath quickened as she moved into the magnetic force that surrounded him. "That's commanding."

"Please kiss me, then."

"In the middle of the road?"

"No, on my mouth. And give me the clothesline," he murmured, reaching for it. His body was warm and hard against hers. "If you forget what you're doing and turn that puppy loose, you'll never forgive me."

"What if *you* forget?"

"I'm a cop. I'm trained to do two things at once." Then his lips found hers.

She quickly realized she couldn't do two things at once, if one of them was kissing Daniel. Her response to him had always been quick, but now it was immediate. She moaned and wrapped her arms around his waist, pressing against the barrier of their clothing.

He lifted his mouth a fraction from hers. "I feel like tying this dog to a tree and dragging you into the woods."

Her heart was thudding so loud she could barely hear him. "It's muddy."

"I don't care." He nipped at her lower lip. "I don't care if we're both smeared with mud. In fact, I think

I'd *like* rolling your tender body in the mud. There's something sexy about ooze.''

The image fed the fever raging within her. If only he'd fill the aching void deep inside, she'd lie in the mud, in a pool of chocolate syrup, in a vat of whipped cream—

"Damn!" Daniel released her with a suddenness that made her stumble. He flung down the end of the rope he'd been holding and raced to the opposite end, which was still tied to the red bandanna lying in the road. St. Paddy had escaped.

10

Rose's stomach churned as she frantically scanned the woods bordering the road. No sign of a tan furry body anywhere. And she'd tied that knot so carefully, yet somehow he'd worked it loose, probably to go after another rabbit. She shouldn't have kissed Daniel, shouldn't have taken her eyes off that puppy for a minute.

"St. Paddy!" she called, a catch in her voice. "Oh, Daniel, he doesn't even know his name yet."

"That's okay." Daniel crossed to one side of the road and studied the underbrush. "Keep calling. Maybe he'll respond to the sound of your voice."

She gave silent thanks for his police skills, which had trained him to observe carefully. She kept calling.

He quickly crossed to the other side of the road and examined the verge. "He went this way," he said, striding through the mud, his boots making a sucking sound as he moved. "I can follow his paw prints, so this shouldn't be too tough. Maybe you should stay there, in case—"

"No chance, copper." Rose plunged after him, although her loafers didn't work quite as well as his boots and threatened to come off her feet with each step.

He glanced over his shoulder as he continued through the woods. "Rose, stay there."

"No."

"Okay, but watch your—"

"Look out!" she called, a millisecond before Daniel tripped over a dead branch and fell headlong into the muck. She crouched down beside Daniel. "Are you okay?"

He pushed up on the palms of his hands and spit out a dead leaf. "Man, that was graceful. Don't you love the country?" His face was so covered with mud, he looked like a character in a minstrel show.

"You said there was something sexy about ooze."

"Thanks for reminding me of that. But I wasn't planning to throw myself facedown in it." He got to his feet and wiped the arm of his jacket across his eyes. Then he studied the ground again. "This way," he said, starting off.

Rose followed, nearly losing her shoes in the process.

Finally he crouched down in front of a large hollow log. "He's in there, I'll bet. Probably followed another rabbit."

Rose squatted down beside him so she could peer into the black opening. The loamy scent of plant decay mingled with what she thought might be the smell of wet dog. "St. Paddy," she called softly. "Come here, little guy. You're too young to be out in the woods alone."

No answer.

Rose's stomach twisted with anxiety. "I hope something didn't get him in there."

"Whatever would fit in this log isn't any bigger than he is, and from the look of his prints, he crawled in under his own steam. He probably just got tired and fell asleep. Let me see what happens when I reach inside."

"Yuck. Think of what could be in there."

"Country stuff." He grinned at her. "Country reality, as opposed to country fantasy."

"You're making fun of me."

"Gently, very gently. There's still some city girl in you, Rose." He dropped to his knees beside the hollow log.

"Daniel, you're going to get—"

"Muddy?" He wriggled down until his chest was on the ground before easing his hand into the log. "Now that would be a real shame, wouldn't it?"

Rose sighed. "Disasters seem to happen to you whenever you're around me."

"I'm not complaining."

"I can't imagine why not."

"Think of the fun we'll have cleaning up." He shoved his arm in a little farther. "Hey, pup. Come on out."

"Can you reach him?"

"Can't seem to. Wish my arm was a little longer. Damn, where's a superhero when you need him?"

Rose gazed at him lying in the mud, heedless of

his own discomfort as he reached deep into the hollow log. "I'd say I have one," she said softly.

"Oh, sure." He grunted as he tried to get his arm in more. "I'm the guy who demanded a kiss when we both should have been watching the dog."

"I'm the one who didn't tie the bandanna knot tight enough," Rose said. "I don't want you blaming yourself."

Daniel began to chuckle.

"What's so funny?"

"Something's licking my fingers. I sure hope it's your puppy."

"It has to be him! Can you grab him?"

"Not unless you want me to pull him out by his tongue."

"Daniel," she said, her voice rising in excitement, "just move your hand back gradually. Maybe he'll keep licking your fingers and follow your hand right out."

"He just might. Did anyone ever tell you that you're very smart?"

"Thank you. It's not usually the first thing men notice about me."

"Can't blame them for that, Rose." He slowly eased his arm out of the hollow log. "You're very beautiful."

"Which doesn't necessarily lead to happiness."

"You sound as if it's a disadvantage, being beautiful."

"In some ways it is."

"I'd like to debate that with you later. Okay, get

ready. Lean over me and when he sticks his head out, grab him by the scruff of his neck like you did in the car.''

Rose positioned herself above him. "I'll be forever in your debt for this, Daniel.''

"And don't think I won't collect.''

Mud and all, his nearness turned her on. "That sounds very promising.''

"And you'd better stop whispering sweet nothings in my ear or I'm liable to screw this up.''

"Right.'' She tried to empty all sensual thoughts of Daniel from her mind as she concentrated on the opening where his hand was now buried only up to the wrist. Gradually he drew his fingers out.

Sure enough, a pink tongue and a stubby snout followed. Rose waited until St. Paddy's floppy ears cleared the ragged edge of the log before she pounced, grabbing a fistful of dog. St. Paddy squealed in surprise and wiggled in her grip. She wrapped both arms around him, lost her balance and fell backwards into a tangle of bushes. But she kept her hold on the dog.

Daniel eased himself up and sat back on his heels. "Why, Rose, you're sitting in a bush.''

She hugged the squirming puppy to her chest. "If you say that must make it a Rose bush, I'll never speak to you again.''

"Wouldn't dream of saying that. Want some help with that critter?''

"Please.''

He got to his feet and leaned down. "Let me take him so you can climb out of there."

She maintained a firm hold on the scruff of St. Paddy's neck while Daniel gathered the dog into his arms. "Got him?"

"Got him."

He lifted the thirty-five-pound animal without effort. After he backed away she extricated herself, ripping the back pocket of her designer jeans in the process.

Muttering to herself, she finally glanced up to see Daniel cradling St. Paddy as he might a toddler and speaking to him in a low, soothing voice. For a moment she stood transfixed by the sight of Daniel comforting the dog. *He would make a wonderful father,* whispered a voice in the back of her mind. If she ever considered trusting a man for the long haul, it would be a man like Daniel. But the timing was way off. He wasn't ready for a wife, and she was more than ready for a child. Nothing about their lives fit together.

Daniel glanced up at her and smiled. "I think he's fine."

That smile found its way into her heart. She could feel it bury itself deep and knew she'd remember the way he looked at this moment—muddy, triumphant and very sexy—for the rest of her life.

"Let's go home," she said.

THANK GOD the dog episode had turned out okay, Daniel thought. He held St. Paddy while he and Rose stood just inside the back door of her cottage. There she subjected him to the sweet torture of watching her peel off her muddy clothes while his hands were completely occupied hanging on to the squirming puppy.

In a way it was fortunate that he couldn't touch her and interfere with her graceful movements as she undressed. Rose had refined the process into performance art, and he felt privileged to be able to enjoy the show. His mouth grew moist and his erection strained against the fly of mud-caked jeans when she stripped down to nothing but her French-cut briefs.

Once her muddy clothes were off, she went in search of an old blanket to wrap around St. Paddy. She returned with it and sat on the floor with the blanket-wrapped dog while Daniel stripped down to his briefs. Then he carried the dog while she walked ahead of him and started the water running in the claw-footed tub.

"I want to make sure he doesn't scratch you," he said as he carefully lowered St. Paddy into the water.

She gave him an elfin grin. "Don't worry. I don't have any swimsuit sessions coming up soon. A little scratch won't ruin my career."

He glanced at her alabaster skin dusted with freckles. "I wasn't thinking of your career. I was thinking it would be a crime to mar skin like that for any reason."

Her smile faded. "See, that's what I mean. Men always expect perfection of someone like me."

"I don't expect perfection. I just—" He was prevented from continuing the explanation as St. Paddy started to climb out of the tub and it took both of them to keep the slippery dog inside. "Let me hold while you wash him," Daniel said.

She glanced sideways at him through a tangle of coppery curls. "Okay. Listen, I'm sorry I snapped at you."

Daniel leaned over the tub and got a firm hold of St. Paddy's chest and hind end. "You're forgiven." Shoulder to bare shoulder like this, he'd have forgiven her much worse transgressions, but he didn't want to let the subject drop, either. "Apparently you've been dating a string of men who only care about what you look like, but you've just come to the end of that run. If beauty was the only attraction, I wouldn't be here."

Rose used a washcloth on the puppy's face. "Then why do I get the feeling I'm like a new car and you're afraid to damage the paint job?"

His answering chuckle was rueful. "Good comparison. Maybe I do feel that way a little. I've never been with someone so…"

"Perfect? Believe me, I'm not."

"Okay, not perfect, but incredibly fragile and delicate." The puppy tried to get away and he tightened his grip. "Whatever that quality is that's made you a successful model. It's intimidating as hell when you get up close and personal with someone who reminds you of fine china."

"I don't want to be treated like fine china!" She scrubbed the washcloth across St. Paddy's back.

"You want rough sex?"

"No. For heaven's sake!"

"Okay, I get your point. You want to be treated like a flesh-and-blood woman."

"Exactly."

"You missed a glob of dirt on his back leg. There. That's it." Her nipple brushed his arm and he fought the urge to let go of the puppy and take an armful of Rose. The cotton of his briefs stirred with the beginnings of an erection.

"I think it's time I had an honest-to-goodness hickey."

Damn, but she had a way with words. "This isn't the best time to announce intentions like that."

"Why not? We're both nearly naked."

"Really? I hadn't noticed."

"We'll be done washing St. Paddy in a minute. I've never had a hickey, Daniel," she persisted earnestly as she continued to wash the quivering pup. "If you gave me a hickey you'd get over this thing about my being so delicate and perfect. You were so afraid I'd get bruised when we made love on the floor."

"How do you know?"

"All those pillows, and holding me the way you did. I could tell."

A ferocious ache gripped him as he remembered just what that session on the floor had been like. "Let's change the subject."

"I think I'd like a hickey on my bottom, in the same place you have that sexy bullet scar of yours."

''What do you know about a bullet scar?''

''Your mother told me about it in the tearoom. She said it made you shy around women, which was why you weren't married. She thought I could get you over that self-consciousness about a scar on your...bum, as she said.''

''Dear God.''

She glanced slyly down at his briefs. ''I think I have, from the looks of things.''

''You little tease. You're talking this way on purpose to drive me crazy, aren't you?''

''Is it working?''

He gave her a searing look. ''Get a towel for this pup.''

He toweled St. Paddy off in record time and carried him into the kitchen.

''Y'all come back,'' Rose called after him.

''Count on it.'' Daniel took St. Paddy into the kitchen, and once the puppy was tucked into his box he drifted right off to sleep. Daniel figured the puppy would sleep for a while, maybe long enough to give Daniel some privacy with Rose. It was time for him to prove to her that he didn't consider her to be made of porcelain.

He washed his face and hands in the kitchen sink and dried off with a paper towel. When he returned to the bathroom she'd cleaned out the tub and was running fresh water in it.

She was leaning both hands on the tub, her legs braced slightly apart as she glanced over her shoulder. ''Is he asleep?''

The pose was so provocative his mouth went dry. "Out...out like a light."

"You can have first bath."

"I think we'll do this together."

She looked him up and down, excitement lighting her eyes. "I don't know if we'll both fit, officer. You seem to have grown."

"We'll work on it." He slipped off his briefs, releasing a full erection, and walked toward her. Her quick intake of breath and a darkening of her eyes were his reward. Holding her gaze he slid two fingers under the delicate lace panel inset of her panties, and in one swift motion ripped the garment from her body. He was through being tentative.

"Daniel!"

"You can tell people I ripped them in a fit of passion." He stepped into the tub and offered her his hand. Wordlessly she stepped in after him as warm water swirled around their ankles. "Turn around," he said.

Her eyes widened, but she turned her back to him.

Taking the curved bar of soap from the holder beside the tub, he knelt in the water behind her, dampened the soap and eased the bar up the back of her leg. She quivered. He dipped the bar in the water again and ran it slowly up the back of her other leg to the top of her thigh. Then he cupped his hand, scooped up warm water and allowed it to trickle down her thigh.

"What are you doing?" she murmured, her voice breathy.

"Cleaning you up." He soaped between her thighs with lazy circular strokes before rinsing with more cupped water.

"I've never had...a bath like this."

"It gets better." He paused briefly to turn off the tap. Then he washed the curve of her backside slowly while he reveled in the way her breathing grew faster and more shallow. He wondered if she'd eventually be so in tune with him that she'd climax with only this kind of caress. He wondered if he'd be her lover long enough to find out.

The soap had become slippery, so he tightened his grip when he slid it between the petals of her femininity. As the curve of the bar came in contact with her flash point, she gasped. He wrapped an arm around her waist to hold her steady as he rubbed the soap back and forth. Then he tossed the soap aside and began to rinse her with splashes of water, followed by intimate explorations with his fingers.

Her legs began to shake. "Daniel—"

"I've got you. Go with it, Rose."

Continuing the caress, he began kissing the tender flesh of her backside. The kisses progressed to gentle nips as she moaned and trembled in the circle of his arm. When she cried out with the first convulsion of her orgasm, he placed his mouth on the exact spot she'd requested and applied firm suction. If nothing else, she'd have a bruise to remember him by.

Perhaps it was her long moan of completion, or the act of marking her, or her stance when he'd first come back into the room, but a primitive lust took command of him, a driving need he could not control. He'd never intended to make love to her in the bathtub, because he hadn't prepared for it, but he was no longer rational.

Desperate to have her in a way that harkened back to the most basic needs of a man for a woman, he got to his feet and leaned her forward over his arm. Once her hands were braced on the edge of the tub, he grasped her hips and entered her, pushing deep. He never remembered such blinding passion. It seemed that burying himself inside her was absolutely necessary, and without this release he would surely die. His strokes were swift, his climax indescribable.

As the red haze slowly cleared, he was swamped by feelings of tenderness...and regret. He had no right to act without a thought for consequences. Withdrawing gently, he kept his arm around her as he stepped from the tub and grabbed an oversize bath towel. He wrapped her in it and lifted her out of the tub to set her on the bath mat.

"Wow," she said, her voice husky.

"Yeah." And now they had to discuss the possible consequences, he thought. But he postponed it, wanting to maintain the soft joy that surrounded them in the aftermath of raw passion satisfied. He dried her carefully, crouching down to run the towel over her legs and buttocks. Sure enough, a definite bruise about the size of a silver dollar was forming there.

"You gave me a hickey, didn't you?"

"Yep." And he figured placing that brand on her was probably what had stirred the instinct passed down by his ancient forebears to complete the possession.

"Hold that hand mirror behind me so I can see."

He took the gilt-framed mirror from the counter and held it while she peered over her shoulder at the round, purple mark.

"Looks like an expert job."

"You came to the master." He stood and put the mirror back on the counter.

"Don't laugh, but I really like it. It's like a badge of womanhood. Now I have another request. Am I too big for you to carry into the bedroom?"

He smiled at her. "Depends on how you want to be carried."

"What do you mean?"

"I can manage it this way." He grasped her arm, stooped and hoisted her over his shoulder.

"Hey! That's not romantic."

"But it gets the job done." Laughing, he hauled her into the bedroom and dumped her onto the feather bed with its bank of lace-trimmed pillows scattered over the headboard. "And in my line of work, that's the main goal. It doesn't have to be pretty."

"I swear you have been taking lessons from old John Wayne movies."

He looked at her lying there amidst the white lace and wanted her again. But the time had come to confront the realities of nature. He climbed in beside her and took her into his arms. "We need to talk, Rose."

She snuggled against him. "What a novel suggestion."

"Hey, this is serious stuff." He shifted her so he could look into her eyes. "I lost control. We need to face what might happen as a result."

Her gaze was warm. "Don't take all the blame on yourself. I could have stopped you."

"Maybe not."

Her eyebrows lifted. "If I'd said no, you would have forced me?"

"No." He gave her a lazy grin. "I would have convinced you to say yes."

"Oh, ho! I guess I don't have to worry about damaging your ego."

"We're talking about desperation, not ego. I've never felt quite so…needy as I did then." He was admitting quite a bit with that statement. He searched her face to see how she'd react to it.

"Neither have I," she said, her expression open and vulnerable.

He took a deep breath and decided to risk a little more. "When I agreed to this weekend, I thought we'd have a fling, a fun roll in the hay, with no complications. It's what we both said we wanted." He paused. "But this doesn't feel like a fling."

"No, it doesn't feel that way to me, either."

He leaned down and pressed his lips gently to hers. "Thank you for saying that," he murmured, kissing the freckles on the bridge of her nose. "But even if we're both rethinking the situation, from now on we're using protection. We don't need the added pressure of an accident right now."

"True, and I can't be trusted to be the voice of reason, obviously. I didn't want to stop, either."

His blood began to heat anew. He sat up and swung his legs off the bed. "And it's obvious that we're headed down that road again. I'm going for supplies."

"Good idea. But really, Daniel, I don't think we have to worry. Getting pregnant with one slipup is unusual, don't you think?"

He stood. "Not so unusual for an Irishman."

11

MAUREEN O'MALLEY wished that Daniel hadn't gone off to his training session on this particular weekend. The parish was having a special Friday night potluck, and she'd figured on talking Daniel into going because she knew he had the time off. At least three young Irish ladies would be there that Maureen wanted Daniel to meet, now that Rose Kingsford had turned out to be such a disaster.

Maureen was putting the final touches on her chowder casserole when the phone rang. Thinking it was Fran Kavanagh, who'd suggested sharing a cab to the church in view of the weather, Maureen dried her hands on her apron, hurried to the phone and answered it slightly out of breath.

"You're panting as if you'd run all the way to the phone. Were you expecting a gentleman caller, Maureen Fiona?"

"*You!*" Once she recognized Bridget's voice, Maureen slammed down the receiver.

It rang again.

Maureen snatched it up. "I'll not be talking to you." She started to hang up again.

"It's about Daniel!" yelled Bridget.

Fear twisted Maureen's insides as she pressed the receiver to her ear. "What about him? Is he all right?"

"Physically, I'm sure he's fine. But his soul is in terrible danger."

Maureen let her breath out in a whoosh of sound. "Well, I care about his soul, naturally, but his body is my first concern. 'Tis just like you, Bridget Hogan, scaring a person half to death. I thought there'd been an accident or the like."

"There well could be if we don't put a stop to what's going on," Bridget said darkly.

"You always were one to drag out a story. As Daniel says, cut to the chase."

A mighty sigh carried across the telephone line. "This isn't easy for me to say about my own flesh and blood. My daughter, Rose—"

"I know perfectly well who your daughter is, you deceitful old banshee!"

"I'm the same age as you! And look twenty times better, too!"

"Ha! You know what happens when you're skinny and you get old? Sag, sag, sag! As my mother used to say, 'After fifty, plump up and stay seated.'"

"Never mind what your mother used to say. What I'm trying to tell you, if you'll be still for one second, is that Rose wants to have a child out of wedlock."

"No!"

"Yes. On purpose, and raise the baby all by herself. I don't know where she got such an idea."

"If you don't know, I do. 'Tis because you married

a Protestant Brit instead of a good Irish Catholic, and that's the truth of it.''

''Cecil has nothing to do with this idea of hers.'' There was a pause. ''No, come to think of it, he probably *is* to blame. I'm glad you mentioned it. But that doesn't matter now. We have to stop them.''

''Them?'' Maureen had a sick feeling she knew what was coming.

''She's picked your Daniel as the father for this unholy plan.''

''He wouldn't be doin' such a thing!''

''What if he doesn't know? What if she puts one over on him?''

''If she tricks Daniel into getting her in the family way, I will wring her neck for her! Good thing he's off on a training weekend with the department.''

''You really think that's where he is, you silly goose?''

Maureen drew herself up to her full height of five feet, two inches. ''He wouldn't be lying to his own mother.''

''Rose lied to me. I finally weaseled it out of her agency that she's on holiday this weekend, not on assignment as she told me.''

''We've already established Rose's character. 'Tis not surprising that she lied to you.''

''I wouldn't be casting stones, if I were you, until you call your son's station,'' Bridget challenged. ''See if there is a training weekend or not.''

''I won't.''

''I know you, Maureen, and you will, as soon as I

hang up. You'd better take down my number so you can call me back and we can figure out what to do.''

''I won't be calling, because Daniel's on a training weekend.''

''You'll call me back, all right.'' Bridget recited her number.

Maureen squeezed her eyes shut and started to hum, as if she didn't need that number any more than a second set of thumbs. ''Goodbye, Bridget. I'll not be speaking to you again in this lifetime.'' She hung up the phone.

Five minutes later she was obliged to dial Bridget's number, which had stuck in her mind like glue. ''Where do you think they went?'' she asked without identifying herself.

''Oh, and who would *this* be?'' Bridget asked.

''You well know who 'tis.''

''Could this be the mother of that boy who would never lie?''

''Bridget Mary, you haven't changed a bit! Are you going to tell me where you think they went, or must I come over there and sit on you until you decide to be nice?''

''I know exactly where they went. Rose has a little cottage about two hours north of the city.''

Maureen gasped. ''They're shacked up?''

''Honestly, get with it. Nobody says 'shacked up' these days. Anyway, we have to go up there. Do you have a car?''

Maureen thought of her husband's old Pontiac parked in the apartment house's basement garage.

Daniel had been trying to get her to sell it, but she couldn't bring herself to do that. She hadn't told Daniel, but sometimes she went down to the garage and just sat in the passenger seat, pretending she and Patrick were about to take a drive.

"Goodness, woman, do you have a car or not? Or am I right in supposing you're losing your marbles?"

"'Tis my husband's car."

"Can you drive it?"

Maureen thought about the few solo trips she'd made in the big old Pontiac. She remembered a wee problem with backing and cornering. But she wasn't about to tell Bridget about that and let her get the upper hand. "Yes, I can," she said.

"Good. Come over and pick me up."

Maureen panicked and grabbed the first excuse she could think of. "But 'twill be getting on toward dark in another hour or so. We can't be gallivanting around upstate in the dark, Bridget."

Indistinct muttering greeted that announcement.

"What's that you're saying?" Maureen asked.

"The deed will be done by then!" she hissed. "But it can't be helped. They probably fell to it once they arrived, so we'd already be too late, and I suppose we shouldn't go at night. All we have left is to confront them and make certain they do the honorable thing."

"Get married?" Maureen squeaked.

"It's a black day, isn't it? When you and I have to contemplate becoming related, I mean. Can't be helped. Pick me up at eight. Here's the address."

Maureen wrote down the address on the back of the electric bill. A Central Park West address. She'd have to drive into the heart of Manhattan. She hung up the phone and crossed herself.

ST. PADDY SLEPT for two hours, allowing his new owner to enjoy a gloriously long lovemaking session on the feather bed with Daniel, and to share a simple meal with him in front of the small fireplace. They'd found they both liked sitting on the floor next to the rustic coffee table.

Daniel had braced a chair against the board barricading Paddy inside the kitchen. They'd found Paddy was strong enough to push the heavy board aside and wiggle out the opening.

They'd just poured another glass of wine and started a game of chess when the puppy scratched at the board. Rose let him out, tied the bandanna collar around his neck, knotting it tighter this time, and took him outside briefly while Daniel stoked up the fire.

After Rose fed the puppy, she decided to let him stay in the living room while she and Daniel finished their chess game.

St. Paddy roamed the living room for a few seconds before flopping down next to Daniel and attacking his shoe.

"Paddy, no!" Rose started to get up and pull him away.

"It's okay. He's just teething and needs something to chew."

"I have some old loafers in the closet that I was planning to give away."

"No, then he'll learn to chew up shoes. A few rags knotted together would be better."

"Let me see what I can find." Rose rummaged through the laundry area and came up with some likely candidates. She brought them to Daniel, who tied them into a chew toy for St. Paddy.

The puppy flopped down and started working away at the knotted rags.

Rose resumed her seat on the floor and studied her next chess move. "You seem to know a lot about dogs," she said after moving her knight.

"As I said, we had family pets when I was growing up." Daniel captured her knight with his pawn.

"Don't you miss that companionship?" She captured his knight with her bishop.

"Pets don't fit the bachelor existence too well." He moved his queen out of danger.

Rose gazed at him. "So you picked a job where you ride a horse."

He shrugged. "Just following in my dad's footsteps."

"You know what I think? I think you'd have a great time in the country, playing with all the animals." She moved her bishop again. "Check."

He leaned his elbows on his knees and looked at her. "Going back to something you said today, is that an invitation?"

She forgot about the chess game. "Do you want it to be?"

He sighed and ran his fingers through his hair. "I don't know, Rose. All this—" His gesture encompassed the fire, the puppy, and her. "It's very appealing. But I couldn't afford something like this on my salary."

"Oh, for heaven's sake! What difference does it make who earns the money?"

His mouth quirked. "In my world, it makes a hell of a lot of difference."

"Then your world is somewhere back in the nineteenth century. Am I to be punished because my career pays better than yours? Are you going to deny me your company because modeling is valued more highly than peacekeeping? Which is ludicrous, by the way, but it's how society works these days."

"You're asking me to go back on decades of indoctrination if I allow a woman to foot the bill."

She could tell he was only half joking. "Well, I won't give up this cottage and toss my investments in the ocean to satisfy your male ego. So, if you want me, you have to accept my money."

"Love me, love my portfolio?"

Her breath caught at his use of the word, even so casually. She tried to maintain the same tone, but didn't quite pull it off. "I guess so." Her voice quavered just a little.

He set down his wineglass. "Rose, I—"

St. Paddy jumped up and knocked the edge of the chessboard, scattering the pieces.

"Hey, you," Daniel said, grabbing the puppy and

falling to the floor with him. "I was all set to win that game until you butted in."

"Likely story," Rose said. "You knew you were going to lose, so you pinched him and made him bump the board." But it wasn't the destruction of the chess game that disappointed her. She wanted to know what Daniel had been about to say before St. Paddy got into the act. Had he been about to broach the subject of a commitment? Neither of them had wanted that at the beginning, but they hadn't realized how strong and how quickly the bond would develop between them. She'd abandoned the idea of asking him to father her child, but a new, more exciting prospect was presenting itself. Perhaps she could have a child *and* Daniel.

He was reaching out to her, but tentatively. The relationship was still fragile, and a telling moment had just been interrupted by her puppy. She couldn't blame St. Paddy. He hadn't asked to be part of this weekend. But as she watched Daniel roll on the floor with the dog, she realized that she was seeing a side of this New York cop she'd never have known otherwise. Daniel had that rare combination of sensuality and tenderness that she'd dreamed of but never found.

Daniel straightened and set St. Paddy firmly on the floor. Then he quieted him by stroking his back. As he caressed the dog, he picked up his wine and drained it.

"You looked as if you were really having fun with him," Rose said.

"On a scale of one to ten, wrestling with a dog on the floor is about a seven. Fun, but not outstanding."

"Really?" She knew she was blatantly fishing and didn't even care. "What's better?"

"Galloping Dan Foley through the streets of New York, which I don't get to do very often, by the way, would be at least a nine."

"Then what's a ten?" She hoped she knew the answer.

"I took a parachute-jumping course once. Leaping from a plane at twelve thousand feet would have to rate a ten."

"Oh." She looked into the glowing embers of the fireplace.

"Rose?"

She glanced back at him.

"Making love to you is off the charts," he said with a smile. "I can't count that high."

"Oh." This time the exclamation came out as a breathy whisper.

"And it's been a long time since we've made love."

Her nerve endings sizzled. "More than three hours."

He stood and held out both hands. "Let's not make it four." When she placed her hands in his, he pulled her to her feet and into his arms.

Much as she longed to walk straight into the bedroom with him, she couldn't ignore her new responsibility. "I should put St. Paddy in the kitchen."

He kissed her swiftly and firmly. "I'll do it. Go in and get that feather bed warm."

After going into the bedroom, Rose turned on the Tiffany bedside lamp and undressed quickly. On impulse, she took a decorative carafe of lavender water from the bedside table and sprinkled a few drops on the sheets and pillowcases. Then she climbed between the sheets, nestled against the cloud-soft mattress, and closed her eyes, a smile of anticipation on her face.

Her eyes snapped open and her smile faded as she suddenly realized what she'd done to herself. She'd never lie here again without thinking of Daniel. She'd never lie here again without *wanting* Daniel. Her hideaway would no longer beckon with the same promise, unless Daniel was part of the picture, but she still didn't know if he was interested in sharing her dream. She'd just thrown a major spanner into the works of her master plan.

The embodiment of that spanner walked through the bedroom door and stripped off his shirt. For the life of her she could summon up no regret, and not just because Daniel was magnificent to look at. When he held her in an embrace both strong and tender, she felt cherished. In her limited experience with physical love, she'd been leered at, fondled and even admired, as one would admire an inanimate object. Daniel was the first man who had ever cherished her.

"Is St. Paddy okay?" she asked.

"He's asleep. The ticking clock seems to be working."

"Good." Hot desire flowed through her as he undressed and she thought of the pleasure to follow.

He discarded the last of his clothes and slipped into bed beside her. "Heaven couldn't be any better than this," he murmured, gathering her close. "It even smells like heaven."

"Lavender water." She molded herself to his virile body.

"Nope." He nuzzled behind her ear. "Eau de Rosie."

"Nobody calls me Rosie."

"Somebody does now." He kissed the tip of her breast. "Touch me, Rosie. Touch me where it counts."

She did, grasping his heated shaft and caressing him until he moaned and pulled her hand away.

"You'd better stop, or I'll finish this before we really start," he said in a husky voice as he reached for the condom on the bedside table.

"Just following instructions, Officer."

"Oh, that's right." He snugged the condom into place and moved over her. "You once said my cop voice was intimidating."

"Extremely."

His dark gaze burned with need, and a fine sheen of sweat covered his shoulders. "So if I give you orders, you'll follow them?"

"I can't seem to help myself."

"A man could ask for no more." He leaned down and nibbled at her lower lip. "Spread your legs, Rosie, girl," he whispered. "And rise to meet me, lass."

She didn't need orders to welcome him deep inside her. Instinct drove her to this melding of bodies, and she suspected a melding of hearts, as well. When they were well and truly locked together, she wrapped her arms around him and looked up into his eyes. "Any more orders?"

"Just one."

She held her breath. From the intensity of his expression, he was in the grip of a forceful emotion.

"Love me."

Her response came without hesitation. "Yes."

He closed his eyes and took a shuddering breath. Then he opened them and gazed down at her. "I won't get in your way, Rose."

"Maybe I want you in my way, you hardheaded Irishman."

A soft smile touched his mouth as he began to move slowly within her. "I'll need convincing."

Her body tightened another notch with each stroke. "How?"

"By making love to me about a million times."

12

DANIEL FOUND his heart was too full for sleep, so he lay in a half-conscious daze of pleasure, his arms filled with the most wonderful woman in the world. He knew he and Rose had some problems to work out if they were seriously considering a permanent relationship. He'd found the woman worth giving up the mounted patrol for, but he wasn't ready to quit the force completely, and Rose had her heart set on this little cottage in the woods. The cottage was a hell of a long way from the city and the life he was used to.

Of course, this cottage had the advantage of also being far away from both of their mothers. God, he didn't even want to think about their reaction if he and Rose made an announcement. They'd have to hold the wedding in shifts, one for Maureen and the second for Bridget.

The wedding. The concept of matrimony had once been unacceptable, and now he couldn't imagine an alternative. Rose was everything he'd always wanted—intelligent, creative, caring and sexy. Not to mention the charisma that made her unique, the charisma that had ensnared him, heart and soul.

He was so engrossed in his thoughts that it took him awhile to hear the whimpering from the kitchen.

Rose stirred and hugged him closer. "St. Paddy's unhappy in there."

"Afraid so."

"He sounds pitiful, Daniel."

"I know. But remember what the breeder said. We have to tough it out."

"You're right. I'm sure he'll stop soon."

Daniel stroked her hair as they lay together and listened to St. Paddy cry. The sound tore at his heart. He thought of how the puppy must have spent the previous night snuggled with his litter mates and his barnyard friends. Now he was completely alone. Frightened. Unable to understand why he was cut off from all love and attention.

"I'm not good at this, Rosie," Daniel admitted.

"Neither am I."

Finally he sat up with a muttered oath. "You'd have to be a sociopath to be good at this. I'm getting him."

"Daniel, is this a good idea? A half pound a day, remember. The breeder said taking him to bed would be like trying to eat one potato chip out of the bag."

"We'll bring his box in and have him sleep in that. It's his first night, and he has to be scared to death." He headed for the kitchen.

Flipping on the kitchen light, he blinked in the glare. St. Paddy was standing right next to the board looking pathetically eager to see him. Daniel opened the makeshift gate, walked over and picked up the cardboard box.

"Just for tonight," he said in his sternest cop voice as he led the puppy, dancing in ecstasy, back to the bedroom.

He positioned the box next to the bed and lifted the puppy into it before climbing back into bed beside Rose. "There," he said, gathering her close.

St. Paddy began to whine and Rose began to laugh.

Daniel released her and rolled over to address the puppy, who by now had his feet on the edge of the mattress. "Lie down and go to sleep."

Rose continued to laugh.

"Don't pay attention to her. She doesn't respect my authority, but I expect you to. Now get down, Paddy." The puppy leaned forward and swiped a tongue over Daniel's nose.

Rose peered over Daniel's shoulder. "Oh, look at him. Poor thing. He wants to sleep with us."

"He's staying in his box."

St. Paddy rested his head between his paws and gazed up at them.

"Aw, Daniel. Doesn't that just melt your heart?"

"He's a con man, Rose, and he has you all figured out. He knows if he gives you that look, you'll let him do anything he wants."

She ran a foot along his calf. "You're the one who let him out."

"And it'll work fine as long as he learns to sleep in his box."

"But look at that face."

Daniel rolled over toward her. "I'm ignoring him. He's staying in the box, Rose."

St. Paddy let out a long, heartfelt sigh.

Daniel lay staring into Rose's eyes as Paddy sighed again, this time with more gusto.

"Daniel."

"No, Rose."

Then the bed began to wiggle as Paddy tried to heave himself up on the mattress. When he lost his footing, he fell back into the box with a little "oof" that sounded human.

Daniel groaned and flopped to his back. "You win, you swindler." He scooped the dog up and plopped him on the bed next to him.

Rose caressed his shoulder. "Thank you."

"I'll tell you this. He's staying on my side of the bed. It'll be a cold day in hell when we sleep with a dog between us."

THANK THE GOOD LORD traffic wasn't as heavy on Saturday morning as on a weekday, Maureen thought as she gripped the wheel of the big Pontiac and inched toward Central Park West. And 'twas so nice of the motorcycle policemen to escort her over to Bridget's apartment house. She hoped she wouldn't sit in purgatory too long for the promise she made to the nice officers, that she'd park the Pontiac and not drive back to Brooklyn until early Sunday, when the traffic would be even lighter. Once she got rid of the police, she and Bridget would head upstate and make sure their children did the right thing.

The police had recognized Patrick's old car once she'd crossed into Manhattan. She hadn't noticed their flashing lights, but the sirens had finally gotten her attention. At first she thought it might have to do with the trash cans she'd mashed on her way out of the garage, but the officers hadn't mentioned those. They'd just offered to see her safely to Central Park. They'd even called in two more officers, so she had motorcycles to the front of her and motorcycles to the rear. Almost like a celebrity. She hoped Bridget was looking out the window. She'd be some impressed, she would.

ROSE AWOKE ONCE during the night and felt a cold nose against her cheek. It was not Daniel's. With a chuckle, she drifted back to sleep. The gruff, tough cop was a softie at heart, and she loved it.

The second time she awoke she smelled coffee— right under her nose. She opened her eyes and Daniel was passing a mug back and forth in front of her face, allowing the aroma to envelop her.

She smiled at him. "Good morning."

"Good morning, yourself." He set the mug on the bedside table.

She eased up on one elbow. "Where's St. Paddy?"

"Eating breakfast. And he's been outside once already."

"Thank you, Daniel."

"You're welcome."

"You know, I probably dreamed this." She gave

him a sly look. "But I could have sworn there was a furry body between us on the pillow last night."

"It was a dream. I have that puppy firmly under my control."

"Uh-huh." She took the mug from the table and sipped. "Mmm. Perfect. You're spoiling me, you know. I usually just throw a teaspoon of instant into a nuked mug of water."

"Not while I'm around, you won't. I've arrested people on less provocation than that."

She took another sip of the fragrant coffee and looked up at him from beneath her lashes. He was already dressed, but that could be remedied. "Did you bring your handcuffs, Officer?"

He folded his arms over his chest and gave her a stern look. "First you want a hickey and now you're talking handcuffs. Should I call in the vice squad, Rosie Kingsford?"

"Only if you can't handle the situation yourself."

He uncrossed his arms and approached the bed. "That sounded like a challenge."

"Are you up to it?"

He took the mug and set it on the bedside table before pulling back the comforter and tumbling her back onto the mattress. "I would say so. Consider yourself under house arrest." He pinned her beneath him.

"Is this how you subdue all your prisoners?"

"Only the sexy ones." He shifted his weight enough to slide his hand between her thighs.

Her breath caught as he began to explore and caress

in a way that brought her to a fever pitch in no time. She pulled his head down. "Come here, you Irish stud." As she kissed him she fumbled with the fastening of his jeans. He caught her wrist and held it, keeping her from her task.

When she tried to twist out of his grip, he lifted his mouth from hers. "Don't seduce the cook."

"You're…cooking something?" she asked, breathing hard.

"Yeah. It's on low, but it'll be ruined if you get me involved in this little game. It's supposed to be your show this time."

"I don't care if the food's ruined."

His breathing had also grown ragged as he gazed into her eyes. "You know what, you sexy wench? Neither do I."

With a laugh of triumph she started to unfasten his jeans, but he moved her hand away.

"I can do it faster."

"Then do it, Daniel. Just do it."

And he did, marvelously. As he carried her to heights of passion she'd never known before, she barely noticed the smell of burned bacon drifting from the kitchen.

"YOU EMBARRASSED ME half to death, coming up to the apartment house with that entourage," Bridget said as Maureen drove along the shoulder of Highway 87 at forty miles an hour. "I thought the Pope himself had come to call."

"Oh, and I suppose you're used to the Pope driving up to your door for afternoon tea?"

"He might. It could happen."

Maureen gripped the wheel and concentrated on driving straight. "The day he wears underwear with shamrocks on it, I'd say."

"What are you thinking, talking about the Pope's underwear! That's plain sacrilegious."

"I never thought of it before, but do you suppose he wears briefs or boxers?"

Bridget groaned. "I don't want to consider the subject. Not for another instant."

"Boxers."

"I didn't hear that. And get off the shoulder and into the lane, for heaven's sake! You drive like an old lady."

"I do not! And you don't drive at all, now, do you? So you can stuff a sock in it, Bridget Hogan. I'm in charge of this vehicle."

Bridget held her head in her hands. "Jesus, Mary and Joseph. What have I gotten myself into?"

"If I remember right, your daughter is at the center of it, so don't be getting high and mighty with me. 'Tis your flesh and blood that's created the whole shebang."

"I put it all down to MTV. It's corrupted the morals of an entire generation. Maureen, you've simply got to drive faster. That man who just whizzed past made a very rude gesture at you."

"You mean he flipped me the Tweetie-bird, as Patrick used to say?"

"Maureen! I hope you don't use that kind of vulgar language on a regular basis."

"What's vulgar? Tweetie is just a cute little yellow canary. Even a person who lives on *Central Park West* should know that much."

Bridget stared at her. "When someone does that thing with their middle finger, it has nothing do with a little yellow canary. Trust me—Maureen! Not so close to the guardrail!" Bridget gasped and covered her eyes.

"You keep yelling and you'll make me nervous, you will."

"You *should* be nervous. I thought you said you could drive?"

"I'm driving!"

Bridget peered at her through her fingers. "Do you even have a license?"

"You didn't ask me that, now, did you?"

Bridget groaned again and crossed herself. "We're going to die. I'm going to be killed in a fiery crash, incinerated by the same woman who ruined my life. I guess that's fitting, after all. I should have known not to believe a woman who would soil a dear friend's reputation just because of a slight accident with a tanning lamp."

"Slight accident! I had second-degree burns, I did! Scabs on my nose!"

"You must have put the lotion on wrong."

"The lotion wasn't any good, and you well knew it."

"Did not."

"Did so."

"Did not."

"Liar, liar, pants on fire," Maureen said.

"I can't hear yo-o-ou," Bridget sang, covering her ears.

"I don't ca-are," Maureen sang back. She drove in silence for a couple of miles before realizing that Bridget was the one with the directions. "Are you going to tell me where to turn, then?"

No answer.

"You'd better tell me, or I'll just turn off any old place and park it."

"I—um—believe there was a grove of trees to the right of the highway when we turned. Yes, a grove of trees."

"But you don't really know, do you? Here we are on this wild-goose chase, and you haven't a blessed idea where the goose is!"

"I do so know! I'm just not…sure."

"I could wring your neck for you, Bridget Hogan. In fact, I think I will. I—"

"Don't take your hands off the wheel, for God's sake!"

"Ha!" Maureen replaced both hands on the wheel and increased her speed to forty-two miles an hour, just for the thrill of it. "Scared you, didn't I?"

"I saw my dear mother coming down from heaven to meet me. I saw the pearly gates and heard the voice of St. Peter. I—"

"Enough of that. Pick an exit. Any exit. I'm tired of this road and all these speeders rushing past me."

"I'll bet they're bloody tired of you, too," Bridget muttered. "There! I think that's the right one. And there's a grove of trees, too."

"There've been about ten groves of trees along this road, all as alike as peas in a pod. This one's no different."

"Turn off at this exit, Maureen."

"You'll probably have fetched us up in some cow pasture, but I'm turning." She swung the Pontiac in a wide arc and heard the screech of brakes behind her.

"You almost ran into somebody!" Bridget cried. "Don't turn so wide, Maureen!"

Maureen continued on. She was rattled, but she'd never let Bridget see it. "You know those signs on big trucks? The ones that say Wide Turns, Stay Back?"

"In case it escaped your notice, you're not driving a truck."

"I know, but next time, I'm getting one of those signs. Slap it right on the bumper, I will."

"There won't *be* a next time! You're a menace on the roadways."

"Am not."

"Are so!"

"Am not!" She turned her mouth up into a devilish smile. "Besides, I'm beginning to enjoy myself."

DANIEL HAD INSISTED on frying up a new batch of bacon to go with the eggs he scrambled with an expert hand.

Rose sat at the kitchen table watching him, her second mug of coffee in one hand and her other reaching down to scratch St. Paddy behind his floppy ears. "I don't remember when I've ever been so happy," she said.

Daniel flipped the bacon in the skillet and glanced over his shoulder. "That's how I like my food-poisoning victims. Happy and clueless."

"I'm beginning to suspect you're a pretty good cook."

"Self-defense. Most women I've met wouldn't be caught dead in a kitchen, and I like home cooking."

"And you thought I'd be different when I offered to make dinner on our second date. Sorry, Daniel. I hope that wasn't part of the appeal."

Dishing up a plate of bacon, eggs and buttered English muffins, he walked over and set it in front of her.

"Looks wonderful, Daniel."

He placed both hands on the table and brought his face close to hers. "For the record, your appeal had zero to do with your abilities in the kitchen."

"You just wanted to get me into bed."

He grinned at her. "Yep."

"A purely physical thing."

"Yep. And you were the same, Rosie. Admit it."

"I admit it." She cradled his face in both her hands and thought about her original intention to ask Daniel to father her child. Not *their* child, but *her* child. What a ridiculous idea. She considered confessing that stupid intention now, but she hesitated. He might laugh, but then again… The proposal sounded so crass in comparison to the wonder of what they'd found together, that she hated to risk injecting a sour note into the blissful harmony they'd created.

"And the physical part has been wonderful," she said. "But now…"

"It goes a little deeper than that," he murmured.

She gazed into his eyes. "Yes, it does."

He leaned closer to feather a kiss against her lips. "We should probably talk about that today." He pushed back from the table. "But let's eat this breakfast before it gets cold."

Yes, today, she thought. They'd plan their future and consider their options, meanwhile taking time out to make glorious love to each other. Smiling to herself, she unfolded her napkin and laid it in her lap. "I feel positively decadent, eating breakfast at nearly eleven in the morning."

"That's your fault." Daniel came over with his own plate of food and sat across from her at the small table. He took a forkful of eggs and paused with it in midair. "You weren't serious about the handcuff thing, were you?"

She laughed. "You really are worried that I'm the kinky type, aren't you?"

"No." He paused. "Well, maybe. When you get right down to it, there are lots of things we don't know about each other."

"It'll be fun finding out, then, won't it?"

"Yeah," he said warily, "as long as what we find out doesn't involve a cat-o'-nine-tails."

"Oh, Daniel," she said, still chuckling. "I think regular sex with you is going to be plenty exciting without getting into whips and chains."

He sighed with relief. "So you were kidding about the handcuffs."

"Yes." She chewed and swallowed a bite of food. "Sort of."

"Sort of?" He sounded nervous again.

"I've never known a man who owned handcuffs before." She winked. "We could, like, fool around with them."

He gazed at her, the light of arousal growing in his eyes. "I don't know how you do it."

"Do what?"

"You have that innocent look about you, but underneath, there's always a suggestion of…"

"Sin?"

"I suppose that's it. We have this perfectly good breakfast in front of us, and until two minutes ago I was starving. Now all I can think about is dragging you back into the bedroom."

"With handcuffs?"

"Yes, dammit! Probably with handcuffs, or a facsimile since I didn't bring any. You're turning me into an animal."

She smiled at him. "I have great material to work with."

He put down his fork and pushed back from the table. "I guess breakfast will be cold."

"I guess it will." She started to leave the table but

paused in midmotion and cocked her head to listen. "That siren seems to be coming closer."

"I heard it, too. Probably old Tim running down another felon doing five miles over the limit. Right now I'm not much interested in old Tim's doings." He stood, his arousal evident from the bulge in his jeans. "Come with me, Rosie Kingsford."

She put her hand in his. "Daniel, that siren's really close."

"Must be on the road that goes past your lane. I—"

Frantic honking added itself to the increasingly loud whine of the siren. Both sounds filled the little kitchen.

Rose and Daniel stared at each other. Then, hand in hand, they walked into the living room and gazed out the window as a green Pontiac wheeled into the drive, followed by a squad car, lights flashing and siren wailing.

"Dear God," Daniel muttered.

"Do you know who it is?"

"I'm afraid so." He cringed as the Pontiac clipped his car's rear fender with a sickening thud before jerking to a stop in the mud next to the driveway. "It's my mother."

13

Rose STARED at the Pontiac with growing horror as the passenger door opened. "And *my* mother," she said.

"Escorted to our doorstep by my old buddy Tim," Daniel added, heading toward the door. "My God. She could have killed herself, not to mention your mother and a cast of thousands."

Rose followed him. "I didn't know your mother could drive."

"She can't." He wrenched open the door. "If you noticed, she hit my car."

"I did notice." She followed him out the door.

Daniel started down the walkway. "She always did have a hard time figuring out which was the brake and which was the gas."

"This can't be real." Rose pinched her arm, hoping she'd wake up from this nightmare.

"Look on the bright side," Daniel said over his shoulder. "Tim will probably arrest them."

"Daniel!" She hurried after him. "We can't let Tim arrest our mothers."

"We might not have a choice. I hate to think of what your pretty little town looks like after my mother

cut through it in that big Pontiac. I—'' Daniel came
to such an abrupt halt that Rose bumped into him. He
spoke in a low, tense voice. *"Will you look at that?*
He's putting his ticket book away. My mother talked
him out of a ticket.'' He started forward again. ''I
think I'll have a conversation with my bro Timmy.''

Rose caught his arm. ''You're going to ask him to
give your mother a ticket?'' she whispered.

''Hell, no. I'm going to protest mine!''

''Wait, Daniel.'' She kept her voice low. ''We have
bigger problems than your ticket. Let's act friendly,
as if we're so glad to see our mothers, so glad to see
Tim again.''

''I'm supposed to be glad that my mother risked
her life and Bridget's, smashed the fender of my car
and corrupted a fine officer of the law?''

She decided not to point out that he'd tried to cor-
rupt that same fine officer. ''We won't get anywhere
if we start yelling.''

''I want to yell,'' he grumbled.

''Well, don't. Not until we find out what our mothers are up to.''

''Just for you, Rosie.''

''Thanks. Let me go first.'' Rose started down the
driveway. ''Mom! Mrs. O'Malley! How nice to see
you.'' She wasn't encouraged by the frosty expressions that greeted her. ''And good to see you again
so soon, Tim.''

''Just thought I'd escort these two ladies to their
destination,'' Tim said.

Daniel stepped up beside Rose. ''Sure gave them

the royal treatment, using the lights and sirens and all. That's not what you usually see in your typical police escort, Tim.''

Tim had the good grace to blush. "Well, actually, I did sort of want them to pull over, but I guess they weren't ready to do that.''

Daniel's eyes widened as he turned to his mother. "You tried to outrun this patrol car?''

Maureen had a devilish gleam in her eye. "No trying about it. I did it. Patrick always did love that big V-8.''

Daniel's expression darkened. "Mom, I ought to—''

Rose nudged him in the ribs.

"Don't worry about a thing, Daniel," Maureen said briskly. "I straightened it all out. You see, without your father, Officer Tim wouldn't even be here.''

Bridget swatted her arm. "Don't say it like that, Maureen. It sounds like Patrick was fooling around with Officer Tim's mother.''

"My Patrick? Never! What happened was Patrick took a bullet for Tim's father, before little Tim was even thought of. I just told Tim the whole story, so naturally he can't give a ticket to Patrick O'Malley's widow.''

"What about Patrick O'Malley's son, Officer Tim?" Daniel asked, turning toward the patrolman. "You gave me a ticket, in case it's slipped your mind.''

"I didn't know about the bullet thing then. I knew somebody had saved my dad's life a long time ago, but I didn't remember who it was.'' He brightened. ''And now I do.''

''And now that you do,'' Daniel said carefully, ''what about my ticket?''

''Sorry, bro. I turned it in already. Now, if you want to come to traffic court, maybe we can work something out.''

Daniel sighed. ''Never mind. I guess the county can use the money.''

''Which reminds me, old buddy. Your mom said you'd take care of the damage.''

''You mean to my car?''

''No, it's the town welcome sign, with the population figure on it, and the founding date and all. I should say, it *was* the town welcome sign. Now it's pretty much firewood.''

Daniel winced. ''Anything else?''

''A couple of those whiskey-barrel planters that sit on the sidewalk along Main Street.''

''They drove on the *sidewalk?*''

''Bridget distracted me. Yelling like a banshee, she was.''

''Because you were headed straight for that bronze statue!''

''The damage shouldn't be much,'' Tim interjected quickly. ''There weren't flowers planted in the barrels yet, and we were going to take that parking meter out anyway. And Mr. Webster may be old, but he hopped out of the way real fast. The sign's the main thing, but I'm sure you have insurance.''

''Nope.'' Daniel leveled a scorching look at his

mother. "Nobody expected that car to be on the road. Or the sidewalk."

Rose stepped forward. "I'll pay for a new sign."

"Oh, no, you won't." Daniel gave her a warning glance. "It's my mother."

"But, Daniel," Rose said, "that could be a very expensive item. I think you should—"

"I think you should just let it be," Daniel said quietly.

She heard the steel underlying his quiet statement and knew it was time to back off. This was one of their sore points, and now, of all times, they needed to stand together. "Okay."

"Get an estimate for a new sign," Daniel said to Tim. "I'll contact you soon."

"That's fine." Tim started backing toward his patrol car. "See you later, then." He seemed eager to leave.

Once the police car had pulled away, Daniel turned toward his mother. "What in hell were you thinking? You could have been killed!"

Rose knew his temper was past restraining and didn't attempt to stop the tirade that was sure to come.

"She almost killed us both!" Bridget said. "I was blessing myself so often I gave myself tendinitis!"

"I'm not surprised," Daniel said. "What do you have to say for yourself, Mom?"

Maureen's expression was unrepentant. "No grandchild of mine is going to be a bastard. Not while there's still breath in my body."

Rose's stomach felt as if she'd just jumped from a

ten-story building. She gave her mother a panicked look and then she knew for sure. Bridget had sold her out.

Daniel stared at Maureen. "What in God's name are you talking about?"

"I wouldn't have believed you'd agree to doing such a sinful thing, Daniel Patrick O'Malley, but after I found out you lied about where you'd be this weekend, then I wasn't certain about anything anymore. This shameless woman just might have talked you into it."

Bridget grabbed Maureen's arm. "Don't you call my daughter shameless! You're the shameless one, running around looking for a wife for your rascal of a son."

"Hey!" Daniel said.

Maureen ignored him. "I thought she was a fine Irish girl!"

"She is!"

"She's little more than a—"

Whap. Bridget's roundhouse connected with Maureen's cheek and she stumbled backward.

"Mom!" Rose cried, starting toward her mother.

"'Tis another donnybrook you want, is it?" Arms flailing, Maureen headed back toward Bridget.

Daniel caught her before she made contact, and Rose grabbed Bridget.

Whatever hope Rose had that the whole incident could be smoothed over ended as Maureen turned to her son.

"So, have you agreed to give Rose the child she wants, without marrying her, then?"

Daniel's jaw clenched. "Look, that's enough. I have no idea what you're talking about, and you're doing nothing to help the—"

"Oh, so she didn't tell you her scheme, then? Never mind. Bridget was good enough to tell me. Rose doesn't want a husband, Daniel, but she does want a wee babe. You're chosen to be the father, whether she notified you of the fact or not."

"I don't believe you. Rose wouldn't want an arrangement like that."

Rose's heart broke.

"Ask her," Maureen prompted.

Daniel released his mother. Then he glanced at Rose, his expression confused. "She's got this all wrong, I know, but—"

"Not exactly all wrong," Rose said, her gaze pleading for understanding. "At one time I was looking for a man to father a child, although I didn't intend to marry him, or anyone, for that matter. I didn't want to go to a sperm bank and take my chances that the donor wouldn't be the sort I wanted, so I was looking for someone who would—" Her courage failed her.

His voice was strained. "Who would what?"

"Who would agree to give me a child without any strings attached."

"And you imagined I would?" The look in his eyes tore her to pieces.

"I...before I really knew you, I thought... But not

after I found out what kind of man you are, Daniel. Being with you made me rethink everything! I would *never* consider such a thing now. Never.''

He grew very quiet. ''When did you change your mind about this? Be specific.''

''Sometime...sometime yesterday,'' she said.

''Before we gave St. Paddy a bath? Or after?''

She looked away. ''After.''

''How convenient. After you'd gotten what you wanted, you mean. No wonder you called me an Irish stud this morning. That's all I've been to you, isn't it?''

''No!'' Her face flamed. ''Daniel, not in front of our mothers, please!''

''A modern thinker like you shouldn't mind,'' he said, his tone icy.

Rose knew she was lost, totally lost.

''We're here to demand that you two marry and give our grandchild a proper home,'' Bridget said.

''In spite of the inconvenient matter of us two having to be related as a result,'' Maureen said with a shudder.

''Well, I hate to disappoint two such upstanding Catholic ladies, and I realize how much pleasure the union of our two families would give you, but I'm afraid it's out of the question,'' Daniel said. ''The prospective groom is too sick to his stomach to propose.''

''Daniel,'' Rose said. ''Please. Don't do this.''

''Oh, I think it's already done.'' He flicked her a

glance. "And you got exactly what you wanted. No strings attached. I won't even charge you a stud fee."

FIFTEEN MINUTES LATER, Daniel left with his mother in the Pontiac. Rose agreed to drive her mother back in Daniel's car, then park it in his apartment garage and take a cab home. He didn't suggest she come up for a visit. He hadn't suggested that they ever see each other again, Rose noticed. Consequently, she had to postpone the drive back to the city until she could stop crying, which took a long time.

Eventually her mother started sniffling right along with her as they sat at the kitchen table. St. Paddy sat between them, his expression worried as his head swiveled from one tragic face to the other. Occasionally he'd whine and walk over to shove his muzzle against Rose's leg.

"I have to stop crying," Rose said, blowing her red nose. "I'm upsetting St. Paddy."

"St. Paddy? What about your poor mother? I'm a wreck!"

Rose glanced across the table at her mother's puffy eyes and red nose. "Yeah, you are."

"Thank you so much for agreeing with me on that. So you really love him, then?"

Rose nodded and choked back another sob.

"And if Maureen and I hadn't arrived and spilled the beans, you'd be setting the date?"

"I...I can't say that for sure. But we seemed to be...moving in that direction." Rose buried her face in her hands. "Oh, Mom. He's just what I want. I never thought I'd find a man who would make me change my mind about getting married, but Daniel did. And now…''

"It's all my fault.'' Her mother sounded completely miserable. "If I'd kept my nose out of it, everything would have been fine. Except, of course, for having to be related to that Maureen person.''

"Don't blame yourself. I should have told Daniel the minute I gave up my original plan. He might have been upset then, too, but maybe I could have made him understand. Or maybe not. A man like Daniel would hate something like that. And that's exactly why I love him! It's so confusing.''

Bridget reached over and placed her hand over Rose's. "The idea of being a single mother was never right for you, Rose. Motherhood is right for you, but so is having a husband. You only had to find the right man. Just because I didn't doesn't mean you can't. I was so young when I married your father. Too young to realize we had nothing in common but my good looks and his money.''

Rose sighed. "Well, it looks like I've ruined my chances with this particular man, and I can't imagine there are many out there like Daniel O'Malley.''

Bridget squeezed her hand. "Does he love you?''

"He was beginning to, I'm sure, but new love can be squashed so quickly. And I—well, I was having fun pretending to be a little wilder than I actually am. No telling how he's put all that together now, or what sort of picture he has of me.''

"Rose, I have to ask you—'' Bridget hesitated.

"Considering what was said out in the front yard, could you be carrying Daniel's child?"

Rose's initial rush of joy at the thought was followed by great sadness. "I doubt it. I would love to be, but we—" She blushed furiously, but decided that if her mother had the courage to ask, she'd have the courage to tell. "We only had unprotected sex once. That would be quite a long shot."

"Ah, but he's an Irishman."

Rose laughed through her tears. "That's what *he* said."

"I think you should get in touch with him when we go back to the city. Convince him that you just weren't thinking straight about this other business."

Rose shook her head. "No. I did the pursuing in the beginning, and if I continue, he'll probably just think I'm after the same thing, because the first dose didn't take. I can't call him."

"That's your stubborn Irish pride talking."

Rose smiled at her. "I know I'm only half Irish, but it sure seems like the biggest half."

"Of course it is, lass."

Lass. She remembered Daniel calling her that, and how sweet the word had sounded coming from his lips. More such memories were undoubtedly on the way, and she was in for the kind of heartache she'd only imagined in the past. As they said in California, this was the big one. She blinked back fresh tears.

"I could call him," Bridget said.

Rose gasped. "No! Don't even think such a thing, Mom! You have to promise to stay out of this."

"But—"

"Promise me!"

"All right." Bridget slipped one hand into her lap. "I promise."

THE SILENCE in the Pontiac was oppressive, broken only when Daniel stopped for gas and asked his mother if she needed to go inside the station and freshen up. She declined. Daniel pumped the gas and swore softly to himself. On top of everything else, his mother had been driving on fumes. It was a wonder she'd made it to Rose's cottage without getting stranded.

They left the gas station and continued down the highway. Daniel flipped on the radio, but no matter how many times he switched channels he kept coming up with love songs. He didn't need love songs. What he needed, at least until the pain eased, was oblivion. But he had to take his mother home, and navigating a New York highway required his attention. Thinking of his mother driving this road froze the blood in his veins. She'd imagined she was doing it for him, so he'd decided not to say anything more about the stupidity of her actions. Next week, however, he was selling the car, fresh dents and all.

"You should be glad to know the truth, Daniel," Maureen said at last.

"Right."

"I couldn't let you go through with such a thing."

"I understand that."

"Daniel, what was it you meant when you said something about her getting what she wanted?"

Pain knifed through him. "Nothing."

"Could she be…carrying your child?"

Oh, God. If only— "Probably not."

"But there's a chance?"

"Not really."

"Don't be beating around the bush with me, Daniel. There's either a chance or there isn't. I keep up with these things. After all, products are sold out in the open now, you know, right next to my multivitamin tablets. You didn't use the sheepskin kind, did you? I read that those aren't as effective as latex."

Daniel blew out a breath. First he'd discovered that Rose was really after a sperm donor instead of a lover, and now his mother wanted to discuss his condom habits. He was so far past the end of his rope he couldn't even see it dangling there anymore.

"Well, Daniel?"

"You know what, Mom? We aren't going to have this conversation. Not now, and not in the future. Whatever did or didn't happen is between Rose and me. I once asked you to stay out of it."

"But when Bridget—"

"I can understand why you felt the need to warn me. Now I want the subject dropped. Permanently."

"Daniel, you're gripping that wheel as if you're likely to bend it clean in half. Are you in love with that girl, then?"

"Drop it, Mom. Now."

"All right. Mercy. I've never seen you like this. A body would think you'd tumbled head over heels."

14

Inside the Statue of Liberty Museum, next to the big foot. Noon, Tuesday. Be there.

B.H.K.

MAUREEN CHECKED the note again after boarding the excursion boat on Tuesday morning. She'd promised Daniel to stay out of his business with Rose. But she hadn't promised not to visit the Statue of Liberty, had she, now? And if she happened to run into Bridget there, and Bridget happened to mention the subject, was she supposed to clamp her mouth shut and not answer at all? 'Twould be rude of her.

She used to love this trip when Patrick was alive. There was something wonderful about having a woman so huge and magnificent at the entrance to one of the great harbors of the world. Maureen had always thought the National Organization for Women had missed a bet, not using that statue as a symbol of female power.

And female power was just what was called for in this mess surrounding Daniel and Rose. As the boat approached the giant copper figure, her torch raised to the sky, Maureen moved to the front of the crowd and let the wind blow against her face. Barbra Streisand had probably felt like this in *Funny Girl* when she was singing "Nobody's Gonna Rain on My Parade," while riding that tugboat out into New York Harbor. Maureen's heart swelled with pride and purpose, and another emotion that surprised the devil out of her—sisterhood.

After the boat docked Maureen hurried to the museum. She knew the exact spot Bridget was talking about in her note. Inside the building was a huge left foot, reproduced the same size as the one on the actual statue, only 'twas polished copper instead of the weathered green of the statue outside. Maureen found Bridget standing by the big toe.

"So you came," Bridget said.

"Of course I came. Something must be done."

"Exactly. For our children and our grandchild-to-be."

Maureen laid a hand on her heart. "You really think Rose is in the family way, then?"

Bridget beckoned Maureen closer and leaned over to whisper in her ear. "They had sex once without a condom."

"Without a condom at all?" Maureen said in a normal voice.

Bridget clapped a hand over Maureen's mouth. "Jesus, Mary and Joseph. What am I to do with you, Maureen Fiona, shouting about condoms at the top of your blessed lungs?"

Maureen pulled Bridget's hand away from her mouth. "Did not."

"Did too."

"Did—" Belatedly Maureen heard the funny little tremble in Bridget's voice, and she looked her square in the face. 'Twas the moment she realized that Bridget was doing her best not to laugh, which set Maureen to giggling.

Once she started, Bridget joined in. Soon they were both gasping and holding their sides as tears streamed down their cheeks.

"No one could ever make me laugh like you, Maureen," Bridget said at last, wiping her eyes. "I don't think I've had a really good laugh since I left Ireland."

"We had some grand times, we did."

"I think…maybe we should forget about that Rose of Tralee business."

Maureen nodded. "I think that would be a grand idea."

"We have other fish to fry, like getting Rose and Daniel back together."

"'Tis not going to be easy. Daniel's a stubborn Irishman."

"And Rose is a stubborn Irishwoman, but I've figured out a plan. Rose will be riding in the back of a convertible during the St. Patrick's Day Parade. One of the beer companies hired her because she looks so Irish."

Maureen saw where the plan was headed. "Daniel will either be in it or patrolling a part of it, I'm not sure which."

"It would be best for my plan if he's patrolling a

stretch of the route. If you'll tell me who his commanding officer is I'll have Cecil make a few calls and arrange it.''

"Cecil? Your husband?"

"*Ex*-husband. But he knows a lot of people in high places here in the city. And even if he is a Brit, he wouldn't want his daughter to have a baby out of wedlock any more than I would. I'm sure I can convince him to help us set the trap for these two.''

"You know, Rose and Daniel may well kill us for interfering again,'' Maureen said.

"I realize that. Are you ready to take that risk, Maureen?''

"I'm ready if you are.''

"Then we must seal it with the secret handshake.''

Maureen put her hand up, palm out, the memory as fresh as if she'd done it yesterday, instead of thirty-seven years ago. Bridget placed her palm against Maureen's, and they laced their fingers together.

"All for one,'' Bridget said.

"And one for all,'' Maureen finished. Then she squeezed Bridget's hand tight. When she got an answering squeeze, she had the dumbest reaction. Tears filled her eyes.

ON ST. PATRICK'S DAY Rose wore a lined green suit with a white fake fur collar, which helped a little to keep her warm in the open convertible as it eased down the parade route. She rode on the boot covering the folded convertible top, which meant she was fully exposed to the chill wind that whipped down Fifth

Avenue. There had been a long wait at the staging area, too. Although she'd thought the O'Hannigan's entry was near the middle of the parade, she'd discovered that morning that she'd been moved almost to the end. She'd been half-frozen before her part of the procession even got under way.

She'd tried to plan for the cold. Beneath her suit jacket she wore a thermal shirt, but there wasn't anything she could do about her legs. The suit skirt barely reached to mid-thigh, which had been exactly what the O'Hannigan's representative had wanted. He'd said something to the effect that a pantsuit would have defeated the purpose of hiring a woman with great legs. Rose had never liked being treated like a commodity, but after years of it she had become stoic about men like the O'Hannigan's rep. A set of earmuffs to cut the wind would also have been welcome this morning, instead of the perky green derby she wore securely pinned to her red curls, but O'Hannigan's Beer was paying a lot for her appearance in this parade, so she was expected to put up with a little discomfort in exchange.

Not long ago she would have been happy about the hefty fee offered by the brewery. She'd have rejoiced in her healthy financial situation, because it meant she'd be able to pursue her master plan more easily. Now her master plan was in tatters. She no longer cared about her little cottage, and drawing the comic strip was increasingly difficult these days.

Years of training were all that carried her through this morning as she smiled and waved at the crowd gathered along the parade route. She envied them their heavy coats and mufflers. March seventeenth had turned out to be a bitterly cold day in New York City this year. But as cold as it was outside, Rose was even colder inside. She'd hoped, prayed, even dreamed that Daniel would call. He hadn't.

Today, as if to mock her, she seemed to be surrounded by mounted patrollers. The contingent picked to lead the parade had been in the staging area, but Daniel hadn't been among them. More mounted officers were stationed along the route for crowd control. She'd studied each of them as the convertible inched down the street, but she hadn't seen Daniel. If she ever did spot him, she fully expected him to ignore her. How she'd keep smiling when that happened, she had no idea.

As the tail end of the parade approached St. Patrick's Cathedral, she glanced to her right and thought she recognized the man on the horse stationed in that block. Oh, God, it was him. She knew the set of those shoulders, the cant of those hips. Her heart began to pound.

Then, from her left, she heard a sickeningly familiar cry.

"I might have known you'd be here hogging the view, Maureen Fiona!"

She turned with a sense of inevitability to see her mother on the steps of St. Patrick's, trying to push Daniel's mother out of the way. Rose closed her eyes and prayed that the stress and the cold morning were causing her to hallucinate.

"Don't be shoving me, Bridget Hogan. 'Tis my corner you're standing on."

Laughter rippled through the crowd and Rose groaned. Maureen sounded like a streetwalker protecting her turf. Rose glanced toward Daniel to see how he was reacting. No help there. Daniel looked like a man chiseled in stone—his mirrored sunglasses concealing his eyes, a blue helmet over his dark hair, and his jaw set in uncompromising lines as he focused on the parade route and ignored the two women on the cathedral steps.

Rose leaned forward, as if that would make the motorcade move faster. But Murphy's Law was working overtime on this holiday, and the parade stopped altogether.

"Did you drive here, Maureen?" Bridget said, loud enough to carry a good half block. "I guess not, since I don't see your car parked on the cathedral steps."

"You know what I have to say to that? Take a look. The Tweety-bird is flying!"

"Oh, God," Rose muttered, her cheeks flaming as she imagined the private hell Daniel must be going through at the moment.

The driver of Rose's convertible chuckled. "Great show, huh? Nothing like a couple of Irish ladies going at it. Probably been drinking some of that green beer. If we're lucky, maybe they'll even throw a few punches."

Rose gasped at the prospect of the mothers becoming physical. Surely they wouldn't start a brawl on the steps of St. Patrick's Cathedral.

They would.

"I'll Tweety-bird you," Bridget said. "Take that, you sheep-faced old crone!"

"Missed me, you blind banshee!"

"I won't be missing you this time!"

As the blows started flying and the crowd made a circle around the screeching women, Rose clambered down from the back of the convertible, cursing her short skirt as she went. "Lean forward and let me out," she said to the driver. "I have to do something about this."

"Hey, it's not your business," the driver said, turning toward her. "Leave it to the police."

"I'm not going to debate this with you. Let me out or I'll climb over your lap."

Muttering something about the crazy Irish, the driver opened the door, got out and helped Rose down to the pavement.

"Thanks. I'll be right back." The crowd now blocked her view of the battling mothers, but all she had to do was follow the sounds of scuffling, shrill insults, and gleeful encouragement from the onlookers.

She shouldered her way through and made a grab for her mother. "Stop this right now!"

Bridget didn't even glance back at her. "Not yet, lass," she gasped. "Not until this is settled."

"Mom, stop!" Rose grabbed her mother around the waist, braced herself and pulled with all her might. It had no effect except that her skirt ripped up one side. O'Hannigan's would really get their money's worth now, she thought as she tugged harder. Then from the corner of her eye she saw the chest of a dark bay gelding part the crowd.

Daniel leaped from his horse and separated the two women with the same expertise he'd used in the apartment house lobby. For some unexplainable reason, the two women stayed separated this time. Daniel looked at his mother, opened his mouth to say something and closed it again, shaking his head.

Maureen's green derby was knocked askew, her coat was missing two buttons, and she was breathing hard. She was also smiling. "Don't stand there like a man with no tongue, Daniel," she said. "'Tis high time to speak to the woman you love."

With a startled cry, Rose stepped back and gazed at her mother, who was just as disheveled as Maureen and was also grinning like the Cheshire cat. "You two *staged* this?"

The crowd began to mutter and laugh among themselves at this new revelation.

"Had to do something," Bridget said. "Considering you were both too stubborn to contact each other."

Rose swung around to face Daniel at the same moment he turned to her. "I say we kill them," she said, her voice tight with fury. "No jury would ever convict us."

"Death is too easy for this pair," he muttered. "Let's torture them first."

"You've already been torturing us in grand style!" Maureen said. "Now stop your fussing and get married so you can give us both the grandbabe we're longing for."

"I couldn't have said it better, Maureen." Bridget walked over and put her arm around Maureen's waist. "I hope I didn't really hurt you. I was trying to be careful."

"Oh, *sure* you were," Maureen said with a chuckle.

Rose's knees felt suddenly weak. She glanced at Daniel. "This isn't real, right? Those are two aliens disguised as our mothers."

"Either that or they're both on drugs."

"Hey, buddy," called somebody from the crowd. "Looks like these two ladies went through a lot of trouble to bring you two together. You gonna propose to the young lady or not?"

Rose's heart began to hammer with a different rhythm. "Listen, Daniel, I—"

"Now don't you let him off the hook, Rose," Bridget said. "You told me yourself you love him, and Maureen's convinced he's in love with you. All you have to do is get him to tell you so."

"Tell her!" shouted an onlooker.

"Yeah, tell her!" called someone else.

The crowd turned it into a chant. *Tell her, tell her, tell her, tell her.*

In an agony of embarrassment, Rose covered her face.

The chant was ended with a blast from a police whistle.

Rose looked up as Daniel removed the whistle from

his mouth. His expression was grim. He must be furious. This was really and truly the end of their relationship, thanks to one final stunt by her mother and Maureen.

Then a hint of a smile appeared on Daniel's face. "How do you expect a guy to propose with all that racket?" he called to the crowd.

Rose felt as if her heart had stopped.

A cheer went up from the crowd.

When it died down, Daniel turned to her and dropped to one knee. "Rose Erin Kingsford, will you marry me?"

"Oh, Maureen!" Bridget cried. "He's proposing on the steps of St. Patrick's Cathedral! It's perfect!"

There was a roaring in Rose's ears and she felt dizzy. She put out a hand to steady herself, and Daniel caught it firmly in his.

"I love you," he said in a low, urgent voice. "And I've been a proud, stubborn idiot. Marry me, Rosie."

She held onto his hand for dear life, afraid she'd tumble to the ground without his support. But she needed to see his eyes. "Take off those sunglasses," she murmured in a voice too low for the crowd to hear.

He pulled off the glasses. The depth of commitment in his eyes settled any doubts she might have had.

She spoke around the lump in her throat. "I would be honored to marry you, Daniel Patrick O'Malley."

"Oh, Bridget, I'm going to cry," Maureen muttered with a sniffle.

"Kiss her!" someone shouted.

"Great idea." Daniel got to his feet and pulled her into his arms.

"Daniel!" she protested, half laughing, half crying as she pushed at his chest. "Surely such goings-on aren't allowed when you're on duty."

The love in his gaze turned the chill day into a tropical paradise. "Ah, but 'tis St. Paddy's Day, and I'm Irish. Say you love me, Rosie."

"I love you, you crazy Irishman."

"That's all I need to know." As the crowd cheered again, he claimed the kiss she'd been yearning for all along.

Epilogue

MAUREEN HAD WON the coin toss to have the slide show of the trip to Ireland in her apartment, which meant she had to put up with Bridget's opinions on organizing her surroundings.

"I think you should hang the *Irish Rose* calendar on this wall next to your telephone," Bridget said. "That way you could see it whenever you made a call. And look at this! You still haven't framed your copy of the *New York Times* comic page. Anyone would think you didn't care that your daughter-in-law got her strip into such a prestigious paper."

Maureen checked on the lamb stew before turning to answer Bridget. "You well know why I haven't framed it. With the wedding, and our trip back to Ireland, and getting ready for the babe, I've been so busy I hardly have time to bless myself!"

"It's your lack of planning, Maureen. If you used your time better, you'd—oh, there's the buzzer. They're here!"

"Is the projector all set up?"

"Of course, although we have precious few slides to put in it."

"'Twas not me who dropped a roll of film into my Guinness."

"No, you were the one who started swaying while she sang 'My Wild Irish Rose' and bumped me."

"Did not."

"Did too."

"Did not!"

The buzzer sounded again.

Maureen placed her hands on her hips. "See how you do? You leave our poor children standing out in the elements while you fuss at me."

"It's your door! Go let them in, for heaven's sake."

Maureen lifted her nose in the air. "What a grand idea."

Shortly afterward Maureen was treated to the sight of her daughter-in-law, looking as if she'd swallowed a pumpkin, coming through the door with Daniel, who looked as if he'd swallowed a spotlight, he was glowing so much. While the stew finished cooking, Bridget showed the trip slides. Maureen never tired of looking at them, even if most of them were out of focus. She and Bridget had already made reservations to go back again next year.

Dinner was a success. Although Bridget complained as usual that Maureen's food was too fattening, she left a clean plate. Maureen was pleased to notice Bridget had gained a few pounds, too. She looked more content with life.

Over a dessert of Daniel's favorite chocolate cake,

the talk turned, as it always did, to the eagerly awaited grandchild.

"Have you picked a name, then?" Maureen asked.

Rose glanced at Daniel.

"You might as well tell them," he said, scraping up the last of his cake with his dessert fork. "Get the haggling out of the way."

Bridget's spine stiffened. "Are you implying that we'll disagree with your choices?"

"The very idea," Maureen added. "'Tis your wee babe, and you can name it Elmer Fudd for all we care."

"But not Tweety-bird," Bridget said, and started to laugh.

"No, indeed." Maureen pressed a napkin against her mouth to stop her giggles.

"But I'm sure you've picked nice names," Bridget said. "What are they?"

Rose took a deep breath. "If it's a boy, we decided on Patrick Cecil."

"That's grand," Maureen said, dabbing at a sudden tear in her eye.

"I won't quarrel with your choice," Bridget said. "Cecil may be your father, but I agree he doesn't deserve top billing."

"And if it's a girl," Rose continued, "she'll be…Bridget Maureen."

"She's first?" Maureen cried before she could stop the words coming out of her mouth. "Did I lose the coin toss, then?"

Daniel cleared his throat. "We thought that was

only fair, Mom. If the boy got Dad's name, then the girl should get Rose's mother's name.''

''Well, I don't see the logic in it.''

''Of course not,'' Bridget said. ''But I think their reasoning is brilliant.''

''We even tried to come up with a combination of your two names,'' Rose said.

''Yeah,'' Daniel added, ''but Maurit and Bridgeen just didn't seem to cut it.''

''I should say not,'' Bridget said. ''They've done an outstanding job with the names, Maureen.''

''That's easy for you to say. You're first in line. No, I think 'tis only fair to toss a coin. What do you say? Two out of three?''

''A coin toss to name a child?'' Bridget said. ''Next you'll have us rolling dice to see which one gets to keep her the first time Daniel and Rose have an evening out.''

'''Tis no contest,'' Maureen said with a superior smile. ''I already have a bassinet.''

''Well, *I* already have a stroller.''

''And I have a—''

''Oh, you know what?'' Daniel said. ''We really have to go. Forgot to feed St. Paddy before we left.''

''Is that dog still sleeping in your bed with you?'' Bridget asked.

Rose looked sheepish. ''We, ah, bought ourselves two new beds, one for the cottage and one for the apartment.''

''Oh, good,'' Bridget said. ''And you're not allowing him in the new ones, are you?''

"Well, no. He sleeps in our old beds."

Bridget rolled her eyes at Maureen. "Have you ever heard anything more strange than that? Giving up your bed to a dog?"

"Never," Maureen said. "I still can't believe they're keeping that dog in their apartment when they're in town. Frightens the neighbors out of their wits, he does. I—"

"And if we don't get back there soon," Rose said, "he just might eat one."

Bridget gasped. "Would he do that?"

"You never know," Daniel said, and helped Rose on with her coat. After quick kisses all around, he escorted Rose out the door.

"I FEEL BAD maligning poor St. Paddy, who would never hurt a flea," Rose said as she and Daniel rode back to Manhattan in a cab.

"Me, too, but it makes them less likely to drop in on us, doesn't it?"

"Good point. You know, I think they took the name business rather well."

"If you mean no dishes were flying around, I guess you're right. Me, I'm hoping for a boy so we don't have to deal with it."

"Daniel, you know the ultrasound showed a girl."

"Maybe it missed something."

"I want a girl, anyway, and I want to name her after both our mothers. After all, this is all their fault."

Daniel caressed her round belly through the fabric

of her maternity dress. "Not entirely. We had a little something to do with it."

Rose leaned closer to him so the cabdriver couldn't overhear. "And you really did know I was pregnant after that time in the bathtub, didn't you?"

"Not really. But I did know you were mine."

"You mean, like caveman stuff?"

"Exactly like caveman stuff. Staking my claim." He cupped her face in one hand. "And I feel like doing that some more…if you're sure the doctor said it's okay."

"It's okay. But, Daniel, your claim is well and securely staked."

"Maybe so," he murmured, leaning close for a kiss, "but I'll need a lifetime to be absolutely sure."

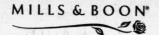

MILLS & BOON®

Makes
any time
special

Enjoy a romantic novel from
Mills & Boon®

Presents™ *Enchanted*™ *Temptation*®

Historical Romance™ *Medical Romance*™

MILLS & BOON®

This Month's Romance Titles

♡

Each month you can choose from a wide variety of romance novels from Mills & Boon®. Below are the new titles to look out for this month from the Presents™ and Enchanted™ series.

Presents™

THE PERFECT LOVER	Penny Jordan
TO BE A HUSBAND	Carole Mortimer
THE BOSS'S BABY	Miranda Lee
ONE BRIDEGROOM REQUIRED!	Sharon Kendrick
THE SEXIEST MAN ALIVE	Sandra Marton
FORGOTTEN ENGAGEMENT	Margaret Mayo
A RELUCTANT WIFE	Cathy Williams
THE WEDDING BETRAYAL	Elizabeth Power

Enchanted™

THE MIRACLE WIFE	Day Leclaire
TEXAS TWO-STEP	Debbie Macomber
TEMPORARY FATHER	Barbara McMahon
BACHELOR AVAILABLE!	Ruth Jean Dale
BOARDROOM BRIDEGROOM	Renee Roszel
THE HUSBAND DILEMMA	Elizabeth Duke
THE BACHELOR BID	Kate Denton
THE WEDDING DECEPTION	Carolyn Greene

On sale from 5th February 1999

Available at most branches of WH Smith, Tesco, Asda, Martins, Borders, Easons, Volume One/James Thin and most good paperback bookshops

MILLS & BOON®

Makes any time special™

By Request

Bestselling themed romances brought back to you by popular demand

Each month By Request brings you three full-length novels in one beautiful volume featuring the best of the best.

So if you missed a favourite Romance the first time around, here is your chance to relive the magic from some of our most popular authors.

Look out for
Sole Paternity in March 1999
featuring Miranda Lee, Robyn Donald
and Sandra Marton

Available at most branches of WH Smith, Tesco, Asda, Martins, Borders, Easons, Volume One/James Thin and most good paperback bookshops

MILLS & BOON®

Nearly

Weds!

From your favourite romance authors:

Betty Neels
Making Sure of Sarah

Carole Mortimer
The Man She'll Marry

Penny Jordan
They're Wed Again!

Enjoy an eventful trip to the altar with
three new wedding stories—when
nearly weds become *newly weds!*

Available from 19th March 1999